Acclaim for Laura Joh Rowland and her novels

"Sano may carry a sword and wear a kimono, but you'll immediately recognize him as an ancestor of Philip Marlowe or Sam Spade."

—*Denver Post*

The Dragon King's Palace

"Rowland uses her fine eye for detail to portray the intricate surface and roiling underbelly of life in a tightly structured, controlled society. Her Japan is a mix of Kabuki theater–like stylized formality, palace intrigue, and physical action that would do a martial arts movie proud."

—*Times-Picayune* (New Orleans, LA)

"Rowland's masterful evocation of the period enables the reader to identify with the universal human emotions and drives that propel her characters while absorbing numerous telling details of a different culture and era."

—*Publishers Weekly*

"The story line remains fresh though this is Sano's eighth tale because of the insightful look at an era when palace intrigue rivaled Machiavelli and samurai code ruled."

—*Midwest Book Review*

"A lively dissection of the samurai code of honor, sexual dishonor, palace infighting, and ancient Japanese mores."

—*Kirkus Reviews*

More . . .

The Pillow Book of Lady Wisteria

"Rowland's dazzling array of entertaining narratives continues to score points with readers, with exotic locales, a flair for dramatics. . . . "

—*The Japan Times*

Black Lotus

"Well-developed characters, a complex, absorbing plot, and rich historical detail should help win the author a place on mystery bestseller lists."

—*Publishers Weekly* (starred review)

The Samurai's Wife

"An exquisite tale of murder, passion, and revenge. Feudal Japan springs to vibrant life under Ms. Rowland's skillful hand, and the sleuthing team of Sano and Reiko will touch your heart. All lovers of mystery, the Orient, romance, and history will enjoy this magnificent tale."

—*Romantic Times*

"*The Samurai's Wife* is the latest in Laura Joh Rowland's bracing books about Sano Ichiro, a 17th-century warrior who serves as a detective for the imperial shogun . . . . A mixed blessing for Sano is his wife's insistence—virtually scandalous in feudal Japan—on accompanying him in his investigations; but she proves invaluable in what turns out to be a probe into deep duplicity indeed."

—*Seattle Times*

Also by Laura Joh Rowland

The Dragon King's Palace

Laura Joh Rowland

St. Martin's Paperbacks

THE DRAGON KING'S PALACE

Copyright © 2003 by Laura Joh Rowland.
Excerpt from *The Perfumed Sleeve* copyright © 2004 by Laura Joh Rowland.

Dragon character by Annie Au.

All rights reserved. No part of this book may be used or reproduced in any manner whatsoever without written permission except in the case of brief quotations embodied in critical articles or reviews. For information address St. Martin's Press, 175 Fifth Avenue, New York, NY 10010.

Library of Congress Catalog Card Number: 2002024542

ISBN: 0-312-99003-0

Printed in the United States of America

St. Martin's Press hardcover edition / April 2003
St. Martin's Paperbacks edition / April 2004

St. Martin's Paperbacks are published by St. Martin's Press, 175 Fifth Avenue, New York, NY 10010.

10 9 8 7 6 5 4 3 2 1

In memory of my father,
Raymond Y. Joh,
May 8, 1919–June 14, 2002

Prologue

Japan, Tenwa Period, Year 2, Month 5 (June 1682)

Across dark water skimmed the boat, bound on a journey toward misadventure. Poles attached to the narrow, open wooden shell supported a red silk canopy; a round white lantern glowed from a hook above the stern. Beneath the canopy a samurai sat, plying the oars. He wore cotton summer robes, his two swords at his waist. Though his topknot was gray and his face lined with age, his muscular body and deft movements retained the vigor of youth. Opposite him, on pillows that cushioned the bottom of the boat, a woman reclined, trailing her fingers in the water. The lantern illuminated her flowing black hair and skin radiantly white and limpid as moonbeams. An aqua kimono patterned with pastel anemones adorned her slim figure. Her lovely face wore a dreamy, contented expression.

"The night is so beautiful," she murmured.

Lake Biwa, situated northwest of the imperial capital of Miyako, spread around them, still and shimmering as a vast black mirror. On the near shore, lights from the inns and docks of port villages formed a glittering crescent; darkness and distance obscured the farther boundaries of the lake. Many other pleasure boats dotted the water, their lanterns flickering. Fireworks exploded into rosettes of green, red, and white sparks that flared against the indigo sky and reflected in the water. Cries of admiration arose from people aboard the boats. A gentle breeze cooled the sultry summer eve and carried the scent of gunpowder. But the samurai gleaned no enjoyment from the scene. A terrible anguish tortured him as he beheld his wife.

"You are even more beautiful than the night," he said.

All during their marriage he'd taken for granted that her beauty belonged only to him, and that he alone possessed her love, despite the twenty years' difference in their ages. But recently he'd learned otherwise. Betrayal had shattered his illusions. Now, as his wife smiled at him, he could almost see the shadow of another man darkening and fouling the air between them. Rage enflamed the samurai.

"What a strange look is on your face," said his wife. "Is something wrong?"

"Quite the contrary." Tonight he would redress the evil done to him. He rowed harder, away from the other boats, away from the lights on shore.

His wife stirred and her expression turned uneasy. "Dearest, we're getting too far from land," she said, removing her hand from the water that streamed past the boat. "Shouldn't we go back?"

The samurai stilled the oars. The boat drifted in the vast darkness beyond the colorful bursts of the rockets. The explosions echoed across the water, but the cries were fainter and the lights mere pinpoints. Stars glittered like cold jewels around a filigree gold moon. "We aren't going back," he said.

Sitting upright, his wife gazed at him in confusion. He spoke quietly: "I know."

"What are you talking about?" But the sudden fear in her eyes said she understood exactly what he meant.

"I know about you and him," the samurai said, his voice harsh with grief as well as anger.

"There's nothing between us. It isn't what you think!" Breathless with her need to convince, his wife said, "I only talk to him because he's your friend."

But the man had been more than a friend to the samurai. How the double betrayal had injured his pride! Yet the worst of his anger focused on his wife, the irresistible temptress.

"You were doing more than just talking in the summer house, when you thought I was asleep," the samurai said.

She put a hand to her throat. "How—how did you find out?"

"You let him touch you and possess you," the samurai said, ignoring his wife's question. "You loved him the way you once loved me."

Always fearful of his temper, she cowered. Panic glazed her eyes, which darted as she sought a way to excuse herself. "It was only once," she faltered. "He took advantage of me. I made a mistake. He meant nothing to me." But her lies sounded shrill, desperate. Now she extended a hand to her husband. "It's you I love. I beg your forgiveness."

Her posture turned seductive; her lips curved in an enticing smile. That she thought she could pacify him so easily turned the samurai's anger to white-hot fury.

"You'll pay for betraying me!" he shouted. He lunged toward his wife and scooped her up in his arms. As she emitted a sound of bewildered surprise, he flung her overboard.

She fell sideways into the lake with a splash that drenched the boat. Her long hair and pale garments billowed around her, and she flailed her arms in a frantic attempt to keep from sinking in the deep, black water. "Please!" she cried, sobbing in terror. "I'm sorry! I repent! Save me!"

A lust for revenge prevailed over the love that the samurai still felt for his wife. He ignored her and took up the oars. She grabbed the railings of the boat, and he beat her hands with the wooden paddles until she yelped in pain and let go. He rowed away from her.

"Help!" she screamed. "I'm drowning. Help!"

Rockets boomed, louder than her cries and splashes; no one came to her rescue. While the samurai rowed farther out on the lake, he watched his wife grow smaller and her struggles weaken, heard her gasps fade. She was a water lily cut loose and dying on a pond. She deserved her misfortune. Triumph exhilarated the samurai. His wife's head sank below the surface, and diminishing ripples radiated toward the circle of light cast by his boat's lantern. Then there was silence.

The samurai let the oars rest. As the boat slowed to a stop, his triumph waned. Grief and guilt stabbed his heart. His beloved wife was gone forever, dead by his own actions. A friendship he'd cherished must end. Sobs welled from the void of despair that burgeoned within the samurai. He didn't fear punishment, because his wife's death would seem an accident, and even if anyone guessed otherwise, the law would excuse an important man of the ruling warrior class. But remorse and honor demanded atonement. And to live was unbearable.

With trembling hands, the samurai drew his short sword. Its steel blade gleamed in the lantern light and reflected his tormented face. He gathered his courage, whispered a prayer, and shut his eyes tight. Then he slashed the sword downward across his throat.

A final explosion of fireworks painted the sky with giant, sparkling colored flowers and wisps of smoke. The flotilla of pleasure craft moved toward shore, and a hush settled over Lake Biwa. The samurai's tiny lone boat drifted in the glow of its lantern until the flame burned out, then vanished into the night.

1

Edo, Genroku Period, Year 7, Month 5 (Tokyo, June 1694)

The great metropolis of Edo sweltered in summer. An aquamarine sky reflected in canals swollen from rains that deluged the city almost daily. The multicolored sails of pleasure craft billowed amid the ferries and barges on the Sumida River. Along the boulevards, and in temple gardens, children flew kites shaped like birds. In the Nihonbashi merchant district, the open windows, doors, and skylights of houses and shops welcomed elusive breezes; perspiring townspeople thronged marketplaces bountiful with produce. A miasma of fever rose from alleys that reeked of sewage; pungent incense smoke combated buzzing mosquitoes. Roads leading out of town were crowded with religious pilgrims marching toward distant shrines and rich folk bound for summer villas in the cooler climate of the hills. The sun blazed down upon the peaked tile roofs of Edo Castle, but trees shaded the private quarters of Lady Keisho-in, mother of the shogun Tokugawa Tsunayoshi, Japan's supreme military dictator. There, on a veranda, three ladies gathered.

"I wonder why Lady Keisho-in summoned us," said Reiko, wife of the shogun's *sōsakan-sama*—Most Honorable Investigator of Events, Situations, and People. She looked over the railing and watched her little son, Masahiro, play in the garden. He ran laughing over grasses verdant from the rains, around a pond covered by green scum, past flowerbeds and shrubs lush with blossoms.

"Whatever she wants, I hope it doesn't take long," said Midori. She was a former lady-in-waiting to Keisho-in and a close friend of Reiko. Six months ago Midori had married Sano's chief retainer. Now she clasped her hands across a belly so rotund with pregnancy that Reiko suspected Midori and Hirata had conceived the child long before their wedding. "This heat is too much for me. I can't wait to go home and lie down."

Midori's young, pretty face was bloated; her swollen legs and feet could hardly bear her weight. She tugged at the cloth bound tight around her stomach beneath her mauve kimono to keep the child small and ensure an easy delivery. "This thing didn't work. I've grown so huge, my baby must be a giant," she lamented. She waddled into a shady corner of the veranda and sat awkwardly.

Reiko pushed away strands of hair that had escaped her upswept coiffure and clung to her damp forehead. Perspiring in her sea-blue silk kimono, she wished she, too, could go home. She shared her husband Sano's work, aiding him with his inquiries into crimes, and at any moment there might arise a new case, which she wouldn't want to miss. But Lady Keisho-in had commanded Reiko's presence. She couldn't refuse the mother of her husband's lord, though her eagerness to leave stemmed from a reason more serious than a desire for exciting detective work.

The wife of Chamberlain Yanagisawa—the shogun's powerful second-in-command—stood apart from Reiko and Midori. Lady Yanagisawa was quiet, dour, some ten years older than Reiko's own age of twenty-four, and always dressed in dark, somber colors as if to avoid drawing attention to her total lack of beauty. She had a long, flat face with narrow eyes, wide nose, and broad lips, and a flat, bow-legged figure. Now she sidled over to Reiko.

"I am so thankful I was invited here and given the chance to see you," Lady Yanagisawa said in her soft, gruff voice.

Her gaze flitted over Reiko with yearning intensity. Reiko stifled the shudder of revulsion that Lady Yanagisawa always provoked. The woman was a shy recluse who seldom ventured into society, and she'd had no friends until last winter, when she and Reiko had met. Lady Yanagisawa had attached herself to Reiko with an eagerness that attested to her lonely life and craving for companionship. Since then, Lady Yanagisawa had visited Reiko, or invited her to call, almost daily; when their family responsibilities or Reiko's work for Sano precluded meetings, Lady Yanagisawa sent letters. Her devotion alarmed Reiko, as did her unwelcome confidences.

"Yesterday I watched my husband writing in his office," Lady Yanagisawa said. She'd told Reiko about how she spied on the chamberlain. "His calligraphy is so elegant. His face looked so beautiful as he bent over the page."

Ardor flushed her pale cheeks. "When he passed me in the corridor, his sleeve brushed mine . . ." Lady Yanagisawa caressed her arm, as though savoring the contact. "He looked at me for an instant. His gaze lit a fire in me . . . my heart beat fast. Then he walked on and left me alone." She exhaled with regret.

Embarrassment filled Reiko. She'd once been curious about her friend's marriage, but now she'd learned more than she liked. She knew that Chamberlain Yanagisawa, who had risen to power via an ongoing sexual affair with the shogun, preferred men to women and cared nothing for his wife. Lady Yanagisawa passionately loved him, and though he ignored her, she never gave up hope that someday he would return her love.

"Last night I watched my husband in his bedchamber with Police Commissioner Hoshina," Lady Yanagisawa said. Hoshina, current paramour of the chamberlain, lived at his estate. "His body is so strong and masculine and beautiful." Her blush deepened; desire hushed her tone. "How I wish he would make love to me."

Reiko inwardly squirmed but couldn't evade Lady Yanagisawa's confessions. The chamberlain and Sano had a history of strife, and although they'd enjoyed a truce for almost three years, any offense against the chamberlain or his kin might provoke Yanagisawa to resume his attacks on Sano. Hence, Reiko must endure the friendship of Lady Yanagisawa, despite strong reason to end it.

Lady Yanagisawa suddenly called, "No, no, Kikuko-*chan*."

In the garden Reiko saw her friend's nine-year-old daughter, Kikuko, pulling up lilies and throwing them at Masahiro. Beautiful but feebleminded, Kikuko was the other object of her mother's devotion. A chill passed through Reiko as she watched the children gather the broken flowers. She knew how much Lady Yanagisawa envied her beauty, loving husband, and bright, normal child, and wished her misfortune even while courting her affection. Last winter Lady Yanagisawa had arranged an "accident" that had involved Kikuko and almost killed Masahiro. Ever since, Reiko had never left him alone with Lady Yanagisawa or Kikuko, and she employed Sano's detectives to guard him when she was away from home. She always wore a dagger under her sleeve during visits with Lady Yanagisawa; she never ate or drank then, lest her friend try to poison her. Extra guards protected her when she slept or went out. Such vigilance was exhausting, but Reiko dared not withdraw from the woman, lest she provoke violent retaliation. Would that she could keep away from Lady Yanagisawa!

The door to the mansion opened, and out bustled Lady Keisho-in, a small, pudgy woman in her sixties, with hair dyed black, a round, wrinkled face, and teeth missing. She wore a short blue cotton dressing gown that exposed blue-veined legs. Maids followed, waving large paper fans at her to create a cooling breeze.

"Here you all are! Wonderful!" Keisho-in beamed at

Reiko, Midori, and Lady Yanagisawa. They murmured polite greetings and bowed. "I've invited you here to tell you the marvelous idea I just had." She dimpled with gleeful excitement. "I am going to travel to Fuji-*san*." Her sweeping gesture indicated the peak of Mount Fuji. Revered as a home of the Shinto gods and a gateway to the Buddhist spirit world, the famous natural shrine hovered, snow-capped and ethereal, in the sky far beyond the city. "And you shall all come with me!"

Stunned silence greeted this announcement. Reiko saw her dismay expressed on the faces of Midori and Lady Yanagisawa. Keisho-in regarded them all with a suspicious frown. "Your enthusiasm overwhelms me." Displeasure harshened her crusty voice. "Don't you want to go?"

The women rushed to speak at once, for Lady Keisho-in had great influence over the shogun, who punished anyone who displeased his mother. "Of course I do," Midori said. "Many thanks for asking me," said Reiko. Lady Yanagisawa said, "Your invitation does us an honor."

Their insincere replies faded into more silence. Reiko said, "But religious custom bans women from Fuji-*san*."

"Oh, we needn't climb the mountain." Keisho-in waved a hand in airy dismissal. "We can stay in the foothills and bask in its magnificence."

"Maybe I shouldn't travel in my condition," Midori said timidly.

"Nonsense. The change will do you good. And we'll only be gone ten days or so. The baby will wait until you're home."

Midori's lips soundlessly formed the words, *ten days,* as Reiko watched her envision giving birth on the highway. Lady Yanagisawa gazed at Reiko. In her eyes dawned the amazement of someone who has just received an unexpected gift. Reiko perceived the woman's pleasure at the thought of constant togetherness during the trip, and her own heart sank. Then Lady Yanagisawa looked into the garden, where Kikuko and Masahiro played ball. Worry clouded her face.

"I can't leave Kikuko-*chan*," she said.

"You coddle that child too much," Lady Keisho-in said. "She must eventually learn to get along without her mama, and the sooner the better."

Lady Yanagisawa's hands gripped the veranda railing. "My husband . . ."

As Reiko guessed how much Lady Yanagisawa would miss spying on the chamberlain, Keisho-in spoke with tactless disregard for her feelings: "Your husband won't miss you."

"But we will encounter strange people and places during the trip." Lady Yanagisawa's voice trembled with fear born of her extreme shyness.

Keisho-in made an impatient, scornful sound. "The whole point of travel is to see things you can't see at home."

Midori and Lady Yanagisawa turned to Reiko, their expressions begging her to save them. Reiko didn't want to leave Masahiro; nor did she want to leave Sano and their detective work. She dreaded ten days of Lady Yanagisawa sticking to her like a leech, and the possibility that the woman would attack her. And Lady Keisho-in posed another threat. The shogun's mother had a greedy sexual appetite that she indulged with women as well as men. Once, Keisho-in had made amorous advances toward Reiko, who had barely managed to deflect them without bringing the shogun's wrath down upon herself and Sano, and lived in fear of another such experience.

Yet Reiko dared voice none of these selfish objections. Her only hope of thwarting the trip to was to appeal to Keisho-in's interests.

"I would love to accompany you," Reiko said, "but His Excellency the Shogun may need me to help my husband conduct an investigation."

Keisho-in pondered, aware that Reiko's detective skill had won the shogun's favor. "I'll tell my son to delay all important inquiries until we return," she said.

"But he may not want you to go," Reiko said, her anxiety rising. "How will he manage without your advice?"

Indecision pursed Keisho-in's mouth. Lady Yanagisawa and Midori watched in hopeful suspense.

"Won't you miss him?" Reiko said. "Won't you miss Priest Ryuko?" The priest was Keisho-in's spiritual advisor and lover.

A long moment passed while Keisho-in frowned and vacillated. At last she declared, "Yes, I'll miss my darling Ryuko-*san,* but parting will increase our fondness. And tonight I'll give my son enough advice to last awhile."

"The journey will be difficult and uncomfortable," Reiko said in desperation.

"The weather on the road will be even hotter than it is here," Midori added eagerly.

"We'll have to stay at inns full of crude, noisy people." Lady Yanagisawa shivered.

"Highway bandits may attack us," Reiko said.

Keisho-in's hand fluttered, negating the dire predictions. "We'll take plenty of guards. I appreciate your concern for me, but a religious pilgrimage to Fuji-*san* is worth the hardship."

She addressed her maids: "Go tell the palace officials to get travel passes for everyone and ready an entourage, horses, palanquins, and provisions for the journey. Hurry, because I want to leave tomorrow morning." Then she turned to Reiko, Midori, and Lady Yanagisawa. "Don't just stand there like idle fools. Come inside and help me pick out clothes to bring."

The women exchanged appalled glances at this foretaste of traveling with Lady Keisho-in. Then they breathed a silent, collective sigh of resignation.

In the cool of dawn the next morning, servants carried chests out of Sano's mansion and placed them in the courtyard. Two palanquins stood ready for Reiko and Midori, while bearers waited to carry the women in their enclosed black wooden sedan chairs to Mount Fuji. Sano and Masahiro stood with Reiko beside her palanquin.

"I wish I could call off this trip," Sano said. He hated for Reiko to go, yet his duty to the shogun extended to the entire Tokugawa clan and forbade him to thwart Lady Keisho-in's desire.

Reiko's delicate, beautiful face was strained, but she managed a smile. "Maybe it won't be as bad as we think."

Admiring her valiant attempt to make the best of a bad situation, Sano already missed his wife. They were more than just partners in investigating crimes, or spouses in a marriage arranged for social, economic, and political reasons. Their work, their child, and their passionate love bound them in a spiritual union. And this trip would be their longest separation in their four years together.

Reiko crouched, put her hands on Masahiro's shoulders, and looked into his solemn face. "Do you promise to be good while I'm gone?" she said.

"Yes, Mama." Though the little boy's chin trembled, he spoke bravely, imitating the stoic samurai attitude.

Beside the other palanquin, Midori and Hirata embraced. "I'm so afraid something bad will happen and we'll never see each other again," Midori fretted.

"Don't worry. Everything will be fine," Hirata said, but his wide, youthful face was troubled because he didn't want his pregnant wife to leave.

From the barracks surrounding the mansion came two samurai detectives, leading horses laden with bulky saddlebags. Sano had ordered the men, both loyal retainers and expert fighters, to accompany and protect Reiko and Midori. He wished he and Hirata could go, but the shogun required their presence in Edo.

"Take good care of them," Sano told the detectives.

"We will, *Sōsakan-sama.*" The men bowed.

Reiko said, "Lady Keisho-in, Lady Yanagisawa, and our entourage will be waiting for us outside the main castle gate. We'd better go."

Sano lifted Masahiro; they and Reiko embraced. Final farewells ensued. Then Reiko and Midori reluctantly climbed into their palanquins. The bearers shouldered the poles; servants lifted the chests. Sano hugged Masahiro close against his sore heart. As the procession moved through the gate, Reiko put her head out the window of her palanquin, looked backward, and fixed a wistful gaze on Sano and Masahiro. They waved; Sano smiled.

"Mama, be safe," Masahiro called. "Come home soon."

2

The Tōkaidō, the great Eastern Sea Road, extended west from Edo toward the imperial capital at Miyako. Fifty-three post stations—villages where travelers lodged and the Tokugawa regime maintained security checkpoints—dotted the highway. West of the tenth post station of Odawara, the highway cut across the Izu Peninsula. The terrain ascended into the mountainous district over which reigned the massive volcano Mount Fuji. Here the Tōkaidō carved a crooked path upward through forests of oak, maple, cedar, birch, cypress, and pine.

Along this stretch of road moved a procession comprised of some hundred people. Two samurai scouts rode on horseback ahead of foot soldiers and mounted troops. Banner bearers held a flag emblazoned with the Tokugawa triple-hollyhock-leaf crest, leading ten palanquins followed by servants. Porters carrying baggage preceded a rear guard of more mounted troops and marching soldiers. Syncopated footsteps and the clatter of the horses' hooves echoed to distant peaks obscured by dense gray clouds.

Inside the first palanquin, Reiko and Lady Keisho-in rode, seated opposite each other. They watched through the windows as occasional squadrons of samurai overtook them or commoners passed from the other direction. Moisture condensed in the cool afternoon; streams and waterfalls rippled; birdsong animated the forest.

"Four days we've been traveling, and we're still not even near Fuji-*san*," Keisho-in said in a grumpy tone.

Reiko forbore to point out that their slow pace was Keisho-in's own fault. Keisho-in had spent hours buying souvenirs and sampling local foods at every post station. She'd often ordered the procession to halt while she greeted the public. Furthermore, she disliked riding fast. The women had now gone a distance that should have taken them half the time and a fast horseman could cover in a day. And the trip had already taxed Reiko's endurance.

The group had gotten little sleep due to late, noisy, drunken parties hosted by Keisho-in every night at the inns where they'd stayed. Reiko, forced to share chambers with Lady Yanagisawa, had hardly dared close her eyes at all. Now fatigue weighed upon her; yet she couldn't even doze in her palanquin, because someone always needed her company. Keisho-in didn't want to ride with Midori, who took up too much space, or Lady Yanagisawa, whose reticence bored her. Midori said Lady Yanagisawa frightened her, and Lady Yanagisawa could bear no one except Reiko. Hence, Reiko divided her time between her three companions.

"This climate makes my bones hurt," Keisho-in complained. She extended her legs to Reiko. "Massage my feet."

Reiko rubbed the gnarled toes, hoping not to arouse desire in her companion. So far Lady Keisho-in had satisfied herself with the soldiers, or the ladies-in-waiting and maids who rode in the last six palanquins. But Reiko feared that Keisho-in's roving eye would turn on her. Estimating at least another two days on the road before they arrived at their destination, Reiko sighed. Mount Fuji, hidden by the clouds, seemed as far as the end of the world, and her return home seemed eons away. She prayed that something would happen to cut short this trip.

The road angled through a gorge bordered by high, steep cliffs. Crooked pines clung to the eroded earth. Pebbles skittered down the cliffs to the road. As the procession moved onward, the cliff on its right gave way to level forest. The road curved out of sight between tall, aromatic cedars on one side and sheer rock on the other. Reiko's senses tingled at a change in the atmosphere. Suddenly alert, she froze.

"Why have you stopped massaging?" Keisho-in said irritably.

"There's something wrong." Reiko put her head out the window and listened. "It's too quiet. I don't hear any birds, and no one has passed us in a long while."

A rush of fear assailed Reiko; her heartbeat accelerated. In front of the palanquin rode Sano's two detectives, and Reiko saw them turn their heads and sweep their gazes across the landscape, as if they, too, perceived danger. Then she heard hissing noises. Torrents of slender shafts whizzed down from the cliff top. A soldier screamed and collapsed with an arrow protruding from his neck. The procession dissolved into chaos as men dodged the arrows and horses bolted. Reiko ducked back inside the window.

"What is happening?" Lady Keisho-in demanded.

"Someone's shooting at us. Get down!" Reiko pushed Lady Keisho-in onto the cushioned floor of the palanquin and slammed the windows shut.

More arrows thudded against the palanquin's roof. Shouts burst from the troops and servants, anxious twittering from the women in the other palanquins.

Outside, the guard captain shouted, "We're under attack! Run forward! Stay together!"

The palanquin lurched, gathering speed, jolting as the bearers trotted. Hoofbeats pounded amid screams. The air whirred with the quickening storm of arrows. Their steel points clattered on the road, rang against armor, struck human flesh with meaty thumps. Men bellowed in agony, then the palanquin crashed to the ground with an impact that broke the windows off their hinges and jarred Reiko against Lady Keisho-in.

"Our bearers have been killed." Horror flooded Reiko as she looked outside and saw the men sprawled beneath their shoulder poles. "We can't move." Up the road, arrows felled running soldiers in their tracks. Horses galloped past the dead, crumpled bodies of their riders, after the mounted troops of the advance guard. Behind Reiko, the procession had stalled. "And we're blocking everyone else's way."

The other bearers set down their palanquins; porters dropped baggage. The advance guard reversed its flight, hastening to defend the procession. "Everyone hide in the forest!" shouted the captain.

Servants, porters, and bearers fled down the banked roadside, into the shadowy haven between the trees.

"They're abandoning us!" Lady Keisho-in cried, indignant.

Troops thundered up alongside the row of palanquins, shouting for the ladies to get out. Reiko grabbed Keisho-in by the hand. "Come on."

As they exited the palanquin, Reiko saw Midori, Lady Yanagisawa, and the female attendants emerge from their vehicles. Then screams blared from the forest. People who'd taken cover there came running out, their faces masks of terror. The woods disgorged upon them a horde of men armed with swords and clad in armor tunics and leg guards, chain-mail sleeves, and metal helmets. Black hoods, with holes for the eyes, covered their faces. The men chased the attendants, slashing their blades at porters who dropped dead on the highway with bloody wounds across their naked backs. The savagery struck Reiko mute; shock momentarily paralyzed her.

"Bandits!" cried Lady Keisho-in.

The other women babbled in fright. The captain shouted, "Ladies, get back in the palanquins!"

Reiko thrust the shogun's mother inside, leapt in after her, and closed the door. Outside, the attackers slaughtered servants, pursued those who fled.

"Merciful gods," Reiko said, astounded as well as aghast. "Who dares attack an official Tokugawa procession?"

The captain shouted orders to his army. While a few

troops guarded the palanquins, foot soldiers and mounted samurai launched a defense. Blades lashed hooded men; horses trampled them. But more attackers erupted from the forest, outnumbering the sixty troops that had seemed adequate protection during peacetime. Now every soldier battled multiple opponents. Mounted warriors circled, surrounded by their foes, their horses rearing; their blades whistled arcs in the air. Hooded men dropped, but their comrades slashed the riders dead in their saddles, or dragged them down and slew them. Foot soldiers whirled in desperate dances, weapons flashing. Scarlet gashes from enemy blades appeared on their bodies, and their garments flew in tatters, until they expired from mortal injuries.

The shooting from the cliffs continued. Arrows claimed fleeing servants, pierced the throat of a horse that toppled, spurting blood, and crushed his rider. Meanwhile, the attackers continued to massacre the entourage. Forest and mountains resounded with the echoes of yells and clashing blades.

Reiko watched, transfixed by horror. "Those men can't be ordinary bandits," she said. "They fight too well. And they didn't just happen to be here, waiting to rob any rich travelers who come along. This ambush was organized in advance, for us."

Lady Keisho-in didn't answer. She stared past Reiko, mouth agape, at the carnage.

"The money we brought might seem worth risking their lives to steal," Reiko said, "but why kill helpless, unarmed people?"

She listened to the other women sobbing in their palanquins, and she worried about Midori, alone and pregnant and terrified. Reiko remembered her wish for something to curtail the trip, and she tasted bitter irony and guilt.

The road, and the grass at the forest's edge, were littered with corpses and red with blood. The attackers had chased down the porters, servants, and bearers and slain most of the army. The arrows had ceased. Now a few surviving troops, including Sano's two detectives, fought the legion of hooded men. Combatants darted and blades slashed, dangerously near Reiko. Bodies struck the palanquin; the flimsy vehicle shuddered. Lady Keisho-in clung to Reiko and wailed. Reiko drew the dagger that she wore under her sleeve, ready to defend their lives.

Soon the number of fighters dwindled; Sano's detectives were among those fallen. Then the battle abruptly ceased. In the eerie quiet that descended, more than fifty men gathered on the road. Some limped, sporting bloody wounds; their chests heaved with exertion. They all wore hoods. Reiko saw their eyes glint through the holes, heard their breath rasping through the black cloth. Terror constricted her heart. The attackers had defeated the army.

"What are they going to do?" Keisho-in pressed her face against Reiko's shoulder.

"They'll take our valuables and leave," Reiko whispered, though an ominous pang deep within her said otherwise.

A faraway temple bell tolled. The hooded men ignored the scattered baggage. Half of them moved briskly off along the road and into the forest, as if to hunt down escapees. The others moved around the palanquins to the doors, which faced the cliff that loomed some ten paces away. Reiko's stomach twisted, for she saw her fears realized.

"They're going to kill us all," she said in horrified disbelief.

Doors clicked open along the row of palanquins. Reiko heard women squealing; Lady Keisho-in mewled. The attackers' excessive cruelty appalled Reiko. As a hooded man strode toward her palanquin, rage overrode her terror. A fierce will to survive tightened her hands on the hilt of her long, slender dagger. When the man opened the door, Reiko lunged at him. She jabbed the dagger up under his armor tunic and between his legs.

The blade pierced soft, vulnerable flesh and came away dripping blood. The man yowled and doubled over. Keisho-in screamed. Reiko leaned forward and shoved the man. He fell beside the cliff, writhing in agony. Clutching her dag-

ger, Reiko jumped out of the palanquin, hauling Keisho-in
after her. They stumbled onto the road. Reiko's heart
thrummed with energy born of crisis. Determined to save
her friends, she looked down the line of palanquins.

The attackers dragged out screaming maids and ladies-
in-waiting and propelled them across the road toward the
forest. Near the second palanquin Lady Yanagisawa struggled, her face blank with panic, against a man who pinned
her hands behind her. She jerked wildly, emitting hoarse
grunts.

Reiko charged toward them. Lady Keisho-in faltered in
her wake, moaning and clutching at her skirts. Reiko lashed
her dagger hard across the backs of the man's thighs, where
a gap of exposed skin separated his tunic and leg guards.
The man cried out in surprise, let go of Lady Yanagisawa
and collapsed, groaning, his severed arteries gushing blood.
Lady Yanagisawa staggered free.

At the fourth palanquin, two men leaned in through the
door to remove Midori. Her shrill cries rent the air. Across
the highway, the attackers lined up maids and ladies-in-
waiting by the roadside. One man brandished a dagger,
walked down the line, and began slashing the women's
throats. Horrendous gurgles accompanied spewing crimson
blood. Women wept, screamed, and begged for mercy.

Sickened and aghast, Reiko turned her back on the awful
sight. To attempt rescuing those women would mean losing
her own life and leaving Midori, Keisho-in, and Lady Yanagisawa to fend for themselves. "Take Keisho-in and run,"
she ordered Lady Yanagisawa.

But Lady Yanagisawa stood motionless. She gazed between the palanquins at women lying in puddles of their
own blood, at their wailing, hysterical comrades. The man
continued along the row, his blade dispensing death while
his comrades watched. Lady Yanagisawa's body swayed;
her eyes rolled upward. Reiko grabbed the woman and
slapped her face.

"You mustn't faint now. Go, before they notice we're
still free!" Reiko pushed Lady Yanagisawa toward Keisho-

in, who crouched, whimpering, nearby. The pair stumbled away. Reiko hurried to aid Midori.

The attackers had caught hold of Midori's legs. She thrashed as they dragged her from the palanquin. The man nearer to Reiko had a rip under the armpit of his tunic, where a sword cut had severed the cloth knots that joined the leather-covered metal plates. Reiko drove her dagger into the slit, through skin and vital organs. The man howled. As she yanked the blade free, he released his grip on Midori and fell lifeless. The other man turned toward Reiko. His eyes glared through the holes in his hood. She lashed her dagger across his neck. He died sprawled in the dirt. Midori fell onto the road.

"Oh, Reiko-*san*!" she exclaimed.

Reiko slid her dagger into the scabbard strapped to her arm. She bent over the man she'd just killed and snatched his sword from its hilt.

"Come, we must hurry," she told Midori.

She gripped the stolen sword as they fled up the road, past the Tokugawa banner that lay amid the carnage. But Midori's cumbersome bulk slowed their pace. Reiko heard shouts and pounding footsteps behind them. She looked backward and saw five attackers chasing her and Midori.

"Run faster!" she cried.

"I can't!" Midori gasped and wheezed. "Go without me. Save yourself."

Their pursuers were upon them. Reiko whirled, slashing at the men. They drew their swords. Midori moaned. Reiko called to her: "Stay behind me."

She lunged and sliced; the men parried. Their blades clashed against hers with resounding strikes that vibrated pain up her arms. Reiko had experienced combat before, but never against thirteen opponents at once. They surrounded her and Midori, and she pivoted, desperate to avoid capture. As Reiko fought, Midori bumped her, restricting her movements. She battered at the men, but her blows glanced off their armor.

"Help!" Reiko shouted, hoping for aid from highway patrol troops or traveling samurai.

Her plea rang unanswered across the vacant, misty landscape. Now two men seized Midori. "Let me go! Please don't hurt me!" she cried.

Desperate, Reiko fought harder. She grew dizzy from spinning, breathless and weak from exhaustion. Her muscles ached; her head echoed with metallic clangs. She heard screams in the distance and glimpsed more thugs hastening toward her around the curve in the road, bringing Keisho-in and Lady Yanagisawa. Anguish filled Reiko: Her friends hadn't escaped.

Suddenly, arms as hard and strong as iron encircled her waist from behind her. In a blur of black-hooded figures, clutching hands, and violent motion, somebody wrested the sword from her grasp and flung her down on the road. Men planted their heavy weight on her and immobilized her arms and legs, though she resisted with all her strength. They tore away her hidden dagger. Rough, thick cords wound and knotted her wrists together, then her ankles. Reiko saw Midori, Keisho-in, and Lady Yanagisawa lying bound and weeping near her, surrounded by the enemy. If only she'd managed to save them!

"Who are you?" she demanded of her captors. "Why are you doing this?"

No answer came. She'd not heard the men utter a single word. Their strange, menacing silence increased her terror. They held her head still. One crouched over her and jammed a small flask between her lips. Reiko tasted thick, bitter liquid opium. She clamped her mouth shut. As she squealed and bucked, she heard the other women retching. The men forced her jaws open and poured in the potion.

Reiko spat and coughed, but the bitter ooze gurgled down her throat. Hands yanked a black hood over her head. Blinded, Reiko struggled in darkness for moments that seemed eternal. The sounds of the other women faded; the pain from the cords biting into her skin dulled as a smothering cloud of sleep encroached. Terror receded; unconsciousness descended. Reiko ceased struggling, felt her body lifted by unseen hands and carried briskly away. Images of Sano and Masahiro briefly illuminated the black oblivion spreading in her mind. As she yearned for her family, one last thought occurred to Reiko.

If she lived, she would be more careful what she wished for next time.

3

"Excuse me, *Sōsakan-sama*, but you must get up at once."

Sano, roused from sleep by instincts ever attuned to the world around him, had opened his eyes just before he'd heard Hirata's urgent call outside his door. His bedchamber was dark, but the corridor was lit by the lantern Hirata carried, and Sano saw his chief retainer's shadow through the paper wall. Sano automatically reached for his wife but found emptiness beside him on the futon. Though Reiko had been gone almost five days, her absence startled him. Sano sat up under the thin sheet that covered his naked body.

"Come in, Hirata-*san*," Sano said. "What is it?"

Entering the room, Hirata said, "A castle messenger just brought word that the shogun has summoned us to the palace."

"What for?" Sano said, yawning and rubbing his eyes.

"The messenger didn't know. But it's an emergency."

Sano and Hirata looked toward the open window. A warm breeze wafted from the garden, where a gibbous moon floated in a black sky above pine trees and silvered the shrubs and grass. Fireflies winked; crickets sang. The dark hush of the atmosphere signified a time equidistant from midnight and dawn.

"That His Excellency wants us at this hour means the problem must be dire indeed," Sano said.

As soon as he'd dressed, he and Hirata left the estate and hurried up through the winding stonewalled passages and the security checkpoints of Edo Castle to the palace. Its half-timbered structures and peaked roofs slumbered in the moonlight. Inside the formal audience chamber, Sano and Hirata found an assembly of men waiting.

Guards stood along the walls of the long room, whose floor was divided into two levels. On the lower level knelt a samurai clad in a blue armor tunic that bore the insignia of the Tokugawa highway patrol. On the upper level, in two rows facing each other, knelt the Council of Elders—Japan's supreme governing body, comprised of the sho-gun's five elderly chief advisors. Beyond them sat Cham-berlain Yanagisawa and his lover Police Commissioner Hoshina, to the right of the shogun, who occupied the dais. All wore troubled expressions; everyone silently watched Sano and Hirata approach. The tension in the room was as thick as the smoke that drifted from the metal lanterns hung from the ceiling.

Sano and Hirata knelt on the upper level of the floor at the shogun's left. They bowed to their lord and the assem-bly. "How may we be of service, Your Excellency?" Sano said.

Incoherent sputters issued from Tokugawa Tsunayoshi. His refined face was deathly pale and his frail, slender body trembled under his white silk night robe. His usually mild eyes blazed, and Sano realized that he was furious as well as distraught.

"You tell them, Yanagisawa-*san*," he said at last.

Chamberlain Yanagisawa nodded. In his beige summer kimono, he looked as suavely handsome as always. His enigmatic gaze encompassed Sano and Hirata. "This is Lieutenant Ibe," he said, indicating the highway patrol guard. "He has just brought news that His Excellency's honorable mother was abducted on the Tōkaidō yesterday, along with your wives and mine."

Shock imploded in Sano. His mind resisted believing what he'd heard. He shook his head while Hirata uttered a sound of vehement denial. But the grave faces of the assembly told them that Yanagisawa had spoken the truth.

"How did this happen?" Sano said, fighting an onslaught of wild anxiety.

"The procession was ambushed on a deserted stretch of road between Odawara and Hakone post stations," Yanagisawa said.

"Who did it?" Hirata demanded. His face was stricken with terror for Midori and his unborn child.

"We don't know," Yanagisawa said. "At present we have no witnesses."

Sano stared in disbelief. "But there were some hundred attendants in the entourage. One of them must have seen something."

Police Commissioner Hoshina and the Council of Elders bowed their heads. Yanagisawa said, "The entourage was massacred during the ambush."

The audacity and violence of the crime struck Sano and Hirata speechless with horror. Sano regretted the deaths of his two detectives. Yanagisawa looked toward the highway patrol guard and said, "Lieutenant Ibe discovered the crime. He shall describe what he found."

Lieutenant Ibe was a lean, sinewy man in his twenties. His bare arms and legs and his earnest face bore streaks of grime and perspiration from what must have been a swift, grueling ride to Edo. "There were bodies strewn along the road and in the forest," he said, his eyes haunted by memory of what he'd seen. "They'd died of sword wounds. Blood was everywhere. The baggage seemed untouched—I found cash boxes full of gold coins in the chests. But the palanquins were empty, and the four ladies gone."

A dreadful thought occurred to Sano. "How can you be sure they were abducted and not—" *Killed,* he thought, but he couldn't say it. Hirata emitted a low, involuntary groan.

"We found a letter inside the Honorable Lady Keisho-in's palanquin," said the guard.

Chamberlain Yanagisawa handed Sano a sheet of ordinary white paper that had been folded, crumpled, then smoothed. Dirt and blood smeared a message crudely scrawled in black ink.

Your Excellency the Shogun,

We have Lady Keisho-in and her three friends. Let no one pursue us, or we will kill the women. You will be told what you must do to get them back alive. Expect a letter soon.

The message bore no signature. Stunned by fresh shock, Sano passed the letter to Hirata, who read it and gaped in astonishment. Lieutenant Ibe continued, "I fetched officials from Odawara, the last checkpoint that the procession passed. They matched the bodies to the names in the records."

Checkpoint officials inspected the persons of everyone who passed through their stations, looking for hidden weapons or other contraband. Female inspectors were employed to search the women. Because the Tokugawa restricted the movements of women to prevent samurai clans from sending their families to the countryside in preparation for revolt, the law required female travelers to have travel passes. The officials copied the information on each pass, which listed the social position, physical appearance, and identifying birthmarks or scars of its owner.

"The female inspectors remembered the four ladies well," said Lieutenant Ibe. "Everyone else was accounted for. The ladies were definitely not among the dead."

This was inadequate comfort to Sano and Hirata, when their wives' fate was unknown. They exchanged apprehensive glances.

"One survivor was found," Police Commissioner Hoshina said. He was broad-shouldered and muscular, with an angular, handsome face. Ambitious to rise in the *bakufu*—the military government that ruled Japan—he took every opportunity to draw his superiors' attention to himself. Now he conveyed facts he'd apparently learned from the highway patrol guard before Sano and Hirata arrived: "The officials identified the survivor as Lady Keisho-in's personal maid, a woman named Suiren. She was badly wounded, and unconscious. Troops are bringing her to Edo. With luck, she'll be here tomorrow."

Perhaps she would identify the attackers, but what might happen to Reiko, Midori, Keisho-in, and Lady Yanagisawa in the meantime? Sano stifled his emotions and willed the detective in him to analyze the situation.

"Has the area around the ambush site been investigated for clues to where the kidnappers took the women?" he asked.

"The local police were on their way to the scene when I left," said Lieutenant Ibe. "They may have found something by now."

"The women's guards, and the two detectives we sent, would have fought whoever ambushed the procession," Hirata said, jittering with his effort to control his distress. "Some of the attackers must have been killed. Were their bodies found and identified?"

"There were signs of a battle, but we found no bodies except those of the ladies' entourage," Lieutenant Ibe said regretfully. "If any of the kidnappers died, their comrades removed them from the scene."

"They massacred the attendants and defeated a squadron of Tokugawa troops. They removed their dead and carried away the four women. *And no one saw that?*" Incredulity lifted Sano's voice. "At this time of year, the highway is usually crowded with peasants going to market and tourists bound for the hot springs. Where was everybody when the procession was attacked?"

"That stretch of the Tōkaidō runs through mountainous terrain," Hoshina said. "There are places where the road is bordered by a high cliff on one side and a steep drop on the other. Someone put up roadblocks made of heavy logs at two of these places. The procession was ambushed between them."

Personally unaffected by the crime, Hoshina seemed to relish it, and Sano disliked him even more than their history of bad blood merited. They'd first clashed during a murder case in Miyako. Ever since the chamberlain had appointed him police commissioner, Hoshina had considered Sano a rival, sought to prove himself the superior detective, and constantly undermined Sano. Of course Hoshina would welcome Sano's misfortune.

"No one passed during the attack because traffic was backed up at the roadblocks until the highway was cleared," Hoshina finished.

Someone had employed many men and gone to great lengths to engineer the ambush, Sano observed.

"You're dismissed," Chamberlain Yanagisawa told Lieutenant Ibe. "You'll stay in the castle barracks in case you're needed for further questioning."

No sooner had a guard ushered Ibe from the room than the shogun burst out, "I don't understand how you can all, ahh, sit and chat while my mother is, ahh, at the mercy of such cruel villains! Are you so heartless?"

"We must all keep calm so we can absorb the facts and decide what to do," Chamberlain Yanagisawa said.

Tokugawa Tsunayoshi glared at him. "It's easy for you to be calm. We all know you're a cold, selfish brute who wouldn't care if your wife, ahh, dropped off the face of the earth."

The shogun doted on Yanagisawa, almost never criticized him, and usually seemed oblivious to his faults, but anxiety had sharpened the shogun's wits and tongue. The elders winced at the personal insult, but Yanagisawa appeared unruffled. "I am very concerned about my wife's safety," he said.

Although he didn't love his wife, she was a Tokugawa relative and therefore a valuable possession that comprised his family link to the regime, Sano knew. And woe betide anyone who stole anything that belonged to Yanagisawa.

The shogun rose awkwardly to his feet. Puffed up with rage, he declared, "I shall send out the army to rescue my mother!"

Sano and Hirata beheld him with consternation. Chamberlain Yanagisawa frowned, while Hoshina watched everyone with the air of a theatergoer enjoying a good play. Murmurs arose from the Council of Elders.

"With all due respect, Your Excellency, I must advise against sending the army after the kidnappers," said Senior Elder Makino, a crony of Chamberlain Yanagisawa and persistent detractor of Sano. He had an emaciated body and ugly skull-like face. "The letter expressly instructs you not to pursue them."

"Those villains do not command the supreme dictator of Japan!" roared the shogun.

"They might make good on their threat to kill the women," Makino said.

"They wouldn't dare!"

"They've already dared to kidnap your mother and murder her entourage," Chamberlain Yanagisawa pointed out.

"Even if we knew where the kidnappers went, we can't mount an assault without endangering the women's lives," Sano said, and Hirata nodded.

"Ahh, yes. You are right." Unhappy comprehension deflated the shogun. He wailed, "But we must do something!"

"May I propose an alternative to the army?" Chamberlain Yanagisawa said deferentially. "Police Commissioner Hoshina and I have formed an elite squad of troops who are trained to handle dangerous, sensitive missions. We can employ them to find and rescue the women."

The very idea repelled Sano. He knew those troops were assassins whom Yanagisawa employed primarily to keep himself in power. Though Sano respected their skill, he didn't trust them.

"I'll lead the squad," Hoshina said, his face alight with eagerness. "The kidnappers won't even see us coming. Just leave everything to us, and the Honorable Lady Keisho-in will be back in Edo in no time."

Nor did Sano want Yanagisawa and Hoshina to take charge of the situation. Their sole concern was rescuing Keisho-in, and perhaps Lady Yanagisawa. They wouldn't care if the other women got killed in the process. Sano burned with hatred toward Hoshina. The police commissioner saw the kidnapping as his big chance. He would climb to power over the corpses of Reiko and Midori!

The shogun brightened, ready as usual to believe someone could solve his problems for him. Before he could speak, Sano turned his rage on Chamberlain Yanagisawa. "I won't let you shut me out of this," he said.

"I'll do what's best," Yanagisawa said with equal ire. "And you're forbidden to object."

Bushido—the Way of the Warrior—demanded a samurai's unswerving obedience to his master and superiors. Yet in this situation, Sano must defy the code by which he lived. "Hirata-*san* and I aren't leaving our wives' fate in your hands," Sano declared.

"I suppose you'd rather entrust the rescue to those hundred reckless amateurs that you call your detective corps?" Police Commissioner Hoshina sneered. "You might as well condemn the women to death right now."

The elders conferred among themselves. The shogun's gaze moved from one man to another as he tried to follow the argument.

"We shall compromise," he said, waving his hands to silence the assembly. "I'll send out the army." He thumped his chest. "You lead your, ahh, elite squad, and you take along your detectives," he said, pointing at Hoshina, then Sano. "Together we'll hunt down the kidnappers and rescue my mother."

The shogun swelled with authoritative pride. But Sano saw his dismay mirrored on the faces of his companions as they all imagined the chaos that would result from their lord's plan.

"That's a brilliant idea, Your Excellency," Chamberlain Yanagisawa said in the warm, admiring tone he used when he disagreed with the shogun and meant to have his own way.

"But . . ." Police Commissioner Hoshina began cautiously.

Sano had no patience for the process of manipulating the shogun. He said, "Pardon me, Your Excellency, but we don't know who the kidnappers are or where they are, or anything else about them except that they've already murdered a hundred people. To launch any attack is too big a risk to our women."

"You're a coward who fears any risk, and too incompetent to deserve any part in this matter. Do not listen to him, Your Excellency," Hoshina said, leaping to defend his own plan and make Sano look bad.

"Don't you insult my master!" Hirata glared at the police commissioner.

With great effort, Sano ignored Hoshina and said to the shogun, "We must obey the kidnappers' instructions."

A storm of voices raised in protest greeted his words. "But if we, ahh, wait for a letter, what might those, ahh, criminals do to my mother in the meantime?" the shogun wailed.

"Surely you don't expect us to give the kidnappers whatever they ask in exchange for the women's release," Chamberlain Yanagisawa said in outraged scorn.

"Or to let them get away with their crime." Hoshina matched his lover's tone.

"To bow down to the kidnappers would portray the Tokugawa regime as weak and vulnerable," Senior Elder Makino said, and his colleagues nodded their agreement.

Hirata turned a wounded gaze on Sano, as if Sano had betrayed him. "We can't just do nothing. Let's fetch our detectives and go!"

Sano hated to deny Hirata's wishes. He hated to bide time while Midori and Reiko were in peril; yet he believed he must convince the assembly that they had no reasonable choice but delay.

"The women are the kidnappers' insurance against retaliation from us," he said. "Criminals who are intelligent enough to plan and carry out that ambush know better than to kill the hostages. They won't harm the women as long as they think they can get what they want."

Observing the other men's skepticism, Sano wished he had more faith in his own argument. He said, "Whatever price the kidnappers ask should be a small price to pay for the return of the Honorable Lady Keisho-in."

Antipathy narrowed Yanagisawa's and Hoshina's eyes, but the shogun knelt; his resolve visibly waned. "Indeed," he said.

"We can hunt down and punish the kidnappers after the women are safe," Sano said, then addressed the elders. "That the procession was ambushed, the troops slain, and the women taken has already shown that the regime is vulnerable. Denying it now would be senseless. The news will spread across the country before we can stop it. A hasty, blind rescue attempt is likely to fail, and if it does, the *bakufu* will look even worse."

Makino nodded grudgingly; the other elders followed suit. Chamberlain Yanagisawa conceded with a faint grimace, and the shogun set his weak jaw. "Sano-*san* is right," he declared. "We shall wait for the, ahh, ransom demand."

"And in the meantime, do nothing," Hoshina said, glowering at Sano, obviously hating to lose his big chance to be a hero.

Sano gleaned no triumph from this victory, because his real enemies were the kidnappers, against whom he felt helpless. "On the contrary," he said. "We must work together to figure out who's behind the crime, so we can locate and capture him when the time is right."

Crisis demanded unity. Tokugawa Tsunayoshi nodded his approval, calmer now that argument had ceased and Sano had reduced the disaster to a solvable problem. An uneasy concord settled upon the other men. The atmosphere in the chamber was hot and stuffy, acrid with smoke and the stink of nerves.

"I propose that we begin the investigation by identifying potential suspects," Sano said.

"The leader of the kidnappers must be someone who has enough troops to massacre an armed procession, or enough money to hire them." Hirata, though clearly opposed to Sano's strategy, was duty bound to support his master.

"He had to have known in advance that the women were going on the trip, so he could position troops to lie in wait for them," Hoshina said. Sano noted how quickly the police commissioner had turned the investigation into an opportunity to display his detective talent. "Since the trip was a sudden impulse of Lady Keisho-in's, and the news didn't have time to spread far, he must live in or near Edo."

Sano had an unfounded but powerful sense that the crime wasn't as straightforward as it seemed. "I wonder who is the real target of the kidnapping plot," he said.

Surprise lifted eyebrows on the faces around him. The shogun said, "How can there be, ahh, any doubt that I am the target, and the kidnapping is an act of war against me?"

"The kidnapper must be an enemy of the regime, who seeks to humble His Excellency and extort ransom money from the treasury," said Senior Elder Makino.

Candidates included citizens who chafed under the *bakufu*'s strict laws, and *daimyo*—feudal lords—oppressed by the Tokugawa. Disgruntled *rōnin*—masterless samurai—were a continuing source of trouble. Yet Sano saw other possibilities.

"Maybe the kidnappers want more than just to strike at the regime, or money for freeing the hostages," Chamberlain Yanagisawa said; his expression turned speculative as he voiced Sano's thought.

"That they didn't bother to loot the baggage and steal the gold indicates that lucre isn't their main concern," Hoshina said.

"Maybe there's a more personal motive behind the crime." Yanagisawa's gaze moved from Sano to Hirata, then to the shogun. "Your Excellency is not the only one of us with enemies who might attack us through our women."

Sano knew that few people alive had as many enemies as did Yanagisawa. A long list included men he'd ousted from power, the kin of rivals he'd demoted, executed, or assassinated, and lovers used then spurned by him.

Ominous intent darkened Yanagisawa's eyes. "I can think of a few people who bear checking into," he said.

Hirata sat openmouthed and frozen, as if thunderstruck by inspiration. His voice emerged bitter with hatred: "Lord Niu."

"Your father-in-law, the *daimyo* of Satsuma Province," Hoshina clarified. "The two of you have been at odds since you married Lady Midori." Proudly showing off his knowledge, the police commissioner added, "Perhaps the kidnapping is his method of reclaiming his daughter."

"If he's behind this, I'll kill him!" Hirata exclaimed.

Sano wasn't ready to focus the investigation on Lord Niu, or Yanagisawa's political enemies. "Let's not forget the Black Lotus," he said.

The name tainted the air like poison. The elders averted their eyes and compressed their lips in distasteful memory; Hirata nodded grimly. Wary interest tensed Yanagisawa and Hoshina, while the shogun looked confused as to what a defunct Buddhist sect could have to do with the crime.

"The sect has been banned since its uprising eight months ago," Sano said, "but although most of the priests, nuns, and followers have been captured and executed for their attempt to destroy Japan, some remain at large, and they've recruited new members. They hate me for my part in crushing the sect, and my wife for killing their leader. They've sworn revenge."

During the past decade, the Black Lotus had tortured and murdered countless people who'd crossed it. The fanatical members, responsible for a conflagration with a death toll of over seven hundred, were capable of slaughtering a procession while sacrificing their own lives. The thought of Reiko caught by them panicked Sano. The sect might have a fate worse than death in store for her.

"It seems we have an abundance of suspects to investigate," Chamberlain Yanagisawa said.

"Well, I, ahh, order you to begin work at once, get my mother back, and execute whoever kidnapped her as soon as possible." The shogun waved his hand at everyone. "Dismissed."

Sano and Hirata left the palace. Hirata brooded in silence until they entered the walled courtyard of Sano's estate. Then he blurted, "Forgive me for speaking boldly, but I don't think we're doing enough to save the women. Limiting our attention to Edo and investigating our enemies may or may not prove worthwhile. Besides, any evidence the kidnappers left is far away on the Tōkaidō."

"You're right," Sano said. "That's why I'm giving you a secret assignment."

Hirata's features, illuminated by the torches that flared in the courtyard, sharpened with eager hope.

"Go to the site of the abduction," Sano said. "Take along Detectives Marume and Fukida. Wear disguises, travel under aliases. No one must know you're investigating the crime because we don't want the kidnappers to find out we're pursuing them and disobeying their orders. Examine the crime scene, look for witnesses, and try to pick up the kidnappers' trail."

"Yes, *Sōsakan-sama!*" Hirata said with ardent gratitude.

"Bring me word of any clues you find," Sano said. "But promise me that you won't approach the kidnappers or do anything else that might endanger the women."

"I promise." The mantle of fear and helplessness dropped from Hirata; he glowed with confidence. "We'll be ready to go by dawn. And I promise we'll find the kidnappers."

Hirata rushed off toward the barracks. Sano stood alone in the courtyard, listening to the sounds of cicadas humming, dogs barking, and mounted soldiers patrolling in the night that spread dark and wide around him. His mind yearned across the distance toward Reiko.

Where was she? As anguish gripped him, Sano hoped she was unharmed. He prayed that she and the other women would come home safely and soon, and that fortune combined with hard work would negate the premonition of calamity that chilled him.

4

The sound of sobbing aroused Reiko to groggy consciousness. She thought Masahiro must have wakened in the night from a bad dream. Maternal instinct compelled her to go to him—but she couldn't move.

A force like bands of steel locked her legs against each other and her arms at her sides. Confusion blinked her eyes open, but thick, rough material covered her face, and all she saw was blackness. She drew a gasp of surprise, then gagged on something coarse and dry that filled her mouth. Now Reiko became aware that she was moving in rapid, jouncing rhythm, carried by hands that gripped her armpits and ankles. The sobbing continued, accompanied by moans. Panic seized Reiko; her heart lurched.

Where was she? What had happened to her?

Then memory seeped, hideous and dreadful, through the fog of sleep that clung to her mind. Visions of the ambush, the massacre, and the kidnapping assailed Reiko. The cries she heard must belong to Keisho-in, Midori, or Lady Yanagisawa. They were still captive, somewhere that defied imagination.

Terror exploded in Reiko. She wanted to thrash and scream, but that would only waste her strength. Reiko forced herself to be still, urged her somnolent brain to rational thought. She must marshal her wits and learn what she could of her circumstances, discover anything that might prove useful for survival, and keep terror at bay.

Reiko focused her attention first on herself. Ropes tied around her immobilized her body. The material covering her face was the black hood the kidnappers had put on her head. Her tongue tasted the dryness of cotton fabric stuffed in her mouth as a gag. She felt nausea and a throbbing headache that she attributed to the opium the men had poured down her throat, but otherwise she seemed unhurt. Stiffness in her muscles, and a need to urinate, indicated that she'd slept for a time long enough to have traveled a great distance beyond the scene of the abduction and beyond the reach of anyone looking for her.

But perhaps nobody knew yet what had happened. Perhaps she would die before someone came to the rescue.

Fresh panic agitated Reiko like wings fluttering inside her chest. She experienced such an intense stab of longing for Sano and Masahiro that she nearly wept. But she willed herself calm. She directed her senses outward.

Through the thick cloth of the hood, she heard footsteps treading dry leaves. Twigs cracked. Grass rustled. Men's breaths rasped. Those noises pierced a mesh of sound composed of crickets and cicadas singing and wind rustling through trees. Owls hooted. Ahead of Reiko erupted phlegmy coughs from Lady Keisho-in; behind her, Midori wept. Where Lady Yanagisawa was, Reiko couldn't tell. She felt branches snag her garments, and cool, damp air; mosquitoes hummed around her. Pine-scented smoke filtered through the hood. Reiko formed a mental picture of the kidnappers carrying her and the other women through a forest at night, their way lit by torches. The commotion signified many more men following. Reiko's imagination showed her an endless line of hooded, stealthy marching figures.

Suddenly the footsteps slowed; movement halted. In the brief quiet Reiko heard a heavy door scrape open. Motion then resumed, and the atmosphere changed. The forest sounds were muted; the men's feet shuffled on a stone surface; echoes reverberated. The air was still, warmer, and suffused with a musty odor: They'd entered a building.

As the door thudded shut, Reiko's body tilted, head upward. The abrupt change of position nauseated her so much that she thought she would vomit and choke. She felt herself ascending, borne by the men whose weight creaked wooden stairs under their feet. They tipped her horizontal at a landing, then climbed more stairs. From above her came the coos of nesting birds frightened by the intrusion, the screech and flutter of bats. The men remained ominously silent. Reiko visualized an abandoned dungeon. Escalating fear prickled her skin.

They reached another landing, mounted another flight of steps, then stopped in a space where the men, redolent of sweat, crowded around Reiko. She heard thuds as they set down burdens. They thumped her onto the floor and released her. The metallic rasp of blades withdrawn from scabbards struck terror into her heart. Hands groped across her body. She keened and writhed helplessly, certain that the kidnappers meant to kill her and her friends. Mews of protest arose from the other women.

The hands on Reiko grasped the ropes that bound her. She felt tugs while a blade sliced through the thick cords. As they fell away, she blindly launched herself toward freedom while grabbing for the dagger under her sleeve.

But the weapon was gone, taken by the kidnappers during the fight. A whirlpool of dizziness drowned Reiko. Her sore muscles collapsed under her weight. She fell back, gasping as the nausea roiled her stomach, awash in cold perspiration. She heard the men bustle away, a door bang shut, and the clank of iron bars dropping into iron latches. Footsteps retreated down the stairs. Tears flooded Reiko's eyes as she mourned the lost opportunity for escape and cursed her own weakness.

But she squandered no more energy on regret; her concern shifted to her comrades. With hands that felt thick and awkward Reiko tore the hood off her head, the gag from her mouth. She squinted at pale, meager light that came from vertical cracks in the shutters of windows set in the four walls of a square room in which she lay. Outside, far below her, waves splashed, and she smelled the marine scent of the water. As her eyes adjusted, she saw three prone figures on the floor around her.

"Lady Keisho-in!" she called. "Midori-*san*! Lady Yanagisawa!"

Feeble cries answered her. Reiko pushed herself upright and breathed deeply for a long moment until the nausea and dizziness ebbed. Then she crawled over to the figure nearest her and removed its hood and gag.

"Ugh!" Lady Keisho-in coughed and sputtered. Her frightened eyes blinked in her haggard, sunken face. "This feels like the worst hangover I've ever had. What's happened to us? What is this place?"

"We've been abducted, drugged, and imprisoned," Reiko said, glad that the shogun's mother was a tough old woman capable of surviving the experience. "I don't know where we are, except high up near a lake or sea in the middle of a forest."

Lady Keisho-in made a clumsy attempt to rise. She said, "I need to make water."

Reiko looked around the room. It was unfurnished, the floor made of bare planks, the walls surfaced with peeling white plaster. Two metal buckets sat in a corner. Reiko fetched a bucket and helped Lady Keisho-in sit upon it.

After she'd urinated, Keisho-in said, "I'm so thirsty. I must have a drink."

Reiko also felt a terrible thirst that parched her mouth and throat. Searching the room, she found a ceramic jar of water in another corner. She and Keisho-in drank eagerly, though the water was lukewarm and tasted of minerals.

Groans emanated from the prone figure whose mountainous belly identified her as Midori. She'd rid herself of the hood and gag, and as Reiko hurried to her, she retched.

"I'm going to be sick," she said.

Reiko dashed for a bucket. Midori vomited while Reiko held her head. Afterward, Midori sat up and clutched her stomach, hands frantically pressing, rubbing.

"My baby." Fright thinned her voice, widened her eyes. "It hasn't moved since I woke up."

She and Reiko sat in momentary speechless terror that the opium—or the trauma suffered by Midori—had killed the unborn child. Then Midori began to sob.

"No, oh, please, no!" she wailed.

"The baby will be fine," Reiko said, hoping she spoke the truth. "It's just asleep. Lie down and rest. Don't worry."

After she settled Midori on the floor, Reiko hastened to Lady Yanagisawa. The woman lay quiet and still, legs straight, her hands fallen at her sides. When Reiko pulled the hood off her and yanked the cloth gag from her mouth, Lady Yanagisawa blinked up at Reiko. Her tongue slowly moistened her lips.

"Are you all right?" Reiko asked.

Lady Yanagisawa murmured, "Yes, thank you."

Her face was strangely blank, her tone calm and polite as if this were an ordinary social occasion. She made a feeble motion to rise. When Reiko helped her sit up, she said, "I must be going home now, if you'll excuse me."

An eerie apprehension stole through Reiko.

"You can't go home," Keisho-in said to Lady Yanagisawa. "We've been kidnapped." She peered quizzically into Lady Yanagisawa's face. "Don't you remember?"

Lady Yanagisawa frowned in bewilderment, shaking her head. "My apologies . . . I don't understand what you're saying." She seemed oblivious to their surroundings; she ignored Midori, who moaned and wept across the room. As Reiko and Keisho-in regarded Lady Yanagisawa with speechless confusion, she repeated, "I must be going home now. Kikuko-*chan* needs me."

"I'm sorry, but that's not possible," Reiko said gently.

She explained what had happened, but the words seemed not to penetrate Lady Yanagisawa's mind. The woman laboriously clambered to her feet. Gripping the walls for support, she stumbled blindly around the room. "Kikuko-*chan*," she called. "Where are you?"

"The shock has driven her mad," Keisho-in said.

Reiko feared that Keisho-in was right. Perhaps Lady Yanagisawa was only suffering from the aftereffects of the opium; but perhaps her already unbalanced mind wanted to deny what had happened, and its refusal to face facts had tipped her over the edge of insanity.

"Where are you, Kikuko-*chan*?" Anxiety inflected Lady Yanagisawa's voice. "Come to Mama."

Reiko hurried to Lady Yanagisawa and put her arms around the woman. "Kikuko-*chan* is safe at home. Please sit and compose yourself. You're not well."

Lady Yanagisawa pulled away and continued searching the room. "Kikuko-*chan*!" she called with increasing urgency.

"We need help," Lady Keisho-in said. She staggered to the door, banged on it, and yelled, "Hey! We've got sick people in here. I order you to bring a physician!"

The banging echoed through what seemed like a deep well of empty space. No reply came. Midori's sobs rose in hysteria.

"I wish I'd never gone on the trip," she cried. "I wish I were at home."

"This is intolerable," Keisho-in declared, her fear giving way to anger. "My head is killing me. I need my tobacco pipe. It's cold in here. The dust irritates my lungs." She coughed and wheezed. "That I, the shogun's mother, should be treated like this is an outrage!" She kicked the door. "Whoever you are, let us out at once!"

"I want my baby to be all right," Midori wailed between sobs. "I want Hirata-*san*."

Responsibility for her companions fell to Reiko with the burdensome weight of an avalanche. Though ill and terrified herself, she said, "We must stay calm. Getting upset will only make matters worse."

Lady Keisho-in turned a vexed scowl on Reiko. "You're so good at solving mysteries. Find us a way out of this."

But Reiko knew how much her past success had depended on weapons; freedom of movement; access to information; and the power of Sano, his detective corps, and the Tokugawa regime behind her. Here, unarmed and trapped, what could she do to save her friends?

Nevertheless, determination and duty compelled Reiko to try. "Please be patient. I'll get us out," she said, feigning confidence.

Keisho-in squatted, folded her arms, and waited; Midori's tears subsided. Lady Yanagisawa turned in slow, giddy circles, her gaze darting deliriously. The lap and rush of waves pervaded the uneasy quiet. Reiko went to the door and pushed. Its thick, heavy wood didn't yield; pressure only rattled the bars on the other side. Her hands probed for cracks in the door's surface and around the edge, to no avail. She moved to the windows and discovered that the shutters were nailed closed. She inserted her fingers into the narrow gaps between the rough wooden slats and tried to pry them apart. This gained her nothing except splinters in her skin.

Lady Yanagisawa collapsed, forlorn and whimpering, in a corner. "I can't find my little girl," she said. "Where can she have gone?"

Reiko examined the walls and floor. Both were marred with holes and fissures, but none large enough for escape. The building seemed ancient, in disrepair, but solid. Soon Reiko was exhausted, panting, and sweaty despite the cold. She stood in the center of the room and gazed upward. The ceiling was twice as high as she was tall. Moonlight shone through crevices amid the rafters. Failure drained her energy; she sank to her knees.

A pitiful wail came from Midori: "What's to become of us?"

Lady Keisho-in jumped up, trotted around the room, and pounded on the shutters. "Help!" she shouted. "Somebody help!"

"Don't panic," Reiko begged. "We must save our strength and ready our wits for when we get an opportunity to escape."

"We'll never escape," Midori said as more sobs convulsed her. "We'll all die!"

Her hysteria infected Keisho-in, who clawed the door with her fingernails. "I must leave this place now! I can't stand this anymore!"

Though Reiko attempted to reason with and comfort her friends, they paid no attention.

"Hirata-*san*!" Midori called, as if her voice could carry across the distance to her husband.

Keisho-in hurled herself repeatedly against the door, uttering foul curses that revealed her peasant origin; Lady Yanagisawa whimpered. Reiko had never felt so useless. When news of the massacre and abduction reached Edo, the shogun would surely order Sano to investigate this serious crime. Here Reiko was at the center of what might be the biggest case of Sano's career; but all her talent and experience mattered not, for this time she was a victim instead of a detective.

Frustration, physical malaise, and terror that she would never again see Sano or Masahiro nearly overwhelmed Reiko. Tears spilled from her eyes; yet her samurai spirit blazed with anger toward her kidnappers and spurned the notion of giving up without a fight. Somehow she must deliver herself and her friends to safety, and the criminals to justice.

"Hirata-*san*!" Midori called again and again.

Her friend's desperation resonated through Reiko. As much as she craved action, there seemed nothing she could do at present except wait for whatever was to come.

5

At dawn, a sun like an immense drop of blood floated up from the eastern hills outside Edo and shimmered in the white haze that veiled the sky. The discordant peals of bells in temples called priests to morning rites and roused the townspeople from slumber. As birds shrilled in the trees within Edo Castle's stone walls, guards opened the massive ironclad gate. Out came Hirata with Detectives Fukida and Marume. Fukida was a brooding, serious samurai in his twenties; Marume, a decade older, had a jovial countenance and a powerful build. They and Hirata rode horses laden with saddlebags for their journey to the scene of the abduction. Disguised as *rōnin*, they wore old cotton robes, wide wicker hats, and no sign of their rank, in the hope that they could blend with other travelers and secretly track down the kidnappers.

Instead of following the main boulevard west to the Tōkaidō, Hirata led his men along a road into the *daimyo* district south of the castle. "One quick stop may save us a long search," he said.

The heat of day vanquished night's fleeting coolness as the city awakened to life. Mounted samurai thronged the wide avenue of *daimyo* estates, mansions surrounded by barracks constructed of white plaster walls decorated with black tiles. Porters delivered bales of rice and produce to feed thousands of *daimyo* clan members and retainers. Hirata, Marume, and Fukida dismounted outside an estate that numbered among the largest. The gate boasted red beams and a multitiered roof; a white banner above the portals bore a dragonfly crest. Hirata approached a sentry stationed in one of the twin guardhouses.

"Is Lord Niu home?" Hirata said.

The guard glanced at Hirata's shabby garments, sneered, and said, "Who's asking?" Then he did a double take as he recognized Hirata. He leapt to his feet and bowed. "My apologies. Yes, the Honorable Lord Niu is in."

"I want to see him," Hirata said in a voice tight with controlled anger.

"Certainly," the guard said, and opened the gate. "I'll tell him you're here."

"Never mind. I'll tell him myself."

Hirata stalked through the gate; Fukida and Marume followed him into a courtyard. Here samurai patrolled and guardrooms contained an arsenal of swords, spears, and lances. As they entered another gate that led beyond the officers' barracks, Hirata burned with ill will toward Lord Niu.

History had lain the foundations for their strife. Lord Niu was an "outside *daimyo*," whose clan had been defeated by the Tokugawa faction during the Battle of Sekigahara and forced to swear allegiance to the victors almost a hundred years ago. Hirata came from a Tokugawa vassal family. Although most other *daimyo* accepted Tokugawa rule without rancor, Lord Niu hated the exorbitant taxes he had to pay, and the laws that required him to spend four months each year in Edo and his family to stay there as hostages to his good behavior while he was home in his province. He also hated anyone associated with the regime—including Hirata. The *daimyo* had opposed the match between Hirata and Midori, who hadn't bowed to his wishes as tradition required. Their love for each other—and the child that was already on the way before the marriage negotiations began—had necessitated desperate action.

Hirata had tricked Lord Niu into consenting to the marriage, and the *daimyo* had never forgiven him. Lord Niu had vowed to separate the couple and sworn vengeance against Hirata. All Hirata's attempts to placate Lord Niu had met with failure. And because of what Hirata had learned about Lord Niu since marriage joined their clans, he believed the *daimyo* to be the best suspect in the massacre and kidnapping.

He and his men entered the mansion, a labyrinthine complex of buildings connected by covered corridors and intersecting tile roofs and raised on granite foundations. They burst into Lord Niu's private chamber.

Lord Niu, clad in a dressing gown, knelt on the *tatami* while a valet shaved his crown with a long razor. Near them sat the *daimyo*'s chief retainer, a dour, homely man named Okita. Guards stood by the walls. Everyone looked up at Hirata and the detectives in surprise.

"Where is she?" demanded Hirata.

Lord Niu demanded, "What are you doing here?"

He was a short man in his fifties, with swarthy skin and broad shoulders. His most remarkable feature was the asymmetry of his face. The right half was a distorted reflection of the other. The left eye focused on Hirata and blazed with hatred; the right contemplated distant space.

"I want to know where my wife is," Hirata said, planting himself in front of his father-in-law, despite the creeping uneasiness that Lord Niu always inspired in him. Detectives Marume and Fukida stood behind Hirata.

"How should I know?" Lord Niu regarded Hirata with puzzlement and hostility. "You stole her from me. It's up to you to keep track of her. Why do you come in here at this early hour, without my permission, to ask ridiculous questions?"

Had anyone else reacted this way, Hirata might have believed he was telling the truth, but Lord Niu was crafty and dishonest. "Midori, Lady Keisho-in, Lady Yanagisawa, and Lady Reiko were abducted yesterday," Hirata said.

"What?" Lord Niu's eyebrows shot up; he leaned forward. "How did this happen?"

As Hirata explained, he observed that Lord Niu's shock appeared genuine. But if he'd arranged the ambush, he would have expected Hirata to come, and prepared to feign innocence. Hirata glanced at the *daimyo*'s men. The guards and Okita looked wary, and Hirata decided they hadn't been aware of the crime. Their master often acted without their knowledge.

"Tell me what you did with the women," Hirata said.

"You think I took them?" Lord Niu rose so fast that he almost knocked over his valet, who'd ceased trying to shave him. He faced Hirata with an incredulous stare.

"Yes," Hirata said.

"Well, I didn't," Lord Niu declared. "Why would I do a thing like that?"

"You want to separate Midori from me and break the union between our clans," Hirata said. "The Council of Elders expects the ransom instructions to demand money, but I know better. You want to force the shogun to dissolve my marriage."

Lord Niu looked dumbfounded. "However much I hate you, I did not massacre a Tokugawa procession or kidnap the shogun's mother. You're not worth risking execution for murder and treason." His voice turned contemptuous; his hand shot out and shoved Hirata. "Only a madman would go to such great lengths for a feud with the likes of you."

That Lord Niu was the madman, Hirata had come to realize when the *daimyo* had begun pursuing vengeance against him. "You've already gone to great lengths," Hirata said. "When Midori came here for her ritual visit after our wedding, you locked her in and threatened to kill her unless I divorced her." The memory fueled Hirata's anger toward Lord Niu. "You didn't let her out until I showed up with troops and forced you to give my wife back to me."

"She wanted to stay," Lord Niu lied brazenly. "You took her against her will."

"A month later, you pretended to forgive me and invited me to a banquet," Hirata continued. "I sat beside you while we ate and drank. That night I fell ill with terrible stomach cramps, diarrhea, and vomiting. No one else at the party got sick. The Edo Castle physician said I'd been poisoned. You did it. You tried to murder me."

"That's vicious slander." Lord Niu puffed himself up in indignation. "You just can't hold your liquor."

"And this spring, a band of assassins attacked me in town," Hirata said. "My men and I fought them, and they ran away—but not before I got a good look at them." Hirata pointed to a hatchet-faced guard standing by the window. "That's their leader. Too bad for you that your men are inept cowards."

The guard bristled at the insult and took a step toward Hirata. A warning look from Lord Niu halted him. Lord Niu folded his arms in defiance; his left eye glared at Hirata, while his right dreamed. He said, "You're mistaken. Those weren't my men you saw. They must have been some of your other enemies. And I've had enough of your false accusations."

Yet Hirata had even more evidence that Lord Niu would shed blood to satisfy a grudge. When Hirata had asked Midori about her father's behavior, she'd confessed that he'd always had a wild, violent, unreasonable nature. Lord Niu had vented his ire at the Tokugawa by beating his concubines, fighting his retainers, rampaging through his province, and slaughtering innocent peasants. Furthermore, Sano had told Hirata about the *daimyo*'s youngest son, now dead, who'd committed such extreme treason that he couldn't have been sane. The clan had hushed up Lord Niu's excesses to protect him, and the *bakufu* had hushed up the treason rather than allow the public to know the regime was vulnerable to attack. Hirata now belonged to a select group of people who knew madness ran in the Niu family. And he believed that Lord Niu's rage against him had worsened the madness and driven Lord Niu to abduct Lady Keisho-in and slaughter her entourage.

"I've had enough of your denials," Hirata said, advancing on Lord Niu. "I want to know what you've done with Midori-*san* and her friends."

Though Lord Niu stood only as high as Hirata's shoulder, his crooked sneer was intimidating. "I couldn't have abducted them. I've been here in Edo the whole time. They'll tell you." He jerked his chin toward his men.

"It's true," Okita said in a firm, matter-of-fact voice. The valet and guards nodded. "He didn't do it. He never even left the estate."

This alibi didn't convince Hirata. Those men owed their loyalty to Lord Niu, had dutifully stood by him through all the evils he'd done, and would lie to protect him. "Then you must have sent troops or hired mercenaries so you could keep your hands clean," Hirata said.

Anger surged in him, and not just because he thought Lord Niu had kidnapped Midori. The *daimyo* had been draining enjoyment from his marriage and his anticipation of fatherhood. His heart was thudding, his hands itching to pound the truth out of Lord Niu. He paced around the *daimyo,* who revolved, glaring at him.

"That is a lie," Lord Niu sputtered. "I didn't order the kidnapping. How could I have, when I had no idea the women were going on that trip?"

"Don't pretend you didn't know," Hirata said, circling Lord Niu, growing angrier by the moment. "You have spies at Edo Castle because you're deluded enough to think the Tokugawa are plotting war against you—even though they wouldn't disrupt the peace they've maintained for almost a century. You must have heard about Lady Keisho-in's plans."

"How dare you mock me?" Lord Niu clenched and unclenched his hands, as though eager to strangle Hirata. "Why do you waste time accusing me, instead of hunting the real culprit?"

Their mutual antagonism vibrated in the atmosphere. The guards rested their hands on their sword hilts; Marume and Fukida hovered alert, anticipating battle.

"May I suggest that there has been a misunderstanding?" Okita said cautiously. His main duty was to control Lord Niu and defuse situations that could ignite the *daimyo*'s temper, Hirata knew. "Perhaps if we all sit down and have some tea, we can resolve our differences."

Lord Niu ignored his retainer. He froze, and a look of horrified comprehension nearly aligned the halves of his face. "Oh, I see what's going on," he said to Hirata. "This is another of your schemes against me." Lord Niu clung to the conviction that Hirata was out to get him, despite Hirata's assurances that all he wanted was a truce. "You want me gone forever, and my honor disgraced—and what better way than to brand me a traitor?" The *daimyo* jabbed a finger into Hirata's chest. "You kidnapped the women yourself, to frame me!"

"What?" Shock halted Hirata and dropped his mouth. How Lord Niu twisted reality never ceased to amaze him. "But I didn't—surely you can't believe—"

"Don't deny it," Lord Niu said, his complexion purple with fury. "You and the shogun hatched the scheme together. You arranged the crime. You used my daughter to implicate me. The shogun plans to execute me for abducting his mother, then confiscate my lands."

"That's ridiculous," Hirata protested.

"What did he promise you in exchange for your help, you dirty sneak?" Lord Niu seized Hirata by the front of his kimono. "A portion of my wealth? My province to rule?"

Outraged, Hirata wrenched free of Lord Niu. "I would never frame anyone for murder and treason. Even though you deserve punishment for everything you've done to me, I would never conspire against my wife's father. You're just trying to divert suspicion from yourself onto me!"

"See how he pretends to be innocent," Lord Niu said to the assembly, his voice filled with scorn. "See how he pretends to believe he thinks I'm guilty. See how he eagerly anticipates my ruin. But you won't get away with it."

Suddenly he lunged at Hirata. The impact of his body

knocked Hirata off balance. He reeled backward and crashed against a wall. The painted landscape mural cracked. Lord Niu's hands closed around his neck and squeezed.

"Where are my daughter and Lady Keisho-in?" Lord Niu shouted while Hirata choked and struggled to pry the *daimyo*'s hands loose. "Tell me what you've done with them."

That Lord Niu had turned him into the suspect, and usurped the role of interrogator, astounded Hirata. Detectives Fukida and Marume hurried to his rescue, but Okita got there first. Okita grabbed the *daimyo* and hauled him off Hirata. While Hirata gasped for air, Lord Niu flung Okita away from him. His gaze lit on his valet, who hunched, terrified, on the floor near him. He snatched the shaving razor from the man's hand.

"I'll make you admit your evil deeds!" Lord Niu roared. He charged at Hirata.

Compelled to defend himself, goaded beyond prudence, Hirata drew his sword. He could tolerate no more of Lord Niu's craziness, insults, or attacks. As hot anger overrode self-control, Hirata almost forgot why he'd come here. He would end this war now, regardless of the consequences.

Then Marume and Fukida caught hold of him, arresting his flight toward the *daimyo*. "No, Hirata-*san*!" they shouted.

The guards rushed and seized Lord Niu. Trained to protect people from their master, and their master from himself, they gripped his thrashing limbs. He cursed and fought them, but they wrested the razor from his hand and restrained him.

"You'll pay for setting me up, you despicable lout!" he yelled at Hirata. "I'll slice your guts!"

"Come on, let's go," Marume said. He and Fukida dragged Hirata from the room.

Now Hirata came to his senses, recalled his purpose. "But I'm not finished." Wild with rage and distress, he resisted his men; he dragged his feet in the corridor.

"It's no use," Fukida said, urging Hirata out of the mansion. "Even if he knows where Midori-*san* is, he won't talk. Staying will only get you killed."

Hirata reluctantly capitulated. Outside the estate, they mounted their horses, and he realized how badly he'd handled the confrontation with Lord Niu. He should have kept calm and treated the *daimyo* with courtesy instead of losing his temper. Even as he understood that his father-in-law would probably have behaved the same way whatever he'd done, Hirata experienced mortifying shame.

"I threw away a chance to solve the case," he said.

"There will be other chances," Marume said, swinging himself into the saddle. "Don't worry—we'll save Midori-*san,* no matter what."

This attempt at reassurance failed to soothe Hirata. As they rode down the street, the sun rising over the roofs of the *daimyo* estates reminded him that time was quickly passing. And he was no closer to finding his wife now than when he'd heard the news of her abduction.

Fukida spoke with the hesitant air of a man voicing what his superior wouldn't want to hear: "There's good reason to believe Lord Niu is the kidnapper . . . but we can't prove it. And as you told us Chamberlain Yanagisawa said last night, there is an abundance of suspects. Fixating too early on Lord Niu might steer us in the wrong direction."

Hirata inhaled and nodded. "You're right," he said. "I shouldn't let my prejudice blind me to the possibility that someone other than Lord Niu took the women." And unless he disciplined himself, he might jeopardize his mission.

He and the detectives turned their horses onto the boulevard and galloped west. Ahead, the road wound and narrowed toward the invisible horizon; shops, houses, and pedestrians dwindled into a shimmering haze of heat and charcoal smoke. The hills were gray smudges against the bleached blue sky. If the weather held, a day of hard, fast riding should take Hirata and his men to the scene of the massacre and abduction.

"But if Lord Niu is behind the crime, I'll prove it," Hirata said, slapping the reins. "And he will pay."

6

In the reception room of Sano's estate, one hundred detectives and soldiers knelt in rows on the floor while Sano, seated on the dais, told them about the kidnapping.

"This case takes priority over everything else," he said. "For now, we will drop all other tasks." Investigating the death of a priest at Ueno Temple, and a theft from the Tokugawa treasury, could wait. "The kidnapping may be the work of the Black Lotus sect. We must round up as many outlaw members as we can and find out what they know about the crime.

"Detectives Inoue and Arai, you'll work with me," Sano continued. The short, muscular samurai and the tall, thin one bowed. Sano divided the remaining troops into teams. "Go to the shrines, gambling dens, teahouses, and other places that the outlaws are known to frequent. Question your informants about secret temples. Use any means necessary to get leads on who the kidnappers are and where they're holding the women."

He sent the men on their way. He was glad to be taking action toward saving Reiko, yet his fear for his wife threatened to shatter the stoic façade he maintained. He told Inoue and Arai to meet him by the gate, then went to the nursery in the mansion's private quarters.

Morning sun shone through doors open to the garden. Masahiro sat at a tray table, eating rice gruel. Three nursemaids wiped up spills and chattered to him. Everyone saw Sano standing in the doorway. The nurses bowed; Masahiro smiled, his face smeared with food, his eyes bright.

"Papa," he said.

Love for the little boy stabbed anguish through Sano's heart. Their son was the embodiment of the happiness Sano shared with Reiko . . . and stood to lose. Sano managed a cheerful greeting to his son, then beckoned the eldest nursemaid. "I must have a word with you, O-sugi."

The old woman followed him outside to the garden; there, Sano told her about the kidnapping. Her lips parted in wordless exclamation and tears filled her eyes. She'd been Reiko's nurse when Reiko was a child. Sano had to look away from O-sugi's grief, lest it weaken his own self-control.

"Please tell the other servants what has happened," Sano said. "But Masahiro is not to know. I forbid everyone to talk about it when he might overhear. I don't want him upset."

"Yes, master," O-sugi whispered.

Sano went back into the nursery. He picked up Masahiro and held him tight.

"I paint picture yesterday," Masahiro said in his earnest baby voice. "Will Mama come home and see?"

As he touched his face against Masahiro's tender cheek, Sano felt the stinging pressure of tears. "Yes, she will," he said, vowing that their son would not lose his mother. He eased Masahiro to the floor. "I have to go now. Be good."

"Where are you going?" Masahiro asked.

"To see your grandfather," Sano said.

Ever curious, Masahiro tilted his head. "Why?"

"Because I need his help with some important work." And because Sano must deliver the news of Reiko's abduction to the man he most dreaded telling.

Sano and his two detectives rode to the Hibiya administrative district south of Edo Castle where Reiko's father served as one of the two magistrates responsible for maintaining law and order in the city. Earthen walls surrounded the tile-roofed, half-timbered mansions that housed offices and residences. Messengers, clerks, and dignitaries thronged the narrow lanes, clustering in excited groups. Sano heard snatches of their conversation; he watched the news of the kidnapping spread. Nothing remained secret in Edo for long.

At Magistrate Ueda's estate, sentries at the portals admitted Sano and his men to a courtyard, where citizens gathered to bring disputes before the magistrate and police guarded shackled prisoners due for trial. Sano instructed his men to wait, then entered the mansion, a long, low structure with projecting eaves and latticed windows. Inside, he met Magistrate Ueda at the carved door to the Court of Justice.

"Greetings, Sano-*san*," Magistrate Ueda said. He was a middle-aged samurai with a stout build, gray hair tied in a thick topknot, and broad features. He wore black robes decorated with gold crests. After he and Sano exchanged bows, he said, "What a pleasure to see you, but I have a trial to conduct."

"Please excuse the interruption. We must talk," Sano said.

The magistrate frowned, perceiving that something was amiss. Concern sharpened his intelligent, heavy-lidded eyes. "What is it?"

Sano glanced at the guards by the courtroom door, and the clerks busy in their chambers. "May we go to your office?"

There, Magistrate Ueda seated himself behind his desk. Sano knelt opposite him and said, "I regret to tell you that your daughter has been kidnapped."

Magistrate Ueda's face went expressionless as Sano related the circumstances of the crime. Anyone not well acquainted with him might have thought him indifferent to his daughter's plight. But Sano knew what shock and alarm the man was experiencing. Magistrate Ueda loved his only child and valued her as all that remained of his beloved wife, who'd died when Reiko was a baby. He'd lavished upon her the education and martial arts lessons normally reserved for a son. Only a lifetime of samurai discipline enabled him to hide his emotions.

"If there is anything I can do to help you save the women and capture whoever took them, just ask," he said.

"Thank you, Honorable Father-in-law." Sano bowed, then explained that he suspected the Black Lotus. "I need to know if any outlaws are in custody." While Sano, the police, and other officials hunted sect members, the magistrate kept track of those apprehended.

"Two men arrested by the police yesterday are in my courtroom awaiting trial now," Magistrate Ueda said.

"May I question them afterward?" Sano said.

"By all means," said Magistrate Ueda.

They entered the Court of Justice, a long hall where guards stood inside the doors and rows of people knelt on the floor. Dusty sunlight beamed through open windows. Men fanned themselves with paper fans. Two defendants knelt on the *shirasu*, an area of floor directly below the dais, covered with white sand, symbol of truth. They wore gray prison robes; their wrists and ankles were shackled. Sano knelt near the back of the room. Magistrate Ueda seated himself on the dais, between the court secretaries. Everyone in the room bowed to him.

A secretary announced, "The defendants are Jun and Goza of Honjo district. They are accused of arson, murder, and belonging to an illegal religious sect."

Both men were muscular commoners in their late twenties. Jun had cropped hair and a face that might have been handsome if not for thick lips held in a surly pout. Goza's head was shaved bald; his small, angry eyes, upturned nose, and bristled jowls gave him the look of a wild pig.

"The court shall now hear the evidence," said the secretary.

He called the first witnesses—a sandal maker and his wife. They came forward and knelt near the *shirasu*. "A Black Lotus nun came to our shop and begged for alms," said the man. "When we refused to give her money, she put a curse on us."

The Black Lotus often extorted money from citizens, and used physical force to back up their magic spells, Sano knew.

"That night, the police caught those men setting the building on fire," said the wife.

A police officer testified that Jun and Goza had killed one of his civilian assistants while resisting arrest. Sano studied the defendants and recognized them as the new breed of Black Lotus followers. They weren't deluded fanatics who believed that membership in the sect destined them for glorious enlightenment. They were unscrupulous men attracted by the violence and wealth associated with the Black Lotus. Perhaps they would serve Sano's purpose.

"You may speak in your own defense," Magistrate Ueda told the criminals.

Jun shrugged, then muttered sullenly, "I did it." Goza echoed him. Sano saw that they realized there was no point in denying their guilt, because they'd been caught in the act.

"I pronounce you guilty and sentence you to execution," Magistrate Ueda said. Then he dismissed the audience and secretaries. They departed, leaving him, his trusted guards, and Sano alone with the criminals, who exchanged glances and shifted nervously. Sano strode up to the dais.

"The shogun's *sōsakan-sama* will question you," Magistrate Ueda told the criminals.

The pair gazed up at Sano with an animosity that matched his toward them. He said, "Who hired you to burn the shop?"

"It was a Black Lotus priest," said Jun. His crude, handsome face glistened with sweat. "He calls himself Profound Wisdom."

Goza nodded his bald, piglike head. Obviously, the men felt no loyalty to their master and didn't mind informing on him. Sano recalled hearing the priest mentioned as one who had a large, dangerous following.

"Where can I find Profound Wisdom?" Sano said.

"He has secret temples," said Jun. "But I don't know where they are. They move around."

To avoid the police, Sano figured. "How do you and his followers know where to find him?"

"He leaves messages at a Buddhist supply shop near the Nihonbashi Bridge. People in the Black Lotus go there and ask the proprietor for Yoshi—that's the password—and he tells them where the temple is that day."

"What other work besides arson does he hire men like you to do?" Sano said.

"When people drop out of the Black Lotus, we threaten them so they won't betray it," Goza said. "We kill anyone who does. We kidnap women for the priest to use in rituals."

Sano's instincts sprang alert. "What women?"

Goza grinned, showing rotten teeth. "Pretty ones."

Magistrate Ueda frowned and leaned forward on the dais. He knew as well as Sano did what happened during the Black Lotus's cruel, depraved rituals.

"Have you ever heard of the Black Lotus kidnapping women for ransom?" Sano asked.

The men shook their heads. Jun creased his brow in puzzlement, as though trying to figure out Sano's intentions; Goza looked merely bored.

"The shogun's mother and three other women were kidnapped yesterday," Sano said, watching the criminals as he moved closer to them. "What can you tell me about that?"

"Nothing, master," Jun said with what seemed to be genuine surprise. "It's news to me." Then he laughed. "The Black Lotus people think their High Priest Anraku has risen from the dead. They say he wants to avenge his murder. Maybe he spirited away those women."

Obviously, he didn't share the sect's beliefs and was mocking them. That he would make a joke of the crime infuriated Sano. He wanted to rub Jun's face in the white sand and grind the smile off it. Then he noticed that Goza sat with his mouth slack and a murky gleam in his porcine eyes, as if a sudden thought had occurred to him. Sano quickly crouched in front of Goza and grabbed him by the shoulders.

"Did the Black Lotus take the women?" he demanded.

Cunning altered Goza's expression even as he recoiled from Sano. "Maybe," he said.

Sano guessed that the man knew something. He shook Goza. "Tell me!"

"If he does, will you spare our lives?" Jun interjected.

The idea of pardoning murderers revolted Sano. "Don't you bargain with me," he said. Anger and impatience overrode his hatred of abusing his power. He slapped Goza hard on each cheek. "Where are they?" he shouted. If this criminal was withholding facts that could save Reiko, he deserved no mercy.

"Hurting him won't do any good," Jun said smugly. "He won't talk unless you save us."

Incensed that the men had gained the upper hand, Sano turned on Jun and would have struck him; but Magistrate Ueda said quietly, "Sano-*san*. Wait." Then he addressed the criminals: "Tell us what you know, and I'll consider revoking your sentences."

His stony expression told Sano how torn Magistrate Ueda was between his duty to uphold the law and his need to save his daughter. Although he often showed leniency toward petty offenders, he never released anyone guilty of a major crime.

Goza rattled his shackles. "Free us first," he said, "or there's no deal."

"Talk, or you go to the execution ground." Magistrate Ueda gave the men the fierce stare that had subdued many an adversary and beckoned the guards.

The criminals quailed visibly and looked at each other. Jun nodded at Goza, who said, "I've heard talk that the Black Lotus is planning a big attack on the Tokugawa. Could be it's the kidnapping, and Profound Wisdom arranged it."

Sano stood back and eyed the man with suspicion. "Who

carried out the kidnapping? Where might they be hiding the women?"

Goza shrugged. "I've told you all I know."

"You've told me what you think will save your skin." Angry contempt heated Sano's blood. The story was plausible but vague, and as much as he longed to believe he had a lead on the kidnappers, Sano distrusted its source. "I say you're lying."

"It's the truth," Goza said, his chin raised defensively.

"Can we go now?" Jun asked the magistrate.

Sano gave Magistrate Ueda a look that warned him against falling for a trick. Magistrate Ueda frowned, compressed his lips, then told the men, "I'll delay your sentences until I find out whether what you've said is of any use." He signaled his guards. "Take them to Edo Jail. Confine them in a cell by themselves, and make sure no harm comes to them."

The criminals protested as the guards dragged them from the court. Sano and Magistrate Ueda expelled gusts of breath. "If that lout told the truth and his information helps us rescue the shogun's mother, His Excellency will praise my cleverness," Magistrate Ueda said. "If he's proven a liar, I'll be ridiculed as a fool and condemned for subverting justice."

With bleak candor he added, "But I don't care what happens to me. All I want is my daughter saved."

Sano forbore to offer sympathy that would embarrass his father-in-law. "Maybe this priest can lead us to her. My men and I will begin looking for him now."

The lane was one of many that branched like crooked ribs off the main boulevard near the foot of the Nihonbashi Bridge, the official starting point of the Tō-kaidō. The bridge's great wooden curve arched over the canal beyond the rooftops. Along the street, businesses that catered to travelers sold hats, noodles, sake, and guidebooks depicting highway attractions. Noisy crowds of religious pilgrims, carrying walking staffs and laden with heavy packs, browsed the merchandise.

The Buddhist supply shop occupied a storefront in the middle of the block. Inside, past the blue entrance curtain, a white-haired man sat behind a counter amid beaded rosaries hung from the low ceiling and shelves crammed with Buddha statues and boxes of incense. Sano and Detective Arai loitered outside while Detective Inoue, clad in a plain cotton robe hastily purchased for this occasion, entered the shop and approached the proprietor.

"I'm looking for Yoshi," Detective Inoue said, as Sano had instructed him to do.

The proprietor scrutinized Inoue, and a leery expression came over his wrinkled face. "I'm sorry, master, there's no one by that name here."

Sano was dismayed because the proprietor had obviously guessed that the detective wasn't a real Black Lotus member. He also discerned that Inoue posed a threat, because he darted toward a curtained doorway behind the counter. Inoue lunged across the counter and caught him. As Sano and Arai rushed into the shop, Inoue held the proprietor by the arms.

"Please, masters, don't hurt me," the old man cried.

"I won't if you tell me where the Black Lotus temple is," Sano said.

"But I don't know."

The proprietor gave a nervous giggle that turned into a shriek as Sano whipped his sword out of its scabbard. "Where is the temple?" Sano demanded. To menace a helpless old man filled him with shame even though his victim abetted the Black Lotus, a crime punishable by death. But the abduction was teaching Sano that his principles had limits. He would do anything to find out who'd kidnapped Reiko, and saving his lord's mother took precedence over personal ideals.

"All right—I'll tell you. It's in the teahouse by the Inari Shrine on the north side of the Kanda vegetable market." The proprietor begged, "Please don't kill me."

Sano sheathed his sword; Detective Inoue relaxed his hold on the proprietor, who babbled in relief.

"Listen carefully," Sano told the old man. "You'll carry on your business as usual. You won't tell your Black Lotus friends about our talk. Do you understand?"

Resignation slumped the old man's body. "Yes, master."

"Detective Arai will be here watching to make sure you obey," Sano added, then turned to Arai. "Arrest anyone who comes and asks for the temple's location."

"Yes, *Sōsakan-sama*," the detective said, though obviously wondering how many outlaws might come and worried about whether he could subdue them by himself.

"I'll send men to help you as soon as possible," Sano said. Suddenly his detective corps seemed smaller than usual and stretched far too thin to net the Black Lotus. "Detective Inoue and I have to find that temple."

The teahouse was located in a row of dilapidated buildings dwarfed by the *torii* gate of the shrine to Inari, the Shinto rice god. The shrine's gong clanged and peasants streamed out the gate while Sano and Detective Inoue secured their horses to a nearby post. As the sun rose higher toward noon, shadows receded and stray dogs lay panting under the eaves. Raucous voices drifted from the vegetable market, and the still, hot air reeked of rotten cabbage. Sano and Inoue appraised the teahouse from a distance. With its thatched roof, barred window, and weathered plank walls, it resembled Edo's thousand other drinking places—except that it showed no sign of life.

Sano signaled Inoue to wait, then walked to the sliding door that stood open just enough for a man to squeeze through. He pressed himself against the building and peered sideways into a small room, unfurnished and empty, with a closed door at the rear. Sano beckoned Inoue, who slipped after him into the teahouse. They leaned their ears to the door and heard high, faint voices, chanting. Sano's heart beat a cadence of caution and excitement because he was certain he'd discovered a Black Lotus ritual. He drew his sword because the sect's priests, nuns, and worshipers would fight to the death rather than be captured. Then he nodded at Inoue.

The detective opened the door, which required all his strength to budge and yielded with a groaning noise. Sano yelled, "Don't move! In the name of the shogun, I order you to surrender!"

He and Inoue rushed into a long, narrow chamber. Unlit lanterns dangled from the rafters. Against the far wall, a black lacquer table held burned-out candles. The space in front of the altar where worshipers would have knelt was unoccupied. Sano halted, lowering his sword, stunned by the letdown; yet the chanting went on, louder now. Sano and Inoue frowned in confusion. Then a slim, vertical rectangle of sunlight at the edge of a back door caught Sano's eye. He and Inoue raced to the door, flung it wide, and looked outside.

In an alley, four little girls crouched in a circle by the opposite house, chanting in some childish game. Sano and Inoue shook their heads at each other. Disappointment grieved Sano as he voiced the obvious: "The sect has abandoned this temple."

The Black Lotus had an uncanny ability to sense danger coming and skip out just in time. Sano looked forward to long hours of chasing it. Worse, he had no proof that the hunt might lead him to Reiko except the word of a criminal . . . and his own instincts, which he realized might lead him as badly astray. Maybe he'd convinced himself of the Black Lotus's guilt because he couldn't bear to think he was just wasting time until the ransom letter arrived. Still, Sano clung to his convictions rather than admit helplessness.

"We'll go ask the neighbors where Profound Wisdom and his followers went," Sano told Inoue. "If they can't tell us, I know a few Black Lotus hideouts to check."

Yet although Sano found comfort in believing he was headed in the right direction, he hoped he was wrong about the Black Lotus and that it didn't have Reiko. The sect's cruelty toward its victims had no limits. And one disturbing notion seemed to Sano the only certainty: No matter who had Reiko, the longer she was captive, the less her chance of survival.

7

Birdsong had replaced the whine of nocturnal insects in the forest outside the prison. The gaps in the shutters had turned from moonlit gray to rose-pink at dawn; now they were bright streaks of sunshine. Reiko sat and watched while day illuminated her surroundings.

Dusty cobwebs festooned the grid of cracked, rotting rafters. The ceiling and the plaster on the walls were stained black with smoke from a fire long ago. Dead bugs and mouse and bird droppings littered the floor. An abandoned nest made of twigs perched high above Lady Keisho-in, who reclined in a corner. With her face powder and rouge smeared, she looked clownish, pitiful, and a decade older than usual. Near her, Midori heaved over on her side, her eyes puffy from tears. Only Lady Yanagisawa had slept during the terrible night. She lay facing a wall, knees drawn up and arms folded, motionless.

"Almost a day has passed since we were abducted," Reiko said. Despite her anxiety, she must raise her friends' morale. "By now someone should have found our entourage murdered and discovered us missing. The crime should have been reported to the authorities, who should have begun searching for us. We'll be rescued soon."

No one answered. No one could guess whether her optimistic prediction would come true, or if worse things might happen.

"It's getting too warm in here," Keisho-in said, fanning herself with the end of her sash. "I'm so thirsty I would kill for a drink." They'd finished the last drop of water in the jar hours ago. "And I'm dying of hunger."

Reiko's own empty stomach growled with a fierce appetite. Did their captors intend them to starve to death? Why had they been kidnapped? What reason could justify the slaughter of a hundred people? Reiko shook her head at the futility of speculating in the absence of clues.

"This place stinks," Lady Keisho-in complained. The buckets filled the room with the odors of urine, feces, and vomit. "I've never had to put up with the likes of this!"

Nor had Reiko, who realized what a comfortable life she'd always taken for granted. Her father's wealth and her advantageous marriage had given her luxurious surroundings, servants to wait on her, and good meals whenever she wanted. But now she hadn't a grain of rice to eat. She couldn't even have a bath, or clean clothes to wear. This intimation of what poor people endured every day enlightened and appalled Reiko.

With intense longing she thought of her home. She recalled awakening in her own bright, airy bedchamber, with Sano's arms around her and Masahiro pattering into the room to crawl under the quilt with them. Sano must be busy working now; probably he didn't yet know about her abduction. Masahiro would be enjoying the wonders that each new day brought him. She blinked back a rush of tears and forbade herself to indulge her misery. She rose and circled her prison, trying to see out the windows.

On three sides of the room, the cracks in the shutters gave narrow views of sunlight and shadow dappling pine boughs that bristled with green needles. Birds winged past in flashes of color and motion. On the fourth side, brilliant blue sky dazzled Reiko. She heard the waves lap and gulls screech as she tilted her head, straining to glimpse buildings or people. But there were none that she could see. Despair assailed Reiko. The prison seemed isolated in remote country, far from help.

"Oh!" Midori exclaimed suddenly. She sat up, and surprise rounded her swollen eyes.

"What's wrong?" Reiko said, hurrying to kneel beside Midori.

"Nothing. My baby just moved." Midori laughed for joy. "It's all right!"

"Thank the gods," Reiko said as relief filled her.

Midori's body tensed; she grunted. In response to a questioning look from Reiko, she said, "I just had a cramp."

"That means the baby will be coming soon," Lady Keisho-in said, nodding wisely.

Trepidation pursed Midori's mouth. A new problem beset Reiko. What if Midori should go into labor here? That Reiko had given birth herself didn't make her an expert at delivering babies. She wouldn't know what to do if something went wrong. Who could help Midori? Reiko considered Lady Keisho-in. Whenever anyone at the palace got sick or hurt, the shogun's mother panicked; the sight of suffering made her ill. She would be of little use as a midwife. Reiko looked toward Lady Yanagisawa—and realized that the woman hadn't changed position nor made a sound for hours.

"Lady Yanagisawa?" Reiko said.

When the woman didn't respond, Reiko gently shook her by the shoulder. Lady Yanagisawa rolled, limp and unresisting, toward Reiko. Her half-open eyes gazed dully at nothing. Her skin had a pallid, greenish cast. A fly alit in drool that glistened on her parted lips. She didn't even flinch.

"Lady Yanagisawa, wake up," Reiko said, her voice quavering as a new fear besieged her.

The woman neither stirred nor replied. Reiko touched her hands. They were limp and ice-cold. Lady Keisho-in crawled over to join Reiko.

"Is she dead?" Keisho-in asked, staring with ghoulish awe at Lady Yanagisawa.

Much as Reiko detested and feared Lady Yanagisawa, she didn't want her to die. Reiko hated for criminals to murder anyone, and Lady Yanagisawa was the mother of a simpleminded daughter who needed her. Furthermore, Reiko felt responsible for Lady Yanagisawa because she herself was the reason the woman had joined the ill-fated trip. If not for their friendship, Keisho-in probably wouldn't have invited Lady Yanagisawa. Dread and guilt fused in Reiko.

"No. Please, no," she said. She shook Lady Yanagisawa, slapped her cheeks, and yelled her name. But the woman remained inert as a cloth doll.

"We're trapped in here with a corpse," Keisho-in moaned. "Our spirits will be polluted by the contamination of death. Her ghost will haunt us!" She scurried to the far side of the room, knelt, closed her eyes, and began chanting prayers.

"Oh, Reiko-*san*, what are we going to do?" Midori wailed, her arms folded protectively across her stomach.

Reiko wanted to berate Keisho-in for scaring Midori, but instead she took a closer look at Lady Yanagisawa. Had the woman been injured during the attack? Could she be revived? Reiko opened Lady Yanagisawa's robes. She examined the pale, flat-breasted torso and sturdy limbs, then checked Lady Yanagisawa's back, but she found no cuts nor blood, and no bruises except where the ropes had bound her. And her body was still warm. Reiko put her ear against Lady Yanagisawa's chest and heard a heartbeat, faint and slow.

"She's alive," Reiko said. Midori sighed in relief, and Keisho-in ceased praying; but Reiko's concern persisted as she redressed Lady Yanagisawa. "She seems to be in a trance. I think she can't bear what's happened and she's withdrawn from the world."

"How lucky for her. She doesn't have to suffer with the rest of us," Keisho-in pouted. "But who needs her, anyway?"

Reiko had never imagined needing Lady Yanagisawa, never expected to feel anything but relief to have the woman incapacitated. But Lady Yanagisawa might have helped her cope with Keisho-in and Midori. Distraught, Reiko wondered what other misfortunes lay ahead.

There came a sudden rustling noise from the forest. Branches snapped; leaves crunched. Reiko, Midori, and Keisho-in froze alert, their breath caught.

"Someone's coming," Midori whispered.

A door scraped open far below them. Footsteps mounted the stairway. Reiko listened to the heavy, overlapping rhythm of the steps, which heralded several men. As the sound grew louder, she and her friends huddled on their knees together. Her heart thudded with dreadful anticipation. The footsteps scuffed to a halt outside the room. The women watched the door, speechless and transfixed. Iron rasped against iron as someone drew back bolts on the other side. Then the door slowly swung outward. In the crack appeared a sliver of a man's face. Its eye appraised the women with sharp hostility. The door opened wider, and the man edged into the room, brandishing a long sword.

He was a tall samurai in his thirties, clad in an armor tunic that left his thickly muscled arms and legs bare. Fresh red scars marked his skin; black stubble shadowed his jaws and shaved crown. A scowl darkened his features. After him followed three more samurai, equally formidable, armed and dressed in similar fashion. An ominous quiet hushed the room as they approached the women, who gazed up at their captors like rabbits cornered by a hunter.

Lady Keisho-in scrambled to her feet and addressed the men. "It's about time you honored us with your presence," she said with haughty bravado, while Reiko and Midori stared, alarmed. "Whom do I have the privilege of addressing?"

"Be quiet and sit down!" the first samurai shouted, lifting his sword.

Keisho-in shrieked and dropped on all fours. The samurai, apparently the leader, pointed the sword at Reiko and said, "You. Crawl over there."

Trembling, her chest constricted with anxiety, Reiko backed on hands and knees into a corner while the samurai advanced toward her. The tip of his sword gleamed close to her face.

"Don't move," he said, "or I'll cut you." Reiko surmised that he'd singled her out for special handling because she'd killed several of his comrades during the battle. Even now that she was unarmed, he didn't trust her. She gazed up the steel length of the weapon at his narrowed eyes, flaring nostrils, and cruel, bow-shaped mouth. He shot a glance at his companions. "Guard the other ones."

Two men moved, swords in hand, to stand near Keisho-in and Midori. The samurai who guarded Lady Yanagisawa nudged her with his foot; when she didn't move, he relaxed.

"You can come in now," the leader called to someone outside the room.

A young man entered. He was a brawny peasant with a soft, round face and the eyes of a boy anxious to please. He carried a lidded wooden pail in each hand.

"Here's food and drink," the leader announced.

The youth set the pails on the floor. Lady Keisho-in said, "At last!" She crawled to the pails and lifted the lids. Reiko saw that one pail contained water. The other held *mochi*— round, flattened cakes of rice—and pickled vegetables. Keisho-in grimaced in disgust.

"I can't eat this garbage," she said.

"You will, because it's all you're going to get," the leader said.

Before Reiko could warn her against provoking the man, Keisho-in reared up on her knees. "I demand that you serve us a good hot meal," she said. "And while you're at it, take away those slop buckets and bring me some warm water for bathing."

The leader gave a disdainful laugh. "You don't give the orders here," he said.

"Do you know who I am?" Keisho-in's rheumy old eyes blazed. "I'm the shogun's mother. I give orders everywhere! And I order you to do as I said, then take us to the nearest post station so we can get a ride home."

Ignoring her, the leader jerked his chin at the other men. They all backed toward the door.

"Don't you walk away while I'm talking to you," Keisho-in shouted, as Reiko silently begged her to be quiet. "Tell me what you're going to do to us. Tell me your names so I can report you to my son!"

The men didn't answer; they kept going. With an exclamation of outrage, Keisho-in picked up a rice cake and threw it at the men.

"No!" Reiko and Midori cried in horrified unison.

But Keisho-in hurled more rice cakes. One struck the leader on the chest. Anger blackened his countenance, flared his nostrils wider. He stalked toward Keisho-in and kicked away the food pail, which toppled and spilled. Keisho-in, startled out of her anger, fell on her buttocks. He grabbed her wrist and yanked her upright. With a savage, whipping motion, he flung her into the corner.

She crashed down with a force that jolted a grunt from her, shook the floor, and knocked plaster off the wall. Horror filled Reiko. Midori covered her mouth with her hands.

"That should teach you to behave yourself." The leader spoke to Keisho-in, but his warning gaze included Reiko and Midori. He and the other men walked out the door.

It slammed shut; the iron bolts dropped. Footsteps descended the stairs. The outer door closed, and leaves rustled as the men retreated. A moment passed while Reiko, Midori, and Keisho-in sat, stunned and wordless amid the scattered food, their ragged breaths the only sound in the room. Lady Yanagisawa lay unconscious. Outside, squirrels chattered, as if mocking their predicament. Reiko stood on legs unsteadied by the crisis and walked to Keisho-in.

"Are you all right?" she asked.

"No. He broke my wrist." Keisho-in spoke in a raspy growl. She proffered the wrist for Reiko to examine.

"It's swelling," Reiko said, gently palpating the joint beneath Keisho-in's age-spotted flesh, "but I think it's just sprained." She tore off an end of her sash and bound the wrist.

"Someday that beast will be sorry he dared to hurt me," Keisho-in fumed.

"Until then, perhaps you'd better not anger him again," Reiko said with a courteous tact that hid her own anger at Keisho-in. She was obligated to protect the shogun's mother, but the old woman stupidly defied prudence. "He's dangerous. He could have killed us all."

Keisho-in sulked, unrepentant, but pity cooled Reiko's anger. For the almost fifty years since she'd given birth to the shogun, Keisho-in had been indulged by everyone and never needed to develop self-control. There was no use expecting her to change now. Reiko sighed and gathered up the food.

"We'd better eat," she said, doling out dirty pickles and *mochi*. "We need to keep up our strength."

Keisho-in grudgingly accepted a share, but Midori shook her head. "My stomach feels too sick to eat," she said.

"Try," Reiko said. "Maybe you'll feel better."

While they sat glumly chewing, Reiko mulled over the incident that had just passed. The five kidnappers seemed the kind of men who had more physical strength than brains. That they'd brought food meant they wanted to keep her and the other women alive. They would come again, and next time, perhaps Reiko could outwit them and escape.

Yet even as she drew hope from these thoughts, others disturbed her. Did the men she'd seen work for someone else who'd ordered the kidnapping, someone who meant to kill her and her friends after they'd served whatever his purpose was? How many more men were stationed around the prison? And her wits alone were no match for steel blades.

Reiko experienced such discouragement and helplessness that she almost wept. But she was determined to escape her captors, and she must make the best of the circumstances they'd dealt her. She finished eating, then searched the room for anything she could use as a weapon. She examined the food and waste buckets. The flimsy wooden containers offered limited possibilities. The kidnappers knew better than to leave anything that would endanger them. Reiko inserted her fingers into cracks in the floor and tried to pry up boards, but dislodged only useless splinters. Desperation cast her eyes up toward the ceiling.

Then, as Reiko contemplated the rafters, a plan formed in her mind. Hope awakened, but she realized that she would need help. She looked over her companions. Her gaze bypassed Midori and Keisho-in, dismissing the latter as too foolish and both as too physically weak, and lit on Lady Yanagisawa. Here was the accomplice she needed—if only she could bring Lady Yanagisawa out of her trance.

Reiko knelt close beside the woman and peered into the glazed, sightless eyes. "Lady Yanagisawa," she said, "can you hear me?"

8

Concealed in a guard tower that topped the wall of his estate inside Edo Castle, Chamberlain Yanagisawa stood looking out the window across a garden below him. A gap in the sunlit foliage revealed the shogun's private quarters, some hundred paces distant. Tokugawa Tsunayoshi sat propped on cushions on the shady veranda while physicians dressed in dark blue coats fed him medicine. The anxious tones of their conversation drifted up to Yanagisawa, who knew the shogun was so upset about his mother's kidnapping that he'd taken ill in the night. Yanagisawa himself had spent sleepless hours thinking over the consequences that the crime posed for him. Now he heard someone walking toward him along the wall, looked out the door, and saw Police Commissioner Hoshina approaching.

Hoshina entered the tower and stood at the window beside Yanagisawa. "I've got our troops ready to march as soon as we need them for a rescue mission," Hoshina said. "And I've ordered all my officers to scour Edo for information about the kidnapping."

His arrival caused a quickening inside Yanagisawa, even after three years as lovers, even at a time when affairs of state preoccupied him. It was as if his heart were a bell, and Hoshina the clapper that awakened song from cold, inanimate metal. The sight of Hoshina aroused an intense desire that Yanagisawa stifled. Need rendered him vulnerable, and vulnerability was fatal for a man in his position. He felt a stab of resentment toward Hoshina, the weak spot in his armor.

Hoshina's eyes took on a look that betrayed his effort to guess what his lover was thinking and his fear of displeasing Yanagisawa. "Is something wrong?" Hoshina said cautiously.

"Your behavior at the meeting last night was reprehensible." Yanagisawa hid his feelings behind criticism, which he often used to keep Hoshina at a distance. "You acted as if the kidnapping was the best thing that ever happened. Fortunately, the shogun didn't notice—but everyone else did. Your attitude endangers us both."

"My apologies," Hoshina said, clearly chastened by Yanagisawa's cold rebuke. "I'll be more careful next time."

Shared memories of every night they'd spent together, drinking and joking between bouts of sex, eased the tension between them. Yanagisawa relented, and although he only nodded his forgiveness, Hoshina's mouth curved in a smile of relief.

"I admit that I do consider the crime to be an opportunity," Hoshina said. Excitement underlay his businesslike tone. "If we rescue Lady Keisho-in and catch the kidnappers, we'll rise in the shogun's favor, while Sano and other rivals sink. Your power will be greater than ever."

As would Hoshina's, thought Yanagisawa. His lover was so transparent in his ambition, and so focused on his goals, that he ignored the pitfalls before him. Yet love excused worse flaws than greed, impulsiveness, or lack of vision.

"If we fail, and Sano succeeds, I'll lose face and standing in the *bakufu*," Yanagisawa reminded Hoshina. "Neither my skill at manipulating the shogun nor my history as his paramour will preserve his good opinion of me. This crime is a potential catastrophe for me—and for you."

"We won't fail," Hoshina said staunchly.

His reassurance heartened Yanagisawa, who'd suffered agonies of fear alone before Hoshina came into his life.

Having someone in whom to confide lessened the torment. But Hoshina's confidence quickly faded into doubt.

"Do you worry because you think Sano is a better detective than I, or that his troops are better than those I've trained for you?" he said.

"Of course not," Yanagisawa said, though he did rate Sano's expertise higher than Hoshina's. He wasn't blind to fact; yet lying came naturally to him, and he would lie to serve affection as well as political necessity. "You've satisfied all my expectations."

Inclining his head modestly, Hoshina basked in the praise.

"I worry because we've met our match in the kidnapper," Yanagisawa said. Possessed of ruthless cunning himself, he could well recognize it in his adversary.

Hoshina nodded, pondered a moment, then said, "What if everyone's efforts fail? What if Lady Keisho-in and the other women never come back?"

They looked across the garden to the palace. The shogun lay on his back, moaning, while physicians applied herbal poultices to his chest. "If he should lose his mother," Yanagisawa said, "grief may ruin his health."

"Should he die soon, his reign would end without a direct heir to succeed him," Hoshina said. The shogun had a wife and a hundred concubines, but he preferred sex with men, and he had no children. "Who would become the next shogun?"

Long before the kidnapping, many contenders had already begun to plan for his death. Tokugawa relatives connived to raise themselves or their sons to the throne. Yanagisawa and Hoshina had their own plans that they dared not openly voice, because spies abounded in Edo, and not even Yanagisawa's own domain was guaranteed safe from them.

"The timing is wrong," Yanagisawa said, answering Hoshina's unspoken hint that the kidnapping could benefit their plans. "If the crime had happened a year or so later, then we might have cause to celebrate. But right now we aren't ready for a change of regime."

"Your bonuses and favors that I've distributed have won you a large following," Hoshina murmured. "Many *daimyo,* Tokugawa vassals, and a third of the soldiers in the army consider you their master."

Yanagisawa had made Hoshina a partner in his scheme to transfer the allegiance of the army, vassals, and feudal lords from the shogun to himself, and Hoshina was performing superbly. But Yanagisawa frowned, dismissing their achievement. "That isn't enough." The success of their plans required a large majority of influential men on his side. "And the crucial basis for our future is by no means secure."

Down in the palace, a tall, slender young samurai dressed in brilliant silk robes walked across the veranda toward the shogun. Yanagisawa and Hoshina watched the shogun sit up, his face brighten. The samurai gracefully knelt before the shogun and bowed. His handsome profile was a mirror of Yanagisawa's.

"The shogun likes your son," Hoshina said.

Yanagisawa contemplated his son, Yoritomo, born sixteen years ago, the illegitimate product of his affair with a palace lady-in-waiting. Because she was a Tokugawa cousin, Yoritomo was blood kin to the shogun and eligible for the succession. Yanagisawa had supported Yoritomo in a luxurious villa outside Edo, given him gifts, visited him, and won the impressionable boy's obedience. This year, Yanagisawa had introduced Yoritomo to the shogun. Tokugawa Tsunayoshi had been quickly smitten. Yanagisawa meant for the shogun to adopt Yoritomo and designate him as heir to the regime. But even if the shogun did, Yanagisawa needed more political and military support to crush the opposition that his many rivals would undoubtedly raise against him. And those rivals were as eager as he was for the role of father to the next dictator and power behind the scenes.

"His Excellency also enjoys the company of many other

young men," Yanagisawa said, watching two more samurai join the shogun. They were sons of other officials, as young and comely as Yoritomo. "He's not ready to pick a favorite."

"Rumor says that Yoritomo has the advantage because he knows how to please His Excellency," said Hoshina.

The shogun waved the newcomers away and extended his hand to Yoritomo. The young man helped him rise, and as they moved together to enter the palace, Yoritomo looked over his shoulder at the guard tower. His anxious face communicated reluctance to do what his lord expected, and need for his father's approval. Then he and the shogun vanished into the palace. As Yanagisawa pictured the scene in the bedchamber, he experienced a stab of guilt. Yet what choice had he except to pander his own son to the shogun? When the current regime ended, his enemies would destroy him and Yoritomo unless he could position them both at the head of the next regime—and prepare to fight a war, if need be, to keep them on top.

"Nothing is for certain until the official heir is installed in the crown prince's residence," Yanagisawa said.

Time would have furthered Yoritomo's progress there; time would have allowed Yanagisawa to profit from Lady Keisho-in's abduction and the shogun's demise. But luck had cheated him.

"I understand," Hoshina said, his initial high spirits deflated. "What shall we do?"

The future that Yanagisawa envisioned necessarily included Hoshina by his side, though he would let Hoshina fear he might be cast off at any time. "We try our best to rescue Lady Keisho-in," said Yanagisawa.

They exited the tower, stepping from shadow into sunlight, just as a messenger hurried along the wall toward them.

"Excuse me, Honorable Chamberlain." The messenger bowed. "Soldiers have just brought Lady Keisho-in's maid back from the Tōkaidō. She's in the sickroom."

Yanagisawa dismissed the messenger, then said to Hoshina, "We need to know what the maid saw during the massacre. She may be able to help us identify the kidnappers." This first possible break in the investigation elated him. "Go and question her immediately, before Sano does."

"Very well." An edge to Hoshina's subservient tone said he disliked taking orders from his lover even though he understood the importance of interviewing the only witness to the crime. Lately, he chafed at the uneven balance of power that Yanagisawa maintained to protect himself. "What will you be doing?"

As they descended the stone stairs to ground level, Yanagisawa said, "I'm going to visit my current worst enemy and determine whether he organized the massacre and kidnapping."

A small entourage paraded with Chamberlain Yanagisawa through the special enclave inside Edo Castle where important Tokugawa clan members lived. In front of him on the flagstone path walked the two secretaries required for formal visits to high officials; close behind him trailed the five bodyguards who accompanied him everywhere. Around them rose the humming whine of insects in the landscaped terrain that lay motionless in the hot, hazy sunshine. Smoke from a fire burning somewhere in the city sharpened the air; war cries drifted from the distant martial arts practice ground. Troops patrolled the area or occupied guardhouses along the walls that separated the estates. Yanagisawa's procession halted outside a gate that boasted a three-tiered roof and ornate double ironclad doors.

One of Yanagisawa's secretaries addressed the gate sentries: "The Honorable Chamberlain Yanagisawa wishes to call on the Honorable Lord Matsudaira."

Soon attendants ushered Yanagisawa into a mansion that nearly equaled the palace in size and refined elegance. Behind his cool demeanor, his heart drummed fast, and he braced himself as he and his party entered an audience chamber.

There, upon the dais, sat Lord Matsudaira, first cousin to the shogun, head of the major Tokugawa branch clan, and *daimyo* of a province in the rich agricultural Kanto territory near Edo. Lord Matsudaira looked as the shogun would if a magic mirror broadened his aristocratic features, sparked intelligence in his eyes, enlarged and toughened his frail body. The man seemed a throwback to Ieyasu, the first Tokugawa shogun, who'd unified Japan almost a century ago. Only birthright had placed Tokugawa Tsunayoshi ahead of Lord Matsudaira in the *bakufu*.

Surrounded by guards who stood against the walls, Lord Matsudaira glared in open hostility at his guests. Yanagisawa knelt before the dais, his men ranged behind him. They exchanged bows, wary and distrustful, like rival generals meeting on a battleground to declare war. During the ritual sharing of refreshments, they behaved with an elaborate courtesy that was more insulting than outright rudeness.

Then Lord Matsudaira said, "I've been expecting you. What took you so long?"

Yanagisawa pretended to misunderstand Lord Matsudaira's intimation that he knew Yanagisawa thought he was involved in the kidnapping and had come to accuse him. "I'm sorry if I've inconvenienced you," he said. "Important affairs of state commanded my attention at the palace."

His tone implied that his status as chamberlain put him at the heart of Tokugawa politics, while Lord Matsudaira hovered on the fringes despite his exalted heritage and Yanagisawa's inferior birth. As Yanagisawa scored the first point in their battle, a flash of offense crossed Lord Matsudaira's face. Yanagisawa knew the man would like to be shogun, thought he deserved the post more than did his cousin, and resented his secondary role in governing Japan.

"More likely they were affairs of the bedchamber that busied you," Lord Matsudaira said with a sardonic smile.

He made no secret of the fact that he loathed Yanagisawa as a parasite who'd seduced his way to the top of the *bakufu* and usurped power from the Tokugawa clan. He seized every chance to condemn Yanagisawa's ignoble deeds. A flame of anger leapt in Yanagisawa, but he raised an eyebrow in feigned amusement.

"Many men have learned the high price of wit like yours," he said, reminding Lord Matsudaira that he'd used political sabotage, physical force, and assassination to keep himself on top and punish anyone who crossed him.

"Only an inferior official rules by coercion." Disgust contorted Lord Matsudaira's mouth. "A superior one rules by honest, fair management, in the ancient tradition of Confucius."

Yanagisawa knew that Lord Matsudaira prided himself on his reputation for honor and integrity and had led crusades against corruption in the government. The self-righteous ass! His inherited position allowed him to scorn people like Yanagisawa, the son of a retainer to a minor *daimyo*, who'd struggled for the authority Lord Matsudaira took for granted.

"Might often triumphs over virtue," Yanagisawa said in a casual tone edged with hostility.

Lord Matsudaira had repeatedly spoken against Yanagisawa to the shogun and courted the allegiance of his other enemies; but so far, his attempts to oust Yanagisawa had failed. Now Lord Matsudaira looked annoyed at the reminder, but he countered with a smug smile: "Not as often as you would like."

He owned the loyalty of two men on the Council of Elders, and through them, he countered Yanagisawa's policies. His influence with the Tokugawa branch clans had thwarted Yanagisawa's wish to become a *daimyo* and ruler of his own province. Vexation goaded Yanagisawa into a malicious retort.

"By the way," he said, "I must offer you my condolences on the recent death of your son."

Lord Matsudaira stared, infuriated, then spoke with bitter acrimony: "That you would even mention my son while his clan still mourns him is an unforgivable insult."

The son, Mitsuyoshi, murdered seven months ago, had

been the shogun's favorite and heir apparent. Had he lived, Lord Matsudaira would have gained even more influence in the *bakufu*. The murder had undermined Lord Matsudaira's goal of eventual control over Japan via ruling through his son, and of ousting Yanagisawa once and for all. And Yanagisawa had benefited from Lord Matsudaira's loss. The death of Mitsuyoshi gave Yanagisawa's son a chance at the succession.

"May I remind you that the shogun is susceptible to evil influences, but also to pressure from his clan," Lord Matsudaira said. "He shall not disinherit our legitimate kin in favor of a bastard with a drop of Tokugawa blood. You had better watch yourself, because your future is no more secure than mine."

For now, they were at a stalemate, Yanagisawa grudgingly recognized. Yanagisawa had the shogun's protection, many allies, a foothold on the ladder to the succession, and he controlled a third of the army. But Lord Matsudaira controlled as many troops and had as many allies. Each side was too powerful for the other to openly attack. But the kidnapping, and its consequences, could decide the victor.

"The abduction of Lady Keisho-in was a bold move on someone's part," Yanagisawa said.

Lord Matsudaira gave him a patronizing look that said he'd expected Yanagisawa to introduce the reason for his visit now, in this way. "What would be the motive behind such a bold move?" he said, adroitly sidestepping Yanagisawa's implicit accusation.

"The shogun will do anything to get his mother back," Yanagisawa said. "He might even sacrifice his top official."

Sano thought the Black Lotus wanted revenge, and Senior Elder Makino thought the kidnapper wanted money; but Yanagisawa viewed the kidnapping as an attempt to alter the nation's power hierarchy.

"So you predict that the ransom letter will order the shogun to expel you from the *bakufu*." Lord Matsudaira chuckled at the hint that the motive fit him and the crime was his strike against Yanagisawa. "That's an interesting theory.

But before you publicize it, consider how foolish you'll look if whoever you accuse was at home in Edo, surrounded by people, when Lady Keisho-in was taken."

Yanagisawa greeted Lord Matsudaira's alibi with disdain. "Whoever I accuse needn't have risked a personal appearance at the crime scene." He paused, then said in a tone heavy with insinuation: "I saw you drilling troops at the practice ground the other day. You have plenty of minions to do your bidding."

"I could say the same of you." Lord Matsudaira's voice softened with menace. "Where were your troops during the abduction? What would you do to destroy me?"

The atmosphere seemed to crackle, as if heralding a thunderstorm. Yanagisawa could almost smell gunpowder in the air as he and Lord Matsudaira poised on the narrow divide between verbal sparring and overt strife. Their men waited motionless yet alert for a signal to attack. Yanagisawa felt currents of exhilaration and dread surge through him.

With a narrow, sarcastic smile, Lord Matsudaira said, "But of course I wouldn't accuse you of murder and treason."

A beat passed. "Nor would I accuse you," Yanagisawa said.

Neither of them had evidence to incriminate the other. Neither dared turn the kidnapping into an occasion for warfare—yet. They bowed to each other in cautious farewell, backing away from a clash that could plunge Japan into civil war. Then Yanagisawa and his men rose and filed from the room. Yanagisawa's expression was sternly tranquil, though his heart thundered and his body perspired from the close call. As they exited the gate and walked away down the path, he reexamined his theory in light of what had just occurred.

Lord Matsudaira might be guilty, despite his alibi and denials; but the fact that the kidnapping was a drastic move even for someone as ambitious as Lord Matsudaira argued in favor of his innocence. Furthermore, Yanagisawa knew the dangers of pursuing one suspect while others existed. He knew what he had to gain or lose by this investigation, and he had many other powerful enemies besides Lord Matsudaira.

"We'll make a few more calls here in the Tokugawa enclave," he told his men. "Then we'll proceed to the official quarter."

He must identify the kidnappers and rescue Lady Keisho-in before she could come to harm—and before anyone else saved her.

9

Hirata and Detectives Marume and Fukida drew their horses to a stop on a deserted stretch of the Tōkaidō. Rain dripped down on them, trickled in rivulets down the steep, rocky cliff at their right, and pattered through the forest on their left. The misty air cloaked the distant mountains and merged with the sky's dense, swirling gray clouds. The cold late afternoon appeared as dim as twilight.

"This must be where the kidnapping took place," Hirata said, his voice echoing eerily in the quiet.

He swung himself out of the saddle, wincing at the soreness in his muscles. He and Marume and Fukida had ridden almost nonstop at a furious pace since leaving Edo early that morning. They'd followed the seacoast, scaled hills, crossed rivers, endured heat and dust. They'd eaten meals on horseback, pausing only to pass inspection and change mounts at post stations. Eventually, they'd passed the remains of the kidnappers' roadblock—massive logs that had been rolled off the highway and down the slope of a gorge. Now, chilled and drenched by the rain, Hirata felt as weary as if he'd traveled through many kingdoms. And his search for Midori had only begun.

Detectives Marume and Fukida stood on the road beside Hirata. Water dripped off the wide brims of their hats as they looked around. "You wouldn't know anything had happened here," Marume said.

"The highway officials have removed the bodies and wreckage." Hirata eyed the road, which was clear of debris and spread with fresh sand.

"And the weather has done away with whatever they missed," said Fukida.

The trio watched the rain slowly dissolve footprints and hoof marks in the sand. "The kidnappers had to have left a trail," Hirata said. "All we have to do is find it."

He panned his gaze across the towering cedars in the forest and the ancient, layered rock that comprised the cliffs. He pictured a horde of faceless attackers battling soldiers, cutting down servants and women. Splashes of blood and shadows in frantic motion painted his vision. The dark, lingering aura of violence radiated from every leaf, stone, and grain of soil. Hirata smelled death. He could almost hear the clashing blades, the victims' terrified cries, and Midori calling his name.

"The women must have been tied up and gagged to keep them from running away or making noise," he said, closing his mind against horror. "The kidnappers wouldn't have transported prisoners along the road and risked someone noticing. They would have gone through the forest."

He and the detectives secured their horses to a tree off the roadside, out of sight from passersby. They trudged up and down inside the forest, paralleling the Tōkaidō and gradually moving beyond the immediate scene of the attack. The rain splashed through the gloom beneath the cedars. Trampled underbrush and broken branches gave clear evidence that people had run and fought here. On fallen leaves shielded by the trees, brownish-red bloodstains marked places where bodies had lain. Hirata found a sandal stuck in the mud, probably lost by a fleeing member of Lady Keisho-in's entourage. Fukida found a straw hat, and Marume a lone sword with the Tokugawa crest on its hilt, the blade already rusting.

"Whatever relics that the highway officials didn't remove, the local peasants must have scavenged," Fukida deduced.

The forest seemed unnaturally still, haunted by the spirits of the dead. A sudden fluttering noise disturbed the quiet. Hirata's heart jumped; he and his comrades started. Their hands flew to their swords as they looked up. A large black crow rose upward on flapping wings and disappeared into the misty sky. The men expelled a collective breath of relief. They resumed hunting for the kidnappers' trail. Some fifty paces away from the road, the forest seemed undisturbed. Hirata and his men separated, peering between trees and scrutinizing the ground. The leaves high over them flinched when pelted with raindrops. Longing and dread for Midori burgeoned inside Hirata. A tickle in his nose and a soreness in his throat presaged a cold. He paused to sneeze, and heard a shout from Fukida, invisible within the woods.

"Over here!" the detective called.

Hirata and Marume hurried over to their comrade. Fukida pointed at a strip of trodden underbrush that led away from the Tōkaidō. Hirata dared not hope too much, but excitation sped his pulse. He and the detectives carefully stepped twenty paces along the crushed weeds and saplings, then saw branches strewn across their path. The thin, leafy shafts were bent and trampled, the ends cleanly severed by a blade. Hirata looked up and saw cut branches on a shrub that had blocked the path. Beyond this point lay more flattened underbrush.

"Someone has broken a trail through here," he said.

Eyes alert, he hastened forward. The detectives followed. Hirata spied footprints in bare earth and crushed, rotting mushrooms. More cut branches marked places where someone had hacked past low-hanging tree limbs. Then Hirata spotted a small, gleaming object of irregular shape. He picked it up and found himself holding a woman's sandal with a silk thong and a chunky red-lacquered sole.

"This must belong to Midori, Reiko, Lady Keisho-in, or Lady Yanagisawa," Hirata said, afire with hope. "One of them must have dropped it while the kidnappers brought them through here."

On through the forest he and his men plunged. As the trail continued, they found long black hairs caught on a tree trunk, as though the bark had snagged one of the women as she passed. A torn scrap of blue-brocaded silk adorned a prickly shrub. Hirata began to feel feverish, and his sore throat worsened; but exhilaration buoyed him. Every sign convinced him that he was following the route the kidnappers had taken . . . until the trail abruptly ended at the vertical rocky rise of a cliff.

Hirata and the detectives stared up at the cliff in dumbfounded disbelief. An icy wind blew mist into their faces.

"The kidnappers couldn't have climbed that, with or without the women," Marume said.

"The trail doesn't go anywhere else," Fukida said as he paced widening arcs in the woods at the bottom of the cliff.

Awful realization struck Hirata. "The kidnappers planted a false trail, to fool anyone who tried to follow them. They came as far as this dead end, then backtracked along the path they'd made." Breathless from fatigue and outrage, Hirata exclaimed, "It's the oldest trick in history. And I fell for it!" He cursed the kidnappers and his own gullibility. He kicked the cliff, venting his anger.

"We couldn't have known it was a trick," Marume said.

"We had to follow the trail because it might have led to the women," Fukida said.

Refusing consolation, Hirata stalked off in a direction chosen at random. "What are you waiting for? We have to keep looking!"

The detectives ran after him, caught his arms, and restrained him. "It's getting too dark," Fukida said. "Pretty soon we won't be able to see clues. We should go back to the highway, get our horses, and find someplace to spend the night."

"Let me go!" Furious, Hirata struggled free of his comrades. "I have to find Midori."

"If we wander around after dark, we'll only get lost," Marume pointed out. "The *sōsakan-sama* will have to send somebody to look for us. Lot of good that will do your wife and her friends. We must wait until morning."

Hirata couldn't bear to call off the search for a moment, let alone a whole night, while Midori was somewhere in the vast countryside, at the mercy of killers he believed had been hired by her insane father. Yet he had to admit that Marume and Fukida were right.

Reluctantly, Hirata accompanied the detectives back down the trail toward the Tōkaidō. "We'll ride to the Oda-wara post station and find lodgings at an inn," he said. "We can ask around town to see if anyone there has seen or heard anything that might help us find the kidnappers."

The Edo Castle sickroom was isolated in a sepa-rate compound, situated low on the hill and far from the palace to protect the court from the spirits of disease and pollution from death. Inside the drab one-story building sur-rounded by a plank fence and tall pine trees, the Tokugawa physicians treated castle residents who were seriously ill or injured. A shrine beside the door contained a rock that served as a seat for protective Shinto deities. In front of the shrine burned a purifying fire. A sacred straw rope encircled offerings of food and drink, a wand festooned with paper strips, and a lock of woman's hair to keep away demons.

Police Commissioner Hoshina, accompanied by two per-sonal retainers, strode into the sickroom. At one end, ap-prentice physicians tended herbal infusions simmering in pots on a hearth. Screens that usually partitioned the build-ing into separate chambers had been pushed against the walls to accommodate the large crowd of palace officials that had gathered. On the crowd's fringes hovered maids and servants. Anxious conversation mingled with chanting and the rhythmic jangle of bells. The sickroom was hot from the fire and redolent with medicinal steam.

"Let me through," Hoshina commanded the crowd.

People stepped aside, bowing to Hoshina as he passed through their midst. At the center of the crowd, on the *tatami* floor, a woman was lying upon a futon. A white sheet covered her body; a white bandage wrapped her head. Her face, with its prominent cheekbones, was deathly pale, the closed eyelids shadowed purple. Near her head, an elderly sorceress clad in white robes banged a tambourine to summon healing spirits, while a priest recited spells and waved a sword to banish evil. At her feet squatted two highway patrol captains. Dr. Kitano, the chief castle physician, knelt beside the prone woman.

"This is Lady Keisho-in's maid, Suiren, who survived the massacre?" Hoshina asked the doctor.

"Yes, Honorable Police Commissioner," said Dr. Kitano. He had a creased, intelligent face, and sparse gray hair knotted at his nape. He wore the dark blue coat of his profession.

Hoshina turned to the officials. "Leave us," he said, annoyed that they'd come to gawk at Suiren, when he himself had important business with her. "You, too," Hoshina told the maids. He gestured for the sorceress and priest to move away. "Not so loud."

Soon he was alone with his own men, the highway soldiers and the apprentices, Dr. Kitano and the patient. While the priest and sorceress quietly continued their ritual in a corner, Hoshina crouched by Suiren. She lay still, apparently oblivious to the world. Her breath sighed slowly through her chapped, parted lips. Hoshina frowned in concern.

"Is she asleep?" he said to Dr. Kitano.

"She's unconscious," the physician said.

The news dismayed Hoshina. He addressed the patrol captains: "You brought her back to Edo?"

"Yes, Honorable Police Commissioner." The captains, brawny and keen-featured, sweating in their armor, spoke in unison.

"How long has she been like this?" Hoshina said.

"Ever since we found her after the massacre," said one captain.

"Describe how you found her," Hoshina said.

"We were examining the bodies to see if there were any

survivors," said the other captain. "We thought she was dead. There was blood all over her, and she didn't move."

"But then we heard her moan. We rushed her to Odawara post station. The local doctor treated her," continued the first captain. "He warned us that she was too sick to travel, but our superiors said she had to be taken to Edo. We were afraid she would die on the way here."

Hoshina had hoped that a quick, easy interview with the witness would give him the identity of Lady Keisho-in's kidnappers. Disappointed, he turned to Dr. Kitano. "Exactly what are her injuries?"

"I was just about to examine her."

Dr. Kitano gently unwrapped the bandage from Suiren's head, exposing hair clipped away from a large, indented purple bruise above her right temple. Frowning, he covered the wound, then drew back the sheet that blanketed Suiren and opened the white cotton kimono she wore. A white bandage swathed her abdomen. Dr. Kitano removed this. Underneath, a gash slanted from just below the left side of her rib cage to her navel. The wound, crusted with dried blood and stitched together with horsehair, oozed yellowish fluid. Hoshina winced; Dr. Kitano's frown deepened. Suiren didn't even stir.

"This is a very bad sword cut," the physician said. "The head wound is also serious."

Dr. Kitano touched the skin around Suiren's sunken eyes, lifted the lids, and peered into her dull, sightless pupils, according to ancient Chinese medical technique. His fingers palpated her cheeks, rubbed her dry, brittle-looking hair, and squeezed her neck. He opened her mouth, revealing pale gums and tongue, then sniffed the air near her face. Finally, he clasped one wrist, then the other. The sorceress's tambourine marked the lengthy passage of time as Dr. Kitano felt the pulses that corresponded to different internal organs. When he finished, he covered the maid and lifted his troubled gaze to Hoshina.

"She is suffering from a deficiency of blood, fluid, and

ki—life energy," Dr. Kitano said. "There is also internal festering and inflammation."

"Can you heal her?" Hoshina said.

"I'll do my best," Dr. Kitano said, "but it will be a miracle if she lives."

Hoshina cupped his chin in his hand and brooded over Suiren while the tambourine rang and the priest chanted. The maid represented a chance to save Lady Keisho-in and solidify Chamberlain Yanagisawa's position in court long enough for the shogun to name Yoritomo his heir. But Hoshina had other, personal reasons for wanting Suiren to recover. If he could extract from her a clue that led to the kidnappers, he would win the shogun's esteem and gratitude for himself. The *bakufu* would have to recognize him as a power in his own right, not just as Yanagisawa's lover. And Yanagisawa would have to treat Hoshina with the respect he craved instead of always demeaning him.

"I must question Suiren about the kidnapping," Hoshina told Dr. Kitano. "Wake her up."

Concern shadowed the doctor's eyes. "It is not advisable to disturb her. She needs rest."

Hoshina experienced overwhelming impatience. Unless he could find the kidnappers and rescue Lady Keisho-in, he might never make his name in the *bakufu*. He and Yanagisawa might fall so far from the shogun's grace that their plans for the future could never work. And failure, like success, posed serious personal ramifications for Hoshina. His lover admired skill and despised incompetence, and so far, Hoshina had managed to do everything Yanagisawa asked—but what if the kidnapping case proved more than he could handle? Would Yanagisawa cease to want him?

Even as Hoshina rued his love for a man as difficult yet alluring as the chamberlain, the thought of losing Yanagisawa stabbed terror into his heart.

"Suiren may be the only person who can give me information about who kidnapped the shogun's mother," Hoshina said. "It's imperative that she speak to me."

"She must not exert her vital energy, which is already

depleted," Dr. Kitano said. "And unconsciousness spares her terrible pain. Please give her time to grow stronger."

"I don't have time," Hoshina said, angered by the physician's calm, authoritative manner. "If Suiren dies without telling what she knows, we may never get Lady Keisho-in back or capture the criminals." And Hoshina might never achieve his desires. He rose, squared his shoulders, and glared down at Dr. Kitano, asserting his rank. "I order you to awaken her now."

Dr. Kitano's composure wavered as he beheld Hoshina. "The honor code of my profession forbids me to endanger the life of my patient."

Hoshina thought the man was less concerned about violating the code than afraid that he would kill the only witness to the kidnapping and the shogun would punish him. "I'll take responsibility for whatever happens to her," Hoshina said. Better that Suiren should die during an interrogation than before he ever tried to question her.

Nodding reluctantly, Dr. Kitano called to his apprentices: "Bring me some musk."

An apprentice brought a ceramic cup full of coarse powder to Dr. Kitano. The acrid, animal scent of the musk tinged the air. Hoshina watched Dr. Kitano hold the cup near Suiren's nose. As the maid inhaled, her nostrils quivered; her lips twitched in an involuntary grimace. Her eyelids fluttered slowly open. Hoshina nodded his approval to Dr. Kitano.

"Try not to upset her," the physician warned.

Hoshina knelt beside the maid, leaning over her. "Suiren-*san*," he said. Her blurry gaze wandered over his face. Fear enlivened her still features. "Don't be afraid. You're safe at home in the castle." Hoshina spoke gently, stifling his excitement. "I'm the police commissioner of Edo."

Breath eased from Suiren; her face relaxed. Her eyelids drooped, veiling her again in sleep.

"Give her another whiff of that musk," Hoshina ordered Dr. Kitano.

The doctor complied with reluctance. "This medicine is very potent, and repeated doses are dangerous to persons in weak health."

When Suiren smelled the musk, her eyes blinked wide. She looked as alarmed as though she'd forgotten, or hadn't understood, who Hoshina was and what he'd told her.

"Do you remember traveling on the Tōkaidō with Lady Keisho-in?" Hoshina asked. "Do you remember being attacked?"

Her eyes clouded with confusion; then terror glazed them. A piteous groan shivered her body.

"Did you see who abducted Lady Keisho-in?" Hoshina pressed as his urgency mounted.

Groaning louder, the maid tossed her head from side to side. She writhed and gasped in pain. Sweat moistened her complexion, which had turned gray.

"It's all right. Be still," Dr. Kitano soothed, stroking her forehead. He fixed a stern gaze on Hoshina. "She can't speak. And whatever she remembers is upsetting her. That's enough."

Hoshina ignored the physician. He wondered why Suiren had lived while everyone else in Keisho-in's entourage had died. An idea occurred to him. "Are you the kidnappers' accomplice?" he said, grasping Suiren by her shoulders. "Did you tell them that Lady Keisho-in would be traveling on the Tōkaidō? Did they spare your life as a reward?"

Suiren shrieked. The blank light of panic shone in her eyes. Thrashing under the sheet, she resembled a moth trying to escape a cocoon.

Dr. Kitano said to Hoshina, "If she doesn't calm down, she'll hurt herself. Leave her alone." His voice was harsh with censure.

"Who kidnapped Lady Keisho-in?" Hoshina demanded. "Where did they take her? Tell me!"

Suiren's mouth formed silent words, but her thrashing weakened. Her eyes rolled back in her head, and the lids closed. Her gasps subsided into slow, somnolent breathing as unconsciousness reclaimed her. Frantic because she'd appeared ready to talk, Hoshina shook the maid.

"Wake up!" he shouted.

"Stop!" Dr. Kitano dragged Hoshina away from Suiren. "You'll hurt her!"

Furious, Hoshina pulled free of Dr. Kitano. "Use the musk on her again. Quick!"

"No more," Dr. Kitano said, with the stony defiance of a man driven to stand by his principles no matter the cost. "Your interrogation will be the death of her. And whatever she knows, she'll take to her grave."

Hoshina stood, panting in frustrated ire. He gazed helplessly at Suiren, who lay unmoving and incommunicative. His hands clenched tight with his need to wrest facts from her, but he accepted temporary defeat. Recovering his composure, he addressed Dr. Kitano: "You'd better keep her alive."

His tone implied the threat he didn't speak. He turned to his men. "Stay here and guard Suiren. Don't let anyone else talk to her." He must prevent Sano from questioning the maid and eliciting who and where the kidnappers were. "I'll be at the palace. If she wakes up, notify me at once."

He stalked out of the sickroom. Outside, he paused under the pine trees. The hot, brassy light of late afternoon streamed through the boughs. Temple bells echoed across the city, heralding another hour gone. That half a day had passed while his inquiries had gotten nowhere shook Hoshina's confidence. And he began to doubt his theory that Suiren knew the kidnappers and had helped them arrange the crime. Would they have wounded an accomplice so badly? Lesser injuries would have sufficed to make everyone think she was an innocent victim who'd escaped death by a fluke of luck. Perhaps Suiren was indeed innocent; perhaps she didn't know who had abducted her mistress. But the circumstances didn't completely discount Hoshina's theory. The kidnappers might have accidentally hurt the maid worse than they'd intended—or meant to kill her so that she could never betray them.

Hoshina decided that his theory merited further exploration. Although Suiren couldn't speak, there were other ways to find out whether she was his best lead or a dead end. He hastened out the gate and up the walled passage toward the palace women's quarters. There resided the ladies Suiren had lived with, as well as the female palace officials who'd supervised her. If she was party to the kidnapping, they might provide the clues Hoshina needed, whether or not she survived.

And one good clue would put him ahead of everyone else who was looking for Lady Keisho-in.

10

"Lady Yanagisawa, if you can hear, please listen to me," Reiko said.

She knelt beside Lady Yanagisawa, as she'd done most of the day. The glaring sun had dimmed and shifted westward, but still Lady Yanagisawa lay in her same, deathlike state. Her vacant eyes fixed on the ceiling, where the holes showed a sky tinged with the gold of approaching twilight. Outside, the windless weather quieted the forest. The waves lapped so quietly that Reiko could barely hear them above the chirping of songbirds and screeching from the gulls. Reiko clasped Lady Yanagisawa's limp hand. It was cold despite the ovenlike heat in the prison. Sweat trickled down Reiko's face, and she wiped her forehead with her sleeve. Anxiety mounted in her after countless failed attempts to communicate with Lady Yanagisawa.

"We're still trapped," Reiko said. "We still don't know why those men kidnapped us or who they are, because they won't say. Two of them came back this afternoon, but they just looked us over, then left."

Though Reiko had often heard the men outside during the day, they hadn't returned again. Flies buzzed around the empty food pail and full waste buckets. The heat worsened the stench. Mosquitoes whined and stung, and the women had red, itchy welts on their skin; yet hunger and discomfort were the least of Reiko's concerns.

"The kidnappers can't be intending to just let us go," she told Lady Yanagisawa. "They mean some kind of harm, I know it. I'm so afraid Lady Keisho-in will provoke them again, no matter how hard I try to stop her."

Reiko looked across the room at Keisho-in. The shogun's mother now lay asleep, snoring quietly, but she'd fumed and pounded on the door for much of the day. When the two men had come back, she'd ranted at them as though she'd forgotten how they'd hurt her that morning. Fortunately the men had ignored Keisho-in's diatribe . . . this time. Reiko didn't know how long their patience would last.

"We have to escape." Reiko leaned close to whisper in Lady Yanagisawa's ear: "I've thought of a way, but I can't do it alone. I don't trust Lady Keisho-in to help me. And Midori can't—she's about to have her baby any time now."

A grunt issued from Midori, also asleep. Her body stiffened and she clutched her belly, then relaxed and sighed. Her occasional cramps had come more frequently as the day passed, and Reiko dreaded the onset of labor.

"I need you," Reiko said to Lady Yanagisawa. Urgency raised her voice. "So please come out of this trance or whatever it is. Please help me save us!"

Lady Yanagisawa didn't reply. Not the slightest glimmer of comprehension showed in her dull, lifeless eyes. Reiko's patience toward the woman was fading fast.

"Maybe it's hard for you to bear what's happening," she said. "Maybe you'd rather hide inside yourself than face up to things. But think of your daughter. Kikuko-*chan* is at home, waiting for you. What will become of her if you don't return? She'll be so sad. She won't understand why her mother is gone. And who will take care of her?"

Lady Yanagisawa's hand drooped flaccid in Reiko's. Only her slow breathing indicated that she wasn't dead.

"I know your child means the world to you. You can't abandon her," Reiko said, trembling with anger now. "For Kikuko-*chan*'s sake, you must recover your wits and do something besides just lie there!"

No response came. Desperate, Reiko said, "Remember

your husband. You've told me how much you love him and how much you wish he would love you. Unless we get home, you'll never see him again. He must know you've been kidnapped. He's probably wondering where you are and what's happened to you. Often, people don't discover how valuable something is until they've lost it. Absence increases affection . . . and do you know what I think?

"I think your husband is realizing that he loves you. Your kidnapping has taught him the error of his ways. He's sorry he mistreated you and wants a chance to repent." Reiko told herself that the circumstances justified the lie. "Isn't that just what you've always dreamed of? But you can't have it if we die here. You'll never get to enjoy your husband's love unless you make an effort to go home to him."

Reiko scrutinized Lady Yanagisawa, hoping that the promise of her heart's desire would stir the woman to action. But Lady Yanagisawa didn't even flinch. Exhausted and frustrated, Reiko dropped Lady Yanagisawa's hand. Talking to someone who couldn't or wouldn't hear was no use. She must try the only other way she knew to revive Lady Yanagisawa.

As a young girl Reiko had learned the martial arts from a *sensei* hired by her father. The *sensei* had also taught her the ancient Chinese healing technique of applying pressure to the surface of the skin to stimulate the human body's natural curative abilities. She'd learned how pressing, striking, or piercing specific places on the body relieved pain in other areas, influenced the functioning of internal organs, and cured maladies both physical and mental. That ancient method could work to dramatic effect, Reiko knew from personal experience. When she'd given birth to Masahiro, the midwife had used it to relieve the labor pains and calm her. She remembered techniques for promoting the circulation of the blood and life force because she often practiced them on herself. But she'd never practiced on anyone else. The method released powerful energies that could be dangerous when mishandled by an amateur. She only hoped she could revive and not harm Lady Yanagisawa.

With the middle finger of her right hand, Reiko palpated Lady Yanagisawa's upper lip just below the nose, at a potent point—a juncture between internal pathways that carried *ki*, the life force. Applying pressure here could revive someone who'd fainted and ease extreme emotional agitation. Reiko pressed, leaning her weight on her fingertip. Beneath the cool, moist surface of Lady Yanagisawa's upper lip she felt the inner tension that blocked the flow of *ki*. She counted to five, lifted her finger, then reapplied the pressure. She detected a faint, throbbing pulse—a good sign of renewed circulation. Again and again she pressed the potent point, and each time the pulse strengthened a little. But Lady Yanagisawa remained as inert as a corpse.

Reiko moved to the junctures known as the Bubbling Springs, located between the fleshy pads on the soles of the feet. These were spots designated for the treatment of shock. Reiko clasped one of Lady Yanagisawa's feet in each hand and pushed her thumbs into the potent points. After twenty cycles of pressure and release, Reiko felt distinct, rhythmic pulses in the feet. The *ki* should be speeding through Lady Yanagisawa, reanimating her muscles, balancing her emotions, wakening her mind. When nothing happened, Reiko supposed that the trauma of the kidnapping had blocked other energy pathways.

She rolled Lady Yanagisawa onto her stomach, then measured four finger-widths from her spine at waist level, locating the potent points named the Sea of Vitality. Reiko pressed, waited, and released, again and again, so many times she lost count. Her hands ached; she gasped with exertion. Now she sensed Lady Yanagisawa's *ki* surging through veins and tissues. Suddenly a deep, ululating groan burst from Lady Yanagisawa. Her limbs began to thrash; her body jerked.

Reiko sprang back, frightened that she'd overstimulated Lady Yanagisawa into convulsions. Then Lady Yanagisawa heaved onto her back. Shuddering all over, she sat upright, hands clawing the floor, and stared wild-eyed at Reiko.

"Where am I?" The question burst from Lady Yanagi-sawa in a loud, hoarse voice. "What happened?"

Reiko smiled with relief that Lady Yanagisawa had come back to life. Keisho-in and Midori, startled awake by the commotion, blinked in puzzlement. Lady Yanagisawa gazed around the room. As she recognized her surroundings, a look of horror came into her eyes.

"Oh, no," she wailed, her face crumpling. "I dreamed that I was home with Kikuko-*chan*. It was so peaceful. Why did I have to wake up?" She lay down, curled her knees to her chest, and covered her head with her arms. Sobs wracked her. "I want to go back to sleep!"

"Please do," Keisho-in said crossly. "Your noise is getting on my nerves."

Reiko pounced on Lady Yanagisawa and forced apart her arms, exposing her anguish-stricken face. "You can't hide anymore. I won't let you."

"Please, no, leave me alone." Lady Yanagisawa squeezed her eyes shut, blinding herself to Reiko and the horrible fact of their captivity. "I want to dream again. I want Kikuko-*chan*."

Reiko was furious that Lady Yanagisawa preferred unconsciousness to taking action, even as she pitied the woman's suffering. She shouted, "If you want Kikuko-*chan,* then stop this nonsense right now!"

She slapped Lady Yanagisawa's cheek. Lady Yanagisawa uttered a cry of pained surprise. Her eyes opened; her sobs halted as she gaped at Reiko.

"It's your duty to fight your way home to your daughter," Reiko said, glad that she'd finally gotten Lady Yanagisawa's attention, yet ashamed of hitting the woman. "It's your duty to help me save Lady Keisho-in and Midori. Do you understand? Are you going to behave yourself? Or do I have to slap you again?"

All the resistance went out of Lady Yanagisawa. She uncurled her body and sat up, though with slow movements and a desolate expression that bespoke her reluctance.

"Will you help me?" Reiko said, hopeful yet cautious.

Lady Yanagisawa bowed her head and nodded.

Triumph at her small victory heartened Reiko, despite Lady Yanagisawa's lack of enthusiasm. Reiko beckoned Keisho-in and Midori. The pair seated themselves close to her and Lady Yanagisawa.

"Here's what we're going to do," Reiko said, then began whispering her plan.

11

"His Excellency has given orders that no one should disturb him," said the guard stationed outside the door of the shogun's private quarters.

Sano, Chamberlain Yanagisawa, and Police Commissioner Hoshina had come to report the progress of their investigation to the shogun. Sano exchanged glances of surprise with the other men: They'd all thought the shogun would be anxious for news, and hadn't expected to be denied entry.

"What's going on in there?" Chamberlain Yanagisawa's face darkened with offense that their lord, to whom he usually enjoyed free access, had shut him out.

"His Excellency is having a private consultation," the guard said.

"With whom?" Yanagisawa demanded.

Just then, the shogun's reedy voice called, "Come in."

The guard opened the door, and Yanagisawa strode through ahead of Hoshina and Sano. Inside the chamber, an ornate metal lantern that hung from the coffered ceiling shone down upon a low platform. On this sat Tokugawa Tsunayoshi, wearing his cylindrical black cap and a jade-green satin dressing gown, supported by heaped silk cushions. Near him, below the platform, knelt a Buddhist priest clad in a saffron robe.

Yanagisawa halted in his tracks. Sano and Hoshina

paused on either side of Yanagisawa. They all regarded the priest with consternation, while his gaze challenged them. This was Priest Ryuko, spiritual advisor and lover to Lady Keisho-in. In his forties, he had a high, shaved scalp and the long nose, hooded eyes, and sensuous lips of a Buddha statue. A gold brocade stole cloaked his broad shoulders and glittered in the lantern light. To find him in intimate company with the shogun gave Sano a presentiment of trouble.

"Ahh, greetings," Tokugawa Tsunayoshi said, his face bright with eager anticipation. He beckoned Yanagisawa, Sano, and Hoshina.

Recovering his composure, Yanagisawa moved to kneel in his usual place, the position of honor at the shogun's right. Sano and Hoshina knelt a short distance from the platform, opposite their lord. They all bowed to him.

"Have you found the honorable Lady Keisho-in?" Tokugawa Tsunayoshi asked, looking around as if he expected to see her.

An uneasy moment of silence passed; then Yanagisawa said, "I regret to say that we have not."

Disappointment dimmed the shogun's expression. Yanagisawa turned to Priest Ryuko. "How pleasant to see you. What brings you here?"

His tone made Sano envision a steel razor swathed in silk. That Yanagisawa detested the priest was no secret. Ryuko possessed an ambition for power that equaled the chamberlain's. His longtime association with Lady Keisho-in had elevated him to the status of highest-ranking priest in Japan and indirect advisor to the shogun. His influence over Tokugawa Tsunayoshi, and thousands of clerics in temples all over the country, threatened Yanagisawa's domination.

"I came to give spiritual solace to His Excellency in his time of trouble," Priest Ryuko said in a suave voice that didn't conceal his hatred for the chamberlain, who waged a covert, ongoing campaign to expel him from the court.

"I see."

Yanagisawa's expression conveyed a skepticism that Sano shared. Priest Ryuko had obviously seized on the kidnapping as a chance to ingratiate himself with his lord, for reasons clear to everyone present except Tokugawa Tsunayoshi. The priest knew his position in court depended on Lady Keisho-in, and should she die, he would lose his power—unless he secured the shogun's protection. Antipathy edged Sano's own distrust of Ryuko. The man cared more about his selfish interests than about the welfare of Keisho-in, Reiko, or the other women.

"Why haven't you, ahh, rescued my mother?" the shogun demanded, oblivious to undercurrents in the atmosphere.

"Please allow me to remind Your Excellency that less than a day has passed since we learned of Lady Keisho-in's kidnapping," Hoshina said with cautious deference. "The investigation requires time."

"You've had plenty of time. Have you done anything besides, ahh, waste it?" Inflated with dangerous petulance, the shogun leaned forward, glaring at Hoshina, Yanagisawa, and Sano. Just as Sano had feared, their lord expected instant results. "What, ahh, progress have you made toward bringing my mother home to me?"

A hint of amusement curved Ryuko's full lips as he observed the interchange. Hoshina scowled at the priest. Chamberlain Yanagisawa said, "A number of promising leads were pursued today. The *sōsakan-sama* will describe what he has discovered."

Trust Yanagisawa to make him speak first and throw him into the fire of the shogun's wrath, as if heaving water on a burning house, Sano thought. "I interrogated two Black Lotus criminals this morning," he said. "They told me about a priest named Profound Wisdom, who's high among the sect's leaders. They say the Black Lotus has been planning a major attack on the Tokugawa regime. It could be the kidnapping, and arranged by Profound Wisdom. He's deserted his secret temple, but my men and I searched the city and arrested forty-eight Black Lotus members today. I'll question them at Edo Jail. Someone among them should be able to tell me where the priest is."

The shogun nodded, pacified. Chamberlain Yanagisawa maintained a neutral composure, and Hoshina relaxed. Then Priest Ryuko said, "Have you any real cause to believe that the Black Lotus kidnapped the women?"

"Black Lotus clergy and followers are mad enough and brazen enough to have committed the crimes," Sano said.

The priest gave him a sardonic smile. "But you've no proof that the sect is involved in the crimes."

"Years of detective experience tell me that it is." Now Sano guessed what Ryuko was up to, and he grew angry at the priest's scheming.

"It appears that the *sōsakan-sama* has spent the day chasing people in the absence of evidence against them," Ryuko said, his voice inflected by an odd mixture of gloom and glee. "I begin to think he would rather persecute old enemies than find the real culprits."

"That's not true," Sano said, incensed at the unjust accusation.

The shogun ignored his denial and beheld him with shock and outrage. "How could you betray my trust?" he demanded. "After everything I've, ahh, given you?"

Before Sano could defend himself, Ryuko spoke: "The *sōsakan-sama*'s behavior is deplorable, but a more serious issue troubles me. Your Excellency, I fear that all the inquiries are headed in the wrong direction."

His critical gaze moved to Yanagisawa and Hoshina. Sano watched them try to hide their alarm: They, too, understood Ryuko's motives. The priest wanted Lady Keisho-in back because she was the source of his power, and he wanted everyone to do a better job of rescuing her. But in case she didn't come back, Ryuko must protect himself from people he feared would strike him down. Thus, he meant to undermine Sano, Yanagisawa, and Hoshina in the eyes of the shogun.

In his years as *sōsakan-sama,* Sano had often been the target of detractors during assemblies like this; but never had he shared the dubious honor with Yanagisawa and Hoshina.

"Perhaps it is you, not our inquiries, that are headed the wrong way," Yanagisawa said. He flicked a venomous glance at Ryuko but forbore to openly attack the priest.

"We have other avenues of inquiry besides the Black Lotus," Hoshina said. His belligerent expression dared Ryuko to fault him. "I've seen Suiren, the maid who survived the massacre. That fool of a doctor prevented her from talking to me, so I've been questioning the palace women about her. If she was an accomplice in the kidnapping, I'll soon find the culprits among her associates."

"*If* she was an accomplice," Ryuko said with disdain. "You seem to have no more proof that Suiren is guilty than the *sōsakan-sama* has evidence that the Black Lotus is."

"Do you have any better ideas?" Hoshina clenched his fists; his eyes blazed at Ryuko. "A gadfly only hinders men of action."

The priest made a moue of contempt, then addressed the shogun: "My duty is not to solve the crime but to point out to Your Excellency that the *sōsakan-sama* and police commissioner have made serious errors of judgment."

Sano and Hoshina looked at each other, flabbergasted by the priest's nerve. They burst into protest, but the shogun waved his hand, angrily silencing them. "Yes, you have, ahh, made terrible mistakes," he said. "You are so blinded by, ahh, prejudice that you would be lucky to find a fish in a bucket!" Saliva sputtered from his mouth. He turned a beseeching look on Chamberlain Yanagisawa. "At least I can rely on you to, ahh, rescue my beloved mother?"

"Of course, Your Excellency." Yanagisawa kept his voice smooth, but Sano sensed his agitation. "I have identified several suspects. One of them probably masterminded the kidnapping. I expect results very soon."

The shogun looked perturbed by this reassuring yet vague answer. Sano had often seen Chamberlain Yanagisawa use the shogun's fear of seeming stupid to keep him from pressing for more information than Yanagisawa wanted to give. Sano guessed that Yanagisawa's suspects included Lord Matsudaira and other Tokugawa clan members, who might have abducted Lady Keisho-in as leverage to force the shogun to eject Yanagisawa from the regime. Clearly, Yanagisawa had no solid evidence against the shogun's relatives and therefore hesitated to accuse them.

A flash of comprehension in Ryuko's eyes said he realized all this. His full lips thinned in a sly smile. "Who are these mysterious suspects?" he asked Yanagisawa.

The words spread a malevolent net of danger. Sano's heart skipped. Hoshina drew a sharp intake of breath. Yanagisawa stared, furious because he saw Ryuko's trap yet was powerless to avoid it.

"To reveal the names of the suspects now would jeopardize the investigation," Yanagisawa said in a voice cold enough to freeze fire. "We must not put the kidnappers on their guard, nor panic them into harming their hostages."

Priest Ryuko chuckled, seeing through Yanagisawa's evasion. "There's little danger of that, because you obviously have no suspects at all. You can't name them because they don't exist."

He couldn't name them—nor defend his competence— because casting aspersion upon his Tokugawa enemies would impugn his loyalty to the shogun, Sano understood. A muscle twitched in the chamberlain's jaw, and anger roiled like lava in his dark eyes. The rare experience of watching someone outmaneuver Yanagisawa gave no pleasure to Sano, because this time they were on the same side.

Yanagisawa said cautiously, "Your Excellency—"

"Be quiet!" the shogun shrieked.

Amazed silence paralyzed the assembly. Yanagisawa looked dumbfounded that the shogun would speak to him thus. Hoshina sat with his jaw dropped and his gaze disbelieving. Sano knew his own expression must appear similar. A smug smile crept over Priest Ryuko's lips.

"Not another word from you!" The shogun pointed at Yanagisawa; his voice and hand trembled with ire. He jabbed his finger at Sano and Hoshina. "Nor you, either.

You have all, ahh, disappointed me. You do not deserve to
be heard!"

Sano, Yanagisawa, and Hoshina sat speechless, afraid to
move. The shogun held the power of life and death over
everyone, and years of faithful service or even sexual companionship wouldn't excuse a retainer who angered him.
He'd executed men for minor offenses, and in his current
bad mood, he might condemn his chamberlain, police commissioner, and *sōsakan-sama* for talking out of turn. Sano
experienced deep distress and a terrible urge to laugh. None
of Chamberlain Yanagisawa's expertise at manipulating the
shogun would do them any good if he wasn't allowed to
speak.

The shogun turned to Priest Ryuko. "The men I counted
on have let me down," he lamented. "Will you help me?"

Ryuko's dignified, somber mien didn't hide his satisfaction. "I'll try my humble best, Your Excellency." He slid
a sly glance at Yanagisawa, whose countenance was livid
with suppressed, murderous rage.

"Then tell me how I can save my mother," the shogun
said, ready to place in Ryuko the faith he'd lost in Sano,
Yanagisawa, and Hoshina.

"With your permission, I shall divine the answer from
the oracle bones," said Priest Ryuko.

He summoned three monks and murmured orders to
them. They fetched a brazier filled with hot coals, and a
black lacquer table that held incense burners, candles, sake
in a cup, fruit, a bowl of cooked rice, cherry-wood sticks,
and the cleaned, polished undersides of five turtle shells.
The monks lit the incense and candles. One placed a turtle
shell in Ryuko's hands; the others heated sticks in the coals.

"Oh, deities of fortune, I respectfully entreat you to tell
us, where is the honorable Lady Keisho-in?" Ryuko said.

A monk handed him a stick whose tip glowed fiery red.
Priest Ryuko pressed the tip into a hollow bored on the
turtle shell's inner side. The shogun watched in avid anticipation, and Sano with the same disapproval that marked
the faces of Yanagisawa and Hoshina. Although fortune-

tellers had performed such rites on turtle shells or animal bones since ancient times, and oracles had revealed secret truths and governed the actions of emperors and generals, divination could be used by charlatans to trick the gullible.

"What must His Excellency do to bring his mother safely home?" Priest Ryuko intoned.

His assistants fanned his stick, which flamed against the turtle shell. The stench of burnt bone mingled with the sweet incense. Sharp cracking noises erupted as the heat fissured the shell. Priest Ryuko repeated the process until the sticks had burned down to stubs, smoke hazed the chamber, and all five shells bore multiple cracks.

"What does the, ahh, oracle say?" the shogun asked eagerly.

Priest Ryuko aligned the shells on the table. As he studied the cracks through which the gods communicated the answers to queries, his expression turned grave. "The gods decline to reveal where Lady Keisho-in is," he said.

Of course, Sano thought, while disappointment clouded the shogun's face and Hoshina and Yanagisawa grimaced in disgust. Ryuko was too smart to name Keisho-in's whereabouts and risk that events would prove him wrong.

"They say you must earn the knowledge," he told the shogun.

"How? What must I do?" Tokugawa Tsunayoshi leaned toward Ryuko, hands clasped with anxious hope.

"Your regime is out of harmony with the cosmos," Ryuko said. "Evil influences surround you and threaten your clan's future. You must purge your court of those evil influences. Restore its spiritual balance, and the path for Lady Keisho-in's return shall be cleared."

"Ahh, that advice eases my mind." Immediately the shogun's relief turned to confusion. "But how can I, ahh, know who around me is evil?" he asked.

Sano felt a pang of dismay as he guessed what Ryuko would answer.

"I will divine names of the evil persons you must expel from the court," Priest Ryuko said.

He flashed a triumphant gaze at the chamberlain and police commissioner. Sano watched their horror and panic at realizing that Ryuko had gained much control over the shogun and could depose them via false oracles. But Sano burned with an outrage that exceeded his fear of losing his own post. He felt a consuming hatred for Priest Ryuko that extended to everyone else in the room. Ryuko, Yanagisawa, and Hoshina all sought to use the kidnapping to advance themselves. All they cared about was their own political careers. And all the shogun cared about was his mother. None of them spared a thought for Reiko, Midori, or the hundred people who'd died during the massacre.

Sano's anger swelled against the barrier of his self-control. He had to leave before he killed someone. He rose, and the other men stared, surprised that he would stand before the shogun dismissed him. Sano bowed to everyone. Then, for the first time ever, he walked from the chamber without permission from his lord. The anger roaring in his head drowned out the sound of the shogun's voice calling to him.

Once outside the palace, he ran through the twilight, along the walled passages. He ignored checkpoint guards who shouted at him to stop for inspection. He arrived, breathless and sweating, at his own estate. The sentries opened the gate for him, and he halted in the courtyard. He bent over, panting, as cold realization quenched his anger.

Walking out on the shogun had only worsened the danger to Reiko. The shogun might order him off the kidnapping investigation—if Priest Ryuko hadn't already persuaded their lord to banish or execute him. Then who would rescue his wife? Sano thought of Hirata. The chance that he and Marume and Fukida would find the women seemed poor, and Sano cursed his own rashness. The darkening heavens and the cool evening air reverberated with his fear that Reiko was lost forever and the world was crumbling around him.

He felt a need to do something, anything, to forestall despair, and remembered that he had a jail full of Black

Lotus prisoners to interrogate. As he started toward the barracks to fetch a squad of detectives, Sano fought qualms
that the Black Lotus hadn't abducted the women and he
was wasting time. A new fear for Reiko took root in him.

His wife was not inclined to sit passively enduring whatever happened to her. Sano knew Reiko would try to strike
back at her kidnappers and escape. Would she succeed? Or
would her daring be the death of her?

Reiko raised her hands high and stretched them
toward the rafters that crisscrossed the ceiling of the prison.
Her skirts were tied around her hips, her sock-clad feet
planted on Lady Yanagisawa's shoulders. Lady Yanagisawa clutched Reiko's ankles and staggered beneath her
weight. As she swayed dangerously, Reiko flailed her arms,
trying to keep her balance.

"Be careful, Reiko-*san*," Lady Keisho-in ordered. To
Lady Yanagisawa she said, "Don't drop her, you fool."

Midori watched, her eyes and mouth round with fright.
Lady Yanagisawa steadied herself. Reiko reached up and
caught hold of a rafter. A hole in the ceiling allowed her
to clasp both hands around the wooden beam. It was rough
and deteriorated from exposure to the weather, and split at
intervals. Reiko yanked downward on the rafter. The wood
held firm.

"Pull harder," Keisho-in said, while Lady Yanagisawa
tottered under Reiko.

Wishing Keisho-in would be quiet, Reiko exerted her
weight on the rafter. A mosquito alit on her chin; she ignored the sting. With a sudden sharp, cracking noise, the
beam snapped. The break in tension canted Reiko backward. Lady Yanagisawa crumpled under Reiko like a
mountain succumbing to an earthquake. She let go of
Reiko's ankles. It happened so fast that Reiko had no time
to experience fear nor prevent her fall. She crashed on her
spine.

The impact jarred her bones, knocked the breath from

her. Midori shrieked. Keisho-in began scolding Lady Yan-agisawa, who had fallen near Reiko and now leaned anx-iously over her.

"Reiko-*san,* I'm sorry I couldn't hold you up," Lady Yanagisawa said. "Are you all right?"

Dazed and panting, her heart thudding in delayed fright, Reiko sat up. She ached where she'd hit the floor, but noth-ing seemed damaged. "I'm fine," she said. Yet perhaps she'd made a mistake by reviving Lady Yanagisawa. Had the woman deliberately let her fall? Could she trust Lady Yanagisawa to cooperate with her plan and not hurt her? How she wished the kidnappers were her only problem! But in her hands was the broken rafter—thick, heavy, and as long as her leg.

"We have the weapon we need," Reiko said, trium-phantly holding up the rafter.

Midori smiled. Keisho-in applauded.

"Now we wait until the men open the door and come into the room again." Reiko observed Lady Yanagisawa. The woman's gaze evaded hers, causing her more distrust. "You'll distract them, the way we discussed. Then . . ." Reiko swung the rafter at an imaginary foe. She hoped her plan would work, and that Lady Yanagisawa would control her murderous impulses for the sake of their survival. "Af-ter the men are unconscious, we all run."

"I don't think I can," Midori said in a tiny, desolate voice. She clambered to her feet and staggered a few steps. Her belly bobbed huge and low. "I can barely walk," she said, collapsing to the floor.

Dismay sank Reiko's heart. "You must try. I'll help you."

"I can't walk either. My knees are too stiff," said Keisho-in, lifting her skirt to show Reiko the swollen joints. "You'll have to carry me."

Reiko looked at Lady Yanagisawa, who gazed back in consternation. The two of them couldn't carry the shogun's mother and help Midori at the same time.

"Please go without me. I'll stay behind. You must save

yourselves." Midori spoke with self-sacrificing bravado.

"I won't leave you here," Reiko said, appalled at the thought. If she and Lady Yanagisawa and Keisho-in escaped, the other kidnappers would eventually discover what had happened. Reiko shuddered to imagine Midori facing their wrath alone. Yet there seemed no way she could get both Midori and Keisho-in to safety. Their infirmities would diminish the chance of a successful escape. Getting caught would endanger all their lives—but Reiko believed that doing nothing would be fatal.

"Lady Keisho-in and Midori-*san* will wait here," Reiko told Lady Yanagisawa. "I'll stay with them and defend them, while you fetch someone to rescue us."

Midori smiled, tearfully grateful that she wouldn't be abandoned. Keisho-in frowned as if unsure whether to protest. Lady Yanagisawa beheld Reiko with horror.

"I can't. I don't know where to go. I'll get lost." Her complexion paled with the terror that choked her voice to a whisper. "To talk to strangers, and ask for their help . . ." Lady Yanagisawa shook her head. "I can't."

"You have to," Reiko said.

"No. I can't. Please don't make me." Lady Yanagisawa shivered and recoiled; her eyes closed.

Reiko saw that what she'd asked was truly beyond the woman's ability. "Then I'll have to go," she said.

Misgivings troubled her, but she stifled them because doubt and fear would only impair her chances of saving her friends. Deepening shadow filled their prison with gloom. Reiko looked up at the patches of sky visible through the ruined ceiling. Stars glittered in the sunset's clear mauve afterglow. Reiko walked to a spot beside the door. She sat, holding the broken rafter in her lap, to wait until the kidnappers came.

12

Sano arrived home just before daybreak, exhausted and discouraged, after interrogating the forty-eight captured Black Lotus members at Edo Jail. Some had told him that the priest known as Profound Wisdom held secret rituals in temples at various locations around Edo, and Sano had sent men to search the places. But those informants apparently knew nothing about the kidnapping or massacre. The other captives were Black Lotus zealots who refused to say anything except that High Priest Anraku had risen from the dead to launch an attack of unknown nature upon the Tokugawa. Although Sano couldn't shake his conviction that the Black Lotus was behind the crimes, he'd realized he must explore other possibilities. He decided to catch a few hours of sleep, then plumb Edo's underworld for tips on who had abducted the women.

Entering the private quarters of his mansion, Sano heard childish squalls. He walked down the corridor, into the nursery, and found Masahiro sobbing in bed. The nursemaid who slept on a futon beside the boy stirred awake. As she moved toward him, she looked up at Sano in surprise, for he usually let Reiko or the maids tend Masahiro when he cried at night.

"I'll take care of him," Sano told the nursemaid. He lifted Masahiro and paced the room, hugging his son's warm, solid body, comforting them both. "It's all right,

Masahiro-*chan*," he said. "You just had a bad dream."

"I want Mama," wailed Masahiro, his face hot and wet with tears against Sano's cheek.

"Mama is away. She'll be back soon." Concern for his son filled Sano. He wondered if Masahiro sensed something was wrong. Maybe he'd noticed the pall that Reiko's kidnapping had cast over the household.

"Excuse me, *Sōsakan-sama*," Detective Arai said from the doorway. "A message just arrived from Chamberlain Yanagisawa. He wants to see you at his estate right away."

Though Sano had never expected to visit Chamberlain Yanagisawa's estate, he and four of his detectives now stood outside the stone wall topped with metal spikes. Dawn had paled the black sky to ashen pink, but the private compound seemed to gather the vestiges of night around itself. Pine trees inside cast deep shadows over the buildings. Sano's sharp eyes discerned soldiers in the watchtowers and archers perched on the gabled tile roofs. The compound was a fortress within the fortress of Edo Castle, designed to protect Yanagisawa from attacks by foes inside the shogun's court.

Guards at the ironclad gate confiscated the swords from Sano and his men, then escorted them into the estate. Sano wished they could keep their weapons. Truce or no truce, this was hostile territory. He and his detectives trod uneasily along a flagstone path, into a courtyard enclosed by soldiers' barracks, and through grounds where more guards patrolled around the interconnected wings of the mansion. Watchdogs, led on leashes by servants, barked and growled at Sano as his escorts led him into a garden.

Here, mossy boulders dotted an expanse of raked sand. Stone lanterns bordered a path that wound through dew-misted lawn, past gnarled shrubs to a raised pavilion with a thatched roof and lattice walls. Through its arched open doorway Sano saw the tall, slim figure of Yanagisawa. The chamberlain paced back and forth, his silk robes dragging the stone floor. Catching sight of Sano, he halted and beckoned. Sano joined Yanagisawa in the pavilion. They bowed to each other, while his detectives and the guards waited a short distance away.

"Thank you for coming so promptly," Yanagisawa said.

His manner was formal and composed, yet his eyes had the intense but unfocused gaze of a man experiencing severe shock. Sano comprehended that something dire had happened.

"Has Priest Ryuko persuaded the shogun to condemn us?" This seemed to Sano the only possible reason for Yanagisawa's summons.

Yanagisawa impatiently waved a hand, dispelling Sano's notion that the chamberlain had invited him here so they could ally against Priest Ryuko and save themselves from demotion, exile, or death. "After you so abruptly left the meeting last night," Yanagisawa said, "I managed to convince His Excellency that Priest Ryuko had been too hasty in judging us and we deserve another chance to rescue Lady Keisho-in." He spoke as if this hardly mattered and the clash with Ryuko had lost all significance. He resumed pacing.

"Then why did you want to see me?" Sano asked.

With a visible effort Yanagisawa halted his restless movements, faced Sano, and said in low monotone, "The ransom letter from the kidnappers has arrived."

"What?" Surprise jolted Sano's heart, which began thundering a rhythm of anticipation and alarm as he stared at Yanagisawa. "When? How?"

The chamberlain reached inside his surcoat and brought out a large folded white paper. "A patrol guard found it an hour ago, plastered on the castle wall. He brought it to me because he's one of my spies."

"Have you shown the letter to His Excellency?" Sano said.

Yanagisawa expelled his breath in a long, quavering gust. "Not yet. No one else knows about the letter."

That he'd withheld important information from the sho-

gun baffled Sano less than did the fact that Yanagisawa
wanted to share the news with him first. "But why—"

"Read it." Yanagisawa thrust the letter into Sano's
hands.

Nonplussed, Sano unfolded the paper. It bore columns
of large characters written with black ink, in bold, elegant
calligraphy. The message read:

> The woman thrashes wildly in dark water,
> Her long hair and robes spread,
> Like the petals of a flower cut and tossed upon the lake.
> Her cries for help pierce the night,
> But alas, to no avail,
> Cold waves engulf her beauty,
> Water bubbles into her lungs,
> Seaweed entwines her limbs,
> She surrenders fear and suffering,
> As she sinks into death.
>
> The pale wraith of her spirit departs its lifeless body,
> She drifts in enchanted slumber,
> Down unfathomable depths,
> Through watery channels,
> Into a cave far beneath the Eastern Sea.
> There she awakens in a glittering garden,
> Of sea urchins, anemones, shells, and coral.
> She floats past brilliant, swimming fish,
> Toward a palace built from luminous mother-of-pearl,
> Where the Dragon King rules his underwater realm.
>
> The Dragon King uncoils within his palace,
> His green scales and golden claws gleam,
> His eyes flash like crimson jewels,
> And flames breathe from his mouth.
> His undulating serpent's body encircles her,
> While she recoils in terror.
> But the Dragon King whispers, "Fear not, my lady."
> He heaps pearls, gems, and gold coins at her feet.

*"You shall be my queen and dwell here in my palace,
For all eternity."*

Your Excellency the Shogun—

Here is what you must do if you want your
honorable mother returned to you. Denounce Police
Commissioner Hoshina as a murderer, then execute
him and display his corpse at the foot of the
Nihonbashi Bridge. Obey my orders, and I will
release Lady Keisho-in and her friends. Disobey,
and they will be killed.

Sano gave minimal attention to the poem, which made
no sense to him. Amazed, he reread the kidnappers' demands and shook his head. He looked up at Chamberlain
Yanagisawa, who watched him with controlled stoicism.

"The target of the kidnapping isn't the shogun, or you,
or me," Sano said. "It's Hoshina-*san*!" They couldn't have
guessed; nothing had forewarned them. And the theories
they'd devised in ignorance had misguided their investigation. "We've been hunting suspects in the wrong places!"

"Indeed." Yanagisawa turned away from Sano and gazed
out of the pavilion.

As morning encroached upon the garden, shadows lifted;
the landscape and colors gained definition. Sano experienced dawning relief because he now understood the
kidnappers' motive and how to save Reiko. Then came the
immediate, awful realization that the terms of the ransom
put her in worse jeopardy than he'd imagined.

"What are you going to do?" As Sano spoke, apprehension struck a new chord.

The chamberlain moved his shoulders in a gesture that
bespoke the quandary weighing upon them. However much
he wanted to rescue Lady Keisho-in and win the battle for
the shogun's favor, should he allow the execution of his
lover? Sano realized that Yanagisawa must care a great deal
for Hoshina, or he would have already taken the letter to

the shogun, and Hoshina would be on his way to his death. Still wondering why Yanagisawa had chosen to break the news about the ransom letter to him this way, Sano faced his own dilemma. He couldn't condone a blood sacrifice in exchange for the women, but Hoshina was his enemy, and Reiko's life was at stake.

Sano said, "When are you going to tell Hoshina-*san*?"

"Right now." Yanagisawa called to his guards: "Fetch the police commissioner."

Soon Hoshina ambled up the path, clad in a beige silk dressing gown that exposed his bare chest, calves, and feet. He yawned, his eyes heavy with sleep. When he saw Sano, he stopped outside the pavilion and blinked in drowsy surprise.

"What's going on?" Hoshina asked, looking to Yanagisawa.

"We've received the kidnappers' ransom demand." Yanagisawa took the letter from Sano and proffered it to Hoshina.

"At last!" Hoshina appeared not to notice Yanagisawa's cold manner; the news had captured all his attention. He vaulted up the steps into the pavilion and eagerly snatched the letter. Scanning the text, he frowned in bafflement at the poem. He read the ransom demand, and Sano watched his eyes widen in shock, his mouth slacken in disbelief.

"The kidnapper wants me dead!" Hoshina burst out. "That's the reason for the crime!" He threw down the letter and turned to Yanagisawa in alarm. "But the shogun wouldn't kill me to get Lady Keisho-in back, would he?"

Yanagisawa avoided his lover's gaze. Sano knew that the shogun not only loved his mother much more than he cared about Hoshina, but would gladly slay any of his retainers for her sake. Now Sano saw the horrified realization sink into Hoshina.

"You won't show His Excellency the letter, will you?" Hoshina said, clutching Yanagisawa's arms. "You won't let him kill me to save his mother, will you?"

The chamberlain's hands came up to clasp Hoshina's

forearms in a gesture of restraint and affection. "I cannot intervene on your behalf." Yanagisawa spoke with quiet regret as he looked directly at Hoshina. "Matters must take their course."

"What?"

Hoshina recoiled from Yanagisawa as though the chamberlain had struck him a physical blow. Sano also experienced shock because he'd expected Yanagisawa to protect his lover.

"You're going to sacrifice me to save Lady Keisho-in." Hoshina shook his head, resisting belief. He uttered a laugh tinged with hysteria. "But—but there's no need. You can talk the shogun into sparing me. We can find some other way to rescue Lady Keisho-in."

His eyes beseeched Yanagisawa, but the chamberlain said in the same quiet tone, "What you ask is impossible."

Sano watched angry comprehension darken Hoshina's face. "You mean you won't defend me because you don't want to risk displeasing the shogun," Hoshina said.

Yanagisawa inclined his head, silent and pensive.

"You'd rather let me die than lose your position or your chance to rule Japan through your son when he becomes the next dictator," Hoshina said. "After everything we've done together and been to each other?"

Blazing with outrage, Hoshina paced circles around Yanagisawa. "I've helped you build your power. I've fought your enemies. I've given you my body and my heart." He thumped his chest. "And now, when I need your help, you cut me loose."

Sano inwardly squirmed with embarrassment at witnessing a private quarrel. Yanagisawa must have known this would happen, and Sano wondered again why the chamberlain wanted him here.

Suddenly Hoshina crumpled to his knees before Yanagisawa. "Please don't abandon me," he wailed, erupting into sobs. His hands scrabbled against the chamberlain's robes. "I love you. I don't want to die. Please, please, if you love me, don't let the shogun execute me!"

Sano recalled the meeting where he'd heard the news of the kidnapping, and how eagerly Hoshina had welcomed the crime as a chance to better his own position. What a contrast between that ambitious, cocky Hoshina and this groveling creature!

Yanagisawa stood speechless, unmoved; yet Sano sensed anguish tormenting him: He did love Hoshina, though he loved power more. Sano pitied them. Then Yanagisawa stepped away from Hoshina.

"It's no use," he said with firm, desolate resolve. "I can't stand in the way of rescuing the shogun's mother. My enemies would jump at the chance to attack me, and their combined power is stronger than mine." Sano knew Yanagisawa referred to Lord Matsudaira, other Tokugawa clan members, and Priest Ryuko. "For me to protect you would mean certain death for us both."

Hoshina sprang to his feet. Panic flashed through the tears that blurred his face. He rushed toward the doorway of the pavilion, but the sight of the guards on the path froze him. Sano watched Hoshina realize that escape was impossible; he wouldn't get out of Edo Castle alive. Sweat glistened on his skin, and he exuded the sour reek of terror. Breathing hard, crouched in a defensive posture, he glanced wildly around him. His eyes lit upon Sano; cunning inspiration focused them.

Sano suddenly knew what Hoshina was going to say, and the reason for his presence. Enlightenment appalled him.

"Do you remember when you were investigating the murder of Lord Mitsuyoshi last winter?" Hoshina said. "I gave you a tip, in exchange for a favor. You promised to do whatever I asked, whenever I wanted. Well, now I'm asking you to honor our deal." Squaring his shoulders, Hoshina lifted his chin and faced Sano with the brazen aggression of a man seizing upon his last resort. "Save my life."

His promise to Hoshina had menaced Sano like a poisonous snake lurking in a forest, waiting to strike him. Finally the snake had sunk its fangs. Sano had expected Hoshina to make the most extravagant request at the least convenient moment, but the nature and timing of this demand were worse than Sano could have predicted.

"How am I supposed to save you?" Outraged and horrified, Sano flung out his hands. "Tell the shogun to let you live and his mother die?" Sano uttered a sarcastic laugh. "You're asking me for a miracle!"

"That's your problem," Hoshina retorted. "Solve it however you can. We made a bargain, and you have to uphold your end."

Sano looked at Yanagisawa, who regarded him with a steady, penetrating gaze that confirmed his suspicions. Yanagisawa had been aware of the bargain. He'd known Hoshina would need help now, and he'd brought Sano here because he knew Hoshina would call in the favor. Yanagisawa had contrived to manipulate Sano into saving his lover for him! Sano gave Yanagisawa a bitter, resentful glare, then turned back to Hoshina.

"This is one time I'll gladly break my word," Sano said, folding his arms in defiance. "After you've done your best to ruin me, you don't deserve my protection."

"I deserve the same good deed I did for you." Hoshina's perspiring face was savage with determination. "If I hadn't given you that tip, you would be dead now. You owe me your life. And you'll repay me by saving mine."

Sano made a sound of vehement denial, but he couldn't ignore Hoshina's logic. Sano had been a suspect in that murder case, and without the tip, he might still have cleared his name and arrested the real killer . . . or not. If he'd failed, he would have been punished by death. He could never know for sure whether he would have prevailed no matter what, or if Hoshina had prevented his downfall.

"I won't sacrifice those women for the likes of you!" Sano shouted, furious at Hoshina, Yanagisawa, and himself for the circumstances that ensnared him. "Nor will I let you interfere with my duty to rescue Lady Keisho-in." He snatched up the ransom letter from the pavilion's floor where Hoshina had thrown it. "I'll take this to the shogun now and advise him to comply with the demands. I'll personally deliver you to the executioner."

In the heat of his anger, Sano didn't want to think that Hoshina had a legitimate claim on him. Sano cared most about saving Reiko. He reached out to grab Hoshina, but the police commissioner shoved him away.

"Behold the mighty *sōsakan-sama*," Hoshina said. Though his eyes registered fear that he'd lost his last gamble, he bared his teeth in a mocking grin. "He pretends to champion justice and uphold honor, but he would condemn me to a disgraceful death, without even knowing what murder the kidnappers have accused me of, or if I'm guilty. And why? Because he wishes to serve duty by rescuing his lord's mother?"

Hoshina addressed his questions to an imaginary audience. He ignored Yanagisawa, who silently watched. "No—he only wants to save his wife." Hoshina stank of desperation, but he sneered in contempt at Sano. "You despise other men for serving selfish interests. Well, you're a hypocrite."

"Shut up!" Sano yelled, incensed because Hoshina spoke the same criticism that his conscience was whispering to him.

"You always insist on knowing the truth, but the truth hurts sometimes, doesn't it?" Hoshina taunted.

"I'll execute you myself!" Sano reached for his sword, which Yanagisawa's guards had confiscated.

"You wouldn't even if you could," Hoshina said, more reckless as he perceived that he'd gained the upper hand. "You won't abet my death even though you love your wife and hate me. We both know you have to keep your promise."

Sano experienced a sensation of careening down a steep hill as he realized that Hoshina was right. Whatever his reluctance, he must concede. The samurai code of honor that he lived to serve forbade reneging on his word or giving in to a demand from a criminal. Lifelong adherence to

Bushido had destined him to perform the favor Hoshina wanted. And he began to perceive other, even more important reasons why he must. Stricken by defeat, he glared at Hoshina.

The mockery in Hoshina's smile turned to triumph. Yanagisawa betrayed no emotion. Sano understood that his own honor had always been their strongest weapon against him. Even as his heart rebelled, his samurai spirit quelled its protests. The onus settling upon him bowed his head.

"We'll go to the shogun now," Yanagisawa said.

He took the ransom letter from Sano, clearly bent on doing just what he'd said he would—letting matters take their course. Sano's mind raced with frenetic thoughts. How could he save Hoshina, and Reiko besides?

13

The shogun sat on the dais in the palace audience chamber, holding the ransom letter in his spindly hands. His head moved, his lips formed inaudible words, and concentration puckered his face while he read the columns of characters. Utter quiet immersed the room.

Sano, kneeling below the dais at Tokugawa Tsunayoshi's left, felt his heartbeat accelerate and his stomach tighten behind his stoic countenance. As he mentally rehearsed what he would say, he eyed Police Commissioner Hoshina, who knelt near him.

Hoshina had donned a silk kimono, trousers, and surcoat in shades of green before coming to the palace. His sweat had already spread damp patches across the garments. Unable to sit still, he kept looking from the shogun to Sano, from the shogun's guards stationed along the walls to Sano's detectives kneeling at the back of the room, and finally to Yanagisawa.

The chamberlain sat at the shogun's right, his aloof demeanor like a shield between him and everyone else. Sano marveled at Yanagisawa's control, for he himself couldn't have remained so calm while depending on his enemy to save his beloved.

"What is this peculiar poem about a, ahh, drowned woman and the dragon king?" the shogun said, baffled. "And what does it have to do with, ahh, the kidnapping?"

No one answered. Everyone waited while he read the ransom demand. "Ahh!" Surprise raised Tokugawa Tsunayoshi's eyebrows; then comprehension illuminated his face. Looking up from the letter, he exclaimed, "Now I can rescue my mother!"

He turned to Hoshina. "You have, ahh, served me well, and it is a pity that I must, ahh, sacrifice you. But you shall have the, ahh, ultimate honor of dying in the line of duty."

Hoshina gulped; his Adam's apple jerked: All his verbal prowess had deserted him. Sano had expected Tokugawa Tsunayoshi would concede to the kidnapper's demands, but he was amazed that the shogun spoke with such callous disregard for Hoshina, though of course he owed his retainers nothing. Sano realized that appeals to the shogun's compassion wouldn't save Hoshina.

The shogun signaled to his guards. "Take Hoshina-*san* to the execution ground at once. After he's, ahh, dead, place his corpse and severed head on a frame at the Nihonbashi Bridge, with a sign that, ahh, proclaims him to be a murderer."

Four guards advanced toward Hoshina, who stared at Sano, willing him to keep his promise. Yanagisawa watched the scene with cool detachment. Now was Sano's last chance to go back on his word, do nothing, and let Hoshina die; yet honor and wisdom overpowered selfish impulse.

"Your Excellency, please wait," Sano said in a voice fraught with his conflicting emotions.

Everyone's attention shifted to Sano. The shogun regarded him in surprise. "Wait for what?" Tokugawa Tsunayoshi said. "The sooner I, ahh, execute Police Commissioner Hoshina, the sooner the, ahh, kidnappers will return my mother to me."

"Not necessarily, Your Excellency," said Sano.

The guards seized Hoshina and yanked him to his feet. He resisted, his muscles straining, his features set in a grimace of terror. The shogun planted his fists on his hips and leaned toward Sano.

"How dare you interfere?" Tokugawa Tsunayoshi demanded. "Are you so, ahh, disloyal to me that you would, ahh, protect Hoshina-*san* at my mother's expense?" Ire reddened his cheeks. "Perhaps you wish to, ahh, join him at the execution ground."

Although fear threatened to choke Sano, he must continue his risky course, for Reiko's sake as well as Hoshina's. "My only wish is to serve you, Your Excellency," he said. "And I must respectfully advise you that killing Hoshina-*san* won't guarantee the honorable Lady Keisho-in's safety."

The shogun tilted his head, looked askance at Sano, but his lack of confidence in his own decisions gave him hesitation. He raised a hand and stopped the guards from dragging Hoshina away. "What are you, ahh, talking about?"

Sano felt the force of Hoshina's hope trained on him. He said, "It's not in the kidnappers' interest to ever free Lady Keisho-in. She must have seen their faces, so she can identify them. They know that if they let her go alive, she'll help you hunt them down. As soon as they know Hoshina is dead, they'll kill her and the other hostages."

This possibility enabled Sano to argue with conviction against obeying the kidnappers. Now the shogun's jaw dropped. "But this says my mother will be released if I, ahh, execute Hoshina-*san*," Tokugawa Tsunayoshi said, holding up the letter.

"A promise from a criminal is worthless," Sano said. "Someone evil enough to kidnap the honorable Lady Keisho-in and murder her entourage will have no scruples about reneging on Your Excellency as soon as you've given him what he wants."

Tokugawa Tsunayoshi pounded the dais in outrage that anyone would treat him thus. "Disgraceful!" Immediately, his face crumpled. He wailed, "But the, ahh, kidnapper will kill my mother if I don't execute Hoshina-*san*."

The kidnapper might indeed murder all the women unless he got his way, Sano knew; whatever they did, they could lose.

The shogun underwent another sudden mood change to suspicion. "You're trying to, ahh, confuse me," he told Sano, then turned on Chamberlain Yanagisawa. "I begin to think there is a, ahh, plot to make me spare Hoshina-*san* and doom my mother."

Yanagisawa involuntarily stiffened with the alarm that Sano also experienced. The atmosphere in the room grew heavy with menace. Outside, beyond the open doors, the sun had risen above the buildings surrounding the garden, but the palace's deep eaves shadowed the audience chamber.

"There's no plot that involves me, Your Excellency," said Yanagisawa, and his voice sounded brittle. "I haven't lifted a finger to prevent Hoshina-*san*'s execution."

"But you've, ahh, sat by and let Sano-*san* argue against it." The shogun lunged to his feet so awkwardly that he almost fell on Yanagisawa, who drew back in consternation. "Do you think I don't know that Hoshina-*san* is your lover? Do you think I'm so stupid that I, ahh, wouldn't guess that you want to save him?" Eyes narrowed by pique, the shogun loomed over Yanagisawa. "You, whom I've loved and trusted, have, ahh, conspired with Sano-*san* to deceive me. Your pact is treason of the most, ahh, heinous kind, and you shall be punished."

Rage swelled his slight body and purpled his face. Before Sano or Yanagisawa could react, the shogun called out: "Guards! Take them to the, ahh, execution ground. They can die with their, ahh, comrade, whom they value above me."

One pair of guards hastened toward Sano, and another toward the chamberlain. Sano saw his own horrified shock expressed on Yanagisawa's face as the guards grabbed them. For years they'd both managed to evade the constant threat of death that haunted everyone in the *bakufu*, but their luck had run out. Panicking, Sano tasted the terror of death, and the awful humiliation that the shogun deemed him a traitor. Hoshina, still in the grip of his guards, moaned as though realizing that all was lost.

"Your decisiveness is admirable, Your Excellency, but I must advise you that you're making a terrible mistake," Yanagisawa said while the guards hauled him upright. His eyes flared with indignation, sweat glistened on his skin, and never had Sano seen him so frightened.

"If you kill Hoshina, you've sentenced your mother to death," Sano hastened to add. Struggling to resist the guards, he wished the kidnappers had asked for anything else but Hoshina's execution. "And if you kill us, who will rescue her for you, before the kidnappers kill her?"

The shogun teetered from side to side; a harried look furrowed his brow. "Priest Ryuko says he can, ahh, help me." His blinking eyes avoided Sano and Yanagisawa. "He said the, ahh, oracle bones named the two of you as, ahh, demons who threaten the regime. If I, ahh, rid my court of you, harmony will balance the cosmic forces. My mother will be delivered from evil."

"Priest Ryuko lies," Yanagisawa declared, now willing to openly denounce the priest rather than give up his life without a fight. "If he's the great magician that he claims, he would have predicted the kidnapping beforehand, and prevented it. It's he, not us, who has tricked you."

". . . Aah?" The shogun pursed his mouth.

Sano was glad to see that Yanagisawa had undermined Priest Ryuko's influence and the shogun's certainty about his own judgment. Yet the guards propelled Sano, Yanagisawa, and Hoshina toward the door, and the shogun didn't intervene. Sano's panic grew. Unless he could sway his lord, he would die in disgrace. Reiko would die without him to save her. All because his honor had forced him to protect Hoshina, who didn't deserve protecting, and because he'd failed to convince the shogun that executing Hoshina wasn't the solution to their problem.

"Yes, Priest Ryuko is a fraud," Sano said in desperation. Speaking out against the powerful cleric couldn't hurt him any more than could keeping silent. "You need us, Your Excellency. We're your only hope of saving the honorable Lady Keisho-in."

Irresolution, and his tendency to quail when anyone opposed him, wavered the shogun's stance.

"Destroy us, and she's doomed," Chamberlain Yanagisawa said. "Spare us, and we'll prove our loyalty by returning her safe and sound to Your Excellency."

A short eternity passed while Tokugawa Tsunayoshi vacillated. Crows in the garden cawed like the carrion birds that flocked the execution ground. At last, the shogun raised a tentative hand to the guards. They paused, bridling Sano, Yanagisawa, and Hoshina at the threshold.

"You haven't, ahh, found my mother yet, so why should I, ahh, believe you can ever rescue her?" Tokugawa Tsunayoshi demanded.

Sano noted that crises affected people in different ways, and this one had improved the shogun's wits. Hoshina mutely waited, his face confused, as if he couldn't guess whether he was about to be saved or on the brink of his downfall.

"That we've learned why the kidnappers took the honorable Lady Keisho-in has opened a new avenue of inquiry," Sano said. "I now know where to begin looking for them." All his hopes for Reiko hinged on that belief. "This time I'll find her." Conviction strengthened his voice. "I swear it on my honor."

Abruptly, the shogun plopped down on the dais. "Very well," he said with the air of a man eager to trust what he heard, make a decision, and spurn responsibility. "I grant you the, ahh, right to continue your search." He waved off the guards who held Sano and Yanagisawa. "Resume your, ahh, seats."

"A million thanks, Your Excellency," Yanagisawa said, meek for once.

Sano exhaled a trapped breath. He and Yanagisawa slunk back to their places, knelt, and bowed to the shogun. Tokugawa Tsunayoshi said, "But what should we, ahh, do about the, ahh, ransom letter? It seems that whether I comply or not, I am damned."

Chamberlain Yanagisawa gave Sano a look that said, *Yes, what should we do?*

"Hoshina-*san* is your insurance of your honorable mother's survival," Sano told the shogun. "Therefore, I advise you to postpone his execution. The kidnappers will keep Lady Keisho-in alive because the promise of her return is their only means of forcing you to meet their demands."

Sano didn't voice his fear that the women were already dead and whatever the shogun did wouldn't help them. "The kidnappers have gone to great lengths to destroy Hoshina-*san*," he continued, "and the fact that they want him dead so badly works to our advantage. They'll wait for you to execute him. Stalling them will give me time to hunt them down."

"That sounds like a, ahh, good plan," the shogun said, mollified.

Hoshina cleared his throat. "Then may I be freed, Your Excellency?" His voice was unsteady, his complexion blanched.

The shogun nodded, but Sano said quickly, "No—you must imprison him and announce to the public that he's been sentenced to death. The kidnappers will hear the news and think you intend to give in to them. The longer they think so, the longer we have to rescue Lady Keisho-in."

Furthermore, Sano couldn't let Hoshina go free because he might panic and run. Hoshina was also insurance of Reiko's survival, and Sano wanted him under close watch.

"Very well," said the shogun, then addressed the guards: "Place Hoshina-*san* under, ahh, house arrest."

As the guards led Hoshina from the chamber, he cast an ireful glance at Sano: He obviously thought Sano should have done better by him. He displayed no gratitude toward Sano for saving his life, nor relief that the shogun had spared it.

The shogun turned to Sano and Yanagisawa. "I shall, ahh, announce that Hoshina-*san* will be executed in, ahh, seven days." The crisis had also spurred him to rare, decisive authority. "That is how long you, ahh, have to rescue my mother."

"Yes, Your Excellency," Sano and Yanagisawa chorused.

Although their moment of gravest peril had passed, Sano foresaw the dangers of the plan he'd foisted upon his lord. His skin was clammy, his hands and feet turned to lumps of ice; nausea lurched his stomach.

"If you don't succeed by then, Hoshina-*san* dies." Menace darkened the shogun's gaze, infused his voice. "And if you've, ahh, advised me wrong, and my mother dies, I'll, ahh, execute you both."

"Yes, Your Excellency," Yanagisawa said in a subdued tone.

Sano could barely nod, for if he tried to speak anymore, he would vomit up the dread born of knowing that if he'd advised the shogun wrong, he'd not only doomed himself but sealed Reiko's destruction.

14

Sunshine fell across Reiko's face and penetrated her closed eyelids. Jarred suddenly awake, she found herself sitting with the broken rafter on her lap, slumped against the wall of the prison. Rays of morning light pierced the window shutters and ceiling and meshed in the dusty air. Reiko bolted up. She'd meant to wait alert for the kidnappers, but sometime during the night she'd dozed off. Now she hastened to Midori, Keisho-in, and Lady Yanagisawa, who lay asleep and motionless.

"Wake up," she said urgently, shaking them. As they groaned and stirred to life, Reiko said, "The kidnappers might arrive any moment. We must prepare."

The loud, abrasive opening of the door reverberated up through the floor. They all jumped.

"They're coming!" Midori cried.

Reiko pointed Midori and Keisho-in toward a back corner. "Sit over there. Hurry!" They obeyed. Reiko seated Lady Yanagisawa against the rear wall, opposite the door. The woman's face was still vacant with drowsiness, her movements slow. "Do you remember what to do?" Reiko anxiously asked.

A hesitant nod from Lady Yanagisawa inspired little confidence in Reiko. She hurried to stand in her own place beside the door. She gripped the rafter in both hands, raising it like a club. As they all waited in suspense, footsteps thumped up the first flight of stairs. Reiko thought she heard only two men this time, and she was glad. The fewer of them, the better her chances.

The footsteps mounted higher. Outside, pigeons cooed and fluttered wildly on the roof; the lapping waves registered each moment. Suddenly Lady Yanagisawa said, "Reiko-*san*?"

"What?" Reiko said, disturbed that the woman should speak at a critical moment.

"Yesterday, when you said you think my husband loves me . . . Did you really mean it?" Lady Yanagisawa eyed Reiko as intently as though the answer was all that mattered.

Reiko was surprised that Lady Yanagisawa had heard what Reiko had told her while she'd seemed dead to the world. Though she regretted the lie, Reiko didn't want to upset Lady Yanagisawa by admitting the truth. "Yes, I did mean it," she said, and trained her gaze on the door.

Outside, the footsteps paused. Reiko's heart raced; her breaths came fast as her hands tightened on her weapon. Keisho-in and Midori watched the door with dread. Lady Yanagisawa sat in apparent tranquility. The door opened. In stepped the cruel samurai who'd come yesterday. Suddenly Lady Yanagisawa flung back her head and let out a bloodcurdling scream. She tore open her kimono, baring her breasts. She clawed at them, and her fingernails raked raw scratches across her skin.

The samurai exclaimed at the sight of this woman who'd evidently gone insane. Reiko, Midori, and Keisho-in gaped, amazed, at Lady Yanagisawa as she kept screaming and her body twitched in violent spasms. She'd managed a better diversion than Reiko had expected. The samurai didn't notice Reiko because Lady Yanagisawa had all his attention. Reiko swung the rafter with all her might at the samurai. The wooden beam struck his temple—and snapped in two. The long, broken half thudded to the floor. The samurai grunted in surprise. He pivoted toward Reiko. His eyes aflame with pain and rage, he drew his sword.

Horror filled Reiko as she looked from him to the useless stub she held. Keisho-in and Midori shrieked. Lady Yanagisawa dropped to all fours, half naked, bleeding, and panting. Suddenly the samurai's eyes rolled upward. He toppled unconscious to the floor.

The peasant youth who'd brought the food yesterday rushed into the room, shouting, "What happened?" He carried a pail, which he set on the floor as he bent over his comrade.

Reiko tossed aside the stub, lunged, and shoved the youth. With a cry of surprise, he stumbled headlong across the room. He crashed against the wall. As he regained his balance and turned, Reiko lifted his pail that contained what looked to be soup. She hurled the pail at him.

It struck him in the stomach. Broth, seaweed, and tofu splattered the room. The youth gawked at the women. Across his childish, naive face flashed his dismay that the prisoners had rebelled and there was no one but him to restore order. Then awareness of his duty braced him. He let out a yell and charged at Reiko, hands extended to snatch.

She picked up the long end of the rafter and swatted his forehead. He fell, with a thud that shook the room, and lay unmoving.

In the sudden quiet, the women stared at their vanquished foes, then at each other. Wordlessly they shared their disbelief at the success of Reiko's plan. That the whole battle had lasted just an instant amazed Reiko.

She bent, light-headed, from delayed excitation. Her heart banged wildly in her chest, but she couldn't spare any time to recuperate. "Help me tie the men up," she told Lady Yanagisawa.

Quickly they rolled over the samurai, removed his sash, and used the long cotton cloth to truss his ankles and wrists behind him; then they did the same to the peasant youth.

"Why not just kill them?" Lady Keisho-in said. "The way they've treated us, they deserve to die."

"We don't want their comrades to take revenge on you."

Reiko pulled off the men's sandals and jammed their socks in their mouths so that when they woke, they couldn't call to their comrades. She snatched up the samurai's fallen sword and thrust it into Lady Yanagisawa's hands. "Use this to defend yourself and Midori and Lady Keisho-in if necessary."

Lady Yanagisawa held the weapon as though afraid of cutting herself. ". . . But I don't know how."

There was no time for Reiko to teach her sword fighting. "Do the best you can," Reiko said. She yanked the samurai's dagger from the scabbard at his waist, then hurried to the door. "I must go now."

"Good luck," Midori said. "And please be careful!"

"Bring back the army," Keisho-in commanded.

Lady Yanagisawa sat in her disheveled garments, the sword wavering in her grip, her expression forlorn.

Hating to leave her friends so helpless, Reiko slipped out the door. She found herself in an empty room whose barred windows gave a view of leafy branches. Walls of thick beams embedded in plaster, blackened by fire, enclosed this room and divided it from the prison. In its center, a wooden staircase slanted upward to a square hole in the ceiling. Daylight poured through the hole. The foot of the staircase ended at another opening in the floor. Clutching her stolen dagger, Reiko hastened to peer down the hole and saw more stairs zigzagging through the building's lower levels. She paused, listening. She heard only the sounds of birds, water, and wind. Then she plunged down the stairs.

Loose, uneven slats wobbled under her sandals. She leapt over spaces where risers were missing. The smells of old smoke and rotted wood intensified. She passed through a room similar to that above. As she clambered down the next flight of stairs, the need for caution vied with her urge to hurry. She slowed her pace near the end of the staircase and hesitantly entered the bottom level.

This contained a room that must have once been an armory; hooks and racks for hanging weapons protruded from the walls. On the stone floor lay a rusted cannon. Double doors, made of heavy timbers and iron plates, beckoned Reiko. One door stood opened outward, framing a rectangle of daylight. Reiko ran to the door and peeked outside. A narrow landing preceded a short flight of stone steps that led to paved, empty ground. Beyond this, a forest of pines, cypress, and maple obscured the distance. To her right and left rose more trees that grew close beside the building. Reiko savored the prospect of freedom. She hurried down the steps into cool, humid fresh air and across the cracked paving stones. A gap in the forest marked the path along which the kidnappers must have brought her and the other women. There Reiko paused, looked backward to see if anyone was coming, and got her first glimpse of her prison.

It was a tall, square tower. Many of the flat rocks that banked its sloped foundation had dropped away, exposing the clay understructure. The tower's walls were plaster, once white but now discolored black and gray by fire and crumbling off the wood framework. Upturned eaves shaded the three lower stories and their barred windows. On the fourth, highest story, a crumbling segment of wall and the remains of a tile roof enclosed one corner. The room stood open to the sky, where dark storm clouds drifted over the sun. Fallen wreckage surrounded the tower. Reiko realized that her prison was the keep of a castle, probably ruined in the civil wars during the last century. But she had no idea where in the world the castle was located.

She crept down the path, over weeds flattened by footsteps. A breeze enlivened the forest; sun-dappled shadows whispered. Unaccustomed to the wild, Reiko flinched at noises. Was that an animal's cry, or a human voice? A bird pecking a hollow tree, or someone drumming a signal? Reiko tiptoed, holding her dagger ready to stab, should anyone leap out of the forest at her. She regretted that her kimono, with its pattern of lavender irises on aqua silk, rendered her conspicuous.

She'd traversed some thirty paces into the forest when the path divided. Looking down the right-hand branch, be-

yond a cypress grove, Reiko saw the peaks and gables of
tile roofs that belonged to the castle's other buildings. There
the kidnappers must have their headquarters. Reiko hurried
down the left path. It circled back around the keep, whose
ruined top she could see above the trees. Then the path and
forest ended.

Before her, a narrow strip of sloping ground, covered
with tall grass, separated the forest from the water she'd
heard while imprisoned. The water, rimmed with reeds,
sparkling blue and indigo beneath the scudding clouds, appeared to be a lake that stretched some two hundred paces
to the opposite shore, where woods rose into hills. The
wind rippled little waves across the lake's surface. Looking
right, Reiko saw that the shoreline at her feet gave way to
marsh as it curved into the distance. To her near left, the
ground had eroded, and the keep jutted into the lake; waves
smacked the stone base. Reiko was alarmed. She couldn't
cross the lake to safety because she didn't know how to
swim—females of her class weren't taught during child-
hood, as were daughters of fishermen. Nor could she follow
the lakeshore in the hope of finding a village, because she
couldn't get around the keep or through the marsh. She'd
chosen the wrong direction and wasted precious time.

Reiko darted back into the forest, heading west and in-
land, climbing over fallen logs, wading through underbrush,
and ducking under low branches, until she stumbled upon a
path. This led her dangerously near the castle, within twenty
paces of a burned building that had collapsed. Reiko saw
smoke rising above the roofs of adjacent, intact structures.
She smelled fish roasting over a charcoal fire. Her stomach
growled with hunger, for she'd eaten nothing since the kidnappers had brought the food yesterday. She raced on, afraid
of encountering the men, past crumbled walls and more
trees, seeking a road to any place she could find friendly people. Soon she burst free of the woods—and foundered on another grassy slope that inclined toward more water.

She stared in disbelief at the sparkling lake, marshy shallows, and the forested land beyond. Had she lost her orientation and returned to the same place she'd just fled? But when she turned, she saw the keep behind her; and on the far horizon across the water were mountains she hadn't seen before. Reiko's heart plummeted as an awful thought occurred to her. She ran along the lakeside, first in one direction, then the other. The way the shoreline curved around the forest and back toward the keep, and the ever-present vista of the lake, confirmed her worst suspicions.

The castle was on an island.

She was trapped.

Gasps of anguish heaved Reiko's chest as she gazed across the lake. The opposite shore, so tantalizingly close, mocked her disappointed hope. Clouds darkened the morning; raindrops dimpled the water. Reiko thought of Midori, Lady Yanagisawa, and Keisho-in, waiting for her to bring help, trusting her to save them. She thought of the risk they'd taken, only for her to fail. In her despair, Reiko wanted to wave her hands and shout to anyone who might heed a plea for rescue.

Suddenly she heard men's voices, coming around the curve of the island. Fright launched her running into the forest. Crouching behind a tree, she peered out at the lakeshore. Three samurai, armed with swords, bows, and quivers of arrows, strode into view. Three more samurai came from the opposite direction. The two groups met and paused. With a thudding heart Reiko listened to their conversation.

"Any sign of her?"

"Not yet."

They knew she'd escaped from the keep, Reiko realized with dismay. They'd found their comrades bound and gagged, and now they were looking for her.

"She can't have gone far."

"She must be hiding in the forest."

The six men turned their gazes in Reiko's direction. She held herself rigid, her breath caught, for fear that the slightest movement would reveal her. The men tramped into the forest, so near Reiko that she could have touched them as they passed her. Had they punished her friends? Reiko was sure they blamed her for the escape attempt and intended revenge on her. But despite her fear, a thought raised her spirits.

There *was* a way off the island. The kidnappers must have transported themselves, the women, and provisions for everyone across the lake to the castle by boat. Reiko might yet escape—if she could find the boat before the kidnappers caught her.

She hastened through the forest, away from the search party, toward the island's north shore, which she hadn't yet seen. Perhaps the boat was moored there. She didn't allow herself to worry that she didn't know how to sail or row a boat. Trusting in luck, Reiko fought past thorny bushes, then froze. Some fifteen paces distant, a lane crossed her path. Two rough peasant men carrying wooden clubs paced up and down the lane. Farther ahead, the forest thinned, buildings fronted the lake, and more figures moved. The kidnappers had marshaled their entire force to patrol the island and find the fugitive.

Reiko veered south, hoping to circumvent the castle and find a boat on the other side. Rain sprinkled the foliage, while the sun's glinting rays penetrated the clouds. As Reiko wove between trees, she heard footsteps crunching the underbrush.

"What was that?" a man's voice said.

"What?" another man asked.

"A flash of light."

The sun must have reflected off the blade of her dagger, Reiko thought with distress. She crouched in the brush, but the first man shouted, "I see her! She's over here!"

Aghast, Reiko heard other voices calling replies and spreading the news. She ran, hindered by tree stumps and saplings. Glancing wildly around, she saw men crashing through the forest, converging on her, though she kept running. Her heart pounded; frantic breaths pumped her lungs. Now the forest gave way to a courtyard paved with cracked

flagstones and surrounded on three sides by attached buildings that blocked her flight. The kidnappers had herded her
straight to the castle. As Reiko skidded to a stop, she
gleaned a vague impression of dingy half-timbered structures that rose two stories high, with balconies, shaded ve-
randas, and latticed windows. She heard horses snorting
and smelled their odor: The kidnappers had swum them
across the lake and stabled them nearby. Cornered and panting, she turned to face her pursuers.

They stood, perhaps thirty strong, ranged in a semicircle
against her. Samurai pointed their swords or held their bows
drawn, arrows ready to fly; peasant toughs brandished their
clubs. Grimy faces snarled. Reiko gulped panic and raised
her blade, determined to fight rather than submit.

"Put it down, or we'll shoot you," barked a samurai.

Reiko recognized his face, saw the bloody bruise on the
side of his head: He was the leader she'd knocked unconscious. While she hesitated, a bow twanged. The arrow
grazed her hand that held the dagger. She shrieked, and her
fingers involuntarily jerked open. The dagger fell to the
ground. The men advanced on Reiko. Terrified beyond
speech, she backed away until stopped against a veranda.

"Not so brave now, are you?" the wounded leader
mocked. Reiko saw vindictive humor in his eyes. "I bet
you ran away because you wanted a little fun. Well, we're
going to have some now."

He grabbed her arm. Reiko cried out and pulled away.
Chuckling, he let her go. Another samurai caught her. Then
the men were shoving her from one to another, laughing
raucously. Hands pawed her body, loosed her hair from its
pinned-up knot, and yanked its streaming tresses. Reiko
struck and kicked the men, but they only laughed harder.
Someone tore off her sash. As she tried to hold her robes
closed, the men made lewd noises. They pushed her back
and forth, spun her, and clutched her. Sky, forest, buildings,
and savage faces swirled around Reiko as she helplessly
stumbled. Fear and vertigo nauseated her. The men ripped

off her kimono. Naked beneath her thin white under-robe, Reiko cowered.

"Leave me alone!" she screamed.

"We're not finished," the wounded samurai said, then told the other men, "Hold her down."

The men seized her, and though Reiko fought until she was breathless, they forced her to lie on the ground. They pinned her arms over her head; they spread and held her legs. Above her towered their leader, huge and menacing.

"Now you'll pay for what you did to me," he said. He lowered himself on his hands and knees, straddling her. His comrades cheered and hooted, egging him on.

"No!" Tossing her head, Reiko strained against her tormentors. "Let me go! Help, somebody, please!"

Hysteria dissolved her speech into inarticulate screams. The leader's ugly, grinning face blotted out the sky. Then a voice rang out above the commotion: "Stop!"

The noise ceased. In the abrupt hush, wind swept the trees; thunder rumbled closer. The samurai atop Reiko turned his head sideways, and confusion replaced the lust on his face. Reiko lay paralyzed, uncertain what to expect.

"Get off her," ordered the voice. It was deep, gruff, and harsh with anger. "The rest of you, move away."

Relief and gratitude flooded Reiko as the samurai climbed off her. The circle of other men broke and they scattered. Reiko cautiously raised herself on one elbow. She watched her tormentors stand at attention, facing the central building. Her gaze followed theirs. On the veranda stood a man. The shade under the eaves obscured him, and all she could discern was that he had the shaved crown and two swords of a samurai. Fresh terror eclipsed her relief.

This man had spared her, but his authoritative manner, and the haste with which the other men had obeyed him, told Reiko that he was their superior. It must be he who'd ordered the massacre and the kidnapping.

Now he descended the steps of the veranda and came across the courtyard toward her. He walked with an odd gait that combined hesitance with samurai swagger. His head looked too big for his body, which was thickset and clothed in black. Across the skirt of his kimono swirled a brocade dragon. Its golden claws and emerald-scaled body undulated as the man moved; its snarling mouth spewed vermilion flames. Reiko scrambled to her feet, clutching her under-robe around herself. Vulnerable yet determined to meet the enemy with courage, she pushed back the hair that had fallen over her face and gazed up at the samurai.

He halted, stood frozen, and stared down at Reiko. She saw that he was younger than his voice had suggested—in his late twenties. Beneath a rugged forehead and slanted dark brows, his eyes smoldered in their deep sockets. His nose was broad and strong, the nostrils flared like those of the dragon on his kimono. But his lips were soft, moist, and pursed; his chin receded. Reiko saw in his gaze the admiration that her beauty often provoked from men. Yet the samurai also beheld her with profound shock, as though he recognized her but disbelieved his eyes. Reiko didn't recognize him: He was a stranger to her.

"Are you hurt?" he said, his gaze roaming over her body before returning to her face.

Unsettled by his intense scrutiny, Reiko looked away from the samurai. "No," she whispered.

He stepped closer and slowly extended a hand, as if to touch her hair. Reiko saw, on the periphery of her vision, the longing in his expression; she heard him breathe through his wet mouth. She flinched. The samurai withdrew his hand, stepping back.

"They won't hurt you," he said in a tone clearly meant to convey an order to his men as well as reassure her.

But Reiko's terror burgeoned. Even if they didn't hurt her, would he? His strangeness sent a chill creeping through her.

The samurai bent and picked up her fallen kimono. He circled around her as she stood wide-eyed and quaking, wondering what he was doing but afraid to look. Then he gently dropped the kimono over her shoulders and pressed the sash into her hand. Reiko felt the warmth of his body while he stood close behind her and she tied the sash around her waist. She shuddered, retching on sudden nausea, because his gentleness revolted her more than did his men's outright brutality.

"Take her back to the keep," he ordered them.

Two samurai moved toward her. One was the man she'd wounded. Despite his master's orders, he gripped her arm in a painful clasp that promised retribution. As the pair led her to a path that cut through the forest, Reiko glanced back at their leader. He stood outside his dingy castle watching her, arms folded, his expression brooding and sinister. The wind ruffled his robes, stirring the dragon alive.

Who was he? What were his reasons for the massacre and kidnapping? An aura of evil that surrounded him filled Reiko with dread. And what fate did he intend for her?

15

Hirata and Detectives Marume and Fukida rode up the steep stretch of highway toward Hakone, the eleventh post station on the Tōkaidō. The lofty altitude chilled the early morning. The sun diffused weak, silvery light through a veil of clouds, while mist saturated the air, blurred the forested hills, and reduced the distant mountains to peaked shadows against the sky. Ahead, a gate protected by Tokugawa soldiers blocked the road. Beyond the portals Hirata saw the rustic buildings of Hakone village.

"Let's hope we have better luck today than last night," Hirata called to his companions.

They'd spent last night at the tenth post station of Odawara. They'd loitered in the shops, bought drinks in each teahouse, and visited every inn, striking up acquaintances with locals and steering the conversation to the kidnapping. But although many people recalled seeing Lady Keisho-in's party before the abduction, no one provided any clues to what had happened to the women. Nor had Hirata and the detectives found any trace of the kidnappers. Hirata had persuaded three drunken town officials to show him the checkpoint travel records. The list showed no group of men numerous enough to massacre Keisho-in's entourage. Hirata surmised that the kidnappers had traveled separately to avoid attracting notice, given different destinations when the inspectors asked where they were going, and joined up at the ambush site. He'd searched the list for Lord Niu's retainers, to no avail. If Lord Niu had sent troops to stage the ambush, they could have traveled under aliases; but for the first time, Hirata experienced doubts that his father-in-law was behind the crime. He wished he knew what Sano's investigation had uncovered, far away in Edo.

Now his frustration and anxiety burgeoned, while fatigue strained his mind. The previous day spent journeying from Edo and hiking the forest, and the long night with little sleep, had taken its toll on him and the other men. His nose was congested, his head ached, and his throat was sore from his cold. Fukida's thin, serious face was haggard, and the brawny Marume had lost his cheer by the time they all reached the Hakone post house, a thatch-roofed building off the roadside.

"Look at that line!" Marume exclaimed.

Some fifty travelers waited, amid their baggage, in a queue at the post house. Inside sat inspectors who registered the travelers, checked their documents, searched them and their possessions for hidden weapons and other contraband, then either granted or denied them passage. Hakone was a *bakufu* trap for people up to no good, and it was famous for its rigorous inspections, which promised a long delay before Hirata and his men could get inside the village and conduct inquiries. They couldn't cut in line, which would get them in trouble and necessitate revealing their identities. Hirata looked toward the nearby camp inhabited by porters and palanquin-bearers for hire.

"We'll try the camp first," he said.

He and the detectives left their horses at a water trough and walked into the camp. Cypress trees sheltered flimsy shacks and tents. A reek of urine and excrement from privy sheds competed with the odors from a nearby stable. Men with coarse, weathered faces squatted around a fire, passing a flask of sake while cooking food in iron pots. Their sinewy muscles bulged through their tattered kimonos. They turned suspicious gazes upon Hirata and the detectives.

"We're looking for four women, probably traveling with

a group of men," Hirata said, then described Midori, Reiko, Lady Keisho-in, and Lady Yanagisawa. "Have you seen anyone who fits those descriptions?"

"It depends on who's asking," said the biggest man. His shrewd, glinting eyes sized up Hirata. His skin was blue with tattoos of winged demons; his crooked nose and scarred face bespoke a lifetime of brawling. Hirata marked him as the gang leader of the camp.

"Someone who's willing to pay for the right kind of information," Hirata said.

Detective Marume jingled coins in the pouch at his waist. The leader's expression turned crafty. "Ah," he said, nodding, "Tokugawa spies. Would you be looking for the shogun's mother and her ladies who were kidnapped off the Tōkaidō?"

"No," Hirata said, perturbed that the man had seen through the disguises and subterfuge that had fooled everyone else.

The leader looked unconvinced. "If you say so." He bowed with mock courtesy to Hirata. "My name is Goro, and I'm at your service." Then he addressed his comrades: "Here's your chance to earn some extra silver. Did you see those ladies?"

Regretful denials and head-shaking ensued.

"What about one or two women traveling in different groups?" Hirata said. Perhaps the kidnappers had split up their party to avoid detection. But this question elicited more negative answers.

"Did you see anything out of the ordinary?" Hirata asked. He saw Goro smirk, and he realized the man had been deliberately withholding information, toying with him. "Tell me!" he ordered, his temper flaring.

Goro held out his hand, palm up, and waggled his fingers. Marume dropped coins one by one into Goro's hand until Hirata said, "That's enough. Now talk."

The man grinned and tucked the coins in his own waist pouch. "The day before yesterday, a group of samurai hired me and some other porters to carry four big wooden chests." Goro's arms gestured, indicating dimensions large enough to contain a human body.

Excitement leapt in Hirata. "What was in the chests?"

"I don't know," Goro said. "The samurai didn't say, and I didn't ask. But the chests had holes cut in the lids."

So that people locked inside could breathe, Hirata thought.

"The samurai were in a big hurry," Goro went on. "And they paid double the usual rate."

As criminals would for carrying contraband such as stolen women. "To go where?" Hirata said.

"Down Izu way." The Izu Peninsula, located west of Hakone, jutted off Japan's southern coast into the sea. "The samurai led us along the main highway that goes through Izu. We had to run to keep up with them. *Aii*, those chests were heavy. It's a good thing there were four of us carrying each one. Otherwise, we'd never have lasted the whole trip."

Now Hirata understood how the kidnappers had transported their victims, in spite of the law that restricted wheeled traffic on the Tōkaidō, hindered troop movements, prevented rebellions, and necessitated cargo to be carried by hand. The kidnappers must have bound, gagged, and probably drugged the women, then packed them in their own luggage. The officials who'd examined the scene afterward wouldn't have noticed chests missing because the checkpoints kept no record of luggage inspected there. Hirata deduced that the kidnappers had carried the chests down the highway from the abduction site. They'd passed as ordinary travelers because the crime hadn't yet been discovered. At Hakone they'd hired the porters because they couldn't manage the heavy loads themselves and move as quickly as they needed.

"It was the middle of the afternoon when we left here, and past sunset when we stopped at a crossroad," continued Goro. "It has a Jizo shrine. The samurai paid us off. We left them there with the chests and came back to Hakone."

Triumph elated Hirata because he now knew which way

the kidnappers had taken Midori. "But how did those samurai get the chests past inspection?" he said.

"The samurai wore Tokugawa crests and had Tokugawa travel passes," Goro said. "They were waved right through the checkpoint."

Hirata, Marume, and Fukida shared disturbed glances. Had *bakufu* officials been involved in the abduction? But Hirata speculated that the kidnappers had stolen clothes and documents from soldiers they'd killed during the massacre.

"Who were those samurai?" Hirata asked Goro.

"They didn't tell us," Goro said.

"How many were there?"

"Twelve of them."

"What did they look like?"

"I didn't get a good look at their faces because they wore helmets with visors and mouth guards."

The kidnappers had made sure that their hired help couldn't identify them, Hirata noted. When pressed for details about the men, Goro recalled little else, and he hadn't heard anything they'd said to one another. The porters who'd gone with him were away on other jobs and unavailable for questioning.

"Did you report what you've just told me to the authorities?" Hirata asked.

Goro shook his head. "When those samurai hired me, I didn't know the shogun's mother had been taken. And afterward, when I heard about the missing ladies . . ." A sly grin uplifted Goro's scarred features. He jingled the coins in his pouch. "I decided to wait for a chance to make a little profit."

The porter's greedy opportunism enraged Hirata, but he had neither time nor energy to waste on punishing Goro, or on speculating what might have happened if Goro had reported his news instead of hoarding it. He and Marume and Fukida left the camp, retrieved their horses, and stood in the inspection line at the post house.

"As soon as we get past this checkpoint," Hirata said, "we'll be on our way to Izu."

• • •

Police Commissioner Hoshina had been imprisoned in a square guard tower on the wall that separated the palace grounds from the forest preserve. The tower had white plaster walls, black trim, a barred window overlooking each direction, and a four-gabled tile roof. Sentries stood on the walkway atop the wall, guarding doors on either side of the tower. Sano approached its third door, set in the base of the wall and also guarded. Beyond the tower, the oaks, conifers, and maples of the forest preserve loomed against an overcast sky. Locusts whined in the hot, humid air as Sano climbed a flight of stairs to the makeshift prison.

Although samurai awaiting execution were usually kept under house arrest in their own homes, Hoshina lived at Chamberlain Yanagisawa's estate, where Yanagisawa had refused to have him. Condemned men were usually barred from Edo Castle, but the shogun valued Hoshina as insurance of Lady Keisho-in's survival and wanted him close at hand. Therefore, the palace officials had hastily improvised a jail for Hoshina.

More guards unbarred the door at the top of the stairs and admitted Sano to the tower room. Inside, Hoshina crouched, his back against the wall, arms resting limp on his knees. As Sano entered, Hoshina looked up, eager and expectant.

"Greetings," Sano said quietly.

Hoshina's face fell. "Oh. It's you," he said.

Obviously, he'd hoped to see Chamberlain Yanagisawa. Sano pitied Hoshina's disappointment and hated to tell him Yanagisawa wasn't coming.

After the meeting at which the shogun had almost condemned Sano and Yanagisawa to execution along with Hoshina, the two of them had walked out of the palace together.

"Hoshina-*san* must be interrogated," Sano had told Yanagisawa as they strode down the gravel path through the grounds.

"You do it," Yanagisawa said, clearly intending to distance himself from Hoshina. His cool expression showed no sign that he'd just narrowly escaped death, nor guilt over how he'd treated his lover. "Report to me afterward." Then he and his guards left Sano and walked away.

First, Sano returned home and summoned his detectives to the courtyard. "I want to know who delivered the ransom letter," he told them. "Interview the soldiers assigned to guard the castle perimeter last night. Ask them whether they saw who posted the letter on the wall, or anyone loitering outside the castle and acting suspicious. If they did, get a description of the person. If not, search the neighborhoods around the castle for witnesses. And if you find the person, arrest him and notify me at once. He may be our best lead to the kidnappers."

Now Sano beheld the other possible lead. Hoshina seemed shrunken by despondency. His head drooped; anguish hollowed his eyes. Sano experienced a pang of concern for him. Many a samurai would consider suicide as a way to escape such ignominious circumstances.

"Is there anything you need?" Sano said. Pretending an interest in Hoshina's physical comfort, he scrutinized the cell.

The palace officials who'd furnished the prison had paid respect to Hoshina's rank. *Tatami* cushioned the floor, and a rolled-up futon occupied a corner. Incense smoked on the window ledges, repelling mosquitoes and masking the foul odor of the stagnant moat below the tower on the forest side. A black-and-gilt lacquer tray contained soup, rice, prawns, vegetables, and tea on matching dishware. Against the stone wall stood a lidded lacquer chamber pot. But Sano saw, to his relief, nothing that Hoshina might use against himself.

"Don't worry—they took away my swords," Hoshina said in a sardonic voice. "They won't even give me chopsticks to eat with." He flapped a hand at the untouched meal. "And the guards watch me every moment. No doubt someone has advised the shogun not to let me commit *sep-*

puku and deprive the kidnappers of the execution they want in exchange for his mother."

The absent Chamberlain Yanagisawa formed a third, almost tangible presence in the room. Sano knew that Yanagisawa had specified the terms of Hoshina's imprisonment, and obviously Hoshina had guessed.

"But I don't intend to die by my own hand, or anyone else's, just yet." Hoshina straightened his posture as some of his old fight rekindled.

"I'm glad to hear that," Sano said.

Hoshina snorted. "I'll bet you are."

His acrid tone implied that Sano only cared about him for selfish reasons, and Sano acknowledged this as the truth. Hoshina was the new key to the mystery of who had kidnapped the women, and he was important to Reiko's survival.

"By the way, I suppose I owe you thanks for persuading the shogun to delay my death," Hoshina said grudgingly. "You'll forgive me if I don't feel much like celebrating right now."

Sano nodded, allowing Hoshina to vent his bitterness. Empathy diminished Sano's hatred for his foe. A different turn of fate could have put him in Hoshina's position.

"What brings you here, when everyone else is avoiding me like a fatal disease?" Hoshina said.

How quickly men in the *bakufu* ostracized colleagues in trouble, Sano thought. "I agreed to save your life," he said. "I'm here to finish what I started."

Hoshina gave him a look that mixed contempt with gratitude. "I might almost think you were the true epitome of honor, if I didn't know you have an ulterior motive."

"We all have our own interests," Sano said, "but mine coincide with yours. I want to catch the kidnappers and rescue the hostages. You want me to do it before the shogun's seven days are up and he executes you."

Hoshina conceded with a wry twist of his lips.

"I need your help," Sano said. "Will you answer some questions?"

"I'm your captive slave," Hoshina said.

Sano crouched beside Hoshina. "Who do you think wrote this?" Reaching inside his surcoat, Sano removed the ransom letter.

"I have no idea." Hoshina exhaled in hopelessness.

"Does the poem mean anything to you?" Sano asked.

He spread the letter on the floor. As they pored over the lines, Hoshina said, "Dragons symbolize power, fertility, good fortune. Every child learns the story of the Dragon King who rules the sea. But this poem makes no sense. Can it mean that the Dragon King is the kidnapper and he's holding the women in his underwater palace?" Hoshina gave a humorless laugh. "It sounds like the rambling of a madman."

Sano nodded, because who except a madman would kidnap the shogun's mother to force the execution of the chief police commissioner? He could have added that dragons brought rain to grow crops and kept the forces of nature in balance. But although he thought the poem must contain clues, he and Hoshina needed to make progress, not discuss cosmology. "Do you recognize the writing?" Sano asked.

"No," said Hoshina, "but then, I never pay much attention to calligraphy."

Another disappointment. Sano had hoped Hoshina would provide more information.

"If you wish I had all the answers, just think how much I wish I did," Hoshina said with a grimace.

"Let's move on to the question of what murder the letter refers to," said Sano.

"I'm not a murderer," Hoshina declared. Anger animated his voice, colored his pallid complexion. "That's what's so outrageous about this whole situation: Somebody I don't know wants me punished for a crime I didn't commit."

Sano eyed him with skepticism. "You've never killed?"

"Well, of course I have." Hoshina looked as though Sano had said something absurd. "I'm a police official. I've killed in the line of duty. That's not murder, because it's sanctioned by the law."

"Many might think otherwise," said Sano, "especially someone who blames you for a death and bears a grudge. The kidnapper appears to fit that category. Tell me the names of everyone you've killed, and their family members and associates. The details on when, where, and how you killed them might also help."

Hoshina gave a dismal chuckle. "I hope you've got plenty of time, because this could take a while."

"I've got time." Sano asked the guards to bring paper and writing supplies. Then, as Hoshina talked, Sano wrote a list. The final count spanned sixteen years and numbered thirty-eight men slain by Hoshina's sword while he was trying to make arrests or maintain order. Some of their names he couldn't recall. Information on their families and associates was sparse.

"That's the best I can do," Hoshina said.

Reviewing the list, Sano said, "These men you killed were gangsters, petty thieves, brawlers, and rioters. They were peasants, artisans, small-time merchants, a few *rōnin*— none wealthy, all members of the lower classes."

"That's the type that keeps the police busy," Hoshina said. "The dregs of society."

Discouragement filled Sano. "It seems unlikely that they would have friends or relatives capable of the massacre and kidnapping."

"Besides, if people of their kind wanted revenge on me, they would attack me on the street, and they wouldn't wait years to do me in," Hoshina said. "They certainly wouldn't concoct such an elaborate, dangerous plot. They haven't the intelligence, let alone the nerve. Or the troops."

Another consideration caused Sano to doubt that the list would point him to the kidnapper. "All the men you killed were citizens of Miyako," he said. The ancient imperial capital was a fifteen-day journey from Edo.

"You know I lived in Miyako until three years ago," Hoshina said. "I did most of my police service there."

Sano knew he must determine whether any of the killed by Hoshina had connections to someone

could have heard about Lady Keisho-in's trip and organized
the kidnapping. But he anticipated a long, fruitless search.

He said, "You haven't killed anyone in Edo?"

"There's been no reason," Hoshina said. "I oversee the
police force now. I don't chase down criminals in the
streets anymore."

Sunlight pierced the clouds and slanted through the
tower windows. The room was stiflingly hot; its walls
oozed moisture. Sano rose and wiped sweat off his brow.
He thought of Reiko imprisoned somewhere, probably under conditions worse than these. He thought of the unknown kidnapper waiting for Hoshina's execution, ready to
slay Reiko, Lady Keisho-in, Midori, and Lady Yanagisawa.
Anxiety mounted in Sano because he and Hoshina hadn't
yet identified a single good suspect.

"Maybe the ransom letter doesn't refer to a killing you
committed with your own hands," Sano said. "Were there
any criminals you arrested who were later convicted and
executed?"

He and Hoshina compiled a list of names that was longer
than the first but posed the same problems. The dead men
had all been of low class, and all Miyako residents—because the chief police commissioner didn't personally arrest
criminals, and Hoshina hadn't sent anyone to the execution
ground since he'd come to Edo. None of his executed criminals had apparent connections to anyone wealthy or powerful enough to manage the kidnapping.

Sano controlled an urge to take out his frustration on
Hoshina. He stood leaning against the wall and contemplated the other man, who gazed up at him in abject misery.

"Can you think of any deaths you didn't cause, but
someone might still hold you responsible?" Sano asked.

Hoshina shook his head, then suddenly started as recollection hit him. "There was one man—a Miyako merchant named Naraya. About seven years ago I arrested his
daughter for theft. She died in jail, awaiting trial. Some
time later, I ran into Naraya in town. He said her death was
my fault and he would make me pay. I'd forgotten about

that. I probably wouldn't have remembered now, except that last year I heard Naraya had moved his business to Edo."

The merchant was a manufacturer and purveyor of soy sauce, Sano knew. He'd been unaware of a connection between Naraya and Hoshina, but had heard enough about Naraya to recognize that here at last was a candidate who fit his idea of the kidnapper.

"Naraya is one good suspect," Sano said. His mood lifted, and his success stimulated his own memory of an incident two years ago. "How about Kii Mataemon?"

"He attacked me with his sword during that argument in the palace," Hoshina said in a tone that spurned culpability. "The guards grabbed him before I had to fight him. It was his own fault that he died." Drawing a weapon in the palace was a crime punishable by death, and Mataemon— son of the *daimyo* Lord Kii—had been forced to commit ritual suicide. "But I suppose his clan might blame me."

Sano felt a spring of jubilation, for the Kii clan represented an even more promising lead than did the merchant. A stunned air came over Hoshina: He'd finally absorbed the fact that his enemies were responsible for the kidnapping and his troubles. During the whole conversation he'd stayed crouched in the same position, but now he sat flat on the floor, his legs extended. He gazed into the distance, like a man marooned on an island, watching a ship sail across the ocean to rescue him.

"I'll interrogate the Kii clan and the merchant Naraya," said Sano.

"Do it and rescue Lady Keisho-in before I go mad in here." Hoshina jumped to his feet and prowled the room, as if the hope of deliverance had unloosed a restless energy. He stalked to a window, grasped the bars, and stared outside. "I wish there were something I could do to save myself." A tortured cry burst from him: "I can't bear this idleness!"

Then his posture slumped, and Sano understood that affairs of the heart weighed as heavily upon Hoshina as did the threat of death. Sano felt compelled to offer solace, despite every bad deed Hoshina had done him.

"Chamberlain Yanagisawa didn't abandon you," Sano said.

Hoshina spat a gust of disbelief. "You don't see him breaking down the door to comfort or rescue me, do you? No—he's lost all concern for me."

"He told me to report to him after I talked to you," Sano said.

"He just wants to know what I told you that might help him find the shogun's mother." Contempt withered Hoshina's voice but didn't hide his grief. "He can't sully himself by associating with me, so he lets you do his dirty work. You'd better watch out that he doesn't steal the credit for everything you accomplish."

"He set us up for you to call in that favor and me to save your life," Sano said.

Hoshina turned, still holding the window bars. He regarded Sano as if he'd lost his mind, then gave a glum chuckle. "No. That's too devious even for the honorable chamberlain." Hoshina resumed gazing outside, his head and clenched hands black against the sunlight that streamed around him. "He cut me loose the moment he read the ransom letter."

Sano realized that in some ways he knew Yanagisawa better than Hoshina did. He also realized that trying to convince Hoshina that Yanagisawa hadn't forsaken him was a waste of time.

"I'll be going now," Sano said, then called the guards to unbar the door. "If Naraya or the Kii clan is involved in the kidnapping, I'll soon find out."

Before leaving the castle, Sano stopped at Chamberlain Yanagisawa's estate. The antechamber was crowded with officials who sat smoking and chatting while they waited to see the chamberlain. But a clerk hurried Sano past the other men and into the reception hall. There, Yanagisawa knelt on the dais. Secretaries held a scroll open on a writing desk before him. Three black-robed officials, seated below the dais, watched him ink his jade seal and stamp the document. When Yanagisawa saw Sano standing at the threshold, he dismissed the secretaries and officials. He gestured for Sano to kneel near him.

"Did you learn anything useful from the honorable police commissioner?" Yanagisawa said.

Sano noticed that Yanagisawa didn't ask how Hoshina was. The chamberlain's businesslike manner indicated that he cared only whether Hoshina had provided clues to the kidnapper's identity. Perhaps Yanagisawa didn't want to display personal concern for Hoshina when someone might overhear, but Sano wondered if Yanagisawa had indeed abandoned Hoshina. Certainly, the way he referred to Hoshina by title instead of name indicated that he considered their relationship a thing of the past. Sano thought he must have misjudged Yanagisawa.

"Here's a list of all the deaths associated with Hoshina." Sano handed the paper to the chamberlain. "We identified two primary suspects." He named Naraya and the Kii clan, then described the deaths that had involved them and Hoshina. As he spoke, Yanagisawa listened intently but without comment. "I'm on my way to see them. Chances are that Naraya or someone in the Kii clan is . . ." Sano recalled the mysterious poem. "The Dragon King."

A faint smile touched Yanagisawa's lips. "What an apt name for the kidnapper." He paused, chin in hand, mulling over the list. Then he appeared to reach a decision. "You interrogate the merchant," he said. "Leave the Kii clan to me. We'll meet tonight, at the hour of the boar, to compare results."

Sano wondered if Yanagisawa did, after all, want to save Hoshina and mend their broken affair; but of course, his primary aim was to catch the kidnapper. Yanagisawa wanted credit for rescuing Lady Keisho-in, as Hoshina had suggested; and Sano recalled instances where his longtime adversary had appropriated facts he'd discovered. Though

Sano cared less about who got credit than about saving the women, he worried that Yanagisawa might somehow jeopardize the investigation. Yet Sano had no control over Yanagisawa.

"As you wish," Sano said. He bowed, rose, and left the room, anxious to solve the mystery himself and rescue the hostages before Yanagisawa did something to endanger Reiko.

16

"You shouldn't have tried to escape," Lady Keisho-in said, fixing a malevolent gaze on Reiko. "You were stupid to put us all in danger for nothing."

Thunder boomed, and the tower shuddered. Lightning illuminated the prison in intermittent flashes, while rain cascaded down through the damaged ceiling. The women sat crowded together in the driest corner of the room. Reiko humbly bowed her head, deploring her own failure even more than Keisho-in did.

"But she couldn't have known we were trapped on an island," Midori said. When the guards had brought Reiko back to the prison, and she'd told the other women what had happened, Midori had wept with disappointment; but now she rose to Reiko's defense. "It's not her fault that our plan didn't work." Midori smiled wanly at Reiko. "I'm grateful to you for trying to save us."

"Thank you," Reiko said, appreciating Midori's loyalty.

"Don't make excuses for her," Keisho-in rebuked Midori. "If she hadn't misbehaved, those men might treat us better. They might at least feed us, or clean this room." The kidnappers had brought no food since the pail of soup that Reiko had thrown at the boy, and the women were all starving because they'd not eaten since yesterday's meal. The stink from waste buckets grew worse by the hour. "And what good are you, Midori-*san*? You just sit around like a quail ready to lay an egg. I don't know why I ever wanted you on my trip."

Chastened, Midori said, "I'm sorry."

Keisho-in turned her ire on Lady Yanagisawa: "And you're even more useless." Fury sparked in her bloodshot old eyes. "When those men came, why didn't you fight them the way you were supposed to?"

Lady Yanagisawa sat hunched in shame, her plain face bleak with misery. Reiko had just learned that the guards had come to the prison soon after she'd run away. They'd found their comrades tied up and unconscious, and herself missing. They'd taken the sword from Lady Yanagisawa, who'd meekly surrendered, and assailed the women with curses, threats, and demands to know where Reiko had gone.

". . . I was afraid," Lady Yanagisawa whispered, wringing her hands. "I'm sorry." She turned a beseeching gaze on Reiko. "Will you please forgive me?"

"There's nothing to forgive." Reiko patted her shoulder. "You did right to surrender. Fighting would have done more harm than good." Though dismayed by Lady Yanagisawa's cowardice, Reiko was glad the kidnappers hadn't hurt her friends.

"Next time I go on holiday, I won't take any of you," Keisho-in declared. "I'll take strong, brave men who can get me out of trouble instead of into it!"

Reiko, Midori, and Lady Yanagisawa sat silent, avoiding one another's gazes and forbearing to mention that none of them had wanted to accompany Keisho-in and would have stayed home if they could. None of them dared remind her that the kidnappers had slain her strong, brave bodyguards, or that there might not be a next time. Nor did they point out that she had eagerly approved Reiko's plan until it failed, and venting her frustration on them didn't improve their plight.

"As far as I'm concerned, you only made everything worse." Keisho-in crossed her plump arms and pouted at Reiko.

Disconsolation filled Reiko because she couldn't deny that Keisho-in spoke the truth. She heard muttered conversation from the guards now stationed outside the door. Sounds of footsteps and stirring below indicated that other men inhabited the tower's lower levels. Even if she somehow managed to get out of the room again, she could never sneak past them all. Reiko stretched out her legs and unhappily contemplated her naked feet. The guards had taken the shoes and socks from all the women. Even if they somehow located a boat and crossed the lake, how far could they get barefoot, before the kidnappers caught up with them?

Reiko mourned that her efforts had decreased their chances of gaining freedom. If she couldn't save them, could anyone?

The merchant Naraya operated his soy sauce factory in the Kanda district, north of Edo Castle. The factory inhabited a building that had a shop at the front and occupied a block across the road from a canal, where barges floated along water edged with houseboats. Bridges led between populous neighborhoods on both sides of the canal.

Sano, riding up the street with four detectives, smelled the factory before he saw it. The rich, salty odor of soy sauce pervaded the warm air. He and his men dismounted outside the factory and ducked under the blue entrance curtain that bore Naraya's name in white characters. Inside the store, ceramic jars filled shelves that lined the walls. Clerks waited on customers. Their chatter ceased as they saw the newcomers.

"I want to see Naraya," Sano told a clerk. "Where is he?"

"He's in the factory," the clerk said, glancing at a curtained doorway at the rear of the room. "Shall I fetch him for you, master?"

"No, thank you. I'll find him." Sano wanted to catch his suspect off guard. As he led his men through the doorway, he counseled himself against jumping to conclusions about Naraya. He'd already erred in blaming the Black Lotus for the kidnapping. He couldn't afford another mistake that would sidetrack the investigation. He must not ruin his chance for a fresh start.

They entered the cavernous factory. Smoke and steam diffused the sunshine from the windows and skylights. Aromas wafted from vats of soybeans boiling on charcoal hearths and wheat roasting in ovens. Sweating workers, clad in loincloths and headbands, poured steaming beans onto wooden pallets, ground the wheat in mortars, lugged tubs of malt and brine, and mixed the ingredients. Amid the activity bustled a middle-aged man dressed in a blue kimono.

"Gently, gently!" he admonished workers who were straining viscous, fermented brew through cloth bags. "Treat the product with respect, or it'll go bad."

His authoritative manner identified him as Naraya. He paused at a row of barrels, tasted their contents, then shook his head. "Not ready yet," he told the workers. "Let the spirit of the soy sauce develop longer."

Then Naraya caught sight of Sano and the detectives. Hastening over to them, he bowed and said, "Good day, masters. How may I serve you?"

Closer inspection showed Sano that Naraya was some fifty years old, with droopy cheeks and jowls. His skin, teeth, sparse gray hair, and the whites of his eyes had a brown tinge, as though he'd absorbed the soy sauce he manufactured. Brown stains discolored his fingernails and cheap cotton robes. Despite his status as one of Edo's wealthy, prominent merchants, Naraya looked like a small-time shopkeeper.

Sano introduced himself, then said, "I'm investigating the kidnapping of Lady Keisho-in, and I need your assistance."

"Oh. I see." Naraya spoke in a hushed tone that recognized the gravity of Sano's purpose, but he frowned as though mystified. "Of course I'll gladly do whatever I can.

May I first offer you and your men some tea at my house?"

"Let's just step outside." Sano didn't want to waste time on formalities. As he and his detectives followed Naraya out the back door, Sano observed that Naraya's confusion seemed genuine, as did his willingness to cooperate. Was Naraya therefore not the kidnapper? But if he was, he would have anticipated that the ransom letter would direct suspicion toward Police Commissioner Hoshina's enemies. He would have expected to be questioned, and prepared to act innocent.

They gathered in the alley between the factory and a warehouse. Trash containers, privy sheds, and night-soil bins fouled the air, but the alley was quiet and afforded Sano the privacy he wanted.

"This kidnapping is a terrible, terrible disaster," Naraya lamented. "Such evil forces plague this world of ours. Your wife was among the ladies taken, wasn't she?" he asked Sano. When Sano nodded, sympathy oozed from Naraya. "My sincere condolences."

"Thank you." Sano scrutinized the merchant. He wanted Naraya to be the Dragon King; he wanted to believe Naraya could deliver Reiko to him. He reminded himself that there were other suspects and he must not rush to judgment again.

"Tell me how I can help," Naraya said, flinging open his arms. "Whatever you want of me, name it, and it's yours."

Was he sincere, or putting on a good show? Naraya seemed too ordinary to be the Dragon King, who'd assumed monstrous proportions in Sano's mind. But a successful merchant, expert at bargaining with customers, was as good at theatrics as many a Kabuki performer.

Sano said, "Tell me about your relations with Police Commissioner Hoshina."

Naraya flinched at the sound of Hoshina's name. His smile vanished. "You seem to already know there's bad blood between us," he said, and his manner turned wary. "Old news travels far. I left Miyako and so did Hoshina-

san, but one can never leave the past behind."

"I understand that you blame Hoshina-*san* for the death of your daughter," Sano said.

The merchant hesitated. Sano sensed Naraya's wish to avoid discussing a painful subject, his fear of how anything he said might hurt him, and his need to air an old grievance.

Need prevailed. Naraya burst out, "It was his fault! My Emiko was my only child, and a sweet, innocent, harmless girl. Hoshina-*san* destroyed her for his own selfish purposes."

Flushed and agitated, Naraya leaned toward Sano, eager to justify his ire. "Emiko was fifteen years old. She liked nice clothes, but I couldn't afford to buy any because I wasn't as well off as I am now." Regret and guilt saddened Naraya's voice. "One day Emiko saw a pretty red kimono hanging in a shop. She went inside, grabbed it, and ran."

So this was the theft Hoshina had mentioned, thought Sano; not a serious crime, but a girl's foolish impulse.

"Emiko wasn't a thief," Naraya said, passionate in his conviction. "She would have soon realized she'd done wrong and returned the kimono. Unfortunately, Hoshina-*san* happened to come riding along the street. He saw Emiko clutching the kimono, running away. He chased her and caught her. He marched her back to the shop. The proprietor identified the stolen merchandise. Hoshina arrested Emiko and took her to jail."

Fury resonated in Naraya's voice. "When I heard what had happened, I went to police headquarters. That was when I first met Hoshina-*san.* I tried to explain that Emiko had just made a mistake. But Hoshina-*san* said she was a criminal and would be sent to work as a courtesan in the pleasure quarter."

Forced prostitution was the usual sentence for female thieves.

"I offered Hoshina-*san* a bribe to free my daughter," said Naraya, "but he refused, éven though the police usually will take bribes when the crime is minor." Naraya glared through tears of outrage. "Later, I learned that Hoshina-*san* had just been promoted to the rank of commander, and he wanted to show everyone how tough he was. He wanted to make an example of Emiko, as a warning to other would-be thieves."

This sounded just like Hoshina, and Sano detested him all the more. Sano had already begun having second thoughts about his decision to protect his enemy. He grew less confident that forestalling Hoshina's death would prolong Reiko's life. Would he have done better to renege on his promise and let the shogun comply with the ransom demand? What if the investigation proved that neither Naraya nor the Kii clan had taken the women?

"The next day, while Emiko was awaiting her trial, a fire started in the neighborhood around the jail," Naraya said. "The warden let out the prisoners."

Tokugawa law decreed that when fire threatened, all prisoners should be released so that if the jail burned, they wouldn't die—a rare example of mercy in a cruel penal system. After the danger passed, the prisoners were supposed to return voluntarily to the jail, and most did.

"But Emiko stayed behind. After the fire was out and everyone came back to the jail . . ." Naraya puffed deep, tremulous breaths, and tears trickled down his droopy cheeks. "The warden found Emiko lying dead in a horse trough full of water. She had drowned."

Even while Sano pitied the man, excitement quickened his heartbeat. Naraya's daughter had perished in the same manner as the unnamed woman in the poem in the ransom letter. Was her death the murder that had precipitated the demand for Hoshina's execution?

"There was no official explanation given for what happened to my daughter." Naraya spoke with extreme rancor. "Maybe she fell in the trough. Maybe someone pushed her. But I think she drowned herself because she couldn't bear her disgrace."

"And you think Police Commissioner Hoshina indirectly caused her suicide?" Sano asked, controlling his excitement.

"If not for that scoundrel, Emiko would be alive today," Naraya said. Animosity burned his tears dry. "I wouldn't have lost my only child. My wife wouldn't have died of grief seven years ago. Every day Hoshina-*san* lives is a big, big insult to their memory. Every day I pray for him to suffer the same agony and humiliation that we did."

Contrary reactions beset Sano. He had more sympathy for Naraya than respect for Hoshina, and he found himself wanting Naraya to be innocent almost as much as he wanted him to be the kidnapper. He would rather see Naraya win vengeance for his daughter than punished for the massacre and abduction.

Naraya abruptly donned a semblance of his normal good cheer. "But the past is water under the bridge," he said. "We must accept what fate deals us and move forward into the future." Naraya paused, then said carefully, "May I ask what my old grudge against Hoshina-*san* has to do with the kidnapping of the shogun's mother?"

"His Excellency has received a letter from the kidnapper," Sano said. "It demanded that Hoshina be denounced and executed as a murderer, in exchange for the return of Lady Keisho-in."

Naraya's eyes bulged and his mouth dropped. He looked as though he'd just swallowed a rock that had lodged in his throat. Obviously, he realized how his story had incriminated him. Then he threw back his head and burst into laughter.

"So Hoshina-*san* has finally reaped his comeuppance!" Naraya exulted. "There's justice in this world after all." He jumped up and down in glee. "When he's executed, I'll be there to watch." Delight burbled from Naraya; he rubbed his hands together, then raised them skyward. "Praise the gods for answering my prayers. Someone has brought down that villain at last!"

"Was it you?" Doubt pierced Sano because Naraya appeared genuinely surprised by the news about the ransom demand. Could even an expert actor fake such a response? If Naraya had kidnapped the women, he should be alarmed that Sano had traced the letter to him, worried that his plot against Hoshina had failed, and afraid he would be punished for the crime, instead of rejoicing over Hoshina's downfall.

"I almost wish it were me," Naraya said. "Such a clever, clever retaliation for the wrongs Hoshina-*san* has done." He pumped his fists and chortled; then belated prudence sobered him as he comprehended his dangerous position. "But I didn't kidnap those women off the Tōkaidō. I haven't even left Edo in months. Ask anyone here." He gestured toward the factory.

But Sano knew that the workers owed Naraya their loyalty and would lie for him. "When did you learn that Lady Keisho-in was going on her trip?" Sano asked.

"Not until the news broadsheets announced that she'd been kidnapped," Naraya said. "I couldn't have done it." Sudden thought narrowed his eyes. "Besides, didn't I hear that Lady Keisho-in's entourage was massacred? A hundred people killed?" Naraya shook his head, deploring the carnage. "I could never, never shed blood—not even to avenge my daughter's death. And I'm not foolish enough to commit treason just to strike back at Hoshina-*san*."

Sano thought of how Magistrate Ueda had compromised his professional honor and bent the law for Reiko's sake. Sano knew that he himself would risk whatever danger and pay whatever price necessary to punish anyone who hurt Masahiro. Paternal devotion was stronger than prudence, and Naraya's denials didn't convince Sano.

"Maybe you wouldn't kill or kidnap with your own hands," Sano said. "But you wouldn't have needed to leave Edo or do your own dirty work."

Naraya snorted in disdain. "I don't have the men or the money to carry off an ambush like that."

Yet although Sano knew that hired muscle came cheap, and Naraya could afford it, he wondered whether Edo ruffians could have so easily slain Tokugawa troops. Sano's misgivings about Naraya's guilt increased. Shifting course, he said, "When did you move to Edo?"

The merchant blinked, disconcerted by the abrupt change of subject. "Two years ago," he said.

"Your family ran the business in Miyako for many generations. Why did you relocate it here?"

"Competition was tougher every year," Naraya said, and Sano watched him squint as he tried to figure out the point of the questions. "Business is much, much better in Edo."

"Your decision had nothing to do with the fact that Hoshina-*san* had moved here the year before?" Sano said.

"No." The merchant frowned in perplexity, then acquired an owlish look of wisdom. Pointing a finger at Sano, he said, "You think I followed Hoshina-*san*. You think I came to Edo to do him harm. But I didn't. The day I heard he'd left Miyako, I celebrated because he wouldn't foul the place anymore. If there were any other city as big as Edo, I'd have gone there instead, so I wouldn't have to breathe the same air as him."

Suddenly Sano lost all tolerance for restrained, deliberate interrogation. His urgent need to solve the case, save Reiko, and avoid execution flared up in him. He grabbed Naraya by the front of his kimono.

"No more denials!" he shouted at the merchant. "If you kidnapped the women, you'd better tell me!"

Startled, Naraya inhaled a loud gulp of breath. Fright widened his eyes. "I didn't," he protested.

If there was any chance that he was the Dragon King, Sano wasn't going to let Naraya dupe him. He slammed the merchant against the building and yelled, "Don't lie to me!"

"It's the honest truth," Naraya said. "I didn't kidnap anybody. I swear on my ancestors' honor."

"What have you done with my wife?" Though Sano hated resorting to brute force, he had two choices: He could be nice to the merchant and leave empty-handed, or pressure Naraya and perhaps elicit the facts he sought. Sano shook Naraya back and forth. "Where is she?"

"I don't know!" Naraya's head thumped on the wall. "Please, let me go. You're hurting me."

"Talk, and I'll stop." Sano shook him harder and faster.

The merchant grabbed Sano's hands and tried in vain to pry them off him. His feet kicked Sano's shins. "Help! Help!" he screamed.

"Tell me!" Sano ordered.

Workers rushed out of the factory, armed with paddles, clubs, and iron shovels, ready to defend Naraya. The detectives drew their swords.

"I'm innocent," Naraya cried. "Torture me until I confess, then kill me—but it won't bring back the women, because I didn't take them. I don't know where they are!"

Sano saw Naraya's terrified face, and a brawl impending. He realized he'd gone too far. Beating Naraya's head to a pulp would do Reiko no good, even if Naraya was the Dragon King. Sano released his hold on Naraya. The merchant sat down hard on the filthy ground.

"Go back to your business," Sano told the workmen.

They obeyed; the detectives sheathed their blades. Sano leaned against the wall, spent by his violent impulse and horrified that his life seemed a nightmare in which he must start and restart this investigation for all eternity, and never find Reiko. He looked at the suspect he'd almost killed. Naraya reclined with eyes closed and limbs splayed, moaning. Blood from his head smeared the wall.

"Are you all right?" Sano said, fearful that he'd beaten Naraya senseless.

Naraya opened his eyes. "No thanks to you," he said, and cracked a weak smile. "But no hard feelings. I understand that you're very, very upset, because I know what it's like to lose someone you love. And I really want to help you." With a pained grunt, he stood up and said timidly, "May I make a suggestion?"

Drained of energy for more verbal combat, Sano said, "Go ahead." His hope that Naraya was the Dragon King had diminished so much that he needed all the advice he could get—even from a suspect.

"If you really want to find the kidnapper," Naraya said, "you should forget me and look into other people Hoshina-

san hurt. He made himself very, very unpopular around Miyako. Maybe his other old enemies came here after his blood. Maybe they took the shogun's mother."

"Maybe you're just trying to cover your own crimes by diverting suspicion elsewhere." Sano spoke with scorn, although he recognized that unless he found evidence against Naraya, he would have to do as the merchant suggested.

"I'm just trying to do the shogun a favor and keep you from making a big mistake," Naraya said. "May I tell you where else I think you should be looking for the kidnapper?"

Sano's silence indicated assent.

"Inside the Black Lotus," Naraya said.

"The Black Lotus?" Sano frowned, startled that the sect should crop up after the investigation had turned away from it. He regarded Naraya with skepticism, wondering if the merchant was just directing blame toward the notorious scourge. "Why do you say that?"

Naraya looked around, as if fearful of eavesdroppers. He spoke in a low, confidential tone: "I've heard that the police are very, very rough on the Black Lotus folks they arrest. Hoshina-*san* has his own secret jail where he and his men torture them into informing on their comrades. While he asks them questions, his men drip molten copper into their eyes. They all talk, eventually."

The news disturbed Sano. Although he abhorred the Black Lotus, he disapproved of torture, and he was finding more to dislike about the man he'd obligated himself to save. And he couldn't dismiss Naraya's story as mere rumor. The police had lately made a large number of Black Lotus arrests. If those stemmed from a personal crusade headed by Hoshina, then he'd been responsible for executions that the Black Lotus would view as murder.

"The Black Lotus has as much reason to want revenge on Hoshina-*san* as I do," Naraya said. "Besides, it has many, many crazy people who would slaughter a Tokugawa procession and kidnap the shogun's mother if their priests ordered them." Naraya echoed the reasoning that had initially caused Sano to suspect the Black Lotus.

Yet Sano warned himself against reverting to his original theory. Even if the Black Lotus priests did want Hoshina dead, they would more likely assassinate him—as they'd done other foes—than concoct the kidnapping plot. They would know that eliminating Hoshina wouldn't end their persecution by the *bakufu*. Sano also thought other elements of the crime didn't fit the Black Lotus. The ransom letter bespoke a personal attack against Hoshina, not religious warfare. The poem didn't sound like Black Lotus scripture, which derived from ancient Buddhist texts, not dragon legend.

Furthermore, a good detective wouldn't let a suspect influence his judgment.

"After your daughter died, you told Hoshina-*san* that you would make him pay," Sano reminded Naraya.

The merchant grimaced in annoyance. "Is that what he told you? Well, I suppose he's so desperate that he'll say anything to help himself. Or maybe my daughter's death meant so little to him that he's forgotten what went on between us. But my memory is as clear as if it happened yesterday. This is what I said to Hoshina-*san*: 'Someday you'll suffer for what you did to my daughter. You can't escape the bad karma you've created. Someday the wheel of fate that crushed my daughter will crush you.' "

Exultation shone through Naraya's fear. "And it looks as though my prediction is going to come true."

Repeated interrogation of Naraya proved futile because Naraya only reiterated his protests of innocence. At last, Sano and his detectives left the factory and gathered outside by their horses. The afternoon sunlight glared dully on the canal; boatmen shouted curses; a beggar limped along the dusty road, empty bowl in hand.

"Keep a secret watch on Naraya," Sano told two of his men. "Follow him wherever he goes. Maybe he'll do something to show he's the kidnapper and lead us to the women."

"Yes, *Sōsakan-sama*," chorused the detectives.

But Sano feared Naraya was another dead end on another hunt in the wrong direction. He regretted all the more his decision to prevent Hoshina's execution and give up a chance to save Reiko. He wondered how Chamberlain Yanagisawa fared with the Kii clan and he hoped for better results than Naraya had produced, because otherwise they were out of luck.

As he mounted his horse, sudden recollection buoyed Sano's mood. There was one more potential lead to the Dragon King, overlooked in the commotion generated by the ransom letter.

"We're going back to Edo Castle," Sano said. Slapping the reins, he galloped down the street, while his two detectives hurried to catch up with him.

17

The storm on the island diminished to a light rain that dripped through the roof of the ruined keep. Inside, amid the puddles and dank gloom, Reiko, Midori, Lady Yanagisawa, and Keisho-in sat clustered together and watched the door creak open. The fierce samurai who had almost ravished Reiko strode into their prison. After him came two younger samurai whose threadbare clothes and surly air branded them as *rōnin*.

"You," the fierce samurai said, jabbing a finger at Reiko. "Come with us."

Alarm struck Reiko. "What for?" Her voice shook with the fear that sickened her heart.

During the hours that had passed since the kidnappers had captured her outside the castle, she'd had little to occupy her except trying to predict what they would do to her and the other women. Common sense told her that the kidnappers couldn't just keep them here like this forever. The leader she'd met must have another purpose. Reiko's instincts warned that something worse would happen. Now it seemed the time had come.

"Don't talk back," the fierce samurai ordered. His scowl deepened. "Just do as you're told."

Midori whimpered; Lady Yanagisawa emitted an ululating groan like a cat's growl. Reiko felt them clutch her hands, trying to prevent her departure.

"She's not going," Keisho-in said with panicky bravado. "Get out. Leave us alone."

The samurai sneered, then nodded to his comrades. They seized Reiko and tore her from her friends' grasp.

"Oh, Reiko-*san*," Midori wailed.

Lady Yanagisawa made inarticulate sounds of protest. Keisho-in shouted, "Let her go, you filthy, disgusting beasts!"

As the men roughly propelled Reiko toward the door, she glanced backward at her friends. Their faces expressed their horror at losing her and their hope of salvation.

"I'll be back," she told them with a confidence she wished she felt. "Don't worry."

Outside the door, two peasant thugs crouched. They leered at Reiko as her escorts urged her to the stairway. One of the younger men descended first. Their leader positioned himself behind Reiko, gripped her shoulders, and forced her to walk down the stairs ahead of him. The third man followed. Splinters from the rickety steps needled her bare feet. On the lower levels, more guards lounged, smoking tobacco pipes. As Reiko and her escorts neared the door, the cruel samurai took hold of her right arm, while one comrade restrained her left. The other dogged her heels. The tip of his sword pricked her back. Her heart hammered and her stomach churned.

Where were they taking her? Did they mean to finish the assault that their leader had interrupted?

They dragged her from the keep. The clouded sky darkened the afternoon. Rain pelted her face; the stone landing felt cold and slick under her toes. The men led her past still more guards who loitered on the steps, and along an unfamiliar path through the forest. Three more samurai joined their procession. The trees dripped water; moisture saturated the air, which smelled of loam and decaying leaves. Reiko barely noticed the sharp twigs that gouged her feet, because an awful thought occurred to her.

The kidnappers intended to murder their victims. They'd chosen her to be the first to die.

Panic compressed Reiko's chest; her breath emerged in wheezes as she tried to control her fear. She longed for Sano, but three days had gone by since her abduction, and he hadn't come. He would not come in time to rescue her now.

Suddenly the forest was behind her, and the path edged the lake, a dull silver mirror of the sky, rimmed by misty woods and mountains on the opposite shore. Would the kidnappers drown her? Reiko imagined Masahiro never knowing why his mother didn't come home. The panic swelled, dizzying Reiko; she stumbled. Borne along by the men, she passed a ramshackle dock that extended into the water. She spied three boats secured to the pilings. The boats were simple wooden shells, with oars laid inside. Her will to survive outbalanced her fear of death, and her spirits momentarily rose. Now she knew that here were her means of transport across the lake, if not how to gain them.

The cruel samurai hustled her past the boats. His grin said he'd read her thoughts and scorned her hope.

On their right loomed what appeared to be the main palace. A paved square, and a crumbling wall studded with ruined guard turrets, fronted the lake. Beyond the wall rose a building crowned with tile roofs whose gables boasted tarnished copper dragon crests. Reiko's captors led her through portals where a gate had once hung. Moss-coated stone lanterns flanked the path through a wilderness that had once been a garden. The buildings seemed intact, though the plaster had flaked off them, exposing weathered wood. Ivy entwined the foundation posts and window grills. The quiet seemed alive with the ghosts of warlords from a bygone era. A shiver chilled Reiko as the men marched her up a flight of steps, into the palace through an open doorway, and along a dim corridor. Torn, moldy paper hung from the lattice walls. Dark stains marred the floorboards, and Reiko sensed that blood had been shed where she now walked. The place breathed a wicked miasma that increased her dread.

Would her blood soon spill here?

They turned a corner and entered a reception chamber. The smoky, bittersweet scent of incense laced the atmosphere. Jagged cracks in sliding doors along the wall gave a view of a veranda outside. Beyond an expanse of rotting *tatami,* the man in the dragon kimono stood waiting on a dais. Behind him stretched a faded mural that portrayed a fanciful underwater scene of blue waves and green seaweed flowing over gardens and pavilions. He watched Reiko and his men cross the chamber and stop before him. Again his sinister, brooding stare burned into Reiko. Again the peculiar longing in his eyes disturbed her.

"Leave her with me, Ota-*san.*" He flicked a glance at her erstwhile attacker, who seemed to be his chief henchman. "You can all go."

"But she's dangerous." Ota stood firm, his hand still gripping Reiko's arm. His comrades also held their positions. "She killed four of our men during the ambush. She attacked Jiro and me this morning. You shouldn't be alone with her."

Nor did Reiko want to be alone with him. Although she feared her escorts, she wished they would stay.

Angry impatience flamed in the man's eyes. "Then wait outside," he ordered his men.

Ota spoke quietly to Reiko: "Behave yourself, or your friends will be punished."

Then he released her. He and his fellows walked out the door, but Reiko sensed him loitering nearby. She saw the other men line up on the veranda, ready to protect their master.

He descended from the dais and approached Reiko. His flared nostrils twitched as though scenting prey; saliva gleamed on his pursed lips. Reiko folded her arms across her bosom and stepped backward. Her heart beat an escalating rhythm as she eyed the swords at his waist.

Had he brought her here so that he could kill her? Had he kidnapped her and her friends because he enjoyed slaughtering helpless women?

He advanced nearer with that proud yet hesitant swagger. The odor of incense was stronger around him, as if soaked into his skin and clothes. "What's your name?" he said, his gaze intent on her face.

She didn't want to tell him, but she was afraid of what he would do if she didn't answer. She opened her mouth. No speech emerged. Swallowing the dry lump in her throat, she tried again. "Reiko," she whispered.

A shadow of displeasure crossed his features. "That name doesn't suit you. I shall call you . . . Anemone." He lingered on the word, savoring it.

Reiko hoped she wouldn't be here long enough for him to call her anything, but if he bothered to rename her, then perhaps he intended her to live awhile. Her mettle revived, emboldening her. "Who are you?" she said.

His brows rose in surprise, as if he thought she should have already known. After a moment's hesitation, he said, "You can call me 'Dragon King.' "

She frowned, baffled by his strange talk. Why would he name himself after the legendary spirit? She was also perturbed that he wouldn't tell her his real identity.

A secretive smile touched his lips. "Yes, I am the Dragon King, who rights the wrongs done by evil men and balances the cosmic forces in the universe."

What he meant by that eluded Reiko's comprehension. "Where am I?" she asked.

"You're with me, where you belong."

He prowled in a circle around her. Pivoting, Reiko watched him, leery that he would attack her. If she was to die, she wouldn't succumb without a battle, and she wanted some answers first. She said, "I mean, where is this place?"

"This is a castle that a member of my clan built as a summer home. He was a general during the civil wars, more than a hundred years ago. One day, enemy troops attacked him here. They fired mortars, gunshots, and flaming arrows from rafts on the lake. The castle caught fire. The enemy invaded. Although my clansman and his army fought bravely, they were doomed. He committed *seppuku* to avoid the disgrace of capture."

Ice congealed along Reiko's nerves as she recalled the bloodstains on the floor.

"But the past doesn't concern us, Anemone," said the Dragon King. "That chance has reunited us is all that matters."

Again, he behaved as if they knew each other, although Reiko was more sure than ever that they'd never met. What part did he think chance had played in his abduction of her? And why insist on calling her Anemone? What significance did the name hold for him?

"I shouldn't have expected you to recognize me," he said in a rueful tone. "When we were last together, I was a mere boy. But I recognized you at once. You are as young and beautiful as ever." Reverence hushed his voice and misted his eyes as he gazed at Reiko. "You are just as you've appeared in my dreams ever since the night I lost you."

Reiko deduced that she resembled someone he'd known. Could it be the reason he'd kidnapped her? The idea that mistaken identity had occasioned the murder of a hundred people horrified Reiko. But when they'd met after her escape attempt, he'd seemed surprised to see her. And why kidnap the other women if she was the one he wanted?

An injured expression altered the Dragon King's aspect. "Why do you not speak?" he asked. "Have you nothing to say to me after all this time apart?"

Reiko blurted, "Are you going to kill me?"

The Dragon King cocked his big head, clasped one fist inside the other, and regarded her for a long, suspenseful moment, while emotions she couldn't interpret flitted across his face. "Hopefully not," he said at last.

Her puzzlement outlived her relief, because the Dragon King thrust out both hands as if to seize her. Reiko cried out and instinctively flung up her arms to strike back, then recalled that her friends' safety depended on her good behavior. The Dragon King withdrew his hands and held them palms up, assuring her that he meant no harm. An anxious, propitiating smile rendered his countenance all the more disturbing.

"Come, we shall celebrate our reunion with a banquet," he said.

He moved to her side. His hand touching her sleeve urged her across the room, up onto the dais. Near the mural lay a cloth set with a sake decanter, two cups, two pairs of chopsticks, and dishes that contained cold rice, roasted fish, boiled greens, and preserved fruits. Reiko unwillingly knelt where the Dragon King indicated. He knelt too close beside her, poured the sake, and handed her a cup.

"A toast to a new beginning," he said, raising his cup while his gaze devoured her.

He drank, and Reiko decided he was playing some private, bizarre game. The need to protect her friends compelled her to play along and drain her cup. The liquor burned her insides like corrosive poison.

"Please eat, Anemone," he said.

Reiko picked up the chopsticks and obeyed. Despite her hunger, every bite stuck in her throat. She didn't want to encourage his weird fancies. What bearing might they have upon his crimes?

The Dragon King poured more sake and drank again. He didn't eat; he just watched her. "You're awfully quiet, my dearest. What are you thinking?"

Summoning her nerve, Reiko said, "Why did you do it?"

The Dragon King started and blinked, as if he'd just awakened from a dream. He seemed not to know what she was talking about.

"What I want to know is why you kidnapped us," Reiko said, and saw comprehension creep into his gaze. She said, "If it's money you want, my family will pay you whatever you ask. So will Midori's and Lady Yanagisawa's families. The shogun will give away the whole Tokugawa treasury to get his mother back."

"I don't want money." The Dragon King dismissed the notion with an adamant shake of his head. "The purpose of my scheme is justice, not wealth. Justice and vengeance. Both require blood sacrifice of the innocent as well as the guilty."

"You wanted revenge? For what?" Reiko said, more perplexed than enlightened. "What did those people your men killed ever do to you?"

"Nothing." His callous dismissal said he harbored no regrets about the massacre. "They were just in the way."

"In the way of kidnapping Lady Keisho-in, Lady Yanagisawa, Midori, and me?" When the Dragon King nodded, Reiko said, "But we've never hurt you. You've no cause to hold us prisoners and mistreat us."

"Haven't I?" Sudden rage flamed in his eyes. "Didn't you entice me into immoral degradation?" He leaned closer to Reiko, and his words sprayed hot liquor fumes into her face.

Disconcerted by his abrupt change of mood, she lurched upward in an attempt to rise. She saw the men on the veranda aiming bows and arrows at her through the cracked doors. She thought of her helpless friends and sank to her knees.

"Didn't you make me your devoted slave, and all the while you bestowed your favors elsewhere?" he demanded. "Didn't I suffer agonizing heartbreak because of you? Didn't you break my spirit, then abandon me?" He shouted, "Whore! She-devil!"

He slapped her cheek so hard that her head snapped and her vision blurred. Reiko screamed in pain and shock as she fell on her side with a bone-jarring crash. Then the Dragon King was bending over her, murmuring tender consolations.

"Forgive me for hurting you," he said. "How can I make amends?"

Comfort from him scared Reiko as much as his violence did. She felt the tingling soreness in her cheek; she tasted blood in her mouth. As she gazed up at him, tears flooded her eyes. "You can let us go."

His brows bunched together. "Why do you want to leave me? Do you find me so repulsive?"

"No, not at all," Reiko hastened to say. Cautiously she sat up, aware that she must not enrage him again, lest he do her greater injury. "I think you're very . . . handsome. But the tower is unfit for people to live in. Lady Keisho-in is old and sick. Midori is going to have a baby soon. Lady Yanagisawa is the mother of a little daughter who needs her."

Ennui shaded the Dragon King's countenance: His interest in Reiko didn't extend to the other women.

"I have a child, too." Reiko's voice trembled as she thought of Masahiro. "We all want to go home!"

The Dragon King folded his arms and straightened his posture. "That's impossible." Coldness edged his gruff voice.

"Have you any children of your own? Don't you miss your own family?" Reiko said, trying to draw him onto common ground and thereby win his sympathy. "Wouldn't you rather be with them instead of in this miserable place?"

"I have no children. I have no family." He spoke in an accusatory tone that said his lack was somehow her fault.

Reiko despaired of reasoning with him, for she comprehended that he was irrational. "Who is it that you want revenge against?" she asked. "What did they do to you that you would kill and kidnap innocent people?"

His superior smile mocked her. "The truth will soon become known to everyone in Japan."

Thwarted, Reiko tried another tack: "How can you serve justice by keeping us imprisoned?"

"You will see," he said, replete with private satisfaction.

"Kidnapping the shogun's mother and slaughtering her entourage is treason against the Tokugawa regime. You'll never get away with it." In her growing anxiety, Reiko resorted to threats: "The army will hunt you down. You'll die in disgrace, while your enemy goes free."

"The army won't touch me." The Dragon King lifted his receding chin and rested a hand on his swords. "I've warned the shogun that if he sends the army after me, I'll kill you all. He must grant my wish, or lose his beloved mother."

Reiko couldn't fathom what wish had spurred this man

to such extreme behavior. "What did you ask the shogun to do?" she said, her curiosity almost equaling her fear.

"Be patient," the Dragon King said with an air of condescension. "Time will tell."

Although Reiko had learned the futility of expecting the answers she wanted from him, she said, "What will happen to us?"

"That depends on the shogun. For now, you will stay here with me. We might as well enjoy this time we have together."

He crept close behind her. His feverish warmth and odor of incense engulfed Reiko; his breaths rasped loudly. An urge to flee almost launched Reiko to her feet, but she saw Ota hovering in the doorway and the men on the veranda, all watching. The Dragon King's fingers tangled in her hair, fumbling and stroking. Reiko felt her skin ripple with revulsion.

No man except her husband had ever touched her in such an intimate manner. She wanted no man except Sano. She would have turned on the Dragon King, grabbed for his sword, and fought him off, but if she did, Keisho-in, Lady Yanagisawa, and Midori would pay.

The Dragon King brushed her hair to one side. His hot, moist breath fanned the back of her neck, that erotic, intimate zone of the female body. His fingertips grazed her nape. Reiko went rigid with terror of ravishment—the worst injury, short of death, that a man could inflict upon a woman.

"The dragon lifts his spiny tail," he whispered. "His majestic body swells and pulsates. Steam bursts from between his glittering scales. His flaming breath ignites passion."

Reiko shuddered at this obscene parody of a love poem. She gagged on bile as she anticipated the agonizing ravishment, and the terrible disgrace.

"An ocean of desire envelops the princess in the underwater palace. Her ivory skin flushes scarlet. She parts her rosy coral lips. Her will drowns in his power. She must surrender."

His moving lips touched Reiko's ear. His hand quivered while he stroked her neck. "Surrender to me now, Anemone, my beautiful drowned princess," he muttered. "Reward me for the justice I will bring you."

Now Reiko comprehended with horror that he wasn't just playing a game. He had such a tenuous grip on reality that he kept forgetting who she was and actually believing she was the woman he called Anemone. He wasn't merely eccentric and irrational—he was insane. What sense could she hope to make of a madman's purpose?

Indecision paralyzed Reiko. If she resisted him, her friends might lose their lives, but enduring his advances might not guarantee their survival. Must she submit to him? Should she fight instead? If she fought, would he or his men kill her?

"You're trembling," the Dragon King said. "You recoil from my touch. Why do you seem not to want me?"

Hurt and confusion echoed in his words. Reiko dared not move or speak. His hand continued stroking her. Then he said, "Ah," in a glad tone of enlightenment. "My haste has offended your feminine sensibility. You would prefer that we delay our lovemaking until we become reacquainted. And your wish is my privilege to honor. Waiting will enhance our pleasure."

The Dragon King's hand dropped from her neck. He stood and called to his men: "Take her back to the keep."

Such overwhelming relief swept through Reiko that her muscles went weak and a sigh gushed from her. Yet even as she silently thanked the gods, she knew the reprieve was only temporary.

The men entered the room and surrounded Reiko. The Dragon King gazed upon her, his eyes burning and face dark with lust. "Good-bye until next time, my dearest Anemone," he said.

As the men led her away, Reiko prayed for a miracle to save her before the next time came.

18

The route to Izu branched southwest off the Tō-kaidō and wound through mountainous, sparsely populated landscape. While Hirata and the detectives galloped along the road, the clouds dispersed, revealing brilliant blue sky, and the afternoon grew warm. Sunlight and shadow painted the cypress forests in vivid shades of green. Steam issued from cracks in the cliffs; hot springs bubbled across the rocky terrain; volcanoes breathed wisps of smoke. Tiny villages, clinging to hillsides, flashed past Hirata as his horse's hooves thrummed under him. The wind roaring in his ears, the tumultuous speed, and the certainty that he was following the path to Midori, elated his spirit. Now he and Marume and Fukida brought their horses to a skittering halt at the junction between the main road and a narrower track that extended west and east into wilderness.

In the sudden quiet stillness, Hirata heard birds singing. He saw, on the west side of the road, a niche carved into a cliff. The niche held a little stone statue of Jizo, the Shinto patron god of travelers.

"There's the shrine Goro mentioned," said Fukida.

"The kidnappers sent away the porters because they didn't want anyone to see where they went from here," Marume deduced. "They carried the chests themselves, down that crossroad. Which way do you think they went?"

Eerie vibrations in the clear, bright air aroused Hirata's

instincts. He peered along the crossroad in one direction, then the other. An internal compass pointed him toward Midori. "This way," he said, and rode ahead of his comrades down the westbound track.

The track climbed a slope, then gradually descended and leveled. Cypress, pine, and oak forest narrowed the track and darkened the sunlight. Leading his comrades in single file, Hirata spied dung and trampled leaves on the ground ahead.

"Someone recently brought horses this way," he said. Moments later he glimpsed deep footprints in a stretch of bare, damp earth. "And someone carried a heavy object through here." His heart beat fast with the increasing conviction that this road would take him to Midori and the other women, and that he would fulfill his duty to Sano and the shogun.

After perhaps an hour's ride, a blaze of sunshine through the trees heralded a clearing in the forest. Hirata, Fukida, and Marume dismounted and walked from cool shadow into warm daylight, blinking as their eyes adjusted. The track extended down a short incline, where tree roots protruded through grass and soil, and ended at a dock built of planks. Beyond this spread a marsh-rimmed lake. A breeze rippled the water, which gleamed like an alloy of gold, copper, and quicksilver. In the middle of the lake, some hundred paces distant from where Hirata and his men stood at the forest's edge, was an island. From its shore jutted another dock surrounded by three small boats. Nearby rose what appeared to be a fortress comprised of white buildings with curved tile roofs, a stone wall, and guard towers, amid woods.

Hirata, Marume, and Fukida gazed across the lake, their mouths agape and hands shading their eyes from the sun.

"A castle on an island in the middle of nowhere?" Fukida said in a tone that expressed their disbelief.

"It must be left over from the civil wars," Marume said. "The forest and lake would protect the castle from attack."

"And it's perfect for a prison," Hirata said. A smile

cracked the rigid mask of misery that had overlain his face since he'd heard the news of Midori's abduction. New strength infused him, and his cold even seemed to abate, because his search had finally paid off. "This must be where the kidnappers took Midori, Reiko, Lady Keisho-in, and Lady Yanagisawa."

As he and his men beheld the castle, they saw no sign of the women, but a thin smoke plume drifted up from the rooftops. "The place is inhabited," Marume said.

Out the castle gate strode four samurai, armed with swords, bows, and quivers. Hirata, Marume, and Fukida quickly hid in the forest. They watched from behind trees as the samurai divided in pairs that marched in opposite directions along the island's shore.

"They're patrolling," Fukida said.

"Maybe they don't know that the wars are over," Marume said, "but I bet they're guarding the castle because they've got the shogun's mother in there and they don't want anybody trespassing."

Hirata, Fukida, and Marume looked at one another. They whooped with jubilation, threw playful punches, and danced in a circle—quietly, so the kidnappers wouldn't hear them. Hirata rejoiced that Midori was so near.

"We have to tell the *sōsakan-sama* that we've found the kidnappers' hideout," said Marume. "Shall we head for home?"

The idea collided against a barrier of resistance within Hirata. He turned away from the detectives and gazed through the trees, toward the island. He sensed Midori's spirit calling to him from that mysterious castle. The irresistible summons, and his overwhelming desire to stay near his wife, rooted him where he stood.

"We're not leaving," he said, facing Marume and Fukida.

They regarded him with surprise. Marume said, "But the *sōsakan-sama* ordered us to report our discoveries to him."

Concern sharpened Fukida's expression as he looked toward the castle, then back at Hirata. "You're not thinking of going over there . . . are you?"

Hirata clenched and unclenched his jaw. Beset by opposing motives, he balanced his weight on one foot, then the other.

"We aren't supposed to approach the kidnappers," Fukida reminded him.

"I know." Hirata also knew that their duty to their master superseded all other considerations.

"You wouldn't go against his orders?" Marume said, clearly shocked that Hirata could even think of such heresy.

A terrible, sick shame coursed through Hirata. Disobedience was the worst sin against *Bushido*. And defying Sano would not only compromise Hirata's honor but also betray the trust of the man who was his closest friend as well as his master.

"We can't just leave," he said. "By the time we reach Edo, the kidnappers might have moved the women elsewhere. We might never find them again."

Marume and Fukida nodded, acknowledging his rationale, but they exchanged troubled glances.

"If the *sōsakan-sama* knew the situation, he would change his orders," Hirata said, convincing himself that this was so. "He'd want us to move in on the castle and attempt a rescue."

"We can't know what he would want. Besides, the kidnappers said in their letter to the shogun that if anyone pursues them, they'll kill the women." Marume's hesitant manner conveyed reluctance to disagree with Hirata, who outranked him.

"They won't see us coming," Hirata said. "We're only the three of us, not an army that would attract their notice."

"Three of us might not be enough," Fukida said. He picked at his fingernails—his habit when nervous—but he spoke with the conviction of a samurai who recognized his duty to voice unpleasant truths to a superior. "We don't know how many kidnappers there are. They survived a battle against the Tokugawa troops in Lady Keisho-in's entourage, which means they're good fighters. Suppose we get caught on the island. If we're killed, we can't rescue the women, or even tell the *sōsakan-sama* where they are."

"He's right," Marume said.

The two detectives stood ranged together against Hirata. "We won't get caught," he said. Angry at himself for defying *Bushido,* he grew angry at them for defying him. "Do you think I'm not capable of leading a successful raid?" The fact that he had his own doubts about their chances of success made him even more furious. "Are you questioning my judgment?"

"No, it's not that," Fukida hastened to say, although his expression belied his words.

"Don't you want to save the women?" Hirata demanded.

"Of course we do," Marume said. "We don't want to slink back to Edo any more than you do." His face, and Fukida's, reflected the same hunger for action that burned in Hirata. "But we can't disobey the *sōsakan-sama.*"

"Our honor is at stake," Fukida said.

The worst thing Hirata could do to his comrades was force them to break their samurai loyalty to Sano. He hated to cause Marume and Fukida such disgrace. But he feared that unless they helped him raid the island, all was lost. Even if Lord Niu had ordered the kidnapping, and his only intention was to separate Midori from Hirata, that didn't mean she was safe. That the violent, unpredictable *daimyo* had never killed a family member didn't guarantee that he wouldn't, and the kidnappers had already proved themselves murderers during the ambush. Hirata couldn't allow a delay that could cost the lives of Midori and their child. And he didn't believe Sano would want him to abandon Reiko or the other women to the kidnappers.

"The *sōsakan-sama* put me in charge of this mission," Hirata said. "As long as we're away from him, you must obey me. I order you to help me invade the island and rescue the women. I'll take responsibility for whatever happens."

Again Fukida and Marume looked at each other. Wordless communication passed between them. When they finally nodded to Hirata, he saw that they were relieved to have matters settled for them, and eager to begin the rescue expedition, if still not entirely convinced about the wisdom of it. He exhaled, feeling his own relief and gratitude.

"How are we going to get across the lake?" Marume said.

"We could swim," Fukida said, his gaze measuring the distance over the water. "But we'll need a way to transport the women to safety."

"What about those boats?" Marume pointed at the far dock.

"I don't think we should depend on them," Hirata said. "If the worst happens and the kidnappers discover that we're on the island before we can get the women off, they'll guard the boats. We would all have to swim, and Midori can't, especially in her condition."

"I wouldn't gamble that the other women can swim, either," Fukida said. "We could tow them, but that would slow down our escape and give the kidnappers a chance to spot us."

A vision of the three of them struggling to pull four women through the water, while the kidnappers fired arrows at them and chased them in the boats, momentarily quieted Hirata, Marume, and Fukida. No one speculated aloud about what hazards they might have to brave while locating the women, removing them from wherever they were imprisoned, and getting them as far as the shore.

"We need our own boat that we can hide on the island and use to carry away the women," Hirata said, concentrating on the problem at hand. He would worry about other obstacles later. He would also postpone worrying about what Sano would think when he found out Hirata had disobeyed his orders.

"Should we ride back to the nearest village and see if the people have a boat to lend or sell us?" Marume said.

"I'm not letting the island out of my sight for that long," Hirata said.

He looked around for an alternative, and his gaze lit on a fallen tree and slender saplings in the forest. "We'll cut some logs and join them together to make rafts. Then we'll wait until nightfall, row across the lake, and invade the island."

19

In the Edo Castle sickroom, the maid Suiren lay
in bed, inert and fragile beneath the blanket. Her closed
eyes were sunken in dark hollows, her facial bones sharp
under her pale skin. Sano knelt at one side of the bed, and
Dr. Kitano at the other. They watched feeble breaths sigh
through her parched, colorless lips. Incense smoke wafted
over her, while the sorceress beat a tambourine and the
priest recited healing spells. Vapor from simmering herbal
infusions hazed the room.

"Has her condition improved at all?" Sano asked doubtfully.

He'd come to visit Suiren because this important witness
to the crime had been forgotten in the turn of events caused
by the ransom letter. He'd intended to follow up on Police
Commissioner Hoshina's attempt at questioning the lone
survivor of the massacre, yet one look at Suiren had deflated his hope that she would provide any information
whatsoever.

"She's no better but no worse," Dr. Kitano said. "She
has a remarkable constitution and a strong will to live, but
she is still in grave danger."

"Has she regained consciousness?" Sano asked.

"Not since Hoshina-*san* forced me to revive her." Dr.
Kitano's stern face expressed disapproval. "He insisted on
trying to make her tell him about the ambush, even though

she was too weak and dazed. His rough handling could have killed her, had I not stopped him."

Sano was furious to hear how Hoshina had endangered Suiren's life and jeopardized the investigation. Although a capable detective, Hoshina relied far too much on brute force. Sano wished Hoshina had never come to Edo. The man had hurt so many people, and not just Naraya's daughter and everyone else on the list of deaths associated with him. The massacre and abduction stemmed from a wrong Hoshina had done. If Reiko, Midori, Keisho-in, and Lady Yanagisawa were murdered, their deaths would be partially his fault. Sano thought the only good thing about the situation was that Hoshina was locked away where he couldn't do any more harm.

"Has Suiren said anything in her sleep?" Sano asked.

"No," Dr. Kitano said.

"Keep a constant watch on her," Sano said. "If she does say anything, write it down. As soon as she regains consciousness, send word to my estate."

"Yes, *Sōsakan-sama*," said Dr. Kitano.

After one last glance at Suiren and a silent prayer for her recovery, Sano left the sickroom to finish Hoshina's investigation of her. He wondered what other mistakes Hoshina had left for him to discover.

The Edo Castle women's quarters occupied a private, inner section of the palace known as the Large Interior. Here lived the shogun's mother, his wife, his two hundred concubines, their attendants, and the palace's female servants and officials—some thousand women in all. Sano presented himself at the door, which was made of iron-banded oak, decorated with carved flowers, and guarded by two soldiers. The Large Interior was barred to all men except a few trusted guards, doctors, officials, and messengers. Even Sano's high rank didn't permit him automatic access.

"I want to see Madam Chizuru," he told the sentries.

They dispatched a messenger inside to fetch Madam Chizuru, the *otoshiyori*—chief lady official—of the Large Interior. Her duties included keeping vigil outside the shogun's bedchamber while he slept with concubines, to ensure that they didn't misbehave. She also kept order in the women's quarters. Sano knew her reputation as an intelligent, able overseer who knew everyone in the Large Interior and missed little of what went on there. Soon she came to the door.

"How may I serve you?" she said, bowing to Sano.

Some fifty years of age and once a concubine to the previous shogun, Chizuru had graying hair worn in a knot atop her head. A modest gray kimono draped her sturdy, muscular physique. Her square face, thick, unshaven brows, and the dark hairs on her upper lip gave her a masculine appearance; but her deep voice was melodious, and her mouth daintily feminine.

"I need you to tell me about Suiren, and show me her quarters," Sano said.

"As you wish."

Chizuru stepped aside, allowing him to enter the Large Interior. They walked down passages with polished cypress floors, through a labyrinth of chambers enclosed by latticed wood and paper walls. In the chambers, pretty young women lounged while maids fanned them. Doors stood open to the garden, where more women and attendants reposed under shade trees. Sano inhaled the odors of perfume, hair oil, and too many people crammed into too little space. Wind chimes tinkled; female voices shrilled loudly. The kidnapping of their lord's mother hadn't quelled the restlessness of these women who were caged like prisoners with nothing to do but pass the time.

"Did Police Commissioner Hoshina already question you?" Sano asked Chizuru.

"He did." Disapprobation compressed Chizuru's mouth. "He accused Suiren of conspiring in the kidnapping."

"You don't believe she did?" Sano said.

"It's not my place to have ideas that contradict those of my superiors," Chizuru said primly.

But Sano knew that an independent mind lurked under her discretion. "I daresay you know the women here better than Hoshina or anyone else does. Tell me what you think."

Emboldened, Chizuru said, "Suiren has attended Lady Keisho-in for more than thirty years. She's devoted to her mistress. And she's a kind, decent woman. The idea that she would help criminals kill her comrades and kidnap somebody is ridiculous." Chizuru spoke with outright indignation.

Sano trusted her opinion more than he did Hoshina's. The theory that Suiren had told the Dragon King about the trip, and he'd spared her life as a reward, lost credibility for Sano. It was just like Hoshina to incriminate a woman who couldn't speak for herself, despite the lack of evidence against her, just so his investigation would appear to be making progress!

"This is where Suiren lives," Chizuru said, leading Sano into a small chamber next to Lady Keisho-in's quarters.

The chamber was sparsely furnished with a lantern, a cabinet, and a low table that held a *butsudan*—a Buddhist altar comprised of a wooden cupboard that housed a sacred scripture. Around the *butsudan* sat incense burners and prayer books.

"She's very religious," Chizuru said. "She plans to enter a convent when she's too old to work."

Sano opened the cabinet and searched through the contents. These included bedding, a comb and brush, an inexpensive writing case, and garments as plain as nuns' habits. He found nothing to counter Suiren's good reputation.

"Did you notice anything unusual about her before the trip?" he asked, closing the cabinet door.

"She was the same as always—calm, cheerful, and efficient," said Chizuru, "even though she had to supervise Lady Keisho-in's packing, and the sudden trip caused a big upheaval."

"Did she go out to see anyone or send any messages before they left Edo?" Sano said.

"Police Commissioner Hoshina asked me that question, and I'll give you the same answer I gave him. Suiren didn't go out. She was too busy. And she didn't send any messages. I know because I inspect all messages from the Large Interior."

It seemed that Suiren couldn't have communicated with the kidnappers, but Sano must explore every facet of her life before he could exonerate her. "Who is her family?"

Madam Chizuru named a clan that had served the Tokugawa for generations and lived on one of the shogun's distant estates. "She never sees her family. Her duties always kept her in Edo."

"Does she have any friends in town?" Sano said, still considering the possibility that the maid had somehow fallen in with a criminal who had forced her to report on Lady Keisho-in's movements to him and then kidnapped the women.

"Not that I'm aware of. Her whole life is spent here." Chizuru's gesture encompassed the Large Interior. "I doubt she even knows anyone outside the castle."

Suiren was looking more and more unlikely an accomplice in the crime, Sano thought. Perhaps there was no accomplice, and the Dragon King had learned about the trip from seeing Lady Keisho-in's procession, or from gossip. Yet Sano couldn't dismiss the accomplice theory just because his investigation of one suspect had come to nothing and he distrusted the man who'd invented the theory. The accomplice could be a palace official, guard, or servant— one of hundreds of people who'd known about the trip before the women left Edo. It could even be a member of Sano's household, where everyone had known Reiko and Midori were going to Mount Fuji with Lady Keisho-in. Sano was disturbed to think that a retainer or servant of his might have betrayed his trust. The prospect of investigating everyone daunted him, especially because the accomplice might not even exist.

But what other avenue of inquiry did Sano have that hadn't already led him to a dead end? He wouldn't know whether the Kii clan harbored any suspects better than the merchant Naraya until Chamberlain Yanagisawa told him. He might as well search for the accomplice. And he might as well continue here in the Large Interior, starting with the other people who'd accompanied the shogun's mother.

"Show me the rooms of all the women in Lady Keisho-in's entourage," Sano told Madam Chizuru.

They began with the ladies-in-waiting. Maybe Suiren had lived like a nun, but Sano discovered that these women hadn't. In their rooms he found gaudy clothing, hair ornaments, makeup, tobacco pipes, playing cards, musical instruments, and sake jars. He also found erotic pictures and carved jade phalluses apparently used for self-pleasure. Sano felt ashamed to discover the secrets of the dead women, especially since Madam Chizuru vouched for the good character of each. And he found nothing to indicate that they'd collaborated with the criminal who'd abducted their mistress. He believed they were all innocent victims, and his opinion of Hoshina's theory sank lower. After replacing their possessions in the cabinets, he turned to Chizuru.

"I'll inspect the maids' quarters now," he said.

The maids lived crowded into a communal room in a separate wing of the Large Interior. While Chizuru watched from the doorway, Sano went through the motions of examining the few cheap garments and trinkets left in the plain wooden cupboards by the maids killed during the massacre. As he pulled a blue-and-white-striped kimono from a drawer, something jingled. He put his hand into the sleeve of the garment and removed a cloth pouch tied with a drawstring. He emptied the pouch into his hand. Five gold coins gleamed up at him.

"Who owned this?" he asked, holding up the kimono for Chizuru to see.

"That belonged to Lady Keisho-in's youngest maid," Chizuru said. "Her name was Mariko." Her tone combined curiosity with apprehension. "What have you found?"

Sano showed her the coins. "How did Mariko come to have these?"

"I don't know." A troubled expression stole over Chizuru's face. "The servants get paid in coppers, not gold. It would have taken years for Mariko to earn that much money, and she'd only worked here six months."

"Where else might she have gotten the money?" Sano asked.

Chizuru shook her head. "Mariko came from a poor family."

A thrill of excitation reverberated through Sano as Hoshina's theory gained new credence. Sano conjectured that the money was a bribe from the Dragon King, and Mariko his spy who'd informed him about Lady Keisho-in's trip. Maybe she'd hidden the coins before she'd left because she didn't want to risk losing them or having them stolen on the highway. Maybe the Dragon King had killed her with the rest of the entourage to prevent her from ever exposing him.

Maybe she hadn't known how he'd meant to use the information she'd given him, or that she would never return to spend her blood money. And Hoshina's theory might prove correct even if he'd misidentified the Dragon King's accomplice. Maybe Sano owed Hoshina more respect than he'd paid him.

"Did Mariko go out of the castle after Lady Keisho-in announced her plans for the trip?" Sano said.

"As a matter of fact, she did." Chizuru spoke hesitantly, and Sano could see her thoughts following the same direction as his. "She asked permission to take the evening off, and I granted it."

"Why did you?" Sano knew that servants were traditionally allowed two days off work per year—one during the eighth month, and the other during the twelfth. The night before the trip qualified as neither holiday.

"Mariko said she wanted to visit her mother, who was very ill and might die while she was away," Chizuru explained. "I felt sorry for her, so I agreed." Horror ascended in Chizuru's intelligent eyes. "Do you think she went to tell the kidnappers about the trip instead of visiting her mother? She'd always been an honest, dutiful girl. I had no reason to think she was lying. If I'd suspected, I never would have let her go." The thought that she'd inadvertently abetted the crime caused Chizuru to lose her poise for the first time Sano had ever seen. She looked flustered and miserable.

"Maybe she didn't lie, and she was innocent," Sano said, tempering his suspicion that Mariko had done exactly as Chizuru suggested. "But I need to know where else she might have gone besides her mother's house."

Chizuru made a gesture that indicated her willingness to do whatever possible to atone for the wrong she feared she'd done. "I can show you the records, if you'll come with me."

She took Sano to a tiny cell near the laundry courtyard and opened a ledger that contained dossiers on everyone who lived in the Large Interior. "That's odd," she said, as her finger traced the lines of characters beneath Mariko's name. "The *metsuke* usually investigates all the palace servants and lists people who vouched for them. But the only information on Mariko is her mother's name and place of residence: 'Yuka, Umbrella-maker's Street, Nihonbashi.' "

Sano's suspicions about the maid deepened. How had she obtained employment here without references? How could the Dragon King have planted a spy in the innermost heart of the Tokugawa regime? A disturbing possibility that had been lurking in the back of Sano's mind now emerged into the forefront. Was the Dragon King someone in the regime, who could bypass rules while plotting against the shogun?

Innate caution warned Sano against jumping to premature conclusions and voicing this idea that would wreak havoc in the court. First he must determine whether Mariko had indeed been the kidnapper's accomplice.

"We'll ask the other women if they know where Mariko went that night," Sano said.

But when he and Chizuru questioned the maids, concubines, and ladies-in-waiting, they found that Mariko hadn't confided her plans to anyone. Everyone who'd known she had permission to leave the castle had believed her story about her sick mother.

"I'm sorry I couldn't help you," Chizuru said unhappily as she escorted Sano out of the Large Interior.

"You did help. You've shown me where to go next," Sano said. "Mariko's mother may have information about her daughter that could lead me to the kidnappers."

The door to the tower prison creaked open, and in strode two guards. Keisho-in and Lady Yanagisawa uttered startled exclamations; Midori squealed. Reiko experienced the frightening conviction that the men had come for her again, as she'd anticipated they would after they'd brought her back from the Dragon King's castle more than an hour ago. She and the other women cowered together, braced for some new horror.

But the men just herded them into a corner and stood watch over them. Six more guards entered. They mopped the floor, carried out the brimming waste buckets, and returned them emptied and cleaned, while the women watched in amazement. They brought bedding, *tatami* to cover the floor, hot water in a basin, and cloths for washing. They set out bowls of dried fish, pickled vegetables, fruits, and eggs, and pots of rice and tea, then departed the room, securing the door behind them.

Keisho-in immediately fell upon the food, wolfing it down with sloppy abandon. "At last, they've decided to show me some proper respect," she said. "It's about time."

"I think there's another reason for their generosity," Midori said with a smile at Reiko. "You must have made a good impression on their leader."

Lady Yanagisawa just eyed Reiko in speculative silence.

Reiko turned away from her friends, bent over the basin, and splashed water on her face, wishing she could cleanse away the fearsome impression the kidnappers' leader had made on her. The other women didn't know what had happened between her and their captor because she hadn't said; she didn't want to upset Midori or spur Keisho-in into another fit of rage. All she'd told them was that the man who called himself the Dragon King had given her food and not hurt her. She'd assured them that they were in no immediate danger, although the truth was that meeting the Dragon King had changed her own situation from bad to worse.

She looked at the cleaned room, and the furnishings and food the guards had brought. The Dragon King was wooing her with physical comforts. Reiko imagined what payment he expected. She shuddered, pressing a cloth over her face. But although she hated that she'd attracted an evil, unwanted admirer, she began to perceive that the Dragon King's attraction to her was a vulnerability that she could perhaps exploit to her advantage. She lowered the cloth from her face as ideas raced and schemes bred in her mind.

A gentle touch on her arm startled Reiko. She turned and saw Lady Yanagisawa kneeling beside her.

"There's more to the story of what passed between you and the Dragon King . . . is there not?" Lady Yanagisawa whispered.

Reiko didn't want to confide in the woman and encourage intimacy between them. But she owed Lady Yanagisawa for aiding the escape attempt and risking her own life. And Reiko needed to discuss her fears and schemes with someone.

She glanced at the other women, nodded covertly to Lady Yanagisawa, and whispered back, "I'll tell you later, when they're asleep."

20

Within hours after Sano had reported to him on the suspects Hoshina had implicated that morning, Chamberlain Yanagisawa rode down the main boulevard of the *daimyo* district with his entourage of bodyguards. The crowds of mounted and strolling samurai parted to make way for him. He and his entourage halted outside an estate whose double-roofed gate displayed the circular crest of the Kii clan. No sooner had they alit from their horses, than the sentries opened the portals for them.

"Good afternoon, Honorable Chamberlain," the sentries chorused, bowing.

Yanagisawa's high rank gave him the right to walk into almost any house, and he was especially confident of a warm welcome here. He strode into a courtyard, where soldiers loitered and a guard captain greeted him.

"Lord Kii is in the martial arts training ground," said the guard captain. "May I please escort you?"

"Never mind," Yanagisawa said. "I know the way."

As he and his men marched past the mansion's buildings, he put to use a lifetime of practice at hiding his emotions. His face was serene and his manner dignified, while his spirit writhed in agony, desperation, and terror. He didn't expect trouble from his impending talk with Lord Kii, *daimyo* of Sendai Province and head of the clan that

Sano had named as a suspect in the kidnapping. All his woe centered around Hoshina.

Try as he might, he couldn't expunge the awful memory of Hoshina begging for his life. He couldn't deny his guilt or shame at refusing to protect Hoshina, or the threat that had turned his own existence into a nightmare. He must save Hoshina, and not only because of his love for the man. Losing Hoshina and their partnership would weaken him politically, rendering him vulnerable to his foes, who included Lord Matsudaira. Should he lose the shogun's favor, they would hasten to attack him. His need to save Hoshina entwined with the absolute necessity of rescuing Lady Keisho-in and maintaining his power. Yanagisawa hoped that a talk with Lord Kii would further at least one of these purposes.

Lord Kii's martial arts training ground was a large, rectangular field, surrounded by stables and full of samurai. Two armies, differentiated by colored flags worn on poles attached to their backs, fought a mock battle. The soldiers charged on horseback across the ground and struck at one another with wooden practice swords. Dust flew and warwhoops rang out. Commanders shouted orders; signalers blew conch trumpets. Entering the ground, Yanagisawa spied Lord Kii.

The *daimyo*, clad in armor and a helmet crowned with golden horns, watched from astride his horse, amid his retainers, at one end of the field. His armor added bulk to his massive physique. As Yanagisawa gestured for his entourage to wait and approached Lord Kii, the *daimyo* turned toward him. An iron mask with a snarling mouth shielded his face. He raised a leather-gloved hand to his armies.

"Stop!" he bellowed.

The battle and noise ceased. The armies separated, lining up in ranks as Lord Kii dismounted and walked over to meet Yanagisawa. Lord Kii removed his helmet and mask, revealing a ruddy, smiling face that was shaped like a pumpkin and youthful despite his sixty years. Crinkles around his eyes, and a gap between his front teeth, increased his amiable appearance. Despite his size, his position as one of Japan's most powerful *daimyo,* and his enthusiasm for military training, Lord Kii was a meek, gentle-natured man.

"Welcome, Honorable Chamberlain," he said. He and all his troops bowed. "What a privilege it is to have you here."

"The privilege is mine," Yanagisawa said, pretending he hadn't just exercised his right to command Lord Kii's attention whenever he wanted. "Please don't interrupt your business on my account."

Lord Kii signaled his troops, and the battle resumed. His retainers moved away to give him and Yanagisawa privacy to talk. "If I'd known you wanted to see me, I'd have come to you," Lord Kii said with his usual eagerness to please. "But I'm glad of this chance to thank you again for your hospitality at the banquet seven nights ago."

"An evening's entertainment is the least I can give such a good friend as you," Yanagisawa said.

Over the years he'd given Lord Kii many gifts and favors, courting his allegiance. The old *daimyo* had repaid Yanagisawa by pledging him military support if and when needed. Lord Kii, though none too bright, knew how much authority Yanagisawa had over the *bakufu.* Yanagisawa had easily convinced Lord Kii that together they would come out on top of any power struggle. Furthermore, Lord Kii was too afraid of Yanagisawa to refuse him anything. The *daimyo* was the perfect ally: He had wealth, lands, and troops, but no ambition of his own. A born follower, he now belonged to Yanagisawa.

"I'm surprised that you have time to call on me, when the court must be in an uproar over the kidnapping," said Lord Kii.

"The kidnapping is why I'm here," Yanagisawa said. "We must talk."

"Certainly."

They walked to a stand of tiered planks, used as seats during tournaments, that extended along the field. They stood on the highest tier, in the shade of a canopy.

"Did you know that the kidnapper has demanded the execution of Police Commissioner Hoshina in exchange for returning Lady-Keisho-in?" Yanagisawa said.

"So I've heard," said Lord Kii. "How unfortunate for Hoshina-*san,* and for you, Honorable Chamberlain. Please accept my sympathy."

Yanagisawa watched the *daimyo* closely, but could detect no guile beneath his sincere manner. Apparently Lord Kii didn't know how the ransom demand related to him. "The investigation has focused on Hoshina-*san*'s enemies," Yanagisawa said. "The *sōsakan-sama* thinks those enemies include you. Because of our friendship, I've come to talk to you myself, instead of letting Sano-*san* interrogate you and blame you for the kidnapping."

But Yanagisawa had motives other than shielding Lord Kii from Sano. He wanted to test his hunch that Lord Kii was innocent of the crime and affirm the man's allegiance to him. He didn't want Sano to rush in here and cause trouble that might upset the balance of power. Even if Yanagisawa eliminated one suspect—and one chance to rescue Lady Keisho-in and stay Hoshina's execution—he would serve his other needs.

Lord Kii squinted in concentration, as he always did when exercising his limited intelligence. His gaze roved the battlefield. The army that sported red flags separated the opposing troops that wore blue flags, surrounded them, and knocked them off their horses in a clatter of wooden blades.

"But I didn't kidnap the shogun's mother," said Lord Kii. "Why should anyone think I would hurt Lady Keisho-in to destroy Hoshina-*san*?"

"Because of his role in your son's death," Yanagisawa said.

Memory and pain overshadowed Lord Kii's cheerful aspect. "The responsibility for the death of Mataemon belongs to himself alone," he said. "Mataemon didn't approve of my allying our clan to you. His disapproval led him to quarrel with Hoshina-*san.* Drawing his sword on Hoshina-*san* was a young man's foolish act that cost him his life."

This was the official story, Yanagisawa knew. He also knew the truth behind the story. Mataemon had pressured Lord Kii to desert Yanagisawa's faction and join Lord Matsudaira's instead. Yanagisawa and Hoshina had feared he might succeed, and had taken precautions. Hoshina had deliberately picked a quarrel with Mataemon, insulted the sensitive young man, and goaded him into drawing his sword in the palace. Mataemon had condemned himself to death, ridding Yanagisawa of a threat.

"I bear no enmity toward Hoshina-*san*," Lord Kii said now, "because I accept that my son was a casualty in the war of politics."

His earnest manner said he actually believed this line that Yanagisawa had fed him after delivering the news of Mataemon's fatal mistake. Lord Kii wasn't a complete fool, but he preferred to take the easy road. His mind spurned realizing that his master had destroyed his son, because admitting the truth would require him to exact revenge. And Yanagisawa thought Lord Kii was neither underhanded nor reckless enough to exact revenge by kidnapping the shogun's mother and demanding Hoshina's execution.

"Your attitude reflects your wisdom," Yanagisawa said. He watched Lord Kii smile with humble pleasure at the compliment. "But people who don't know you as well as I do might think you bear a grudge and wonder if you secretly want to punish Hoshina-*san*. The *sōsakan-sama* will wonder how and when you learned about Lady Keisho-in's trip."

Puzzlement creased Lord Kii's forehead. "Why, I learned about it from you, at your banquet, the night before Lady Keisho-in left Edo. Don't you remember telling me?"

"Of course I remember." Yanagisawa rested secure in his belief that his passing remark hadn't delivered Lady Keisho-in into the hands of the kidnapper. "And I'll tell the *sōsakan-sama* that even though you knew in advance about the trip, the information was safe with you because you would never hurt our lord's mother. But there's one small matter that might point his suspicion toward you."

"What is it?" Lord Kii said, looking more confused than ever.

"The *metsuke* has reported that a squadron of your retainers left Edo a few hours ahead of Lady Keisho-in," said Yanagisawa. "They traveled in the same direction along the Tōkaidō." Had he not known Lord Kii's lack of nerve as well as imagination, Yanagisawa would have deemed this evidence that the man had arranged the ambush. "Where did they go?"

"I sent them on business to Miyako."

"What business?"

"Why does it matter?" Now a beleaguered expression came over Lord Kii's face. Sweat trickled down his cheeks. On the battlefield, the Red Flag and Blue Flag armies charged and clashed again. Their ranks disarranged, while their commanders scolded them and the conch trumpets blared. "Why are you asking me these questions?"

"I need to know why your men were on the highway, near the place where the women were kidnapped," Yanagisawa said. "If you give me a good reason, I can explain to the *sōsakan-sama*, and he won't assume the worst. What were they doing?"

He expected his verbal finesse to counteract the offense his questions had given; he expected Lord Kii to answer because his ally never refused him anything. But Lord Kii gave him a blank stare that gradually filled with wonder, then dismayed enlightenment.

"I understand now," he said in the tone of a man just wakened from sleep and facing a harsh reality. "It's not the *sōsakan-sama* who thinks I've done something wrong, it's you." His finger pointed at Yanagisawa. Indignation raised his voice: "You're accusing me of sending my men to kidnap the shogun's mother!"

The conversation, which had been proceeding smoothly under his control, now hit dangerous ground with such abruptness that Yanagisawa didn't know quite how it had happened. He blinked, knocked off balance.

"I'm not accusing you of anything," Yanagisawa said,

aware of the need to placate Lord Kii and correct his misperception before the danger worsened. "You've misunderstood me."

Lord Kii appeared not to hear. Slowly he shook his head. "I sold my clan to you, even though Mataemon warned me that I shouldn't. Even after he died because I chose you over his wishes, I still honored our bargain because I had sworn loyalty to you. But now I see that Mataemon was right." Lord Kii reeled away from Yanagisawa; hurt welled in his gaze. "Now you repay my loyalty by accusing me of treason against the shogun!"

"I would never do that," Yanagisawa said with a vehemence born of his horror at seeing the fabric of their relationship torn apart. "Believe me, because I'm telling you the truth."

His thoughts flashed to the six thousand troops that Lord Kii commanded, and the vast fortune that would finance a coup. Yanagisawa must repair the damage to the alliance that was crucial to his bid for power and his defense against his enemies. He took a step toward Lord Kii, but the *daimyo* flung up his chain-mailed arms, repelling Yanagisawa's advance.

"You're a liar!" Lord Kii shouted as his hurt gave way to rage. "I knew your reputation when I accepted your favors. I should have known you would one day turn on me like a snake who bites the hand that feeds it. I was stupid to convince myself that allying with you would do me good. I was a disgraceful wretch to excuse your lover, who caused the death of my son, and to place my duty to you ahead of my own flesh and blood!"

Yanagisawa saw with fresh horror that he'd been wrong to think Lord Kii had forgiven his son's death or spared Hoshina the blame. The offense Yanagisawa had unintentionally given Lord Kii had ignited a cauldron of bitterness within the *daimyo*. Yanagisawa was abashed to discover that he'd misjudged the man he'd thought his tamed, subservient creature. He realized that the accusation Lord Kii had perceived was a heavy onus placed atop the other ills

Yanagisawa had caused him, and his tolerance for them had just snapped.

The old *daimyo* smote his gloved fists against his chest, punishing himself for his sins. "What a coward I was to bend to your will! How wrong I was to cast my lot with you, who've come to destroy me!"

"My only purpose is to clear you of suspicion and protect you from the *sōsakan-sama*," Yanagisawa said, anxious to win back Lord Kii's good will. "Please calm down, so you can recognize the truth."

Lord Kii folded his arms. "I do recognize the truth." Anger colored his face such a deep, purplish crimson that he looked ready to burst a vein. "You've got one eye on my troops, and the other on my treasury. You've used me and humiliated me. That you dare insult my honor has shown me the mistake I made in trusting you."

A thrill of fear coursed through Yanagisawa.

"I'll not be a fool or coward or disgrace any longer," Lord Kii declared. "Our alliance is severed."

Yanagisawa stood dumbfounded by shock as his mind absorbed the fact that he'd suddenly lost a major source of military backing. A new battle commenced on the training ground. This time the Blue Flag soldiers rallied. Their blades struck down Red Flag troops, who fell in the dust. As Yanagisawa experienced a sensation of the earth crumbling under his feet, outrage enflamed him. That his faithful dog should step out of line and deal him this blow! If reassurances wouldn't put Lord Kii back in his place, then perhaps intimidation would.

"Don't be so quick to break with me," Yanagisawa said in the quiet, venomous tone that had subdued many a man braver than Lord Kii. "You're in a dangerous situation. You have reason to want Hoshina-*san* dead. You had time to plan the ambush. Your men rode out on the Tōkaidō the same day as Lady Keisho-in. That makes you a primary suspect in the kidnapping. One word from me to the shogun, and you'll be arrested and stripped of your title, your lands, and your wealth."

A sharp intake of breath from Lord Kii, and a sudden fearful look on his face, gratified Yanagisawa.

"But if you uphold our alliance, I'll protect you. I won't let the *sōsakan-sama* persecute you, or the shogun think you kidnapped his mother." Yanagisawa infused his voice with all the coercion he could manage. "Just tell me why you sent your men on that journey. Give me proof that you're innocent, and everything will be the same as before."

Lord Kii vacillated, his gaze shifting, his eyes agleam with his terror of Yanagisawa's wrath. Yanagisawa waited, confident that he could overpower the *daimyo*. But although Lord Kii trembled like a tree cut at the base and ready to fall, he stood firm.

"I shouldn't need to prove to you that I'm not the kidnapper," he said, huffing with rage, fright, and wounded dignity. "My word should be good enough because I've never deceived you, and you should know I'm an honest man. If you don't trust me after all I've endured for you, then whatever I say won't convince you that I'm innocent. Go ahead and denounce me to the shogun, but first you'd better listen to this."

Vengefulness radiated from the *daimyo*'s armor-clad bulk. On the battlefield, his Blue Flag soldiers scattered and chased their opponents; they whooped in glee. "Yesterday, Lord Matsudaira came to see me. He proposed a marriage between his second son and my granddaughter." Lord Kii grinned in triumph at Yanagisawa. "I want you to be the first to know that I've just decided to accept Lord Matsudaira's proposal."

Terror thunderstruck Yanagisawa. That Lord Kii would agree to the marriage meant he was switching sides to the Matsudaira faction. The balance of power would tip away from Yanagisawa. When his other allies learned that Lord Kii had defected, other defections would follow. The odds that he could install his son as the next shogun had drastically diminished in a mere instant. So had his chances of surviving a change of regime. Yanagisawa recognized that his situation was desperate and called for extreme measures.

"Wait, Lord Kii," he said. "Before you act on your decision, please accept my apologies for offending you."

How the words rankled in his mouth! He rarely apologized to anyone; his rank exempted him from appeasing most other people. Lord Kii beheld Yanagisawa with obvious surprise that he would humble himself, but didn't answer.

"Know that I respect your fine intelligence, courage, and honor," Yanagisawa hastened to continue. "Your friendship is more precious to me than your army or treasury."

The flattering lies that usually rolled off his tongue now stuck in his throat because he resented groveling to someone of inferior status. Lord Kii stood silent and unmoved, waiting to see how much lower he would stoop. Tasting a mortification that sickened his spirit, Yanagisawa dropped to his knees before Lord Kii. He never knelt to anyone except the shogun, and every muscle stiffened with resistance; humiliation galled his pride.

"Please let us remain allies." Yanagisawa forced out the plea in a voice that he barely recognized as his own. Hot with shame and fury at his abasement, trembling in his terror, he gazed up at Lord Kii. "Please don't desert me."

Lord Kii only stared down at him with scorn. He uttered a laugh that expressed contempt toward Yanagisawa's begging, and enjoyment of their reversed positions. He said, "Leave my estate at once. Never come here again."

A sense of doom resounded through Yanagisawa. Before he could protest, Lord Kii called to his troops on the battlefield. They galloped over to him, primed for more combat.

"Training is over. Escort the honorable chamberlain off the premises," Lord Kii told the troops.

Yanagisawa had no choice but to descend from the stands and slink across the battlefield like a whipped dog, while Lord Kii gloated. The troops followed him and his entourage until they exited the gate. As the gate swung shut behind them, a funeral procession of chanting priests, bearers carrying a coffin, and somber mourners filed down the street. Bells tingled; drums throbbed. Yanagisawa stood isolated and stunned, regretting how badly his scheme had backfired.

He'd lost the ally whose support he'd wanted to confirm. Even worse, he'd accomplished nothing to advance the search for the kidnapper. He'd not obtained proof of Lord Kii's innocence and eliminated him as a suspect. Furthermore, the whole disastrous episode had shown Yanagisawa how seriously he'd misjudged the *daimyo*'s character, with disturbing consequences. It was now obvious that Lord Kii had nursed a grudge against Hoshina. Perhaps he'd also plotted revenge. If he had the nerve to repudiate Yanagisawa and the wits to understand that he could protect himself by joining the Matsudaira faction, then he wasn't as dull or meek as Yanagisawa had thought. Perhaps he had arranged the kidnapping.

But Yanagisawa had failed to find evidence that Lord Kii was the Dragon King, or leads to Lady Keisho-in's whereabouts. He'd gotten himself thrown out of the estate before he could even look for clues, and if he dared return, he might start a war that he couldn't win, because his power was on the downslide. The pounding of his heart, and the thunder of his blood, produced a roar in his ears like a distant avalanche tumbling toward him. Yanagisawa knew not what to do, except hope for Sano to solve the case, prevent Hoshina's execution, and spare Yanagisawa the downfall that would begin if no one rescued Lady Keisho-in.

21

Umbrellas, patterned in hues of red, pink, yellow, orange, blue, and green, bloomed like giant round flowers outside shops along the narrow street in the Nihonbashi merchant district. Inside the shops, the umbrella makers cut bamboo handles, glued paper to spokes, and painted designs. Customers haggled with clerks and departed carrying portable shade to protect themselves from the afternoon sun that rained heat upon the city. Sano and a squadron of detectives left their horses outside the neighborhood gate. They walked up Umbrella-maker's Street, jostling past an itinerant tea seller. Sano stopped a boy who toted a load of bamboo poles and asked, "Where can I find Yuka?"

The boy pointed down the block. Sano looked, and saw what he at first thought was a little girl wielding a straw broom, sweeping debris out of a shop. He led his men toward her, and closer appraisal showed her to be a diminutive woman, dressed in a faded indigo robe and white head kerchief. When Sano called her name, she stopped sweeping and lifted a round, pleasant face to him. Brown spots and faint wrinkles on its tanned skin marked her age at some thirty-five years. Sano observed that she seemed in good health, and certainly not on her deathbed, as her daughter, Mariko, had told Madam Chizuru.

"Yes?" She bobbed a quick bow. Her bright eyes regarded Sano and his men with shy curiosity.

Sano introduced himself, then said, "I've come to talk to you about your daughter."

"My daughter?" Yuka's gaze dimmed.

"You are the mother of Mariko, aren't you?" Sano said.

"Mariko?" The woman clutched her broom to her stubby, childlike body. Sano couldn't tell whether fright or simplemindedness caused her to echo his words without apparent comprehension. Then she nodded, her expression wary.

"I must ask you some questions about Mariko," said Sano. "Did she come to visit you seven days ago?"

"Visit me? No, master." Confusion wrinkled Yuka's brow.

Sano decided that Yuka wasn't simpleminded; she just feared authority, as did many peasants, and her repetition was a nervous habit. Yet although Sano recognized that this would be a difficult interview, and he must exercise restraint while asking a bereaved mother for information about her dead child, he felt none of the impatience that had hounded him while questioning the merchant Naraya.

He now knew that Mariko had lied about visiting her mother. The lie, coupled with the gold coins she'd hidden, fueled his suspicion that she was the Dragon King's accomplice. A growing certainty that he'd found a path to the truth infused Sano with an energy that calmed as well as elated him. Even while each passing moment heightened his desperation to find Reiko, for the first time he had faith that he would succeed.

"Then you didn't see Mariko before she went away on the trip," Sano clarified.

"Trip? What trip?" Yuka shook her head. "I didn't know Mariko was going away. I thought she was working at Edo Castle. I haven't seen her in six months." A shadow crossed her good-natured countenance: She'd begun to understand that a visit from the shogun's investigator boded ill for her. "Has Mariko done something wrong?"

Sano realized with dismay that Yuka didn't know her daughter was dead. Perhaps the Edo Castle officials who were responsible for notifying the families of Lady Keisho-in's murdered attendants hadn't gotten around to Yuka. She probably couldn't read and would have ignored the news broadsheets that had reported the massacre. The task of delivering the bad news fell to Sano.

"Come, let's sit down," he said, gesturing for his detectives to move away and give him and Yuka privacy.

He took the broom from Yuka and leaned it against the wall of the umbrella shop. They sat together on the edge of the shop's raised floor, in the shade beneath the eaves, and Sano gently explained to Yuka that her daughter had been killed. As he spoke, he watched shock and disbelief glaze her eyes, and horror part her lips. A whimper of anguish arose from her. Quickly she turned her face away to hide her grief.

"Please excuse me, master," she whispered.

Sano saw tears glisten down the curve of her cheek. His heart ached because he could imagine himself in her place, losing his own child. Feeling helpless to comfort her, he called to the tea seller and bought her a bowl of tea. Yuka drank, swallowing sobs, then hunched over the bowl in her hands, as though she craved its warmth even on this hot day. After she'd calmed, she began to speak in a wan, desolate voice.

"I knew Mariko would come to a bad end someday. But I don't know what went wrong."

Time pressed against Sano, and questions percolated in his mind, but he waited and listened. Yuka deserved the solace of speaking about her child, and he had a hunch that letting her tell her story in her own way could produce more valuable facts than would a formal interrogation.

"Her father died when Mariko was seven," Yuka said. "He used to work in the umbrella shop. The proprietor took pity on me and hired me as a servant. He let Mariko and me live in the back room. I have to work day and night. I couldn't watch Mariko. But at first I didn't worry, because she was so quiet, so obedient, so good. Even when she got older, I trusted her to look after herself. She wasn't a pretty girl—not the kind that boys chase."

Nor did Mariko sound like the kind of girl who would accept bribes to spy on her mistress. Sano experienced a qualm of doubt that she'd been the Dragon King's spy in Edo Castle. Would she turn out to be yet another dead end, despite her lie and her stash of gold coins?

"But two years ago, when she was thirteen, she started going out and staying away for days at a time. When I asked where she'd been, she wouldn't tell me. She got quieter and quieter as the months went by." Yuka's tone recalled the anger, puzzlement, and frustration that her daughter's behavior had caused her. "Even when I scolded and hit her, she kept her mouth shut and stared into space."

Sano's instincts quickened with the sense that he was going to learn something important. Here, he felt certain, began Mariko's odyssey from Umbrella-maker's Street to the Dragon King.

"One night, after Mariko had been away five days, I was wakened by the sound of moaning. I saw Mariko lying on the floor, writhing in pain and clutching her stomach and calling for help. I got up to see what was wrong. I thought she was sick. But a little while later, she gave birth to a baby boy. It was no bigger than my hand. It was born dead."

Yuka stared, her teary gaze remote, as though she watched the scene in her memory. "I'd had no idea that Mariko was with child. I asked who the father was. She just closed her eyes. I wrapped up the baby and put it in the garbage bin. I didn't want anyone to know she'd disgraced herself. I hoped she'd learned a lesson and would stop running around."

This common tale of a girl gone bad had a mysterious undertone that whetted Sano's appetite to hear more.

"But the next day, Mariko sneaked off again," Yuka continued. "She hadn't said a word about what happened! I only found out who the man was by accident, from a clerk in the shop. He said to me, 'I saw your girl in Ginza the other day.'

"Hiroshi-*san* had gone there on business and stayed so late that the gates were closed and he couldn't get home. He went to an inn to ask for lodging. A man came to the door and said, 'There's no room left.' Hiroshi-*san* thought that was strange, because the place was so quiet, it seemed empty. He looked past the man, into the building, and saw Mariko sitting there."

A signal chimed in Sano's mind, alerting him to a possible clue. He resisted the urge to interrupt Yuka with questions.

"I was so glad to find out where Mariko was," she said. "I begged Hiroshi-*san* to take me to her and help me bring her home. He's a kind man, so he agreed. The next day, we went to the inn together. We walked up to the door, and the man came out to meet us. I said, 'I've come to fetch my daughter, Mariko.' He said, 'She's not here.' I got angry because the moment I laid eyes on him, I knew he'd fathered the child. 'You're lying,' I said. 'Bring Mariko to me. I won't leave without her.'

"But then he called two big, mean-looking fellows out of the house and told them to get rid of me. They threw Hiroshi-*san* and me out the gate. He said, 'If you come back, they'll kill you.' Hiroshi-*san* and I went home. I knew Mariko had gotten mixed up with bad people, and I wanted to save her, but I didn't know what to do, where to turn. I just hoped she would be all right. I prayed for her to come home."

Yuka sat with head bowed and eyes downcast. "A whole year I waited, until last autumn. It was during the eighth month. Mariko came stumbling into our room at daybreak. She was panting, as if she'd run a long way. There were cuts and bruises on her face. Her clothes were torn and stained with blood. She smelled like smoke. She wouldn't tell me what had happened, but she clung to me and cried."

Last autumn . . . the eighth month. That time was indelibly etched into Sano's memory, associated with events he would never forget. A possible explanation for Mariko's strange behavior, and her condition that morning, occurred to him. He frowned as his perceptions shifted with an eerie feeling that the case had folded back upon itself and returned him to ground he'd abandoned after the ransom letter arrived. His heart began racing with excitement countered by disbelief.

"I washed Mariko and put her to bed," Yuka said. "For four days she wouldn't eat or do anything but lie there and weep. When she slept, she would cry out, 'No, no!' and act as if someone was attacking her." Yuka pantomimed, tossing her head and thrashing her arms. "She would wake up screaming."

Sano cautioned himself against seeing connections where none existed. He needed more evidence before he reverted to a theory that circumstances had proven wrong.

"I comforted her," Yuka said, "and after a while, she seemed calmer. Her wounds healed. She started eating and washing and dressing herself. I told her, 'The world is dangerous. If you go, you'll get hurt even worse. Stay here, where you'll be safe.' I thought Mariko understood. She stayed a month. She was polite and obedient and helped me with my work. But just as I began to believe she'd changed, she left again. The next time she came back was just before the New Year. There were two samurai with her. She said, 'Mother, I've come to say good-bye.' "

Weariness inflected Yuka's voice. "By that time I wasn't surprised by anything Mariko did. I said, 'Where are you going?' 'To Edo Castle,' she said. One of the samurai said, 'She's going to be a maid to the shogun's mother,' and they took her away. That's the last time I ever saw Mariko."

Another signal rang in Sano's head as he perceived another clue that tied Mariko to the kidnapping. He let a moment pass in silence, allowing Yuka her sad thoughts. Then he said, "The shogun has ordered me to find the person responsible for crimes that include the murder of your daughter. I need your help."

"Help?" Yuka looked up. Her face, streaked and mottled

red by tears, seemed to have aged a decade. "What could I do to help you?"

"Give me directions to the inn where you went looking for Mariko." Sano conjectured that the inn was where Mariko had gone the night before the trip.

"It's on a road that crosses the main Ginza street, eight blocks past the silver mint," Yuka said. "Turn left on the road. There's a picture of a carp on the sign at the inn."

"Can you describe the man you met there?" Sano said. Perhaps the man was the Dragon King or his henchman, as well as the father of Mariko's stillborn child.

Yuka pondered. "He was maybe thirty-five years old, and tall." Sano noted that almost anyone probably seemed tall to her. "He was handsome, but there was something about him that frightened me." She frowned in an effort to articulate her impression. "It was his eyes. They were so black, like he could see out of them, but I couldn't see in. I felt as if they could pull me into their darkness."

"Did you get his name?" Sano asked.

Yuka shook her head. Although Sano questioned her at length, she couldn't remember any more about the man. But perhaps the strange eyes would better serve to identify him than would details on his other features or his clothing.

"Who were the two samurai that came with Mariko the last time you saw her?" Sano said.

"I don't know," Yuka said. "They didn't introduce themselves. And I was too afraid to even look closely at them. But they wore crests like yours."

She pointed to the Tokugawa triple-hollyhock-leaf insignias on Sano's surcoat. A chill of dismay stole through Sano. If the men who'd taken Mariko to Edo Castle were indeed Tokugawa retainers, then here was more evidence that someone in the *bakufu* had planted her as a spy in the Large Interior. Sano quailed at the thought of telling the shogun that a traitor lurked within the regime. He dreaded extending the search for the Dragon King into the ranks of his comrades, and the peril that would result. Yet Sano had never backed away from danger while in pursuit of the truth. To save

Reiko and his lord's mother, he would take the investigation wherever he must.

"Mariko must have done terrible things that I never knew about." Yuka began to weep again. "Her death must have been the punishment she deserved."

"Perhaps not," Sano said, rising. "I think your daughter got involved with someone who forced her to do things she shouldn't have."

No matter if the evidence suggested that Mariko had been an accomplice in the kidnapping, Sano believed she'd also been an innocent victim, unaware of the Dragon King's evil schemes and in thrall to him. The mystery surrounding her life hinted at how she'd become his unwitting tool, and how various threads of the crime intertwined. Sano also believed Mariko had brought him a step closer to the Dragon King. Now he had additional reasons to persevere with his investigation, no matter the risk to himself.

"I promise to bring Mariko's killers to justice and avenge her murder," Sano told Yuka.

22

"I couldn't tell Midori or Lady Keisho-in everything the Dragon King did because I don't want to frighten them," Reiko said to Lady Yanagisawa. "But I'll tell you—if you can be brave enough to stand some bad news."

"Yes. I can," Lady Yanagisawa said eagerly, pleased that Reiko would confide in her, as she too seldom did.

It was early evening, and chill air crept into the prison. In the melancholy ocher light of sunset, Reiko and Lady Yanagisawa sat together in a corner, speaking in low tones while Midori and Keisho-in lay sleeping on the mattresses, covered by quilts. Mutters and shuffling noises came from guards stationed throughout the building. Birds cawed and flapped wildly in the trees outside; cicadas and crickets began their nocturnal dirge. A quickening breeze slapped waves against the base of the tower.

"I begged the Dragon King to let us go," Reiko said, "and he refused. He wouldn't even tell me where we are. When I asked why he's holding us prisoners, he said he wanted revenge—on someone he wouldn't identify, for some reason I couldn't understand. When I asked if he was going to kill us, he said he hoped not."

"What did he mean?" Lady Yanagisawa said.

Reiko uttered a forlorn laugh. "I suppose that whether we live or die depends on his whim."

Lady Yanagisawa experienced a dwindling hope of survival, yet their companionship eased her misery. She clasped Reiko's hands. "If we must die, at least we'll die together."

She felt Reiko flinch, and sensed that her friend was still withholding information. "Was there something else that disturbed you?" she said, and not only because she wanted to know what else had happened between Reiko and the man who called himself the Dragon King.

Ever since she'd first laid eyes on Reiko almost four years ago, she'd wanted to know everything about her. Reiko epitomized all that Lady Yanagisawa lacked. Reiko was beautiful, while Lady Yanagisawa was ugly. Reiko had a husband who adored her; Lady Yanagisawa agonized in unrequited love for the chamberlain, who barely seemed aware that she existed. Reiko had a child who was as perfect as Kikuko was defective. Envy had turned Lady Yanagisawa's interest in Reiko into an obsession.

Lady Yanagisawa had ordered her servants to find out from Reiko's servants everything that Reiko did. When Reiko went out, Lady Yanagisawa had followed her at a distance, spying on her. Last winter she'd formed an acquaintance with Reiko that permitted welcome opportunities to learn about her. Whenever she visited Reiko, she sneaked around the house and rummaged through Reiko's possessions. She memorized things Reiko said. She loved Reiko with an ardor that nearly equaled what she felt for her husband and daughter.

Yet deep within her smoldered a volcano of jealousy, fueled by anger that Reiko should have so much, and she so little. She bitterly resented that Reiko didn't value their friendship as much as she did; at the same time, she cherished a vague idea that if they grew close enough, some of Reiko's good fortune would magically transfer to her.

"The Dragon King behaved so weirdly," Reiko said with a shiver. She told how the Dragon King had stared at her, prowled around her, and talked in riddles. "He frightens me as much because I can't understand him as because he and his men murdered our entourage. The most I can figure out is that his reason for kidnapping us has something to do with a woman he once knew. It seems that her name was Anemone, and that I resemble her."

As she described how he'd given her a banquet, raged at her, and recited erotic poetry, Reiko slipped her hands from Lady Yanagisawa's grasp and twisted them together. Her eyelids lowered; her throat contracted. "Then he made improper advances toward me."

Her tone and expression conveyed the fear, disgust, and anger of a woman threatened by an assault on the virtue that society required of her. Lady Yanagisawa burned with outrage at the Dragon King. Yet although she wanted to kill him for upsetting her friend, her internal forces shifted with a queasy sensation, as if she'd suddenly spun around to behold a different view. Even while trapped in the middle of nowhere, Reiko was special. Her beauty set her apart from the other women. She had attracted the Dragon King, who'd given them better treatment because of her. He cared nothing for Lady Yanagisawa and hadn't summoned her, even though she outranked Reiko. Lady Yanagisawa wouldn't have wanted him to, but a perverse resentment stabbed her pride.

Would she never be allowed to forget that men desired Reiko and not her? Must circumstances always force her to remember that Reiko, not she, possessed the qualities that could win a husband's love?

Even now, with the threat of death menacing them all, her jealousy toward Reiko surged hot and turbulent within Lady Yanagisawa. She bowed her head, pressed her hands against her temples, and felt the blood throb under the skin.

"I never expected this," she muttered.

"Neither did I," Reiko said, obviously interpreting the comment as a response to her story and unaware of the direction that Lady Yanagisawa's thoughts had taken. "The Dragon King stopped short of ravishing me," she continued, "but what about next time? If no one rescues us first, what then?"

Reiko paced the prison, wringing her hands. "He'll take

me, while his men watch. If I resist, they'll kill me—and punish you, Midori, and Lady Keisho-in." Anger flamed in Reiko's eyes. "I hate being so helpless!"

Pity for Reiko abated Lady Yanagisawa's other emotions. She rose, moved behind Reiko, and lay a consoling hand on her shoulder. "There must be something we can do to escape."

Reiko whirled, turning a fierce gaze on Lady Yanagisawa. "Such as what?" she demanded. While Lady Yanagisawa stood mute, at a loss for answers, Reiko said, "Shall we break down the door and overpower the guards with our bare hands?" She pantomimed the actions. "Shall we walk across the lake and back to Edo Castle before the Dragon King's troops can catch us?"

Lady Yanagisawa shrank from Reiko's sarcasm. "I don't know what to suggest," she murmured. "I wish I did." She was hurt that the friend she loved should lash out at her, and beneath the hurt, the tide of her jealousy rose. Yet she hastened to appease Reiko, whose friendship she dreaded to lose. "I'm sorry if I've upset you. Please forgive me."

"It's I who should apologize," Reiko said, equally contrite. Midori stirred, Keisho-in mumbled in her sleep, and Reiko lowered her voice: "I shouldn't have taken out my anger on you."

They clasped hands. Lady Yanagisawa tried to believe that Reiko wanted to placate her because they needed each other, but the memory of their children and the pond in Reiko's garden on a day last winter nagged at Lady Yanagisawa. Had Reiko remembered that Lady Yanagisawa had the power to hurt her?

"Desperation is no excuse for rudeness," Reiko said. "Quarreling among ourselves does no good." She sighed, rubbed her forehead as if it ached, and resumed prowling about the room. "But how am I to protect myself from the Dragon King? He has swords; I have no weapons. He has an army, and we're four lone women. All the strength is on his side, all the weakness on mine."

"But you are so clever," Lady Yanagisawa murmured.

She knew that Reiko helped Sano with his work, which endeared her to him as much as did her beauty, charm, and the perfect son she'd borne. "Surely you can outwit the Dragon King."

Reiko halted her steps, and a thoughtful look narrowed her eyes. A ray of dying golden sunlight streaming through the roof illuminated her features as she motioned Lady Yanagisawa to follow her to the side of the room farthest from the door.

"The Dragon King does have one weakness," Reiko said in a conspiratorial whisper that the guards wouldn't overhear. "Desire for a woman can make a man vulnerable and careless. Maybe I can use his feelings for me as a weapon against him." Animated by hope, Reiko said, "Maybe I can trick him into setting us free."

Lady Yanagisawa enlaced her hands together under her chin as she brimmed with adoration for Reiko and faith in her abilities. "Oh, yes," she breathed. For the first time since their escape attempt had failed, she began to think they might soon go home. She might see her daughter and husband again. Reiko would deliver them all from this nightmare.

"Before I can trick the Dragon King, I'll have to gain his trust." Reiko focused her gaze inward, as if watching the sequence of events unfold in her mind. "To gain his trust, I would have to pretend I desire him. I would have to seduce him into letting down his guard." The animation faded from her. "I would have to welcome his lovemaking, and let him do whatever he wants with me until I can find a way for us to escape."

She was obviously disturbed by the realization that her chastity could be the price she must pay for the success of her plan. A needle of panic stabbed Lady Yanagisawa. Although she hated for Reiko to put herself in peril, the plan seemed their only chance of survival.

"Surely you could manage him so that we can get away before you have to . . . before he can . . ." Unaccustomed to talking about sex, Lady Yanagisawa could only hint at the horrible degradation that her friend risked.

"How can I control a madman?" Reiko whispered, incredulous. "What if the plan doesn't work? I'll have given myself over to him for nothing." She turned toward the wall, her back stiff. "I don't think I can do this." Her thin voice was a poignant plea for reprieve.

For once in her life, Lady Yanagisawa was glad to be ugly, because she couldn't attract the Dragon King's fancy, and she wouldn't have traded places with Reiko for anything in the world. Yet she still envied Reiko's beauty, which now represented a pass to freedom as well as love and marital happiness. Lady Yanagisawa wished she herself had the power to bend a man to her will, as she thought Reiko could bend the Dragon King. If she had it, she could make her husband love her. The jealousy burgeoned, poisoning her affection for Reiko. There seemed no end to Reiko's wonderful attributes. Lady Yanagisawa resented her dependency on Reiko, even as she relied on her friend.

Reiko haltingly turned, her face marred by pain and worry, her eyes glittering with tears. "But what alternative do I have, except to try to manipulate him? He's going to take me no matter what. I could tell from the way he looked at me, the way he touched me. My ravishment is inevitable."

Her body slumped in resignation. Then she straightened her posture, as if casting off fear and despair. "So I might as well try to turn the situation to my advantage, rather than surrender without a fight." Now she acquired the brave, determined air of a soldier marching into battle. Her gaze encompassed Lady Yanagisawa, Midori, and Keisho-in. "I'll do whatever it takes, and endure whatever I must, to save your lives."

"We shall all be most grateful to you." Though Lady Yanagisawa spoke the truth, she experienced another onrush of jealous anger. Reiko was not only beautiful, she was so noble that she would sacrifice herself for the sake of other people. As Lady Yanagisawa gazed upon Reiko, her tolerance for Reiko's perfection abruptly snapped, like ice on a pond whose waters have suddenly heated to a seething boil. She clenched her hands so tight that her fingernails dug painful crescents into her palms.

Even here, in this miserable prison, Reiko shone like a bright flame, while Lady Yanagisawa was but a dreary shadow. Lady Yanagisawa couldn't bear the contrast between them. Now her anguish swung her to the opposite pole of her love for Reiko. Fevered by hatred, she wanted to see Reiko brought down, her perfection despoiled, her husband, son, and other blessings torn from her. Lady Yanagisawa knew that her wish to ruin what she couldn't have was pointless; destroying Reiko's good fortune wouldn't improve her own. She'd tried that once, and realized the error of her thinking. Yet she still believed in her heart that the universe contained a limited supply of luck, and Reiko had more than her share. She clung to the idea that by taking action against Reiko, she could sway the balance of the cosmic forces and win the happiness that was rightfully hers.

But how could she attack Reiko when they must stand united against their enemy? How could she satisfy her urges without jeopardizing her chance for freedom?

"I've never done anything like this before," Reiko said, her face taut with apprehension. "How should I go about it?"

"You'll know what to do when the time comes," Lady Yanagisawa said.

And so will I, she thought.

23

Before Sano traveled to the inn where Mariko had been seen, he went home and assembled a squadron of twenty detectives, because he had a hunch about what he would find at the inn, and he anticipated needing military force. Now, after another sultry night had descended upon the town, he and his men arrived in the Ginza district, named for the silver mint established there more than eighty years ago by the first Tokugawa shogun.

Ginza was a drab backwater located south of Edo Castle. To its north spread the great estates of the *daimyo*; to the south, upon land reclaimed from Edo Bay, the Tokugawa branch clans maintained wharves and warehouses for storing rice grown in their provinces. To the west, the Tōkaidō ran through the outskirts of Edo, while to the east lay a district of canals used to transport lumber. Sano rode with his troops up the Ginza main avenue, past the fortified buildings of the mint and the local official's estate, and through a sparse neighborhood of shops, houses, and fire-watch towers. Lights shone in windows and at gates to the side streets, and voices sounded from balconies and open doors, but the streets were empty.

At the eighth block, Sano and the detectives dismounted outside the gate, left the horses with one man guarding them, and stole on foot up a street that wound into darkness relieved only by the bleached, ovoid moon that hung low

above the distant hills. They filed noiselessly past warehouses closed for the night, to Ginza's southern edge. Here,
the merchant quarter yielded to rustic cottages interspersed
with woodland. The road ended at a high plank fence that
enclosed thatch-roofed buildings amid trees. A signboard
on the gate displayed a crude drawing of a carp and the
characters for "inn."

Faint light diffused up from within the enclosure, but as
Sano and his men gathered silently outside, he heard nothing except insects shrilling in the trees and dogs barking
far away. He and Detective Inoue peered through cracks in
the gate. Sano saw a garden and a short gravel path to the
inn. A glowing lantern hung from the eaves above its entranceway. Two samurai stood on the veranda, motionless
yet alert—guarding the inn from trespassers. Their presence
told Sano that the inn was what he'd deduced it was from
hearing the strange tale of Mariko. His heartbeat accelerated
with excitement as he and his detectives retreated from the
inn.

"Sneak inside over the fence. Subdue the guards in front,
and any others you find," Sano told Detective Inoue and
four other men. "When you're done, let the rest of us in
the gate."

The detectives slipped away. Ages seemed to pass while
Sano waited in the dark road, but soon the gate opened.
Inoue beckoned Sano, who hurried over with the other de-
tectives.

"We found eight guards," Inoue whispered to Sano as
they ushered their troops through the gate. "They're all unconscious now. Otherwise, the place seems deserted."

Drawing their swords, Sano and his men moved cautiously up the path, toward buildings grouped among the
trees and connected by enclosed walkways. The windows
were shuttered, and the buildings gave no sign of occupa-
tion, but a strange, rhythmic pulsation resounded up
through the ground.

"Do you hear that?" Sano whispered.

His men nodded, their faces grim because they recognized the sound from previous, similar missions. They roved the compound, trying to locate its source. Sano pointed to a small storehouse with a tile roof and thick plaster walls. Inoue yanked on the ironclad door. As it swung open, the sound intensified. Sano discerned voices chanting and drums beating; cries, moans, and a familiar, pungent odor of incense drifted into the night. He peered inside the storehouse. In the center of the bare wood floor, a ladder extended down a square hole from which arose smoke, flickering light, and the noise.

"We're going down there," Sano said.

Eight of his men plunged into the hole to scout the way. Sano clambered down the ladder, his other men following, into a dank, earthy-smelling shaft. The chanting, drumming, and cries enveloped them. At its bottom they crowded into a cellar illuminated by a glow that filtered through a curtained doorway. From this emanated the noise, deafening now. Sano hastened to the doorway and lifted the curtain. In a cavernous room hollowed out of the earth, women wearing red kimonos danced in frenetic gyrations, waving black-beaded rosaries. Men dressed in gray monks' robes, their heads shaved, beat drums as they cavorted around the room. On the floor, countless naked people writhed and embraced in sexual orgy. Wails of rapture or pain rose from couples and groups of various shapes, ages, and erotic combinations. Along the far wall, hundreds of candles flared amid hundreds of smoking incense burners on an altar beneath a mural that depicted a huge black flower.

The cavern was a secret Black Lotus temple. The orgy was one of the sect's rituals.

"Praise the glory of the Black Lotus!" chanted the drummers and dancers.

Disgusted at the obscene spectacle, Sano stepped into the temple with his detectives. The outlaws were so caught up in their drumming, chanting, and sexual hysteria that they didn't notice the intrusion. Among them strode their priest, a tall man who wore a glittering brocade stole over his saffron robes and held a flaming torch. His eyes were closed, but his bare feet wove deftly through the orgy. His bold-hewn features wore an expression of unnatural serenity. His lips formed soundless words; ash and sparks from his torch scattered on his congregation.

Sano inhaled a deep breath, then roared, "Stop!"

Dancers faltered to a standstill. The drumming pattered into silence as the monks froze. The mass of humanity on the floor ceased squirming. Its cries and wails faded. The priest paused midstep; his eyes opened. Everyone gazed in consternation at Sano, his troops, and their upraised swords. The cavern amplified the hiss of inhaled breath.

"This temple is condemned," Sano said. "You're all under arrest for practicing an illegal religion."

The naked orgiasts leapt to their feet and surged toward the door, heedless of the detectives' weapons: They knew that the punishment for their crime was execution, and they would risk injury to escape. The men bellowed and the women screamed. Hot, moist flesh hurled up against Sano. The detectives seized dancers and drummers, who kicked and fought. Sano looked around for the priest. Beyond the tumult, he saw the flash of a brocade stole disappearing through a doorway. Shoving his way past thrashing bodies, he plunged through the door and found the priest scrambling up a ladder. Sano grabbed the priest by the ankles and jerked. The priest came toppling down on Sano. They fell together.

"The Black Lotus will triumph over the faithless!" the priest shouted, punching Sano. "They who attack us will die!"

Blows pummeled Sano's face while he tried to shield it. He heaved upward and rolled the priest under him. The weight of his armor-clad body flattened the priest. Sano pinned the priest's arms over his head. In the light from the temple, where noisy chaos still raged, Sano beheld the face of his captive.

Eyes with pupils dilated so large that there seemed no color surrounding them glared fiercely back at Sano. *They were so black, like he could see out of them, but I couldn't see in,* he recalled Yuka saying. This was the man who had pulled her daughter, Mariko, into the darkness of the Black Lotus sect.

Was he also the Dragon King?

"Who are you?" Sano shouted into the priest's face. "Tell me your name!"

The priest snarled, baring broken, sharp-edged teeth. "I am Profound Wisdom, lord of cosmic forces that will destroy you and all your fellow nonbelievers."

Amazement silenced Sano. He had found the Black Lotus priest and secret temple he'd sought at the beginning of the investigation.

Sano's troops had overpowered the Black Lotus worshipers. Two monks had committed suicide to avoid capture. Four people had been trampled to death while trying to escape. Sano had sent most of his men to take the remaining Black Lotus members to Edo Jail and notify Ginza officials about the raid. Now he and two detectives stood in a chamber at the inn, where they'd brought Profound Wisdom for interrogation.

The priest knelt beneath a lantern suspended from the ceiling. His hair was rumpled, dirt streaked his perspiring skin and dimmed the glitter of his stole, but his upright posture exuded insolence. The unnatural serenity masked his emotions. His fathomless black eyes watched Sano, who paced around him while one detective blocked the door and the other leaned against the barred window. Outside, torches flared and figures moved in the yard as local officials came to inspect the clandestine temple that had operated under their noses.

"Did you kidnap the shogun's mother?" Sano said.

He forced himself to be civil, though the priest's demeanor stoked his hatred for the Black Lotus. Captured sect members relished goading authorities into physical violence that would allow them to test their faith and demonstrate their spiritual superiority. Sano knew that if he got into a fight with Profound Wisdom, he was capable of killing the priest, a collaborator in the enslavement, torture, and murder of countless innocent people. If he killed Profound Wisdom, he might never get the information that would help him save Reiko.

Scorn rippled the surface of Profound Wisdom's serene façade. "If I did kidnap Lady Keisho-in, I would not tell you." He had an odd, deep, resonant voice, as if his throat were made of iron instead of flesh. "My spirit is mighty. You won't wring a confession out of me."

Sano controlled his impatience. He recognized Profound Wisdom as one of the Black Lotus's true zealots—armed with the courage of his faith, resistant to coercion. "Then suppose we just talk about your followers," Sano said.

"I'll not reveal the identities of the Black Lotus faithful who are still at liberty." Profound Wisdom sat unmoving as Sano continued to circle him. "Torture me, kill me, but I won't betray my people and send them to their death."

"I'm not interested in making a martyr out of you," Sano said. "And the only follower I want to know about is already dead. She died in the massacre of Lady Keisho-in's entourage. Her name was Mariko."

"I don't know any Mariko," the priest said.

His indifferent tone and manner would have fooled Sano, had he not known that Profound Wisdom was lying. Sano said, "She joined the Black Lotus two years ago." When her mother had told him about Mariko's changed personality and mysterious absences, Sano had recognized the behavior of youngsters lured into the sect. "She's been seen with you."

"Many people come to me," Profound Wisdom said. "So many that it is impossible for me to know them all."

"She was at the Black Lotus Temple during the disaster," Sano said. This explained why Mariko had returned home wounded, bloody, and hysterical that night. "She was one of the few survivors who escaped. And she was your mistress. You fathered her child."

"Our rituals require me to have so many women that I

can't recall each one," Profound Wisdom said with a patronizing smile. "Sexual energy fosters spiritual enlightenment."

A clever excuse for orgies, Sano thought in disgust. "Did Mariko come here seven days ago?" he said.

"If so, I don't recall," Profound Wisdom said smugly.

As ire enflamed Sano, he squatted before the priest. He stared through the deep eyes, into a reservoir of madness. "Either you start telling the truth about Mariko, or—"

"Or you'll kill me?" Profound Wisdom sneered. "I'll be executed no matter what I do. So I choose not to talk. There's nothing you can threaten me with that will keep me from taking my secrets to the grave."

Sano said, "I can hold you in jail while I spread word that you named your leaders and told the *bakufu* where to find them. They'll send their assassins after you. You'll be condemned as a traitor to the Black Lotus and never achieve spiritual enlightenment."

The mockery in Profound Wisdom's eyes ignited into alarm. "No!" he bellowed.

"Yes," Sano said, gratified by the priest's reaction. He'd learned from past experience that the worst thing one could do to a Black Lotus member was turn the wrath of the sect on him. The Black Lotus could infiltrate any place and dispense death in painful ways that put the Edo Jail torturers to shame. And zealots like Profound Wisdom believed that the sect had the power to deny them the glory of enlightenment and doom them to burn in a hellish netherworld for all eternity.

Profound Wisdom lunged toward the door. The detectives caught him and shoved him down on his knees. Sano stood over him. "Did Mariko come here seven days ago?" Sano repeated.

Fists clenched, the priest huffed at Sano as though ready to explode from hatred. Then the breath seeped out of him; defeat slackened his face and posture. "She did," he muttered.

"Why?" Sano said.

"To report on the shogun's mother. She said Lady Keisho-in was planning to travel the next day."

Vindication elated Sano: His theory had proved correct. "So Mariko got permission to leave Edo Castle that night because she wanted to see you," he said. "She was your spy."

And Profound Wisdom appeared a likely suspect in the kidnapping. A leader in a sect persecuted by Police Commissioner Hoshina, the priest boasted many followers willing to kill for revenge. The bizarre poem about the Dragon King seemed a product of his insanity.

But Profound Wisdom shook his head. "Not my spy."

"Then why did she report to you?" Sano asked as his elation turned to confusion.

"The news Mariko brought was for someone else."

"For whom?" Sano said, increasingly baffled.

"A man. He worships at my temple," Profound Wisdom said. "Mariko came here to see him. He wasn't here. She left the message in case he should come, then went to look for him."

Now it appeared, to Sano's disappointment, that Profound Wisdom was neither the Dragon King nor the final stage in the search for Reiko. "Who is this man?" Sano said.

"I don't know," the priest said sullenly.

Sano gripped his stole. "Tell me, or the word goes out right now that you betrayed the Black Lotus."

Although Profound Wisdom recoiled in terror, he cried, "I speak the truth! I don't know his name."

Sano flung Profound Wisdom down; he folded his arms and waited. Eager to placate Sano, the priest explained, "He joined the Black Lotus about three years ago. One day this past winter, he said he needed a quiet, obedient girl to work for him. I introduced him to Mariko. He got her a position as a maid to the shogun's mother. She was supposed to find out whenever Lady Keisho-in was leaving the castle, where she was going, and what route she would be taking. Mariko would either tell me or send me a message, and I would relay the news to the man when he came to the temple."

Now Sano speculated that this unknown man was the Dragon King. He must have been looking for the right opportunity to abduct Lady Keisho-in. But Sano wondered how he'd gotten Mariko a position in Edo Castle. And Profound Wisdom's tale struck a note of disbelief in Sano.

"Since when do you, a high Black Lotus priest, do favors for a follower whose identity you don't even know?" Sano said.

"Since he became a patron of the Black Lotus," said Profound Wisdom. "He gave me large donations. He paid me for Mariko, and for taking her messages for him. I did other things for him, too."

Money bought service even from Black Lotus priests who usually tyrannized their followers, Sano noted. It also helped the sect survive in a hostile climate. Sano deduced that Mariko had met the man that night, and he'd paid her in gold coins, which she'd hidden in her room until she could give them to her priest.

"Later on the night that Mariko brought her message," Profound Wisdom said, "the man came here. He wanted some good fighters. I asked why, but he just counted money into my hand. I gathered eighty-five *rōnin* and some peasant toughs and sent them to Shinagawa to meet him the next day."

A thrill of revelation sped through Sano's veins. Shinagawa was the Tōkaidō post station nearest Edo. The man, whom Sano now believed was the Dragon King, had borrowed an army to pursue Lady Keisho-in's party, massacre her attendants, and kidnap the women. His initial hunch had been half right: The Black Lotus was involved in the crimes, though not chiefly responsible for them. The merchant Naraya had spoken a partial truth when he'd blamed the kidnapping on the Black Lotus. But Sano's thrill immediately turned to horror.

Black Lotus samurai were a vicious scourge that killed at the slightest provocation. Now Sano's earlier fears gained substance. The Black Lotus had Reiko. Although her role in High Priest Anraku's downfall had been hushed up, the secret could have leaked. If the Black Lotus kidnappers knew what she'd done, Reiko was doomed no matter what plans the Dragon King had for her.

"How can you not know who the man is?" Sano said as his terror boosted his ill will toward Profound Wisdom. "I thought you Black Lotus priests were supposed to be all-seeing, all-knowing. What happened? Did your spies let you down?"

Crestfallen, Profound Wisdom twisted his mouth. "I had them follow the man every time he left the temple. Every time, they lost him. He was good at sneaking away."

"Describe what he looks like," Sano said, avid in pursuit of the Dragon King, who seemed almost close enough to touch yet still eluded him.

The priest scrutinized Sano, using him as a standard of comparison. "He's younger and heavier than you. His eyes are rounder, his lips puckered."

That description fit thousands of men. Sano's hopes waned. "Is he a samurai or commoner?"

"I don't know. He always wears a hood under his hat." The hood had concealed whether the Dragon King had the shaved crown and topknot of the warrior elite. "But he didn't wear swords."

Then he could be a peasant, artisan, or merchant—or a samurai disguising his class. "Was there anything notable about his voice or manner?" Sano asked.

"His voice was deeper and quieter than yours. He moved as if . . ." The priest searched for the right words. "As if he was afraid but wanted everyone to think he was brave."

This detail might help identify the man—if Sano could find him first. "Did he say or do anything that gave you any information about him?"

Profound Wisdom meditated, the blackness of his eyes deepening with recollection. "He paid me to conduct a ritual for him. He wanted to communicate with someone who had died."

Certain Black Lotus priests claimed the ability to speak

to the dead and receive messages from them, Sano knew. "Who was it?" His instincts vibrated alert as he sensed the advent of a clue.

"A woman. He said her name was Anemone."

"What happened?"

"The ritual was held in the temple here," Profound Wisdom said. "I went into a trance, and I felt a gate within my mind open to the spirit realm. I called out, 'Hail, spirit of Anemone. Please come and speak.' "

Sano had once raided another temple during a similar ritual, and he could picture Profound Wisdom seated on a dais, eyes closed in concentration, while monks and nuns chanted prayers. He imagined the flickering candlelight, heavy incense smoke, and the mystical atmosphere that induced the crowd of eager onlookers to believe in the priest's fraud.

"A woman's voice spoke from my mouth," Profound Wisdom continued. "It said, 'I am here. Why do you summon me?' The man grew very excited. He cried, 'Anemone! It is I. Do you recognize me?' "

Sano envisioned a hooded figure kneeling in supplication before Profound Wisdom, who'd impersonated the dead woman.

"The spirit answered, 'Yes, my dearest,' " said Profound Wisdom. "The man began to weep. He said, 'Anemone, I will avenge your death. Your spirit can rest in peace after the man who was responsible for your murder is punished.' She whispered, 'Avenge my death. Punish him.' Then the gate to the spirit world closed. My trance broke. The man jumped up and shouted, 'No! Anemone, come back!' "

Even though the priest was a charlatan, he knew how to tell people what they wanted to hear, Sano thought; and by echoing the man's words instead of inventing conversation, and cutting short the ritual, Profound Wisdom had avoided exposing the spirit as a fake. Yet Sano was more struck by the significance of what the man had said than impressed by Profound Wisdom's cleverness. He stood immobile while his thoughts registered the one potential clue in Profound Wisdom's story and raced on to strategies for connecting it to the Dragon King. Outside, lanterns lit the yard bright as day as laborers hauled loads of dirt to fill in the underground temple. Profound Wisdom eyed Sano with a contempt that didn't hide his fear.

"I've told you everything I know," he said. "Is it enough that you won't brand me a traitor?"

"Enough for now," Sano said, though the clue was tenuous.

"What are you going to do to me?"

"I'll let you live awhile, in case you remember anything else about the man." Sano addressed his detectives: "Take him to Edo Jail. Okada-*san*, you guard him so that nothing bad happens to him. Watanabe-*san*, tell Magistrate Ueda that I ask him to delay Profound Wisdom's trial because he's a witness in the kidnapping investigation. I'm going back to the castle. I'm late for my meeting with Chamberlain Yanagisawa."

"I'm certain that the murder of Anemone is the murder that the ransom letter refers to, and the motive behind the kidnapping," Sano said.

"And you suggest we investigate your theory that the mysterious Black Lotus follower is the Dragon King?" said Chamberlain Yanagisawa.

"I do."

Midnight had passed while Sano rode from Ginza to Edo Castle. Now he and Yanagisawa sat in the chamberlain's estate, in an office whose walls were hung with maps of Japan. Sano had just finished telling Yanagisawa about Mariko, the gold coins, the visit to her mother, and the raid on the Black Lotus temple. In the grounds outside the open window, cicadas droned; torches carried by patrolling guards smeared smoky light across the darkness. Sano reflected that crises forged strange alliances. He and Yanagisawa had become a partnership he'd never thought possible.

"If my memory serves me well, there was nobody named Anemone on your list of deaths associated with Police Commissioner Hoshina," said Yanagisawa.

He was as immaculately groomed and stylish as always, but dark hollows circled his bloodshot eyes. His long fingers tapped a nervous rhythm on the desk. Sano deduced that something even worse than the problem of Hoshina had beset him since they'd last met that morning. But he'd volunteered no explanation, and politeness forbade Sano to ask.

"You're right. Anemone wasn't on the list," Sano said.

"Then according to Hoshina, he didn't kill the woman," Yanagisawa said, "so why would the kidnapper blame her murder on him, or want him executed for it?"

"Your guess is as good as mine." A thought occurred to Sano. "It's possible that the Dragon King blames Hoshina for a death that wasn't his fault at all." Sano realized with chagrin that his own dislike of Hoshina had led him to assume Hoshina was guilty as accused. "Maybe the Dragon King has kidnapped Lady Keisho-in to force the execution of the wrong person."

"In that case, the list is useless," Yanagisawa said, "and we've been hunting suspects in the wrong places."

The thought of a day wasted, and the women still missing, weighed heavily upon the hot, close atmosphere. "But at least we have a new, better suspect," Sano said.

Yanagisawa emitted a mirthless chuckle. "A suspect with no name, and his whereabouts unknown. How do you know that Black Lotus priest didn't invent him to save his own skin? We can't afford to squander any more time on fruitless chases."

"What choice do we have except to investigate the man?" Sano said, although he shared Yanagisawa's misgivings. "I've run out of ideas. My men have been looking for the person who posted the ransom letter, but with no luck. I talked to the merchant Naraya today, and I don't think he kidnapped the women." Sano described his interview with Naraya. "May I ask if you questioned the Kii clan members? Are they any likelier culprits than Naraya?"

Yanagisawa inhaled on his tobacco pipe and expelled smoke that obscured his features. "I don't know."

His curt tone prohibited Sano from asking for details. "Then what do you suggest we do?" Sano said.

"My troops can go hunting Lady Keisho-in, as I proposed at the start. That would be a better strategy than searching for a man who may not exist." Grimness hardened Yanagisawa's bloodshot eyes. "I spent the evening with the shogun, listening to him fret about his mother. He's threatening to execute Hoshina, send out the army, and banish you and me for floundering in the dark. We may not be able to stall him for the seven days he gave us."

"We must," Sano said, as strongly opposed to Yanagisawa's plan as ever. Increasing desperation would make the chamberlain more ruthless in his desire to save Lady Keisho-in, and more careless toward Reiko and Midori. "Going after the kidnappers is too dangerous for the hostages. At least wait until we know who the Dragon King is. Maybe then, when we understand him, we can find a way to persuade him to return the women without a battle that could kill them."

And although Sano had no news from Hirata, he still hoped his retainer would find the hostages so that when the time came for a rescue mission, he could plan how best to stage it.

The chamberlain sat silent, his thumb and forefinger bracketing his chin, while he considered Sano's arguments. Obstinacy hardened his gaze.

"If your troops should bungle the rescue because they don't know where to go or whom they're dealing with, and Lady Keisho-in dies, you'll be in worse trouble than you are now," Sano reminded Yanagisawa.

A moment passed as they stared each other down. Outside, the whine of the cicadas rose to a frenetic pitch. Then Yanagisawa dropped his hand from his chin.

"All right," he said, "you win—for now." But Sano had

barely relaxed, when Yanagisawa added, "You have until noon to look for your mystery suspect. After that, I take over the investigation, and my troops will march." His eyes narrowed in challenge. "Where do you propose to begin your search?"

The short time frame dismayed Sano. He rejected the idea of asking Hoshina about Anemone's murder, because wouldn't Hoshina have already mentioned it if it had anything to do with him? Then inspiration awakened in Sano. He looked out the window. The density of the darkness had lessened, but dawn was some hours away.

"It's a little early to call on a *metsuke* intelligence agent," Sano said, "but I daresay the circumstances justify rousting him out of bed."

24

A loud moan broke the silence of the tower prison. Reiko emerged from fitful slumber, her eyes squinting in the faint gray moonlight. Across the room she saw Midori sitting up on her futon, arms cradling her belly. Pain drew her features into a grimace as she moaned again. Reiko flung off her quilt. Shivering in the chill, she hastened to kneel by Midori's side.

"Midori-*san,* what's wrong?" Reiko said.

"A bad cramp woke me up. It's stopped now." Midori's grimace relaxed into a look of shame. "I've wet the bed."

Reiko looked down and saw a bloody stain spreading over Midori's futon and puddling on the floor. She felt its liquid warmth seep through her kimono and dampen her knees.

"Oh, no," she said, grieved by the realization that the event they'd hoped would wait until they got home was happening now.

Lady Yanagisawa sat up in bed, clutching the quilt to her chin, blinking in sleepy confusion. Lady Keisho-in flopped onto her side and said in a hoarse, cranky voice, "What is it?"

"Midori's water has broken," Reiko said. "Her labor has started."

The streets of the Hibiya administrative district were deserted except for watchmen dozing in guard booths outside the walled mansions, and dark except for lamps burning over the gates. Sano dismounted outside the mansion that belonged to Toda Ikkyu. An especially high wall secluded the premises from neighbors, who probably didn't know Toda was a spy for the *metsuke*—the Tokugawa intelligence service that guarded the shogun's power over Japan. Sano knew that Toda maintained an unobtrusive profile, the better to spy upon his *bakufu* colleagues.

"Tell your master that the shogun's *sōsakan-sama* wishes to see him at once," Sano ordered the watchman.

His title and authoritative manner brought quick results despite the fact that he'd arrived in the dead of predawn. A household retainer ushered him into a reception room that was decorated with bland, conventional landscape murals which seemed meant to hide rather than reveal its owner's character. Soon a man appeared, barefoot, clad in a gray dressing gown, his eyes puffy with sleep.

"Good evening, *Sōsakan-sama*," he said. "Or should I say good morning?"

"Good morning, Toda-*san*." As they exchanged bows, Sano covertly studied his host to make sure he was really Toda. The spy was so nondescript that Sano always had difficulty recognizing him. He looked like anyone and no one, an advantage in a profession that depended on his avoiding notice. But his world-weary voice and manner jibed with Sano's vague memory of Toda.

"I doubt this is a social call," Toda said. "To what do I owe the honor of your presence?"

"I have a favor to ask," Sano said.

Toda grimaced. "Why am I not surprised?"

Sano had consulted Toda during past investigations because Toda had access to facts about many citizens, gathered by a legion of spies and informers all over the country.

"What do you want this time?" Toda said with veiled annoyance. He didn't like sharing information; the *metsuke* jealously hoarded knowledge, the basis of their unique power.

"I need your help identifying a man I believe to be the kidnapper of Lady Keisho-in," said Sano.

Toda's eyes registered awareness that he had better cooperate. If Lady Keisho-in wasn't rescued and the kidnapper brought to justice, the shogun would likely punish the whole *bakufu,* including the *metsuke* spies, who were responsible for discovering and neutralizing threats to the Tokugawa.

"What's the matter? Have you abandoned your theory that the Dragon King is one of Police Commissioner Hoshina's old enemies?" Toda could never resist a sly rejoinder. "Did the Kii clan and the merchant Naraya prove not to be the culprit?"

Sano wasn't surprised that Toda knew about the theory, and the suspects. Toda probably had spies among the soldiers guarding Hoshina, and they'd eavesdropped on his conversation with Sano that morning. "I've got a new suspect," Sano said, "but unfortunately not his name."

He described what had happened at the secret Black Lotus temple. "The only clue I have to the man's identity is the dead woman that he tried to communicate with through the Black Lotus priest. Her name was Anemone. I think someone among her family or associates is the Dragon King. I'm hoping you can tell me who she is."

Toda pondered, searching the voluminous storehouse of his mind for the answer. Then he said, "I don't remember a murder of anyone called Anemone. It's a pity you didn't get her family name. When was she killed? How did she die?"

"I don't know," Sano said.

"Perhaps you can tell me where her murder took place?"

Sano shook his head, realizing that what he asked might be more than even Toda could give him, considering the paucity of background information on the crime.

"There have been thousands of murders in the country throughout the years, as you well know," Toda said. "For me to know where to begin looking for information about Anemone, I need more than just her given name."

"Let's suppose there's a connection between Anemone and Hoshina," Sano said, "even if he didn't kill her."

"That would narrow the time span down to the past twenty years or so, presuming the murder didn't occur while Hoshina was only a child," Toda said. "It would also locate the crime in Edo or Miyako, the two places Hoshina has lived."

"The Dragon King couldn't have planted Mariko as a spy in Lady Keisho-in's retinue unless he has close connections to the Tokugawa," Sano said. "He must be someone in the *bakufu,* and a member of a high-ranking samurai clan. There can't be many murders of women named Anemone that involve a man who fits those criteria."

"True," Toda said, his weary expression leavened by the possibility that this favor to Sano might not cost him too much trouble after all. "And crimes involving a man of that sort would be noted in the records at *metsuke* headquarters. Give me a moment to get dressed, then we'll be on our way."

Soon they were in the partitioned room in the palace that housed the *metsuke* headquarters. A single lamp burned in the compartment where Sano and Toda pored over ledgers that detailed incidents concerning Tokugawa vassals and the law. The palace corridors were silent, the other compartments unoccupied. Desks piled with scrolls, maps, and writing materials awaited *metsuke* agents who still slumbered at home while Sano and Toda searched the Edo records for the three years Hoshina had lived in the city. Sano turned pages of accounts of people killed in duels or crimes of passion, wives divorced, and disputes over money, property, and protocol, but he found no mention of Anemone's murder.

By the time he and Toda started on the Miyako records, daylight began seeping through the windows; temple bells around the city tolled, summoning priests to morning prayers. The room filled up with men, muttered conversation, and tobacco smoke. Strain burned Sano's eyes as he read through yet another ledger and tried to stay awake.

The noon deadline that Chamberlain Yanagisawa had given him loomed nearer, until at last, the characters of the name he sought focused his bleary gaze.

"Here it is," he exclaimed to Toda, who gladly set aside his own ledger. Sano read: " 'Tenwa Year two, month five, day four,' " then clarified, "That's twelve years ago. 'Dannoshin Jirozaemon, commander of the militia, dead by suicide. His wife Anemone, dead by drowning. The lifeless body of Dannoshin was found in his pleasure boat, adrift on Lake Biwa. His throat was cut, his short sword in his hand. He had left a note at home that explained his actions.

" 'It said that his wife and a man who was Dannoshin's own paramour had carried on a secret affair together. When Dannoshin found out, he decided to punish his wife by throwing her into the lake, then kill himself because he must atone for her death and could not bear that the two people he loved most had betrayed him with each other. The body of Anemone was never recovered.' "

Sano pounded his fist on the ledger as triumph exhilarated him. "This has to be the murder behind the kidnapping plot! Anemone is the drowned woman in the poem in the ransom letter. Since she was never found, she's still in the lake, under the water—in the palace of the Dragon King."

"But Hoshina didn't kill Anemone," said Toda. "Her husband did, according to his own confession. Why would anyone demand Hoshina's execution for Anemone's drowning? It makes no sense."

"Maybe Hoshina still played a role in the murder," Sano said. "I'm thinking he was the man who was the lover of both Dannoshin and Anemone."

"Hoshina has been known to bed women, even though he prefers male partners," Toda said. "If he was the lover, then Anemone's death is indirectly his fault because her affair with him caused her husband to drown her."

"Someone who grieved for her might resent the fact that Hoshina went about his business as if nothing had happened." Sano reread the account. "Whoever wrote this neglected to mention the lover's name."

"Perhaps the omission was deliberate," Toda said, then hinted, "What was Hoshina doing twelve years ago, when Anemone and Dannoshin died?"

"Hoshina was a detective on the Miyako police force," Sano recalled. "Perhaps he investigated the deaths. There would have been an ugly scandal, and he probably wanted to keep himself out of it. He could have destroyed evidence that implicated him."

"And made sure his name never appeared in any official records," Toda said.

"Supposing he was indeed the third party in the triangle, there's another reason for him to cover up the fact," Sano said. "At the time, he was the companion of the *shoshidai*." The *shoshidai* was the Tokugawa official who ruled Miyako, and a cousin of the shogun. "He wouldn't have wanted his master to know he'd been indulging his lust elsewhere."

"That might have cost him his position," Toda said, "and his chance of rising in the *bakufu*."

Exhaustion, as well as pressure to identify the Dragon King before noon and save Lady Keisho-in before the shogun lost patience and did something rash, took the edge off Sano's triumph. Rubbing his tired eyes, he said, "This is all conjecture. And even though I'm sure that the Dragon King is someone connected with Anemone or Dannoshin, we still don't know who he is, let alone where he is."

"I'll look up the names of their relatives," Toda said. "I can also check on which are members of the *bakufu* and live in Edo. But it will take time to unearth the clan lineage records from the archives and match names on them to the thousands on the *bakufu* list."

And time was running out for Sano. "Get your *metsuke* comrades to help you," he said, rising to leave.

"Very well," Toda said.

"Meanwhile," Sano said, "I'm going to try a shortcut to

the Dragon King. Knowing what we know now, I think a talk with our friend Hoshina is in order."

The sun had ascended over Edo Castle, but the forest preserve cast deep shadow over the guard tower that imprisoned Hoshina. Although the morning was clear and the air windless beneath the hazy aquamarine sky, gray clouds spilled mist and rain over the distant hills, portending storms for the city. Sano strode toward the tower along the walkway on top of the palace wall. There, three guards lounged outside the door to the prison.

"Open up," Sano said. "I want to see Hoshina-*san*."

The guards obeyed. Sano stalked into the dim room, whose stone walls exuded the transient coolness of night. Hoshina lay asleep on his futon, with his back to Sano. When Sano kicked his buttock, Hoshina jerked awake, let out a cry of alarm, and clambered to his feet. Groggy panic showed on his face as he reached for the sword he normally wore, and his hand clutched empty air. Then he saw Sano. Even as his breath puffed from him in relief, anger stimulated him to alertness.

"Why did you wake me up like that?" he said. "To torment me for your own amusement?"

"We need to talk," Sano said, his sympathy for Hoshina depleted by everything he'd learned about the man since yesterday.

"What's happened? Have you found out something?" Hope of rescue enlivened Hoshina's haggard, unshaven face. "Have you caught the person who got me into this predicament?"

Pressed for time, Sano forbore to argue that Hoshina's own execrable behavior was the root of his troubles. "No, I haven't caught the Dragon King," Sano said, "but I've found out plenty. Why didn't you tell me about Anemone?"

"Who?" Hoshina regarded Sano in genuine bewilderment. Then recognition encroached. "Oh. Anemone," he said in the perturbed tone of a man suddenly confronted by a ghost from his past.

"So you were her lover?" Sano said. When Hoshina nodded, Sano said, "Were you her husband Dannoshin's lover as well?"

Again Hoshina nodded, warily.

"Dannoshin drowned Anemone because you and she cheated on him by having an affair with each other," Sano said. "Were you the detective who investigated their deaths? Did you cover up your part in them to protect yourself from scandal and punishment?"

"Yes, but what has that got to do with anything?" Hoshina said, annoyed now.

Incredulity filled Sano as he beheld Hoshina. Did the man really not understand the significance of the events? "It's a murder connected with you, that you should have mentioned when we made the list yesterday."

"But we were focusing on people I killed, or sent to their execution," Hoshina said, hands on his hips and feet planted wide in defensive obstinacy. "I didn't kill Anemone. She didn't belong on that list."

"One might argue that you were indirectly responsible for her death," Sano pointed out.

"I wasn't responsible. Her murder was her husband's doing, not my fault. They were just a pastime for me. I couldn't help it if he overreacted." An aggrieved whine tinged Hoshina's voice. "How did you find out about her, anyway?"

It was just like Hoshina to disclaim culpability, Sano thought in disgust. "Never mind how I found out. You should have told me about Anemone's murder, instead of hiding a source of potential suspects."

"I wasn't hiding anything," Hoshina protested. "I haven't thought of Anemone in years. I didn't mention her because I'd forgotten her."

"She and her husband died because of her affair with you, and *you didn't even remember her?*" Sano thought he'd already learned the worst about Hoshina, but there seemed no limits to the man's callousness.

"All right, I should have remembered. I should have told you about Anemone." Hoshina flung out his arms in a gesture of mock surrender and glared at Sano. "What are you going to do, kill me?"

"It's tempting," Sano said, "but I need your help. I've got an army of *metsuke* agents searching for information on people connected with Anemone and Dannoshin, but that will take too long. Here's your chance to make up for the lost time that your bad memory has cost us. You knew Anemone and Dannoshin. Who in their household would have wanted to avenge her death?"

Hoshina's features went slack with astonished dismay. "It was ages ago that I knew them. That time is a blur in my mind. How am I supposed to remember anyone in their household?"

"Try," Sano said. "Your life may depend on your remembering."

Pacing the room, Hoshina clamped his hands to his head, as though to physically squeeze out facts. "Dannoshin had a couple of sons from his previous marriage. They were in the Miyako militia. We were on friendly terms—I don't think they had a grudge against me. Dannoshin's parents lived in his house, but they were so old, they're probably dead now. I can't think of anyone else."

"Think harder!"

"I'm doing the best I can!" Hoshina stomped the floor, sounding close to tears.

Sano realized that his own impatience was only worsening the situation. "Let's try a different approach," he said. "Who besides Dannoshin knew about your affair with Anemone?"

"Nobody." Hands falling limp at his sides, Hoshina seemed near the breaking point. "We were very discreet. She sneaked me into a cottage in the garden late at night, while everyone was sleeping."

"Who knew?" Sano repeated, because somebody had

known, and that somebody had transformed into the Dragon King twelve years later.

Hoshina shook his head in despair. Then his drooping posture straightened. "Wait," he exclaimed, his dull eyes lighting. "Anemone had a son by Dannoshin. He was about fifteen years old—a strange, repulsive boy." Hoshina made a moue of distaste. "Whenever I went to the house, he would creep around and stare at me. And once, when Anemone and I were making love, we heard a noise in the bushes outside the cottage. It must have been him, spying on us."

At last they were making progress, Sano thought with relief. "What was the boy's name?"

"Dannoshin Minoru," Hoshina said, and grinned, proud of himself for remembering.

"The son of Anemone is a likely person to want her death avenged," Sano said.

"He must be the Dragon King." Hoshina bounced on the balls of his feet and smacked his hands together, obviously exhilarated by the thought that his ordeal might be nearing a happy end. "He must have been plotting my downfall ever since Anemone died."

"Now all I need to do," Sano said, "is find out what became of him, pick up his trail, and follow it to wherever he's hiding the hostages. I'll go tell the *metsuke* to start combing the archives for information on Dannoshin Minoru."

"Don't bother," Hoshina said. His mocking attitude resurfaced. "I've just remembered something else: I saw the fellow recently. I know where he's been."

"When?" Sano said, frowning in surprise. "Where?"

"About two years ago. Here in Edo. He's grown up and changed since we last met, and I couldn't place him. But now it's come back to me." Hoshina said, "He's an inspector for the Ministry of Temples and Shrines."

Thoughts crystallized in Sano's mind as he comprehended how the Dragon King, the Black Lotus, and the kidnapping fit together. The Ministry of Temples and

Shrines was responsible for monitoring religious sects, making sure they obeyed the laws and didn't rise up against the ruling regime. Therefore, the Ministry had a major share of the task of eradicating the Black Lotus and employed inspectors to travel around the city, looking for illegal religious activity.

"Dannoshin Minoru's work put him in contact with Black Lotus outlaws," Sano deduced. "That's how he found the secret temple and met Profound Wisdom. But instead of reporting them to the police, he used them. He got Mariko to spy on Lady Keisho-in. He probably used his connections in the *bakufu* to plant the girl inside Edo Castle. He got a band of Black Lotus *rōnin* to help him ambush Lady Keisho-in's procession and kidnap her."

"Are you going to tell the shogun now?" Hoshina grabbed Sano by the arm. "Take me with you. When he hears that I've identified the kidnapper, he'll be so grateful that he'll set me free and give me back my position."

Trust Hoshina to try to turn the situation to his personal benefit and reap all the credit instead of just the fraction he deserved, Sano thought. "You're not going anywhere," he said, flinging off Hoshina's hand. "I still have to find out where the Dragon King is holding the hostages and rescue them."

Maybe Hoshina had redeemed himself by providing the vital piece of information. But the Dragon King would be awaiting news of Hoshina's execution. How much longer would he wait before he decided the shogun had disobeyed his order and he made good on his threat to kill his captives?

Had the identification of Dannoshin Minoru come too late to save the women?

25

Detective Marume dragged a load of long, thin logs into the forest clearing where he and Hirata and Fukida were building the raft upon which they would cross the lake and bring back the women. A day had passed since they'd arrived on the Izu Peninsula, and they still had yet to invade the kidnappers' island. The air was cool and misty, and the sun hidden behind layered gray and white clouds, but Marume was sweating from the hard labor of cutting and hauling wood. Stripped down to his loincloth and sandals, his dagger gripped between his teeth, he looked like a savage. He dropped the logs beside Hirata.

"Do you need more wood?" Marume asked, panting.

Hirata aligned the logs with the others that comprised the raft and tied them together with braided reeds. He wiped his dripping nose on his sleeve. "I don't think so." He looked at his hands, which were filthy and marked with bloody cuts, then at the raft. "It's big enough, isn't it?"

The raft was a lopsided square platform, approximately twice as long as Hirata's height. Rough logs of various widths, bristling with trimmed stubs, were joined side by side with clumsily knotted reeds. Hirata felt more crestfallen than proud of his work. Fukida brought over the oars he'd fashioned by cutting two forked branches and weaving dense, unruly mats of sticks and reeds between the forks. He tossed the oars atop the raft and gave Hirata an apologetic glance. All three men gazed doubtfully at the product of their efforts.

"Will it float?" Marume said, voicing the thought on everyone's minds.

"It has to," Hirata said firmly.

They'd invested the whole previous afternoon and evening, as well as this morning, in his decision to attempt the rescue instead of returning to Edo. The raft had taken longer to build than Hirata had anticipated. First, they'd had to backtrack from the lake and camp in a secluded place off the road, where any kidnappers who happened to leave the island wouldn't notice them. The search for suitable timber, and the struggle to hack it to the right size, had consumed hours. By the time they'd devised methods for constructing the raft and oars, darkness had forced them to stop work until sunrise. They'd spent a cold, uncomfortable night trying to sleep on the ground, while a ceaseless mental debate had kept Hirata awake.

Had he made the wrong decision? What would happen when Sano found out he'd disobeyed orders? Had building the raft wasted precious time that he should have spent on traveling home and reporting that he'd found the kidnappers and hostages? Hirata had also worried about Midori. He'd wondered if he and Marume and Fukida could manage the rescue. But his unwillingness to leave his wife's vicinity had solidified his resolve. And he must wrest Midori away from the kidnappers. He couldn't leave her at the mercy of Lord Niu or whatever other insane villain had her.

Now Hirata said, "We'll wait until late tonight. Then we'll invade the island."

Accompanied by thirty of their detectives and troops, Sano and Chamberlain Yanagisawa rode into the *bancho,* the district west of Edo Castle where the lower Tokugawa vassals resided. The afternoon sun, chased by gathering storm clouds, flickered patterns of light and shadow over small, run-down estates enclosed by live bamboo fences. The streets were narrow, muddy, soiled with horse dung, and teeming with mounted samurai. Flies buzzed in ditches overflowing with sewage. The vassals lived in squalor because the regime could afford only meager stipends for a huge military class during peacetime.

Sano and Yanagisawa had already reported to the shogun that they'd identified the Dragon King as Dannoshin Minoru, inspector for the Ministry of Temples and Shrines. The shogun had ordered them to find out, by the end of the day, whether Dannoshin really was the Dragon King, and where he was hiding the women. If they failed, the shogun said, he would execute them, and Police Commissioner Hoshina. Now Sano's party arrived at Dannoshin's estate.

With its thatched roof and plain, half-timbered construction, the estate was nearly identical to the others crammed into the labyrinthine *bancho,* differentiated only by Dannoshin's name written on the gate. After dismounting there, Sano and his detectives followed Yanagisawa and his contingent into a gravel courtyard shaded by the bamboo leaves. An old man dressed in a faded indigo kimono came hurrying out of the house.

"Who are you?" the man said, clearly startled to behold the army of samurai and the Tokugawa crests on their garments. He backed up the steps in alarm before bowing. "What can I do for you, masters?"

"We're looking for Dannoshin Minoru," said Chamberlain Yanagisawa. "Tell us where he is."

"He's not home," the old man said.

Advancing up the flagstone path with his troops, Yanagisawa demanded, "Where did he go?"

"I don't know. He didn't tell me. I'm just his servant."

"Then we'll just have a look around," Yanagisawa said.

While he and his men rushed into the house, Sano went up to the servant, who hunched timidly on the veranda.

"When did your master leave?" Sano asked.

"Seven days ago." Anxious to propitiate, the servant volunteered, "The night before that, a girl came here. She and my master talked. After she left, he told me to pack him some clothes and provisions for a journey."

The girl was Mariko, Sano deduced. She'd brought the news of Lady Keisho-in's impending trip. Dannoshin had then made preparations to outpace and ambush Keisho-in and hired Black Lotus mercenaries to help him. One of them must have ridden back to Edo after the kidnapping, posted the ransom letter on the castle wall, then vanished unnoticed by anyone.

Sano led his detectives into the house. Beyond the entryway, Yanagisawa's men swarmed the corridor, pushing open doors in the paper-and-wood wall partitions, tramping through rooms, hunting occupants. The smell of incense tinged the air. The house's interior was dingy and ill-furnished. Sano supposed Dannoshin had hoarded his money to fund his revenge against Hoshina and pay for help from the Black Lotus. But perhaps the sect had cooperated partly because he could have turned its members in to the police if they refused.

From somewhere in the back of the house, Yanagisawa called, "*Sōsakan* Sano!"

"Go and help search the premises," Sano told his men.

He jostled past the troops and found Yanagisawa in a chamber, standing before a teak table. The table held candles with blackened wicks, incense burners full of ash, and an ornately carved black lacquer cabinet.

"It's a funeral altar," Yanagisawa said.

According to custom, the cabinet should have contained a portrait of the deceased, but it was empty. Sano touched a finger to the carved flowers surrounding the blank interior.

"These are anemones," he said. "This is Dannoshin's funeral altar to his murdered mother."

"He must have taken her portrait with him," Yanagisawa said.

Sano inhaled the incense smoke absorbed by the walls and *tatami*. Anxious for clues to the Dragon King's character as well as location, he opened a cabinet. He found quilts and a futon. Dannoshin must sleep in this shrine to his mother. He must have worshiped her spirit for twelve years, nursing a murderous, obsessive need for revenge. Sano stepped into the study, a niche in a corner lined with shelves of books. On a desk lay two sheets of paper scribbled with black calligraphy. Sano picked these up. Yanagisawa read aloud over his shoulder:

> *"The woman struggles desperately in the lake,*
> *Her long hair and robes spread,*
> *Like flower petals strewn on the dark water.*

"This is a draft of the poem in the ransom letter," Yanagisawa said.

"And it's proof that Dannoshin is indeed the Dragon King." Sano examined the second page and said, "Listen to this.

> *"Despoiler of feminine virtue,*
> *Selfishly taking his pleasure at will,*
> *The scoundrel Hoshina leaves destruction in his wake,*
> *Never caring nor looking back at the pain he causes,*
> *While fortune blesses him with wealth and prestige.*
>
> *But Hoshina will not escape his comeuppance forever,*
> *The Dragon King will rise up from the ocean to exact*
>   *retribution,*
> *He will grasp Hoshina in his golden claws,*
> *And breathe flaming wrath upon the despoiler,*
> *Whether it be the death of them both.*

"So much for any doubt that Dannoshin is out to get Hoshina," Sano said.

Yanagisawa's troops burst into the room, bringing three women. One was gray-haired and matronly, the others teenaged girls. All were whimpering with terror. "These are the housekeeper and maids," said a soldier. "They say they don't know where their master went."

Sano's detectives appeared at the door. "The barracks behind the house are empty," Detective Inoue told Sano. "So are the stables. It looks like Dannoshin has taken all his retainers with him. There's no one else here."

Yanagisawa cursed under his breath. Sano's heart plummeted under the gravity of frustration and despair. To have tracked the Dragon King to his home territory, only for the trail to end there, was a crushing letdown. Sano and Yanagisawa hunted through the study niche, rummaging in drawers, riffling papers, thumbing ledgers, searching for clues to where the Dragon King was now. The detectives and soldiers searched the rest of the estate. At last they gathered, all empty-handed, in the courtyard.

"Does the great *sōsakan-sama* have any ideas?" Yanagisawa's mocking tone had a sharp, desperate edge.

Memory suddenly transported Sano back to a time when he'd worked at a place where they could find the information they needed. "Actually, I do," he said. "Come with me." He led the rush out the gate to their horses.

Midori uttered a long, keening wail of anguish as a spasm convulsed her. Her back arched; her body heaved up from the bed. The pain squeezed her eyes shut, bared her teeth. Her fingers clawed into the futon. Tears and sweat drenched her face. Lady Yanagisawa, kneeling on one side of Midori, dabbed her brow with a cloth. Keisho-in squatted on the other side.

"The pains are coming more and more frequently. The birth will happen soon," she said with the smug air of an expert.

Reiko pounded on the door, as she'd done countless times since Midori's labor had begun in the night. "Help!" she called to the guards. Now it must be past noon, and her voice was hoarse, her anxiety turning to panic. "My friend needs a midwife. Please bring one immediately!"

Earlier, the guards had responded by yelling at her to be quiet. This time someone thudded a fist against the outside of the door. Ota, the Dragon King's chief henchman, said, "We're not falling for any more of your tricks."

"It's not a trick," Reiko cried in desperation. Childbirth was an event fraught with hazard, and without a skilled midwife to handle any trouble that arose, Midori and the baby were in grave peril. "Come in and see for yourself."

Nothing happened. Midori gasped and lay still, temporarily released from pain. Thunder grumbled outside; rain tapped on the roof and dripped through the holes onto Midori. Then the door opened. Ota, his face belligerent with suspicion and annoyance, pointed his sword at Reiko, backing her into the room while he entered with two other men. As they approached Midori, she wailed, shuddering violently, seized by another contraction. Ota and his companions leapt back from her genuine agony. Their faces expressed the primitive awe and fright of men confronted with the spectacle of childbirth.

"She needs a midwife," Reiko said. "She needs clean water and bedding and a dry, comfortable place to have the baby." Determined to protect Midori's well-being, Reiko forgot caution and ordered the men, "Go tell your master! Now!"

They fled, although obviously less intimidated by Reiko than eager to get away. Reiko knelt beside Midori and pressed against the potent points on her spine, trying to relieve the labor pains. Midori panted; Lady Yanagisawa wiped her face; Keisho-in peered under her robes, watching for the child to emerge. Soon Ota returned. His cruel grin mocked the women's hopeful expressions. "My master wants to see you," he told Reiko.

As he and two other guards escorted Reiko into the palace, her heart pounded with fear. Inside, they climbed a staircase to a chamber that stank of the Dragon King's incense. The fear settled like a cold, hard weight in her stomach. She glimpsed doors open to a balcony overlooking the lake, before a partition slid aside with a loud, grinding creak. From the adjacent room stepped the Dragon King. Today he wore a plain gray silk kimono over black trousers. His unblinking stare fixed on Reiko. He paused at the threshold, then moved toward her with his odd, hesitant swagger. Madness and desire smoldered in his eyes.

The icy weight in Reiko's stomach grew heavier, and her legs trembled. Now would begin her ordeal of compromising herself to win the Dragon King's trust. Although she felt woefully unprepared, despite hours spent scheming, she must maneuver him toward liberating her and her friends.

"Good day, Anemone," he said in a hushed voice that reeked of intimacy.

Reiko imagined a black abyss yawning at her feet. With a sense of futility, she stepped over the edge. She felt her spirit plunge into depths from which it might never rise.

"Good day, my lord," she said, imitating his tone. She donned a semblance of an enchanting smile; she forced her eyes to shine at the Dragon King. Stifling hatred, she dropped to her knees and bowed low in the hope that submissiveness would disarm him.

He moved near to her, cloaking her in his suffocating aura of incense. When she raised her head, Reiko saw his loins positioned very near her face. She almost flung herself backward, against the guards who stood behind her. Instead, she held her breath and gazed at his swords, and the rampant dragon embroidered in lighter gray thread on his robe.

"Leave us," the Dragon King told the guards.

Reiko glanced around and saw Ota pause on his way out the door. He gave her a warning look. Whether or not her humble pose had convinced his master, Ota clearly suspected her motives. Reiko knew that he and the other guards wouldn't be far away. She also knew that she couldn't hope to defeat the Dragon King unless she figured his men into her plans.

The Dragon King upturned his hand, the long fingers extended toward Reiko. Unwillingly she laid her hand on his and let him raise her upright. They stood close like lovers, their bodies touching through the thin layers of garments that separated them.

"Did I send you enough food and bedding yesterday?" he said. "Did my men clean your quarters to your satisfaction?"

His breath on her scalp felt as hot to Reiko as fire from a dragon's nostrils. Taking her cue from him, she said, "Yes. A million thanks. You have been most kind. My friends and I are beholden to you." She almost whimpered with distress brought on by her worst fears.

When the Dragon King had his way with her, her life would be ruined even if she survived. She would have broken her wedding pledge to be faithful to Sano, even though against her wishes. How could she return to him, defiled by another man?

No matter if she explained that she'd cooperated with the Dragon King and sacrificed herself to save her friends, she couldn't expect Sano to forgive her. No matter how understanding he was or how unconventional their marriage, Sano was a man, and men were possessive, jealous. A part of him would suspect that she'd welcomed and enjoyed the Dragon King's attentions. He would wonder whether she could have avoided them—had she chosen. His doubts about her fidelity to him would erode his trust, and their marriage. He might even divorce her. She would lose not only Sano but her son, and be cast off to live in disgrace, on her family's charity.

"Ota-*san* says you have something to ask of me," said the Dragon King. "But first, let us make ourselves comfortable." They knelt facing the balcony, his hand still holding hers, his presence immovable at her side. "Let us cherish this time that fate has bestowed on us."

A voice inside Reiko's mind whispered that whatever happened between her and the Dragon King, she didn't have to tell Sano. Maybe no one else would, either. Sano need never know. But Reiko would know. The secret would fester like a disease inside her spirit. And what if the Dragon King impregnated her? Reiko imagined carrying the child, hoping desperately that it was Sano's, then watching it grow up and seeing the dreaded resemblance to her kidnapper. The child would be son or daughter to Sano, brother or sister to Masahiro, yet always a reminder of Reiko's defilement.

"Last night I dreamed we were at home," the Dragon King said. "It was spring, and the cherry trees were blooming outside. You were teaching me calligraphy, as you used to do. You put your arm around me and clasped your hand around mine, helping me guide the brush."

His lips curved in a private, nostalgic smile. He contemplated the lake, as if he saw the scene from his dream mirrored in its choppy, steel-colored waters. "You caressed my loins, while your hair tumbled over my shoulders and your bosom pressed against me. We laughed together."

Reiko cringed at the image of him and a woman who resembled her engaged in erotic play. She gazed at the fog billowing over the distant mountains and wished herself far beyond them.

"When I awake from such dreams, I usually suffer terrible disappointment that you are gone and I am alone," the Dragon King said. "But now you have been restored to me in a way I never expected." He mused, "When I kidnapped the shogun's mother, I only took you along because you were with her, and obviously a high-ranking person who might be useful to my plans. Not until I got a closer look at you did I discover that you are the image of my beloved Anemone. And not until yesterday, when we first spoke, did I realize that you are possessed by her spirit."

Reiko didn't know whether to be glad or sorry that he could distinguish her from the real Anemone. It might spare her the violent rage he'd expressed toward Anemone, but also lessen her influence over him. She was glad that stealing her wasn't his reason for kidnapping the women and slaying their entourage, but horrified that her present peril was but an accident of fate. If only she'd refused to go on the trip! Better she should have faced punishment from Lady Keisho-in than disgrace and torture at the hands of the Dragon King. Yet there was no use wishing to go back in time and alter the future.

The Dragon King was watching her, awaiting a response. Hastily she improvised, "Last night I hardly slept at all. My mind was filled with thoughts of you. I kept remembering your touch, and your look, and the rapture of your nearness."

Her words derived from vague memories of love poems she'd read; her fluttering eyelids and husky, breathless voice imitated the actors in romantic Kabuki plays she'd seen. The Dragon King stared at her; his breathing quickened, his tongue moistened his lips, and palpable waves of hot arousal emanated from him. Reiko's insides churned with revulsion and fear as she wended closer to danger, but she clasped her free hand to her bosom, as if truly enraptured.

"I longed to see you. I prayed we would soon meet again," she whispered. "How thankful I am that my prayers were answered, and we are reunited."

The Dragon King caressed her cheek. "Your death parted us twelve long years ago. But even before then, we were divided. That man—whose very name I despise—came between us." Anger welled in the fiery gaze that devoured Reiko. The Dragon King's hand tightened painfully around hers. "He wasn't worthy of you, Anemone. He was a cruel, selfish cad who was only toying with you. How could you take him as your lover? How could you forsake me?"

Reiko wondered who this man could be, and what he might have to do with the kidnapping. "I never loved him," she said, because this seemed the best way to avoid the Dragon King's savagery. "You're the only one who matters to me."

Now tears quenched the rage in the Dragon King's eyes. "Ah, my dearest. That man deprived us of so much." Clouds moved over the balcony as rain trickled through the foliage; a shadow crossed his expression. "If only I could make up to you for those lost years, and the life stolen from you."

Here Reiko spied opportunity. "Perhaps there is something you can do," she murmured.

"What is it you wish, my dearest?" His grip on her hand relaxed into moist fondling.

The plan Reiko had devised to free herself and the other women from the Dragon King must wait, because Midori's plight took precedence. "My friend is ready to bear her child," Reiko said. "I wish to have a midwife for her."

To her distress, Reiko felt the Dragon King withdraw from her, although his body stayed in place. A barrier lowered behind his gaze. "That is out of the question," he said brusquely. "I cannot allow some woman to come here, then tell others what she's seen."

He had a sense of self-preservation despite his madness, Reiko understood. Even though he was deluded enough to think she embodied the spirit of Anemone, he knew he'd committed serious crimes for which the Tokugawa would punish him if he got caught. He recognized his need for secrecy.

"But my friend needs help. She and the baby may die otherwise." Reiko saw the annoyance flicker across her companion's features, and realized he didn't care what happened to Midori. Altering course, she curved her lips into a seductive smile and eased closer to him. "You are such a good, kind, generous man. Surely you wouldn't let an innocent woman and child come to harm?"

"I'd like to grant your wish, but it's impossible," the Dragon King said, his voice hardening. "Besides, we're far from anyplace where a midwife might be found."

Reiko's heart sank at the implication that they were also far from anyone who might rescue her. "Would you at least move us to a better room?" Comfort might help Midori, and if Reiko could get away from the tower, escaping might be easier. "The roof of the tower leaks. The rain falls on me. It's too cold at night, and too hot in the daytime." Reiko peered at the Dragon King from beneath demurely lowered eyelids and coaxed, "This is a small thing that I ask."

The Dragon King shook his ungainly head. "It pains me to deny you, but I must. The tower is the easiest place to guard prisoners. You and your friends are secure there."

Reiko was frantic because all her wiles had done nothing except encourage the Dragon King's attachment to her. Winning his trust seemed impossible. Was her plan doomed to fail? Would her ruin be for naught? Then inspiration struck.

"There's something I must tell you," Reiko murmured. She crooked her finger at the Dragon King. Her smile promised intimate revelations. She felt like a Yoshiwara courtesan wooing a client. "Lean close, and listen."

She knew Ota and the other guards were eavesdropping, and she didn't want them to hear. The Dragon King inclined his head toward her. Reiko whispered in his ear. "You are surrounded by enemies. They're here on this island, among your men."

The Dragon King shot her a sidelong glance of surprise.

"They don't approve of your relations with me," Reiko whispered. "They're jealous. They want to separate us. Last night I heard them talking. They're plotting to kill me."

"This can't be. My men have orders not to harm you or your friends without my permission." But consternation tinged the distrust with which the Dragon King beheld Reiko.

"It's true," Reiko said, hastening to play upon the doubts about his authority over his men and the fear of betrayal that she sensed in him. "They're going to kill me, throw my body in the lake, then tell you that I ran away."

His brows slanted downward in distress. "Ota and the rest of my personal retainers would never go against my wishes. But the other men . . ." He fingered his chin, brooding. "Perhaps I shouldn't have employed people of their kind. I've never quite trusted them."

Reiko was gratified to have planted a seed of suspicion that would poison the Dragon King's mind toward his henchmen. "I don't want to die," she said. Tears of genuine desperation spilled from her eyes. "Please, you must protect me!"

He conceded with a decisive air: "Yes, I must."

Encouraged, Reiko said, "Then please keep your men away from my friends and me." Getting rid of the guards would benefit an escape attempt. "Put them where they can't hurt us."

"But I can't leave you unguarded," the Dragon King said as rational thought penetrated his fear of treachery.

"I promise I won't run away," Reiko said. "Now that we've found each other again, I can't bear to leave you."

"Even if you stay, your friends will escape."

"They're too afraid to go without me," Reiko said. "And you can move us all someplace where you can watch us yourself."

The little influence she had over the Dragon King was more than she had over the guards. The odds that she could trick one madman outweighed the chance that she could fight past his army. Wherever else he put the women was bound to be less secure than the tower, and possibly closer to the boats.

The Dragon King vacillated, scowling as he pondered whether the threat to Reiko—and Anemone—necessitated changing the arrangements he'd made. Reiko turned their clasped hands so that his lay on top. With the fingertips of her other hand she stroked his hand with gentle, lingering, sensuous movements, as she often did to Sano. Her spirit grieved, because voluntarily touching the Dragon King seemed a betrayal of Sano, and the first willing step toward losing her virtue.

"The tower is too far from you." Reiko trailed her fingers along the Dragon King's wrist. "Move me into the palace, where we can be close." Her whisper promised nights of wild passion. Her seductive manner hid anguish.

The Dragon King moaned. While Reiko continued her caresses up his arm, bumps rose on his skin; he closed his eyes, and a shudder coursed through him. Even as she dreaded to arouse him into ravishing her, she sensed him fighting the impulse. He suddenly tore himself away from Reiko, strode outside to the balcony, and slumped against the rail, his breath rasping.

Although heartily relieved that the seduction need go no further, Reiko experienced confusion at his response. What had held him back from the carnal union that she knew he wanted? She thought of Midori laboring in the wet, bleak prison, and her spirits sank deeper. If this first attempt at manipulating the Dragon King failed, what chance had her plan to free herself and her friends?

"I will think about what you've asked," the Dragon King said, his back still turned toward Reiko. Then he called, "Ota-*san*! Take her away."

26

The government archives inhabited a mansion in the official quarter of Edo Castle. Here Sano had worked when he'd first joined the *bakufu*, before the shogun had assigned him to investigate crimes. In its main study, clerks moved aside the desks where they copied, sorted, and filed documents. The chief archivist, a pudgy, middle-aged samurai named Noguchi, spread huge maps of Japan on the cleared floor space. Sano and Chamberlain Yanagisawa knelt to examine the maps, which were brilliantly painted in blue to represent rivers, lakes, and oceans, green for plains, and brown shades for mountains. Inked characters marked cities and the names of landowners.

"Dannoshin Minoru must have had a particular destination in mind when he abducted the women," Sano said.

"He wouldn't count on finding a suitable prison on the spur of the moment," Yanagisawa agreed. "A man who's been plotting revenge for twelve years is neither impulsive nor inclined to trust in luck."

"And a man as clever as Dannoshin would know enough to avoid attracting notice while he's holding the shogun's mother captive," Sano said. "He wouldn't take rooms at an inn or rent a house in a village, because people who'd heard about the kidnapping would get suspicious."

Yanagisawa perused a map of the Hakone region. "There are caves in the wilderness around the kidnapping site. Maybe he scouted one in advance and hid the hostages there."

"Maybe," Sano said, "but I would bet that Dannoshin owns a property where he can be sure no one will happen upon him and report him to the authorities."

"If he does, and that's where he went, it can't be far from the kidnapping site," Yanagisawa said. "He needed to hide the women quickly to avoid being seen, and minimize the risk of their escaping."

Sano traced his finger along the white line on the map that represented the Tōkaidō. He stopped at the winding stretch where Lady Keisho-in's party had been ambushed. Then he drew an invisible circle whose radius corresponded to a day's journey from the spot. The circle contained the names of local landholders.

"Let's begin looking here," Sano said.

The shogun sat on the dais in the audience chamber, presiding over a meeting that concerned national defense and included Uemori Yoichi, a member of the Council of Elders and chief military advisor to the Tokugawa, and several top army officials. While Uemori droned on about troop supplies, fortifications that needed improvement, and arsenal inventories, the shogun worried about his mother. He imagined Lady Keisho-in trapped somewhere, wondering why he didn't rescue her. He fidgeted, barely able to tolerate sitting idle and waiting for Chamberlain Yanagisawa and *Sōsakan* Sano to bring him news. How he wished that he himself could do something to save his mother and catch her kidnapper!

"Your Excellency, will you please sign this?" Uemori reached up to the dais and set documents on the table there.

The shogun contemplated the documents with timid uncertainty. Having paid no attention to the discussion, he didn't know whether he should approve them. But even if he had listened, he probably wouldn't have known. Ruling a nation was so difficult!

"What is this?" he said, cautiously fingering the pages.

"Authorizations for treasury funds to cover the costs we just reviewed." Uemori spoke in a tone of patient forbearance.

The shogun sighed. What else could he do except follow other people's advice? Yet suddenly he was sick and tired of his own impotence, and furious at the world.

"How dare you, ahh, bother me with trivia at a time like this?" he shouted at his subordinates. They regarded him in surprise. He crumpled the documents and flung them at Uemori. "Take this and, ahh, insert it up your, ahh, rear end!"

Uemori ducked; the other men sat grave and wary of their lord's anger. Just then, Dr. Kitano, the chief Edo Castle physician, entered the room. "Excuse me, Your Excellency," he said.

"What do you want?" the shogun demanded.

Dr. Kitano knelt and bowed. "Please pardon the interruption," he said, "but Suiren has regained consciousness. I had orders to notify *Sōsakan* Sano, but I can't find him, so I thought I'd better report directly to you, Your Excellency."

The shogun frowned, puzzled by the news. "Who is Suiren?" he said.

Dr. Kitano looked surprised that the shogun didn't know. "She's your mother's maid. The one who survived the attack."

More annoyed than enlightened, the shogun said, "Why should I care that she's, ahh, conscious? Why do you, ahh, bother me about her?"

"There is a possibility that Suiren heard or saw something that could help us determine where the kidnappers took your honorable mother," Uemori interjected.

"Ahh. And now that she's conscious, she can, ahh, tell us what she knows." Comprehension quickly gave way to anxiety. "*Sōsakan* Sano must go to her at once!" Then recollection struck the shogun. "But Sano-*san* is out tracking down Dannoshin Minoru. So is Chamberlain Yanagisawa."

The shogun pointed at one of his secretaries. "Go fetch them."

As the secretary started to obey, Uemori said, "With all due respect, Your Excellency, perhaps the chamberlain and *sōsakan-sama* should be allowed to finish what they're doing."

. The shogun chewed his lip, humbled by Uemori's better judgment. "Never mind," he told the secretary.

"Someone else could question the maid," Uemori said.

"Ahh. Yes. You are right," the shogun said, then asked in bewilderment, "But who shall I send? I can't entrust such an important task to just anyone."

Out of nowhere came a sudden, novel idea: *Why don't I go myself?* So disconcerted was the shogun that his jaw dropped. Yet the idea seemed the perfect solution, because interrogating the maid would satisfy his desire for action. While his audience watched him as if wondering what had gotten into him, he stepped toward the edge of the dais . . . only to hesitate. Talking to a servant was beneath him. He must uphold the dignity of his rank and let his underlings do his dirty work. Wishing Sano and Yanagisawa were here to spare him this dilemma, he started to step back, but the thought of them arrested him.

They had taken charge of the kidnapping investigation, but why should they? It was his mother who was in danger, not theirs. Tokugawa Tsunayoshi experienced a rare pang of resentment toward Yanagisawa and Sano. From time to time he had a sneaking suspicion that they thought they were smarter than he, and more fit to make important decisions. He recalled that when the ransom demand came, he'd at first wanted to execute Police Commissioner Hoshina, then changed his mind . . . or had he? Could Sano have changed it for him, with Yanagisawa's collusion? The shogun wondered how many of his other decisions they'd influenced. Resentment and suspicion turned to anger at his trusted chamberlain and *sōsakan-sama*. Well, he wouldn't leave matters to them anymore. It was time to stand on his own two feet.

"This meeting is, ahh, adjourned," he said. Hopping off the dais, he pointed at his chief attendants and Dr. Kitano. "Come with me."

"Where are you going, Your Excellency?" Uemori said, obviously startled.

"To the, ahh, sickroom to question Suiren." As everyone stared in amazement, the shogun strode regally from the chamber.

Righteous indignation carried him out of the palace, through the castle grounds and passageways, to the threshold of the sickroom. There, sudden apprehension halted him and his retinue at the shrine outside the low, thatched building. The sickroom was haunted by spirits of disease and polluted by the deaths that had occurred there. The shogun, whose health was delicate, felt dizzy and sick to his stomach at the thought of entering. But enter he must, for his mother's sake.

He took a clean white cloth from under his sash and tied it over the lower half of his face to prevent the bad spirits and contamination from getting in his nose or mouth. "Let us, ahh, proceed," he said.

His chief attendant opened the door of the sickroom, walked in, and announced, "His Excellency the Shogun has arrived."

Faltering into the room, the shogun saw physicians and apprentices staring in shock to see him in this place where he'd never come. They fell to their knees and bowed. The shogun approached the woman who lay in the bed.

"You must be, ahh, Suiren," the shogun said. He crouched some distance from her, because he could read death in her wasted body and unwholesome pallor.

She gazed up at him in awe. "Your presence does me an honor, Your Excellency," she whispered in a low, cracked voice.

With his retinue and the doctors all watching him, the shogun felt self-conscious and uncertain because he'd never before questioned a witness about a crime. "Do you remember how you, ahh, got hurt?" he ventured.

Suiren nodded weakly. "Some men attacked us on the highway. They killed the troops and attendants. They took Lady Keisho-in." Tears welled in her eyes.

At least she hadn't lost her memory, the shogun thought. Perhaps this wouldn't be so difficult. "I want you to tell me everything that happened during the, ahh, attack," he said.

The maid poured out a tale of carnage and terror, her words frequently halted by weeping and pauses to muster her strength. "I was pulled out of my palanquin. A man stabbed me. I fell and must have hit my head and fainted. When I woke up, I was lying in a pool of blood. There were dead bodies all around. I saw the men emptying the trunks. Lady Keisho-in, Lady Yanagisawa, Lady Reiko, and Lady Midori were lying by the road. They seemed to be asleep. The men put them inside the trunks."

Envisioning his mother treated like cargo, Tokugawa Tsunayoshi gasped with outrage.

"I tried to crawl toward the men and stop them, but I was too weak." Sobs wracked Suiren. "How I wish I could have saved Lady Keisho-in!"

"Here is your, ahh, chance to help me save her," the shogun said. "Did the men say anything to, ahh, indicate where they were taking my mother?"

Weariness overlaid Suiren's features like a veil. Her voice dropped to an almost incomprehensible murmur: "There was an argument. Some of them complained . . . the trunks were too heavy to carry all the way to . . ." She breathed the last word.

"Izu!" the shogun interpreted. "They were going to Izu!" Behind his facecloth he grinned with glee because he'd found out something that Yanagisawa and Sano hadn't.

"The leader . . . told some others to hire porters to help carry the trunks," Suiren said. "They asked how . . . how to find the place where they would all meet again." Suiren paused, as if listening to echoes from the past. ". . . main highway south through Izu . . . west on the crossroad at the Jizo shrine . . . a lake with a castle on an island. . . ."

Such joy overwhelmed the shogun that he chortled and clapped his hands. Now he knew precisely where to find his mother! He couldn't wait to see Sano's and Yanagisawa's faces when he told them.

"You've done me a, ahh, great service," he said, impulsively leaning over to pat Suiren's head. "I will, ahh, reward you with anything you ask."

Suiren closed her eyes and sighed, weakened by the effort she'd expended on speech. "All I ask is for Lady Keisho-in to come home," she murmured. "Then I can die happy."

The shogun belatedly remembered the danger of disease and pollution. He bolted from the sickroom, his retinue in tow. Outside, he removed his facecloth, wiped his hands on it, and prayed that his health wouldn't suffer. Yet he was proud that he'd talked to Suiren, and taking this initiative had whetted his appetite for more. He was tired of waiting for others to act on his behalf, and fed up with complicated strategies for hunting the Dragon King. The reasons for delay fled his mind, as did his usual indecisiveness. For once Tokugawa Tsunayoshi knew exactly what to do next.

Two guards eased Midori down the tower stairs and carried her on a litter through the forest. More guards herded Reiko, Lady Yanagisawa, and Keisho-in behind her in the rain and locked them inside a wing of the main palace. The room was dingy and smelled of the dampness and mold that discolored its bare walls, but it was furnished with tattered cushions, frayed *tatami*, enough bedding for all the women, a basin of hot water, and a pile of rags. An undamaged roof kept out the rain.

As Reiko helped the other women settle Midori on a futon, she breathed a prayer of thanks that the Dragon King had decided to relocate them. She glanced out the barred windows at the gray, stormy lake, visible through the trees. Here, on ground level and nearer to the boats, freedom beckoned. But devising an escape would have to wait.

Midori shrieked, convulsed, and wept harder with each strengthening pain. She sat up, huffed, bore down, and grunted again and again, then fell back on the bed.

"It hurts so much," she cried. Terror and panic filled her eyes. "I can't bear any more!"

"Calm yourself," Reiko said, pressing on Midori's spinal potent points. But only delivering the baby would bring relief. She stifled her fear that Midori would succumb to the agony. "It will be over soon."

Lady Yanagisawa sat helplessly wringing her hands. Keisho-in peered between Midori's humped legs and exclaimed, "Look! The baby is coming!"

Reiko saw a small, round portion of the infant's head, covered by fuzzy black hair and bloody, oozing fluid, at the mouth of Midori's womanhood. "Push," she urged Midori.

But Midori's labors weakened even while the pains wracked her. She strained, but feebly. "It won't come out!" Her voice rose in hysteria. "It's stuck!"

"Try a little harder," Reiko begged.

"I can't!" A frenzy of sobbing and thrashing betook Midori. "I'm going to die! Oh no, oh no, oh no!"

"Oh, for the grace of Buddha," Lady Keisho-in said, grimacing in annoyance.

She drew back her hand and slapped Midori hard on the cheek. The blow abruptly silenced Midori. She stared in gasping, wounded surprise at Keisho-in.

"You're going to have this baby whether you like it or not," Keisho-in said. "Quit your silly whining. Show some courage." She knelt at Midori's feet and grasped her hands. "Now *push!*"

For once she'd used her authority to good purpose. Midori wheezed in a deep breath. Clinging to Keisho-in's hands like a rider trying to rein in a galloping horse, she raised herself forward. She pushed so hard that her face turned bright red and a savage growl arose from her throat.

"Good!" Keisho-in said. "Again!"

Midori clung, pushed, and growled. Reiko could hardly believe that Keisho-in had risen above her bad temper and given Midori the will to succeed. Now Midori strained with all her might. She screamed in triumph and release. Out of her slid the baby, its translucent pink skin streaked with blood and lined with blue veins, its eyes closed.

Keisho-in, Reiko, and Lady Yanagisawa cheered. While Midori lay panting and exhausted, Keisho-in held up the baby and said, "Look, you have a little girl."

The baby opened her mouth, and a loud wail emerged. Her tiny hands flexed. Midori gazed at her with awestruck love. Reiko belatedly noticed three guards standing in the open door, gaping at the scene.

"Don't just stand there, someone bring a dagger and cut the cord," Lady Keisho-in ordered them.

A guard complied; then he and his comrades departed. Keisho-in laid the child at Midori's breast. While Midori cuddled her, the child suckled.

"She's so beautiful," Midori murmured.

Tears stung Reiko's eyes as she and Lady Yanagisawa smiled. Keisho-in said, "Here comes the afterbirth."

The shared miracle of a new life raised their downcast spirits; new hope for the future banished the pall of fear, misery, and danger. But Midori's face crumpled. She began sobbing as if heartbroken.

"What's wrong?" Reiko said.

"I wish Hirata-*san* could see his daughter," Midori cried. "Maybe he never will."

Harsh reality shattered the joyous mood. Reiko, Lady Yanagisawa, and Keisho-in bowed their heads, unable to look at the innocent child that had been born into peril. Even while Reiko remembered the nearby boats, she knew that running away would be more difficult now than ever, with the fragile newborn. And since she couldn't count on anyone to rescue her and her companions before they came to harm, their lives depended on her manipulating the Dragon King into freeing them.

• • •

"Your Excellency, we bring good news," said Chamberlain Yanagisawa. He and Sano knelt before the dais in the audience hall and bowed to the shogun. "We've found proof that Dannoshin Minoru is the Dragon King. And we've discovered the location of a piece of property he owns. We believe he has imprisoned your mother there."

"You're too late!" the shogun crowed. There was rosy color in his usually pale cheeks, and an uncharacteristic sparkle in his eyes. "I, ahh, already know!" Hopping up and down in a little dance of triumph, he said, "The Dragon King has taken my mother to a castle on an island in a lake on the Izu Peninsula."

Sano reared back in surprise to hear the shogun name the site that he and Yanagisawa had just found on the map in the archives. He felt his mouth open and a frown contract his forehead. He glanced sideways and saw Yanagisawa reacting in the same manner.

"How did you find out?" Completely flummoxed for once in his life, Yanagisawa stared at the shogun.

"The maid Suiren is conscious," the shogun said. "I, ahh, talked to her." He giggled in delight at Yanagisawa's and Sano's discomposure; his attendants hid smiles. "She told me she'd overheard the, ahh, kidnappers say where they were going."

Sano and Yanagisawa exchanged a look of amazement. That their lord should take such initiative was something Sano had never expected. That Suiren should turn out to possess vital information, after he'd virtually given up hope on her, was almost beyond belief.

"Well," Yanagisawa said, recovering his poise. "Now that we all know who and where the Dragon King is, I ask that Your Excellency allow me to lead my troops on an expedition to rescue Lady Keisho-in."

"You're too late again!" The shogun gleefully beheld Sano and Yanagisawa. "I've already sent out the army. They're riding toward Izu at this moment."

Now Sano's amazement turned to horror. There was another reason he hadn't wanted the army involved, aside from the fact that the Dragon King had threatened to kill the hostages if he were pursued. Tokugawa soldiers were good at keeping order because their sheer numbers inspired fear among the public, and good at ganging up against troublemakers in the streets; but most of them had no battle experience. Their commanders had only commanded wars on the martial arts training ground. Sano didn't trust the army with a mission that required superior fighting skill or strategy. When they got to Izu, they wouldn't bother negotiating for the hostages' freedom; they would simply overrun the island. Even if they vastly outnumbered the defense, the Black Lotus mercenaries could kill enough Tokugawa troops and stave off defeat long enough for Dannoshin to kill Lady Keisho-in, Lady Yanagisawa, Midori, and Reiko. There was only one way to prevent this calamity.

"I request Your Excellency's permission to join the expedition to Izu," Sano said.

"Myself, too," Yanagisawa said, and Sano saw that he, too, understood that the shogun had jeopardized the hostages' survival. Furthermore, Sano reckoned that the chamberlain still wanted to be the hero, as well as earn back their lord's esteem.

"What for?" the shogun said with sly malice. "The army can, ahh, manage very well without you. Better that you should, ahh, stay here and attend to the duties you've, ahh, neglected lately. Sano-*san,* don't you have crimes to investigate? And Yanagisawa-*san,* I'm getting tired of, ahh, ruling the country by myself. I could use your help."

Sano and Yanagisawa looked at each other, and between them passed the tacit understanding that they must go to Izu, or woe betide everyone.

"Please allow us to congratulate you on your cleverness and prompt action, Your Excellency," began Yanagisawa.

As the shogun preened, Sano continued, "But we must express some concerns about your strategy."

"Ahh?" Self-doubt deflated the shogun's triumph.

"The army isn't trained to handle sensitive situations like this," Yanagisawa said.

"Nor do the commanders know anything about Dannoshin," Sano said.

"They won't be prepared for how determined he is to get revenge on Police Commissioner Hoshina or die trying," said Yanagisawa.

"A siege will provoke Dannoshin to kill your mother before the army can rescue her," Sano said.

The shogun gazed aghast at Sano and Yanagisawa. He wilted like a kite when the wind dies. "I never, ahh, thought of that," he mumbled. Falling to his knees, he clutched his head in both hands. "What have I done?" he said, his voice rising in panic. "Has my haste doomed my mother?"

His attendants averted their eyes from his misery. Although Sano pitied the shogun, whose stab at independent action had gone wrong, and hated to run roughshod over his lord, there was no time to cosset him. "It's not too late to correct your mistake," Sano said. "Just send us to Izu."

"We'll get there ahead of the army and prevent it from doing anything to endanger Lady Keisho-in," Yanagisawa said.

"We'll bring her home safe." *And Reiko and Midori with her,* thought Sano.

Now, seized by urgency, the shogun cried, "Yes! Yes! What are you waiting for?" His hands flapped, shooing Yanagisawa and Sano away from him. "Go!"

As Sano strode out of the room beside Yanagisawa, he looked back and saw the shogun slumped on the dais, face buried in his hands, mourning his own rashness.

27

The Dragon King regarded Reiko with stern disapproval. "There is blood on your clothing," he said.

Again he'd summoned her from the women's quarters, where Keisho-in and Lady Yanagisawa were bathing the baby and Midori slept. Reiko surmised that he'd brought her to his chambers to satisfy the passions she'd aroused in him earlier. Mustering the courage for another attempt to maneuver him, swallowing her fear, she looked down at her kimono and the red stains from Midori's childbirth.

"You must wash," said the Dragon King. "Come with me."

He led Reiko downstairs, into a room that smelled of decay and contained a bathtub sunken in a floor of wooden slats. Vines growing on lattice-covered windows imparted a murky green hue to the evening light. Black mold dotted the plank walls.

"Take off your clothes," the Dragon King said.

Reiko abhorred the very thought, but she was keenly aware of his power to hurt her should she displease him. And unless she proved her willingness to obey, she would never overcome his distrust, and her plan to free herself and her friends would never work. She turned her back to him, untied her sash, and dropped her outer robe.

He didn't speak, but she heard his breathing grow harsh. She reluctantly slipped off the white under-kimono and stood naked within the aura of his palpable lust. Her flesh rippled, and her muscles tensed; her spirit withered as she thought of Sano and deplored that this man should see what only her husband had the right to behold.

"Exquisite," the Dragon King murmured, trailing his fingers along her torso, down the curve of her hip.

Involuntarily clenching her buttocks, Reiko winced and braced herself for the assault that she'd feared since she'd first met him. Her throat constricted, nearly choking her.

The Dragon King snatched away his hand. "Go ahead and bathe now," he said in a subdued voice. "There's soap and a bucket on the shelf. Excuse me."

Reiko heard him leave the room. Her fear eased, although minimally. For some reason he kept skirting the brink of ravishing her, then retreating, but this might be her last reprieve before he yielded to desire. She noticed that he'd taken her clothes. She would have run away stark naked, if not for the guards she heard outside, and her captive friends. Reiko filled the bucket from the tub of water that smelled of the lake. She poured the water over herself, then scrubbed her body and hair with the cloth bag of rice-bran soap. Despite the circumstances, she found relief in washing after days without a bath. She rinsed, then immersed herself in the tub.

The Dragon King appeared at the door. He carried a bundle of folded fabric. "Here are some cloths to dry yourself, and fresh robes to wear," he said.

"Thank you," Reiko said, shivering in the chilly water as he stared through it at her body beneath the surface.

"Are your new quarters satisfactory?" he said.

"Yes, very." The sliding door and wall panels were solid and firmly locked by vertical beams inserted through the latches and floor on the outside; but Reiko had discovered that the wooden bars on the window were rotted and breakable.

"I've been thinking about what you said earlier." Squatting at the edge of the tub, the Dragon King spoke in a low, conspiratorial tone: "From now on, when you're not with me, you'll be guarded only by Ota, whom I trust. The others won't be allowed near you."

"Many thanks," Reiko said, glad to hear he'd reduced the watch on her. "I feel much safer now."

The Dragon King nodded absently, watching Reiko. "You look cold. You'd better come out."

He stepped back from the tub and waited. Reiko turned away from him as she rose, then climbed out of the water. Quickly she dried herself and put on the clothes he'd brought—a white under-robe and a teal silk kimono printed with white flowers. She tied the aqua sash, wondering where he'd gotten women's clothes. As she combed her fingers through her wet hair, the flowers on the kimono caught her eye.

They were anemones.

The clothes the Dragon King had given her had belonged to his dead beloved.

A chill passed through Reiko as she realized that he must have kept them during the twelve years since Anemone had died. She smelled a faint, stale whiff of perfume and body odor on the robes: They'd not been washed after Anemone last wore them. Reiko pictured the Dragon King fondling the clothes, sniffing their scent, arousing himself. She understood he was perpetuating the illusion that she was the embodiment of Anemone by dressing her in them. Revolted, she turned to face him.

His strange features were luminous with admiration. He intoned, "The pale wraith of your spirit departed its lifeless body. You drifted in enchanted slumber, down unfathomable depths, through watery channels, to the palace where we reunited." He touched Reiko's wet hair. "Come. There's something I must show you."

He led her up to his chamber and beyond the sliding partition. There, in a smaller room, Reiko saw the source of the incense odor that pervaded the palace and shrouded him. Brown sticks smoked in a brass bowl atop a small iron trunk. Near the bowl, candles burned around a painted color portrait of a young woman.

"This is you during the prime of your life, Anemone," the Dragon King told Reiko. "You are as beautiful now as you were then."

Reiko discerned a vague likeness to herself in the stylized portrait.

"I've kept your funeral altar since you died," he said. "My faithfulness has brought you back to life."

Glancing around the room, Reiko saw his bedding rolled up in a corner. Here was morbid evidence that he slept with the altar, worshiping the dead.

"Who was she?" Reiko said, driven by curiosity to risk disrupting the charade that she herself was Anemone.

The Dragon King gazed at the portrait. "She was my mother."

"Your mother?" Surprise struck Reiko, because his behavior toward her wasn't filial in the least. "But I thought . . ."

"That she was my lover?" The Dragon King smiled at Reiko's reaction. "Indeed she was." He'd switched from speaking to her as if she were Anemone to addressing her as the stranger in whom he thought Anemone's spirit reposed. "We were much closer than mothers and sons usually are."

He had engaged in carnal relations with his own mother! Reiko was shocked into silence. She recalled the Dragon King telling her about his dream in which Anemone had taught him calligraphy. Her mental image of the scene underwent a sudden alteration. Instead of an adult couple indulging in love play, Reiko saw a mother fondling an adolescent son, initiating him into forbidden sex. And now the son, grown into this evil, tortured man, wanted to recreate his sordid past with her. The magnitude of his perversion and insanity horrified Reiko.

"Anemone is the only woman I've ever loved," the Dragon King said, ignoring Reiko's discomfiture. "I never married because I couldn't forget her."

That was why he had no children and blamed Anemone for his lack, thought Reiko.

A pained smile twisted his face. "She was less faithful than I. She gave her love to someone else."

And that explained the anger with which he'd lashed out at Reiko and cursed her as a whore.

"But I can't entirely blame her," he said. "Women are weak, and susceptible to villains bent on seduction. When that man came along, she was helpless to resist him."

Reiko listened, compelled by morbid fascination, yet sure that the rest of the Dragon King's story couldn't top his earlier revelation.

"The man was my father's lover first," continued the Dragon King. "But he wasn't satisfied to make one conquest in our household. When he visited my father, he would sneak flirtatious looks at Anemone. He paid her compliments. When she served tea, he would touch her hand as he accepted the bowl from her and gaze into her eyes. My father was oblivious, but not I." The Dragon King's expression turned resentful. "I saw that man trying to win Anemone's affection. I saw her blush and smile. I saw her sneak him into the garden late at night and make love with him in the summer cottage."

She'd underestimated the Dragon King, Reiko thought, as she experienced fresh shock that the story involved an adulterous three-way love triangle as well as incest.

"Anemone was fooled by the man's ardor, but I knew better. I tried to tell her that he was just toying with her to feed his own vanity. I warned her that their affair would come to a bad end. But Anemone wouldn't listen. We never lay together again, because she abandoned me for him." Clenching his hands, the Dragon King flared in indignation: "She abandoned me, her own son, who loved her as that man never did!"

"What happened to Anemone?" Reiko asked, certain that these events had somehow led to the woman's death.

"My father learned of the affair between his wife and lover," the Dragon King said, his voice tight with the effort to control his emotions. "One night he took Anemone out on Lake Biwa in their pleasure boat. He drowned her, then killed himself."

A gasp caught in Reiko's throat.

"That man not only stole my beloved," the Dragon King said; "he was the cause of her death, and my father's." Rancor harshened his features. "He destroyed my family."

Reiko felt an unexpected pity toward the Dragon King, tormented by his memories, a prisoner of his torment. Then he said, "If not for Hoshina, my mother would still be alive. Anemone and I would be together."

Hearing a familiar name startled Reiko. "Anemone's lover was Hoshina? Do you mean Police Commissioner Hoshina, of Edo?"

"I do," the Dragon King said. He reeked of bitterness, as though it oozed like venom from his pores. "Hoshina was never punished for his part in Anemone's death. Everyone blamed her, because she was an adultcress who deserved to die, and my father, because he killed her. Not only did Hoshina walk away unscathed—he has prospered."

The Dragon King gnashed his teeth, consumed by rage. Reiko marveled that Hoshina, someone she knew, was the man who'd come between the Dragon King and Anemone, deprived them of their togetherness, and stolen the life from her.

"These twelve years, I've watched Hoshina rise in the *bakufu*," the Dragon King said. "I've watched him gain wealth, influence, and power, while I grieved for Anemone. I swore that someday I would make him pay for destroying her."

"Why did you wait so long?" Reiko said, puzzled.

"When Anemone died I was a mere boy, while Hoshina was an officer on the Miyako police force," the Dragon King said. "He had a powerful patron and other friends in high places; I had none. There was nothing I could do to hurt him then, so I bided my time. I kept my eye on Hoshina. Nine years passed without the right opportunity to attack. Then Hoshina moved to Edo. I followed him, and there I finally conceived my plan.

"One day, when I was riding through the city, I saw Lady Keisho-in traveling in her palanquin. I asked myself, 'What does the shogun value enough that if it were stolen from him, he would do anything to get it back?' The answer was right before my eyes. I decided to kidnap Lady Keisho-in and demand that the shogun execute Hoshina for murder in exchange for her return." The Dragon King gloated; the flames of the candles on the altar reflected in his eyes. "And that's exactly what I've done."

Reiko had thought herself inured to further surprise, but his new revelation shocked her beyond all else. "Do you mean you kidnapped us because of Hoshina?"

"Of course," the Dragon King said as though it were the most reasonable deed in the world.

At last Reiko understood the reason behind his crimes. What great lengths he'd gone to to satisfy an old grudge! What savagery he'd committed with the ultimate aim of bringing down one man!

"How could you kill so many people, just to punish Hoshina?" she cried. "How could you kidnap the shogun's mother, and the rest of us, when we've never done anything to hurt you? Why should we suffer for what Hoshina did?"

"Vengeance justifies extreme action," the Dragon King said. "The deaths of your attendants were necessary sacrifices. That you must suffer is unfortunate, but can't be helped. Nothing short of what I've done could destroy Hoshina."

He seemed so proud of what he'd done, and so eager to boast, that he didn't mind confessing to her. Either he was mad enough not to care that she knew, or he thought she would never have a chance to tell anyone. The grandiose scale of his plot flabbergasted Reiko, as did his belief that it was his only means of revenge.

"Why didn't you just tell everyone how Hoshina caused your parents' deaths and ruin his reputation?" she said. "Why not go to the magistrate, lodge a formal complaint against Hoshina, and demand that he make amends?"

"Hoshina is an important man. If I spoke out against him, no one would listen to me. No magistrate would take my side in a dispute."

"Then why not challenge Hoshina to a duel?" Reiko said. Duels were a common means by which samurai resolved grievances outside the law. "Wouldn't killing him yourself be simpler than making the shogun execute him?"

"I don't just want Hoshina dead," the Dragon King said, his manner defensive. "I want him officially denounced as a murderer, stripped of his rank and privileges, and executed like a common criminal. I want his honor disgraced, and his corpse exposed to the public revilement he deserves. This is what my scheme will accomplish."

Yet Reiko glimpsed the truth underlying the Dragon King's self-righteous assertions. He wouldn't challenge Hoshina to a duel because Hoshina would probably win, and he didn't want to die. Nor would he speak out against Hoshina, because he feared retaliation from his powerful enemy. He wanted to attack Hoshina without risking his own skin; he wanted revenge without consequences. He thought he could kidnap the shogun's mother, force Hoshina's execution, then sneak away to savor his triumph.

The Dragon King was a coward.

"And now that my scheme is under way," he said, "all I need do is wait for my spies in Edo to bring me the news that Hoshina has been executed. When I see his corpse displayed by the Nihonbashi Bridge, I shall have my revenge."

He was also a fool if he believed his scheme would work, Reiko thought. Didn't he know Hoshina was the paramour of the shogun's second-in-command? Chamberlain Yanagisawa would prevent Hoshina's execution. But even if he didn't, the crafty Hoshina was sure to avoid death somehow. The Dragon King's scheme would fail. A premonitory chill crept through Reiko.

"What are you going to do if the shogun won't do as you've demanded?" she said.

"He will." Smug confidence infused the Dragon King's voice. "Because I've warned him that unless he does, I'll kill his mother and her friends."

Reiko at last understood what he had meant when he'd previously told her that he hoped not to kill her. He would prefer that his plan achieve Hoshina's death rather than carry out the threat of slaying his hostages. But she comprehended with a rush of sickening horror that she, Lady Keisho-in, Midori, and Lady Yanagisawa had been doomed from the start. There had never been any possibility that the Dragon King would free them. He would wait for news of Hoshina's death, in vain. And when he realized that his revenge attempt had failed . . .

Panic filled Reiko as she wondered how much time was left before he gave up hope. Maybe those twelve years of waiting for revenge had exhausted his patience. She couldn't afford to gamble that he would wait much longer. She must forge ahead with her scheme, even though she feared it was premature.

"Dearest," she said, caressing the Dragon King's hands, "I'm so afraid something will go wrong. And I don't like this place. Why don't we leave—just you and me?"

If she could get him to take her off the island, away from his men, she would have a chance at freedom. He couldn't watch her all the time. She could sneak away, find a Tokugawa garrison, and send soldiers to rescue her friends. His men wouldn't stay here once they discovered their master was gone; rather, they would realize that he'd left them holding the hostages, ready to take the blame for the kidnapping. They would flee, abandoning Midori, the baby, Keisho-in, and Lady Yanagisawa, who would be safe enough until help came.

"We can go somewhere pleasant together," Reiko said eagerly. "We don't even have to tell anyone."

The Dragon King regarded her with consternation. "We can't leave. Not until Hoshina is dead."

"Why not just forget him? Why is revenge so important

anymore?" Reiko wheedled. "That we're together is all that matters."

"Twelve years I've waited to bring Hoshina to justice." The Dragon King's hand was hard and unyielding in Reiko's. "I won't give up my victory over him, even for you. I'll not have peace until he no longer fouls this world."

"But I'm so afraid you'll get in trouble," Reiko said. "Punishing Hoshina isn't worth your life. I can't bear the thought of losing you." With a sob of genuine desperation, she lifted her hand and stroked his cheek. The stubble on it abraded her fingers. "Please, take me away from here now!"

He frowned, leaning away from her touch. "My plan is foolproof. There won't be any trouble." His adamant tone bespoke his faith in his insane scheme. "We will stay here until I know Hoshina has been denounced and executed. My decision is final."

Hirata, Marume, and Fukida carried their raft out from the woods. Staggering under its unwieldy mass, they laid it at the edge of the lake. The sky was a vast cobalt-blue dome spattered with brilliant stars; the full moon diffused radiance through clouds that drifted like smoke. Reflected lights glimmered on the black water. A cool wind evoked whispers from the forest, which vibrated with the nocturnal insect chorus. Hirata and the detectives eased the raft off the bank, into the water. They held their breath in wordless suspense.

The raft rocked on the undulating surface, but didn't sink.

"Thank the gods," Hirata said with fervent relief.

He and Fukida fetched the oars, then crawled gingerly onto the raft. Marume pushed it away from the shore, waded into the lake, and clambered aboard. The raft plunged under him. The men hurriedly shifted position until their weight balanced and the raft stabilized. Hirata and Fukida began paddling. Water sloshed over the raft and seeped through cracks between the logs, but it stayed afloat, inching toward the opposite shore. Hirata feared that each accidental splash of the paddles would alert the kidnappers that intruders were approaching. As he rowed, he watched the island.

Darkness blended the terrain and castle into a black, impenetrable mass. Although the island seemed devoid of life, Hirata dreaded that its occupants would spot him and his companions on the open water, vulnerable as a duck without wings. A pang of doubt chimed inside him. Despite his determination to save Midori, he wondered whether he'd made the right choice. Should he have obeyed Sano's orders instead?

Jittery with fatigue and apprehension, Hirata plied his oar with hands that were still raw and tender from building the raft. He sniffed mucus up his nose and wished his cold would go away. He told himself it was too late to change his decision. Afraid for Midori's safety, he wanted her back now, not after he returned to Edo.

The island loomed larger. Soon the raft bumped to a halt in the shallows near the end of the island opposite the dock. Hirata saw the sloping bank and dense trees articulated by the moonlight, and luminous reflections breaking at the shoreline. He and his companions climbed off the raft. Cold water immersed them up to their shins. Mud sucked at Hirata's sandals as he waded ashore. He and Fukida and Marume hauled the dripping raft out of the lake, into the forest, and leaned it upright against a tree. They draped vines over the raft and buried the oars under fallen leaves. Then they crept through the woods, toward the castle.

The light from the stars and moon barely pierced the dense shadows in the forest. Hirata and the detectives groped their way around trees, over dead logs. His fear of getting caught magnified every crackle of twigs under his feet, and every rustle of leafy branches against him, into a thunderous noise. The atmosphere tingled with the presence of nearby humans. A sudden sense of danger and malevolence stirred Hirata's nerves. At the same moment, he smelled burning oil and spied a light flickering in the near distance.

Hirata froze, his arm flung out to halt Marume and Fukida behind him. They all crouched in the underbrush as footsteps tramped toward them. The light was a flame that guttered in a metal lantern carried by a tough-looking samurai. His visage, eerily lit by the lantern, disappeared and reappeared between the trees. Hirata held his breath until the samurai passed. With his heart pounding from the close call, Hirata cautiously rose. He and his men continued their advance for some twenty more paces, until they spied more lights, traversing the island in multiple directions. Again and again they paused to hide as more samurai patrolled around them. Hirata was dismayed that so many of the kidnappers maintained a vigilant watch even at night, when he'd hoped they would be asleep.

Could he find Midori before they found him?

Ages seemed to pass while he and his comrades crept across the island. Finally, a lessening in the darkness ahead of them signaled an open space. Hirata, Fukida, and Marume stopped within the fringes of the forest and peered out at the castle. The glow of the moon limned buildings that squatted like a mausoleum in a graveyard. Their damaged roofs pointed jagged peaks toward the sky. At intervals along the dilapidated, vine-covered walls stood many sentries, guarding the place. The occasional low rumble of their voices underlay the distant splashing of the waves.

Gesturing for Marume and Fukida to follow him, Hirata crept around the castle's perimeter, staying within the cover of the forest. He saw collapsed structures, a pavilion in an overgrown garden, and more sentries. Breaching the kidnappers' defenses and rescuing the women began to seem impossible.

Fukida leaned close to Hirata and murmured in his ear: "If we go to Edo, we can bring back more troops."

This idea had occurred to Hirata, but he couldn't bear to retreat after he'd come this far. "Not yet," he whispered.

They resumed circling the castle. Outside a wing that

was joined to the main palace by a covered walkway, a lone samurai crouched on the veranda. His two swords jutted at his waist. The clouds shifted, unveiling the moon, which shone on the peeling plaster wall behind him. Above him to his right, in a rectangular window, vertical bars alternated with stripes of dark interior space. As Hirata sidled onward in search of an unguarded access to the castle, a pale shape moved into the frame of the window.

It was a woman, her face framed by long hair that streamed down her shoulders. The moon illuminated her features. Hirata's heart slammed inside his chest. Recognition froze him so abruptly that Fukida and Marume bumped against him.

"Midori," he whispered. Jubilation surged within him. He'd found his wife! Giddy with relief, he clung to a tree trunk and stared at her.

She gazed out through the window, her expression pensive and melancholy. Hirata knew she was thinking of him, longing for him. He stifled the impulse to shout her name and run to her. Then Midori turned away from the window. Hirata reached out his hand to stop her, but she vanished into the darkness inside the room. Anguish and frustration flooded him. Even though he and Marume and Fukida could easily overpower the guard, the noise would bring the other kidnappers running. He mustn't start a battle that he would certainly lose because the enemy outnumbered his side.

"We've got to find a way inside the castle and sneak Midori and the other women out," he whispered.

28

"My influence over the Dragon King is too weak to make him abandon his plans," Reiko told Lady Yanagisawa.

They sat in their room, while the night immersed them in shadow and the light coming in the window glowed pale with the moon's cold rays. The Dragon King had sent Reiko back to the room, and she'd just told Lady Yanagisawa what had happened between her and their captor. Nearby, the baby wailed, and Midori rocked her.

"She's hungry," Keisho-in said. "Time to feed her again."

"She eats a lot," Midori said, opening her kimono and suckling the baby. "That's a good sign, isn't it?"

"Oh, yes." Keisho-in sniffed the baby's bottom and wrinkled her nose. "She also makes lots of dung. That's a good sign, too."

Lady Yanagisawa said to Reiko, "Perhaps if you ask the Dragon King again . . . ?"

Reiko shook her head as desolation overwhelmed her. "I'm afraid that if I continue begging him to leave the island, he'll get angry. Maybe angry enough to do something terrible." She touched her cheek, which was still bruised where the Dragon King had struck her. She watched Midori and Keisho-in fuss over the baby; she spoke quietly so that they wouldn't hear: "Lady Keisho-in is the only one of us that he can use to force the shogun to execute Police Commissioner Hoshina. The rest of us are expendable."

"Surely he wouldn't want to harm you or your friends?" As horror crept over her features, Lady Yanagisawa moved closer to Reiko. "Not while he's in love with you because he thinks you're possessed by the spirit of his dead mother?"

"He's a madman," Reiko said, easing away from Lady Yanagisawa's suffocating nearness. "However he seems to feel about me, there's no telling what he'll do."

Lady Yanagisawa said, "But even if you can't trick him into leaving . . . now that there's only one man guarding us, perhaps we can get away?"

They looked toward the window that Reiko had identified as an escape route. At that moment Ota's scowling face peered through the rotten bars she'd hoped to break.

"Listen to me, you little witch," Ota said, pointing a finger at Reiko. "Even if you've fooled my master by playing up to him, you can't fool me. I know you're up to no good. I'll be watching you. So be warned." His hostile gaze flickered over Midori. "One wrong step, and that baby is dead."

He disappeared from view. Midori shrieked in terror. As Keisho-in shouted curses after Ota and enfolded Midori and the baby in her arms, Lady Yanagisawa turned to Reiko. "What shall we do?" she said anxiously. "Wait for someone to rescue us?"

"We can't." Reiko sat mired in the awful conviction that they would all die unless they got away before the Dragon King discovered that he wasn't going to get the revenge he wanted. But Ota made sneaking out of their prison impossible. An even worse dread filled Reiko as her mind lit on an alternative.

"I can think of only one way to free us," she whispered. "The next time I'm with the Dragon King, I must steal his sword and kill him. Then I must get us all out of the palace and into the boats."

Lady Yanagisawa nodded, her faith in Reiko shining in

her eyes. But Reiko experienced a dire, sinking sensation because she also could think of only one way to conquer the Dragon King. It would surely bring her ruination. And even if she defeated him, she still must contend with Ota and any other guards who tried to prevent her and her friends from leaving.

"Your life is in danger, and I haven't even named you yet," Midori lamented to the baby clasped against her bosom. Tradition required that parents wait until the sixth day after the birth to name a child and celebrate its arrival. "Oh, Reiko-*san,* will we be home for her naming day?"

As Reiko beheld Midori and the baby, resignation spread through her, as if turning the blood in her veins to stone. The need to save the innocent child outweighed all the hazards and sacrifices associated with her new plot against the Dragon King.

"I promise we'll be home by then," Reiko said.

As Hirata, Marume, and Fukida rounded the curve of the clearing, the castle's revolving view presented more wings, guarded by more sentries. Then Hirata saw a section where roofs had caved in on structures with gaping holes in the walls and trees growing out of the rooms. Vegetation enmeshed scattered rubble in what appeared to be an utter, deserted ruin that the kidnappers neglected to guard.

"Let's try there," Hirata said.

They sprinted across the narrow strip of open ground in the clearing and darted into the ruins. They thrashed through high weeds and stumbled amid debris. Fukida tripped on a pile of wreckage and fell; Marume yanked him to his feet. As they circumnavigated a corner formed by two broken walls on an exposed foundation, sudden light dazzled Hirata.

Toward him marched a brawny young samurai, carrying a lantern. Hirata, Fukida, and Marume faltered to a standstill. The samurai saw them and froze; his eyes registered that they were intruders. He drew his sword. His mouth opened to call his comrades.

Marume lunged. He lashed out his sword. It cut the samurai across the throat. A look of horror came over his face as the wound spurted blood. He gurgled, and the lantern dropped from his hand. He collapsed dead on the ground.

Hirata and the detectives stared at the corpse, then each other, unnerved by the sudden violence and their narrow escape. Then Hirata took a closer look at the dead man's face. A disturbing chord resounded through him because he didn't recognize the man—this wasn't one of Lord Niu's. Hirata reasoned that he didn't know all his father-in-law's many retainers, but he felt increasing doubt that the *daimyo* was responsible for the kidnapping.

"We should hide the body," said Fukida.

Before he or Hirata or Marume could move, someone nearby called, "What was that noise? Ibe-*san,* are you there?"

Footsteps hurried toward Hirata and his comrades. They backed away from the corpse and sped around the wrecked building. Huddling at its base, they peered around the corner and watched another young samurai kneel beside the corpse.

"Ibe-*san!* What happened?" he exclaimed, holding his lantern near his comrade's lifeless face. He looked fearfully around him. Hirata saw that this man, too, was unknown to him. Then the samurai took off running. "Ibe's been killed!" he shouted. "Someone has invaded the island!"

The night came alive with answering voices and sounds of motion. Men streamed out from the castle grounds. A bolt of horror stunned Hirata. He felt Marume and Fukida tense beside him as their worst fears became reality.

"What do we do now?" Marume said.

Shouts rang out as the kidnappers raised the alarm. "We run," Hirata said.

They raced out of the ruins, crossed the clearing, and plunged into the woods. Torchlights flashed; shadowy figures came speeding toward them. They zigzagged between trees, ducking beneath foliage, crouching to avoid notice as their pursuers multiplied in number. Hirata wished with all his heart that he had obeyed Sano's orders rather than attempted the rescue himself. If he'd done his duty, he would have arrived back in Edo by now and reported the location of the kidnappers. Sano could have sent the whole detective corps to rescue the women. But instead, Hirata was running for his life and was no use to Midori. If he, Marume, and Fukida got caught, there would be no one to tell Sano where the women were. Hirata bitterly regretted his choice.

"We have to get across the lake," he said, "but our raft is too far away. Let's steal the boats and maroon the kidnappers."

They raced toward the shore. Arrows whizzed through the air, striking ground and tree trunks near their feet. When they reached the forest's edge, they saw two men standing on the dock, guarding the boats. Winded and panting, they veered back into the forest.

"We can swim to the mainland," Fukida said.

But their pursuers wove a tightening net around the island, chasing them away from the shores. They found themselves in the woods near the main palace. Skeletal guard turrets protruded from a crumbled wall. Four sentries loitered outside a gateway that led to grounds filled with a jungle of shrubbery. Beyond the grounds, the moon floated above the palace. Carved metal dragons set in the roof gables proclaimed a silent warning. Light shone through grills that covered the second-story windows. Hirata deduced that this was the kidnappers' stronghold, a place to avoid. But exhaustion forced him and Marume and Fukida to stop and rest.

"Let's hide someplace until they think we've escaped," he said.

Just then, runners came crashing through the forest behind them. Instinctively they fell flat on the ground and lay still. Two men galloped right past Hirata's face. Their feet kicked damp leaves onto him. They burst through the clearing and rushed into the palace. Hirata raised his head and

saw them standing inside the dimly lit entranceway, with a
third man who'd joined them.

"We have bad news," Hirata heard one of the arrivals
say in a breathless voice.

"What is it?" The third man's voice was gruff, tinged
with irritation and anxiety.

"There are trespassers on the island."

"Who are they?" demanded the gruff-voiced man, who
seemed to be the leader.

"We don't know."

The leader said, "How do you know they're here?"

"They killed one of our men. And we found a raft hidden in the forest near the shore."

Hirata learned that life could go from bad to worse in a
mere instant. The kidnappers not only knew that he and
Marume and Fukida were here; they'd discovered his
means of conveying the women to safety. His hope of trying another rescue attempt later died within him.

"I've got two men hiding near the raft, in case the trespassers go back to it," said the man who'd brought the
news.

"Round up all the others," the leader said, his manner
curt and authoritative. "I want everyone out searching."

Furthermore, Hirata didn't recognize the leader's voice.
This fact confirmed that someone other than Lord Niu had
organized the kidnapping. Lord Niu might have hired a
mercenary army to help, but he was smart enough not to
delegate command of such a risky operation to somebody
other than one of his longtime trusted vassals. Hirata knew
all those, and the man in the castle wasn't one. Now Hirata
absorbed the full, horrific truth about his predicament.

The kidnapping wasn't just a scheme by his father-in-
law. It was part of something he couldn't begin to understand. He and Marume and Fukida were trapped on the
island by a stranger with unknown motives even more evil
than Lord Niu's.

"Capture the trespassers and bring them to me," said the
leader.

The men hastened from the castle. But even as the consequences of his actions appalled him, Hirata postponed his self-recriminations. There was no use wishing he'd done what he should have. There seemed but one remedy.

"We'll have to kill off the kidnappers," Hirata said, "until there's few enough of them left that we can sneak inside the palace, get the women, and escape."

"Or until the kidnappers catch us," Marume and Fukida said in unison.

29

A storm the next day assailed the Tōkaidō, where Sano and his detective corps trotted on horseback behind Chamberlain Yanagisawa and his elite squadron of fighters, bound for the Dragon King's palace. Gusts of wind lashed streaming rain against the two hundred mounted men. Thunder boomed across distant hills obscured by mist; lightning crazed the sky above the cypress woods that bordered the highway. Sano and his comrades rode hunched against the downpour. Water cascaded off the brim of his wide wicker hat, pelted his face, drenched his cloak and armor. The horses' hooves splashed in puddles, flung up mud. But discomfort bothered Sano less than did the fact that although he and Yanagisawa had gathered their forces and headed west toward the Izu Peninsula as soon as the shogun had granted them permission, they'd made poor progress.

They'd traveled all yesterday evening and last night, and they'd barely passed Oiso, the halfway point of their journey. Traffic outside Edo and steep stretches of road along the sea had hindered them, although Chamberlain Yanagisawa's authority had sped them through inspections at checkpoints. Riding any faster would tire the horses, and the village stables didn't have enough fresh mounts for rent. And the twenty small wooden boats, brought for ferrying

troops, guns, and ammunition to the island, further precluded speed.

The boats had traveled on oxcarts for the early part of
the trip, but the carts had been abandoned because they
couldn't cross the rivers. Now foot soldiers carried the
boats over their heads. The Tokugawa policy that prohibited bridges along the main highways, restricted troop
movement, and prevented rebellions had backfired on the
rescue mission. At this rate, the mission wouldn't reach the
island until tomorrow. Sano feared that the delay would
cost Reiko, Midori, Keisho-in, and Lady Yanagisawa their
lives. If only he'd discovered the Dragon King's identity
and whereabouts sooner, or if Hirata had brought the information! Sano wondered what had become of Hirata,
Marume, and Fukida.

Suddenly he heard shouts ring out above the thunder.
The procession slowed to a halt.

"Why are we stopping?" he said to Detective Inoue, who
rode at his side.

Inoue squinted into the pouring rain. "It looks like
there's someone blocking the road."

Sano stood in the stirrups, peered impatiently over Yanagisawa's troops, and saw banners emblazoned with the
Tokugawa crest. "It's the army," he said. "We've caught
up with the forces that the shogun sent."

He was glad the army hadn't yet reached Izu and he and
Chamberlain Yanagisawa could prevent its siege of the
Dragon King. But the procession remained stopped. Angry
voices rose from a stir between the procession and the
army; mutters of confusion spread through the ranks. Eager
to learn the cause of the delay, Sano steered his horse past
the troops to the front of the procession. There he found
Yanagisawa, astride a black stallion and clad in dripping
rain gear, facing off against a bulbous mounted samurai
who wore a helmet crowned with golden horns. Sano recognized the samurai as General Isogai, supreme commander
of the Tokugawa army.

"I'm taking over the rescue expedition," Chamberlain

Yanagisawa shouted. He gestured at the army, some thousand strong, waiting on the road ahead of him and General Isogai. "Turn your troops around. Go home."

"I'll do no such thing," the general retorted. "The shogun has sent us to rescue his mother, and I intend to do my duty."

"You'll do as I say, or be sorry later," Yanagisawa said.

General Isogai laughed scornfully. "I don't take orders from you. And in case you haven't noticed, your threats don't carry as much weight these days." Galloping to the head of his army, he called, "Onward!"

The army surged down the highway. Yanagisawa stared after it in helpless rage. Sano experienced disbelief that anyone would treat the chamberlain so rudely, shock that Yanagisawa seemed to have lost much power, and awareness that the kidnapping had spawned unexpected repercussions, which weren't yet common knowledge outside the *bakufu*'s top echelon.

Then Yanagisawa yelled to his troops, "Overtake the army!"

His men charged past Sano. Galloping horses buffeted him until he found himself at the front of his own detectives and joined the wild chase. His and Yanagisawa's forces streamed up the road's sloping banks around the army and plowed through its ranks. Skirmishes erupted. Yanagisawa's squadron broke free from the pack and sped away. Sano and his detectives knocked soldiers off their horses, fended off grabbing hands, cleared the way for the men carrying the boats, and followed Yanagisawa.

Lightning stabbed a jagged silver line down the heavens; thunder shook the earth. Murderous yells came from the army, in hot pursuit but falling behind. Through the rainy landscape Sano and Yanagisawa hastened, until they reached the Sakawa River. The rain had swelled the river into a rushing torrent that overflowed the stone dikes. Perilous rapids stretched as far as Sano could see in either direction. The ferrymen who usually rowed travelers to the opposite bank were absent.

"We'll ride the horses and row our own boats across," said Yanagisawa.

At his orders, their army plunged into the river. The water became a roiling tumult of men and horses. Some riders were swept off their mounts and carried downstream. The men in the boats fought to row against the current. Sano urged his horse into the river. While the horse trod the water, Sano felt the current tugging at them. Cold waves sloshed over his lap. Midway across, he heard hoofbeats pounding on the road behind him. He looked around, saw mounted troops approaching, and thought the army had caught up. Then he noticed the banner carried by the lead rider. Surprise beset Sano, for the banner bore a dragonfly symbol instead of the Tokugawa crest.

The newcomers dove into the water; they joined the crush of struggling riders and whirling boats. A samurai rammed his horse against Sano's. "Get out of my way!" he yelled.

"Lord Niu," Sano said, beholding the crazed, distorted face of the *daimyo*. "What are you doing here?"

"I heard that you and the chamberlain and the army were going to Izu to rescue my daughter. I decided to go along." Slapping the reins, Lord Niu shouted at his horse to swim faster.

Sano was horrified at the chaos that had resulted from too many people getting involved, to the detriment of the common good. The impetuous, hot-tempered Lord Niu could jeopardize the rescue even worse than could the Tokugawa army. This mission had become a race to get to Izu first, as well as a fight to stay alive long enough to save the women.

Inside the Dragon King's palace, the women listened to the commotion that had begun last night and continued through the present afternoon. Shouts echoed; running footsteps sounded throughout the castle buildings and grounds. Reiko heard the distant whir and thump of flying arrows. She peered out the barred window, as she'd done repeatedly since the unrest began.

"What do you see?" Midori asked anxiously, while she nursed the baby.

"It's going to rain again," Reiko said. Dark storm clouds encroached upon the overcast sky. She watched Ota step off the veranda and stride through the garden to meet another man who hurried toward him. They conversed in low, urgent tones. "Ota is talking to one of his friends. I can't hear what they're saying, but they seem troubled."

The other guard hastened away. Ota shot Reiko an ireful glance. Earlier, she'd asked him about the strange disturbance, but he'd refused to tell her anything. She sidestepped away from the window.

"I wish I knew what's going on," she said.

"Could the kidnappers be fighting among themselves?" Lady Yanagisawa said hesitantly. "Or maybe they've rebelled against their leader?"

A mutiny would explain the commotion, Reiko thought. It would also explain why the Dragon King hadn't summoned her since yesterday, when he'd revealed the reason for his crimes and she'd failed to convince him to leave the island. Defending himself against traitors would keep him too busy. But another possibility gave her hope.

"Maybe someone has come to rescue us," Keisho-in said, voicing Reiko's thought.

"Oh, I hope it's Hirata-*san* and Sano-*san*!" Eagerness shone on Midori's face. "Maybe they'll get us out of here soon."

Reiko also hoped their husbands had come to their rescue. But if so, what was taking them so long? And she couldn't feel Sano's presence, as she always did when he was near.

Lady Yanagisawa joined Reiko near the window. "Might the noise signify a battle between the rescuers and the Dragon King?" Lady Yanagisawa whispered.

"I'm afraid that may be the case," Reiko whispered back. "Almost a day has passed since the noise began, and we're still captive. That could mean the Dragon King is successfully defending his stronghold."

Distress etched Lady Yanagisawa's face. "If his men kill the rescuers, salvation will never come."

Reiko nodded unhappily as another unwelcome thought occurred to her. "No matter whether someone's trying to save us or there's a mutiny—either one means trouble for us. An attack by the *bakufu* could panic the Dragon King into carrying out his threat to kill us. But we could also be killed in a war between him and his own men."

What she'd decided yesterday still seemed to hold true: "Unless I can get to the Dragon King, kill him, and free us, we'll die." Even though Reiko prayed that he would send for her again, she longed for rescue to come and spare her the need to do what she planned.

Crouched behind a moss-covered boulder in the gardens within the castle, Hirata, Marume, and Fukida spied two peasant hoodlums striding in their direction through the tall grass. Both carried iron clubs and wore the watchful air of hunters. Hirata was glad the island afforded many hiding places, and the sunless day helped him and his comrades blend into the landscape. But he wasn't so glad that the kidnappers had begun stalking them in teams. They'd lost the advantage they'd had against lone pursuers. Every time they got close to the part of the castle where Midori was, the kidnappers chased them away. A night, morning, and afternoon of covert warfare had diminished their stamina. Exhaustion, hunger, and strain plagued Hirata, as did his cold. How much longer could they continue their deadly game?

The hoodlums passed them. Marume sprang from behind the boulder. Grabbing the nearest hoodlum, he flung his strong arm across the man's throat. One brutal squeeze, one strangled cry, and the hoodlum dropped dead. His partner turned, saw Marume, and raised his club. Hirata lunged and swung his sword, gashing the hoodlum's belly. As the bleeding, groaning man crumpled, Hirata saw two samurai sneaking up behind Fukida, who squatted near the boulder.

"Look out!" Hirata called.

Fukida whirled, sword in hand. He parried strikes from the samurai, then struck one down with a deep, slanting cut to the torso. Hirata and Marume felled the other in a frenzy of clashing swords. Weary and panting, bloodstained from minor injuries, Hirata and the detectives beheld the corpses.

"That's eighteen so far," Marume said. "I wonder how many more kidnappers are left."

"Too many," Hirata said.

That they'd eliminated some of the enemy seemed to have hardly diminished its numbers. Hirata felt no remorse at slaying men who'd stolen his wife and murdered a hundred people, but the ceaseless round of killing had eroded his spirit. He only hoped he could endure long enough to save Midori.

Suddenly he heard movement behind a wrecked cottage nearby. He saw the cylindrical barrel of a gun poking around the corner. Panic lurched his heart. "Run!" he said.

He and Fukida and Marume launched themselves across the gardens. The shot boomed; the bullet pinged off the boulder. More gunfire roared; running footsteps followed them. They sprinted, crouching low to the ground, through trees that screened the castle from the lake, which rippled like gray lava. Halted at the shoreline, they looked desperately around for somewhere to hide. At the water's edge, tall reeds waved in the breeze. Low, sooty clouds scudded over the woods and hills on the mainland. Hirata, Marume, and Fukida plowed through the reeds, into water up to their thighs. They crouched in the cover of the reeds.

Two samurai burst from the forest. Each carried an arquebus; containers for gunpowder and bullets dangled at their waists. They paused to survey the area. Their gazes bypassed the spot where Hirata and the detectives waited in motionless suspense. Then they retreated into the forest. Hirata and his comrades exchanged a look that expressed more apprehension than relief.

"That they're using guns now means they've given up trying to capture us," Hirata said. "They're shooting to kill."

"Our close calls are getting closer every time," Fukida said.

"We can't keep this up forever," Marume said. "Eventually they'll get us."

Hirata couldn't deny that likelihood. But he said bravely, "We don't have to keep this up forever. Just long enough to reduce the castle's defense and smuggle out the women."

30

Time on the island crept at an agonizing, relentless pace, through a cold night, a bleak dawn, and a day of intermittent storms. Now another night descended. Gunshots blared closer to the palace with each passing hour. Inside the women's room, the baby wailed in Midori's arms.

"The shooting frightens her," Midori said. "I wish it would stop."

Keisho-in and Lady Yanagisawa, bundled in quilts against the night chill, looked up at the window. Their anxious faces shone white in the moonlight. Reiko stirred in her own quilt. She understood how samurai women must have felt during wartime, anxiously waiting while men fought. What she wished for was one chance to slay the Dragon King. But two days had passed since she'd seen him. What effect would the attack have on his demented mind? Instead of summoning her for another erotic tryst, would he order his men to kill her and her friends?

More gunfire resounded. As Midori and Keisho-in cried out and the baby shrieked, the door opened. Ota stood at the threshold. His hostile eyes flashed at Reiko.

"My master wants to see you," he said.

Anticipation and dread melded inside Reiko. As she rose and walked toward Ota, she felt herself embarking on a course that would decide her destiny, tonight.

Ota pointed at the other women. "Behave yourselves while I'm gone."

He cut an ominous glance at the baby, then positioned Reiko against the wall of the corridor outside the room. He held the blade of his sword to her throat while he closed the door and rammed the metal beam through the latches. Evidently, he intended to leave her friends alone; he didn't call other men to guard them. Reiko wondered why the sudden lapse in security. But whatever the reason, she was glad, because if she managed to kill the Dragon King, she could liberate the other women.

Ota walked her along the roofed, open passageway that connected the castle buildings and traversed a garden. Reiko looked for the men who usually loitered around the castle, which seemed eerily deserted. Through a screen of tall, tangled shrubs on her left she spied two guards hurrying past. Between them they carried a long, limp bundle. Reiko's eyes widened: The bundle appeared to be a dead body. She deduced why the guards were absent.

Someone was killing them off.

Ota propelled her through a door to the palace. As they climbed the stairs, she heard the Dragon King say, "Haven't you caught the intruders yet?"

"No, master," said another man's voice, more distant.

"How can they keep killing our men when there are only three of them and so many of us?" the Dragon King demanded. "How can they evade you on this tiny island?"

"I'm sorry to say they're very clever," the other man said. "But we've managed to keep them away from the women's quarters, where they're trying to go."

Jubilation surged within Reiko. Someone really was trying to rescue her! Immediately, doubts eclipsed happiness. Could the rescuers prevail against the Dragon King's army?

"Perhaps we should move to a safer place?" said the man.

"There is nowhere safer," the Dragon King said. "And I won't be chased off by anyone, nor change my plans."

Ota thrust her into the chamber. The Dragon King stood

on the balcony, his back to the door. The brocade dragon on his kimono snarled at Reiko. "Keep hunting the intruders," he said to someone outside. "Don't let them near the prisoners or off the island."

He turned, spied Reiko, and said to Ota, "Go help catch the invaders." Although Ota objected, the Dragon King waved him away. He departed with a scowl at Reiko. As the Dragon King advanced on her, she tried to smile, though quaking with anxiety. It was more important than ever for her plan to succeed. She must help the rescuers by slaying the Dragon King before he killed them. She must get herself and her friends out of the palace, which his men had so far managed to defend.

"Greetings, Anemone," the Dragon King said.

His manner was preoccupied, his attention divided between Reiko and his troubles. She drew a deep breath for courage, then stepped close to him and began the dangerous seduction by which she hoped to win her liberty.

"What's wrong, my lord?" she said, feigning concern about him.

"Nothing that need trouble you," he said curtly.

Reiko tried to forget all the perils she risked, and the husband that her actions would betray. She loosened her sash and let Anemone's silk robes slip down her shoulders in alluring fashion. She spoke sweetly through nausea that rose in her throat: "Is there something I can do to help?"

Affection relaxed the Dragon King's tense face. Desire rekindled in his gaze as he looked down at her bared skin. "Your presence is enough to ease my mind."

"When so much time passed and you didn't send for me, I was afraid something had happened," Reiko said. "I was afraid we would never see each other again."

"My apologies for ignoring you so long, Anemone," the Dragon King said. "I had business to attend to. There's no reason for fear. Everything is under control."

But even as the Dragon King spoke, another gunshot roared somewhere on the island. He swiveled his head to look outside at the wind-tossed trees and dark sky beyond the balcony. He turned back to Reiko and attempted a re-assuring smile.

"Come, let's have a drink," he said.

He'd already been drinking, Reiko noticed from the smell of his breath. They knelt side by side at the table, and he poured two cups of sake from the decanter. While she sipped hers, he downed his in one quick gulp. She poured him another, hoping he would drink much more, dull his wits, and weaken himself.

"Do you feel better now?" he said.

"Much better, my lord." Reiko watched him drain the cup again. "But I sense evil influences in the air." She shivered, glancing nervously around. She began spinning a line of words that would bring him under her power: "The forces that would separate us are gaining strength. I fear that our time together is short."

"We have all the time in the world, Anemone," the Dragon King said.

Yet Reiko heard a qualm of uncertainty beneath his confident tone: He was following where she wanted to lead him. She said, "But we mortals can never be sure of the future. Our lives might end at any moment. And then we'll never enjoy all the pleasures we postponed."

The Dragon King frowned, nodding as if absorbing her speech, yet wondering at its significance.

"I want you to make love to me." Reiko's voice cracked as she spoke the words that she never wanted to say to any man except Sano. "I want us to be together—before it's too late."

His lips parted as he stared in awe at her bold proposition. She heard his breathing grow loud and rapid, saw the pupils of his eyes dilate. But a strange, fearful reluctance stayed him. Slowly he shook his head.

"We must wait until Hoshina has paid for the harm he did us," he said.

Desperation assailed Reiko. She must seduce him, for how else could she overpower a man stronger than herself?

How else could she make him let down his guard and remove his swords so that she could kill him?

"I don't want to wait any longer," Reiko said. Now was
her best time, when his men were busy fighting the invaders
and wouldn't interfere. "This might be our last chance to
fulfill our desire. If we give up the chance, we may regret
it forever."

Urgency sparked her with a passion that no ordinary
man could resist. But the Dragon King leaned away from
Reiko, his facial muscles twitching in alarm. She rose and
tugged his hand. "Come," she said. "Let me give myself to
you."

He let her raise him to his feet. She felt resistance dragging him down, and need pulsing in his warm, sweaty palm.
"Not yet," he said. "We mustn't."

"We must." Reiko stepped toward the bedchamber beyond the open partition.

The Dragon King stiffened his arm; he stood immobile.
His panicky gaze darted wildly in search of reprieve from
what he wanted to do and she would rather avoid, except
for necessity's sake. Reiko smiled, flashing her eyes in invitation. As she gave his hand another tug, he exhaled. Step
by deliberate step, they moved toward his bedchamber.

          Across the lake, Sano and Chamberlain Yanagi-
sawa rode from the woodland darkness and reined in their
horses on the lakeshore. Their procession of mounted men,
foot soldiers, and boats halted along the track behind them.
In front of them, beyond water that shimmered black and
silver in the moonlight, rose Dannoshin's island.

Sano expelled a breath of relief that they'd finally
reached their destination, after traveling hard for two days,
while General Isogai, Lord Niu, and their troops followed
like a long tail on a kite. Now, exhausted from his nonstop
journey, Sano could hear the beat of their horses' hooves
fast approaching. As he and Yanagisawa studied Dannoshin's island, he saw lights moving there. He heard

shouting, and sporadic booms. Wisps of smoke rose from the island and hovered in the moonlight. The wind carried a bitter tang of gunpowder. Sano's heart sank because he realized what had happened.

"It seems that someone has beaten us here," Yanagisawa said. Suspicion and recollection edged the gaze he fixed on Sano. "I haven't seen your chief retainer lately."

"I sent him and two detectives to trace the women," Sano confessed. "He was supposed to come back to Edo and report their whereabouts."

"Apparently, he decided to attempt a rescue instead," Yanagisawa said, "and he's fighting a war with Dannoshin."

"Apparently."

Shock pierced Sano to the core. That Hirata had disobeyed his orders seemed impossible. That Hirata had broken the sacred bond between retainer and master was a grievous breach of honor. But Sano could think of no better explanation for the war on the island, nor any other reason why Hirata hadn't returned to Edo. He understood how much Hirata wanted to rescue Midori, but he was horrified and outraged that Hirata had not only betrayed his trust but put Reiko in jeopardy. Had Dannoshin slain her and the other women as soon as he realized he was under attack?

"There's no hope of negotiating a peaceful return of the hostages now," Yanagisawa said. Turning to the troops, he shouted, "Prepare to invade the island!"

Inside the Dragon King's bedchamber, the candles and incense burned before the portrait of Anemone. The futon lay spread near the altar. With terror speeding her heartbeat and nausea clenching her stomach, Reiko coaxed the Dragon King toward the bed. Along the way, she let the teal robe slide from her body, then shed her white undergarment. He moaned, and a visible shudder passed through him. Reiko endured his avid gaze on her nakedness. Her mind imposed a barrier between her spirit and the loathsome scene she was enacting. She took the Dragon King's hands and placed them on her hips.

He uttered a hoarse exclamation. His face was flushed and glistening with perspiration. Reiko willed her skin to turn numb against his warm, damp touch. She untied his sash.

"Please don't," he muttered.

But he didn't stop her. He stood wobbling fearfully before her while his swords clattered to the floor. As Reiko murmured endearments, she glanced down at the weapons. They lay near the end of the futon. She slipped the Dragon King's kimono and under-robe off him. His body was muscular, but chunky and graceless; wiry hair sprouted from his torso. Just as Reiko bent to grab the long sword, he clambered out of his trousers with rapid, clumsy movements that blocked her reach for the sword. Moaning, he tore away the band of white cotton fabric that bound his loins; he freed his erect manhood, which was short and veined, purplish from the blood that engorged it. He seized Reiko and pulled her down onto the futon.

They toppled together. The lost chance to kill him, and the hot, intimate press of their flesh, horrified Reiko. An involuntary cry burst from her.

"Anemone, my beautiful Anemone," the Dragon King moaned.

He clumsily pawed her neck and shoulders. He squeezed her buttocks, groped between her legs. All the while, his erection pressed against her thighs. Reiko tried to maintain her detachment and courage, but she felt as if every touch from him spread filth over her. When he sucked voraciously at her nipples, she choked on silent screams. His body lay between her and his swords. How could she reach them before he consummated his terrible desire?

"Let me pleasure you, my lord," she gasped out.

Extricating herself from him, she rose up and straddled the Dragon King. He lay passive, his chest heaving and eyes half shut. Reiko swayed her body against his. He keened in delight, while she glanced sideways. The short sword lay closest, an arm's length from the bed. Keeping one eye on the sword, she grasped the Dragon King's erection. She pumped him, detesting the feel of the rigid, pulsating shaft. His pelvis arched. Groans erupted from him. Reiko pumped faster, hoping to bring him to climax before he could penetrate her. Then, while he was distracted by the throes of release, she could grab the sword, unsheath the blade, and stab him.

The Dragon King bucked and wailed. He reached up, grabbed Reiko's buttocks, and pulled her down on him. To her startled dismay, he rolled her over, away from the sword. Then he was thrusting hard against her, his organ jabbing her pubis, seeking entry. His face, close to hers, contorted with ugly rapture.

"Anemone, Anemone!" His breath hissed from between bared teeth and sprayed saliva.

Terror shot through Reiko like lightning that seared every nerve, spasmed every muscle. His foul smell of sweat, incense, and liquor engulfed her. Abandoning the pretense that she enjoyed his attentions, she writhed, trying to push him away. She flung out her arm, desperately reaching for the sword. But her groping hand knocked the weapon out of reach. The Dragon King's knees pried her legs apart. His weight and crushing embrace immobilized her. His organ probed near her womanhood. Reiko had no choice but to submit, then hope for a chance to kill him afterward. She closed her eyes and gritted her teeth; she turned her face away from his. She tried to separate her mind from her body so that she wouldn't feel the pain or repugnance. She prayed for the Dragon King to spend himself quickly and end her torture soon.

Suddenly she felt his organ go limp against her. He gave a cry of distress. Reiko opened her eyes in surprise as he reared up from her and sat back on his heels. Straddling her legs, he gazed with horror at his shriveled, dangling member.

"Not again!" he cried. "Not now!"

His hands frantically jerked at his organ, trying to revive

its erection. Simultaneous relief and shock flooded Reiko. The Dragon King was impotent!

Wracking sobs arose from deep within him. "I've wanted this for twelve years . . . and I can't!"

Reiko finally understood why he'd resisted his desire and her seduction. Waiting for his revenge against Hoshina was only an excuse. He'd feared that he wouldn't be able to perform. And now, while he stimulated himself and mourned his humiliation, he was vulnerable. He still sat on Reiko's legs, pinning her to the bed, but she sidled her upper body toward the edge. She cautiously extended her arm along the floor. Her fingers grazed the sword hilt. One swift move—one quick slash across his throat . . .

The Dragon King's hands slammed down on her shoulders, arresting her reach for the sword. Reiko gasped.

"It's your fault, Anemone!" he shouted, his eyes burning and jaws tight with fury. "You seduced me when I was too young and foolish to resist. You put your spell on me so that I could never love anyone except you. Then you betrayed me for that villain Hoshina. Your faithlessness caused your murder. And do you know what my life has been like ever since?"

Looming over Reiko, he spat the words into her face as she struggled and cringed. "I've tried to bed many women, but always failed. Not even the most beautiful, expensive courtesans could help me. I've taken virility potions, to no avail. And now that your spirit has come back to me in the body of this other woman, I can't make love even to you, because I can't enter her. You robbed me of my manhood forever!"

He smote her face. As pain exploded across her cheekbone, Reiko screamed.

"You deserved to die," he said, closing his hands around her neck and squeezing.

Reiko gurgled and choked, fighting for breath. She kicked her legs. Her heels pounded the bed. Suffocation dizzied her; black blots obscured her vision. She clawed at the Dragon King's wrists. He recoiled, yelping in pain, and let go her neck. Gulping air, she sat up, wildly striking him. Her fist hit his nose. His head jerked. Blood poured from his nostrils.

He howled in outrage: "How dare you hurt me, after you've already ruined my life?"

Reiko kept hitting. In a storm of thrashing arms, he snatched her wrists and slammed her down on the mattress, hands pinned on either side of her head. His knee bore down on her stomach. She heaved and jerked and grunted, but she couldn't throw him off. His blood-smeared face was swollen, monstrous.

"One death wasn't enough for you, Anemone," he said in a voice that rasped like steel on stone. His hot, sour breath flamed her face. "You must suffer again."

He pummeled blows against her head and breasts. Reiko cried out and threw up her hands to fend off the attack. She wrenched her body sideways. Unbalanced, the Dragon King fell onto the mattress. Reiko lurched for the sword, but he caught her ankle. She sprawled on the thin, hard *tatami*. While her outstretched fingers strained to reach the weapon, he yanked her toward him. Reiko rolled her body over. She flexed her other leg, then kicked his stomach.

The Dragon King's breath snorted out of him. Thrown backward, he released her. Reiko scrambled to her feet and ran blindly. He flung himself after her. His arms encircled her knees. She tumbled, and they thrashed in a frenzy of blows and kicking. Reiko sobbed and gasped. She was losing the battle; yet her determination flared anew. She reached down between their straining, colliding bodies. Her hand fumbled at the Dragon King's loins. She gripped his scrotum and squeezed hard.

A violent spasm jerked his body. A deafening screech burst from him. Agony wrenched his features into a horrible mask. His fingers pried at hers. Reiko hung on, digging her nails into the soft, tender globes of flesh. He twisted her wrist. Reiko yelped as pain shot up her arm and broke her hold on him. He scuttled away, moaning. Exhausted and disoriented, Reiko raised herself on her elbows.

The Dragon King was hunched a short distance from her. He whimpered and cupped his injured private parts in both hands. She looked for the swords. Both lay far away across the room. As she mustered the strength to crawl toward them, the Dragon King staggered to his feet.

"I'll . . . kill . . . you!" Wheezes expelled each word from him. He lumbered toward Reiko.

Through her mind flashed the knowledge that she would never reach the swords in time. But her will to survive heightened her perception. The Dragon King's furious bellow, and the gunshots outside, roared in her ears; the candles on the altar shone dazzling bright. She saw the Dragon King's naked body and crazed face with preternatural, vivid clarity as he came at her. Time seemed to expand, slowing his approach. The teal kimono that lay on the floor along his path caught Reiko's attention. The moment he stepped onto the kimono, she leapt up and lunged in a single fast, instinctive motion. She grabbed the edge of the kimono in both hands and yanked.

The smooth silk cloth whipped out from under the Dragon King's feet. Emitting a yowl, he flipped up in the air, his body horizontal and arms outspread for an instant. Then he crashed down. His head struck the floor with a thud. He lay immobile, his face frozen in blank surprise.

Reiko felt her expression mimic his as she stood staring at him and her heart hammered with lingering panic. Her senses subsided to their normal intensity; time resumed its normal pace. Was the Dragon King dead, or stunned unconscious? Reiko rushed for the sword, intending to make sure he never rose.

Just then, excited voices called from the lower story. Fresh panic beset Reiko. Footsteps pounded along the corridor beneath her. She mustn't let the guards catch her. Quickly she donned the teal kimono and tied its sash. She picked up the long sword, then ran from the bedchamber into the anteroom. Now the men were hurrying up the stairs. Aware that she couldn't get past them out the door, she raced onto the balcony.

Wind tossed her hair; the dark trees and lake spread before her under the star-pricked sky. The guards reached the corridor outside the room.

"Troops are crossing the lake in boats!" Ota shouted. "We're under siege!"

Reiko didn't pause to wonder who the invaders were or worry about the danger of exiting from the balcony. She climbed over the rail, gripped the sword, then jumped. A short drop through a rush of darkness, and she crashed down into a bush. Rough, thorny branches enmeshed her. She tore herself loose. From above her came the guards' exclamations in the palace: They'd found the Dragon King. She drew his sword, let its scabbard fall, and sped across the garden. By now, Ota must have figured out what had happened to his master; he'd have discovered she was missing. He knew where she would go. She had to get there before he did.

The shouts and gunfire continued as Reiko hurried around the castle buildings. She heard rhythmic splashes from the lake, saw torchlights moving through the grounds. At last she located the familiar open passageway. She raced up it, into the building, and groped along the dim corridor. Her hand found the door. Panting, she yanked out the metal beam that secured the latches. She flung it aside and threw open the door.

Inside the room, Lady Yanagisawa, Keisho-in, and Midori sat huddled together, outlined by moonlight that streamed through the window. They exclaimed at the sight of her—bruised, bloody, disheveled, holding the sword, and alone.

"Reiko-*san*!" cried Midori. "What happened?"

"There's no time to explain," Reiko said. "We must run!"

31

    Reiko hurried through the castle grounds, carrying the sword and supporting Midori, who clutched the squalling baby as she toiled beside Reiko. Behind them, Lady Yanagisawa towed Keisho-in along. Lights moved in the gardens, flashed on ruins, and streaked across Reiko's vision. The night reverberated with a tumult of arrows whizzing, men crashing through woods, and spurts of gunfire. The women scrambled out from the castle buildings. Ahead, past a crumbled wall, Reiko saw the lake glittering through a stand of trees, and the dark shape of the dock. But as she hastened her friends toward the boats, footsteps thundered from their right.

    "Hey, you! Stop!" Ota's voice ordered.

    Aghast, Reiko saw Ota and another samurai speeding at her. Midori screamed. Reiko heard Lady Yanagisawa cry, "No!" She turned to see Keisho-in limping back toward the castle, and Lady Yanagisawa chasing her. Both women vanished into the grounds. Horrified to see her escape thwarted and panic disperse her friends, Reiko ran, tugging Midori, after the other two women. They wove around trees whose branches snagged them, and they tripped on weed-covered rubble. Reiko heard cries from Lady Yanagisawa and Keisho-in, but she couldn't see them in the darkness. She also heard Ota and his partner trampling debris and panting in close pursuit.

"Stay here and hide," she whispered to Midori. Reiko knew she was the one Ota most wanted to catch, and if they separated, maybe he would spare Midori.

"No, don't leave me!" Midori cried.

But Reiko shook her friend loose and sped onward. The men followed her, as she'd hoped. She squeezed through shrubbery, darted around buildings. With her small size and quick agility, she gained distance from her pursuers. She turned a corner—and crashed smack into someone. Alarmed shrieks burst from them both. Then she recognized Lady Yanagisawa.

"Reiko-*san,* I'm so glad I found you!" Lady Yanagisawa exclaimed. "But I've lost Lady Keisho-in."

As Reiko felt her heart sink at the thought of the shogun's mother wandering alone, she heard the men coming. She and Lady Yanagisawa raced hand in hand through the night. Out of the castle the men chased them, into the forest. Fatigue dragged at Reiko's legs. She grew breathless from exertion. Lady Yanagisawa moaned, clutching a cramp in her side. They staggered out from the forest. Before them, the high, ruined tower of the keep rose from its surrounding trees. The jagged segment of wall on the top story pointed at the moon.

"I can't run anymore." Dropping Reiko's hand, Lady Yanagisawa wheezed to a standstill.

"Yes, you can," Reiko urged. She heard crunching leaves and snapping branches: Their pursuers were coming. "Hurry!"

A mewl of terror issued from Lady Yanagisawa. She faltered up the steps to the keep.

"No!" Reiko cried. "We mustn't let them trap us inside!"

Such panic gripped Lady Yanagisawa that rational thought fled her. All she wanted was shelter where she could rest and hide from the enemy. She stumbled through the portals of the keep. The dark, damp-smelling room enclosed her. She saw Reiko running toward her up the steps.

"Where are you?" Reiko called, her voice fraught with urgency. She rushed into the room, and the darkness erased her from Lady Yanagisawa's view. "Come out!"

Though Lady Yanagisawa was thankful that Reiko hadn't abandoned her, she didn't answer. If she went, Reiko would make her run until those men caught and killed them. She ducked behind the old cannon.

Ota's partner staggered, panting, in through the doorway. Lady Yanagisawa glimpsed a swift motion behind him, and a flash of moonlight on steel. The samurai yowled. There was a loud thud as he fell on the floor. Lady Yanagisawa realized that Reiko had cut him down.

"We have to go now," Reiko hissed. "Ota is coming. He knows where we are. Quick, before he gets here!"

Lady Yanagisawa didn't want to leave her shelter. As her eyes adjusted to the dimness, she saw a shaft of faint light beaming down through the ceiling. Into it rose the stairway. Lady Yanagisawa clambered up the rickety slats. Through the second level she ascended. Vermin skittered and nesting doves cooed, disturbed by her noise. Reaching the third story, she heard Reiko's rapid footsteps on the stairs, and Ota's pounding after them. The racket echoed through the keep. Lady Yanagisawa climbed faster. She saw the moon, round and radiant, framed by the square hole above her. She flung herself up the last steps, out the hole, and onto the summit of the tower.

Its uppermost story was exposed to the sky and wind, and littered with broken roof tiles, flaked plaster, and charred, splintered timbers. From the crumbling edges of the floor, the tower's lower portion extended in a steep drop. On three sides spread the forest's treetops; below the fourth side, the lake shimmered. The height dizzied Lady Yanagisawa. She crouched within the corner of the remaining wall.

Reiko burst up through the hole. Ota followed, grabbing at Reiko's skirts. She ran across the rubble-strewn floor and teetered at the brink. Pivoting, she raised her sword at Ota.

He laughed and said, "If you'd rather die than surrender, that's fine with me." He drew his sword.

Reality penetrated Lady Yanagisawa's dazed fright. She'd brought Reiko up here; now Ota was going to kill Reiko. Horrified by the prospect of losing her only friend, Lady Yanagisawa watched Reiko swing her weapon. Ota parried. The clanging impact of their blades knocked Reiko perilously close to the tower's edge. They whirled, lunged, and slashed as they skirted the perimeter. The moon illuminated Reiko's determined, terrified face in flashes as she spun. Although she fought with skill and courage, Ota managed many more strikes than she did. He kept her busy parrying and dodging. He was using his greater strength to tire her out. Lady Yanagisawa realized that there was nobody to help Reiko except herself.

She hefted a wooden beam in both hands. When Ota came near her, she swung with all her might. The beam hit the backs of his knees. They buckled under him. He staggered and pitched forward with a grunt of surprise. As he flung out his hands to break his fall, Reiko slashed her blade across his throat. A horrendous, liquid squeal came from him. Blood spurted, gleaming black in the moonlight. He collapsed facedown, dead.

In the sudden stillness, Lady Yanagisawa and Reiko gazed across Ota's corpse at each other. Reiko let her sword fall. She breathed in shallow, rapid puffs, her mouth open, shocked at their sudden victory. Lady Yanagisawa dropped the beam. She and Reiko hugged, sobbing in relief.

"You saved my life," Reiko said. "A million thanks!"

Lady Yanagisawa basked in their closeness. For once she felt truly cherished. But Reiko suddenly withdrew from her.

"Look!" Reiko cried, pointing toward the lake.

Dots of light on the water surrounded the island like a glowing rosary of beads. As Lady Yanagisawa and Reiko watched, the lights moved closer, borne on small boats crammed with men. Lady Yanagisawa could see them rowing. Above the gunfire and yells that pierced the night, she heard the oars splashing.

"They're coming to rescue us!" Reiko hurried to the tower's edge. Jubilant, she waved at the boats. "We're saved!"

Gladness filled Lady Yanagisawa but quickly drained away. Now that rescue was near, mixed feelings assailed her. She wanted badly to see her daughter, yet she experienced dismay at the thought of going home to Edo. There waited the familiar pain of her unrequited love for the chamberlain. There, Reiko would return to her adoring husband and perfect son. There, Reiko wouldn't need Lady Yanagisawa. Now the ever-present jealousy of Reiko skewered Lady Yanagisawa's heart.

Reiko turned, still poised at the edge of the tower. Her beautiful, joyful face ignited the ever-present furnace of anger in Lady Yanagisawa. Possessed by irresistible impulse, she thrust her hands against Reiko's chest and pushed.

Surprise jolted Reiko as her feet faltered off the tower and she listed backward over the edge. She flung out her arms, trying to regain her balance. Lady Yanagisawa's face, twisted with cruel, gleeful triumph, hovered over her for a moment. Then Reiko was falling through empty space, arms and legs flailing. The tower wall rushed upward past her horrified eyes. A scream tore from her. Then she hit the lake.

The tremendous splash against her back knocked the breath from her lungs. Cold water swirled around Reiko as she plunged through its depths. Its roar filled her ears; its turbulent blackness blinded her. As she bobbed up, her heart hammered with panic, and she fought the urge to inhale. She beat her hands and pumped her legs against the water, trying to reach air. Her long hair, sleeves, and skirt entangled her.

She couldn't believe Lady Yanagisawa had pushed her

off the tower! After everything they'd gone through together, Lady Yanagisawa's ill will had once again prevailed over their friendship.

Reiko's head broke the surface. She gulped a huge breath. The moon and stars glittered through the water that streamed down over her eyes. The tower loomed above her; the world rocked with her frantic struggles to keep afloat. How she wished she knew how to swim! Her thrashing produced not the slightest motion across the short distance to the island. As she began to weaken, she saw the tiny figure of Lady Yanagisawa, standing high up on the tower, watching her.

"Help!" Reiko cried.

Lady Yanagisawa vanished from sight. Reiko wished she'd been imprisoned with anyone else in the world except that demented woman. She'd felled the Dragon King and escaped his palace, only to be attacked by the ally that circumstances had forced her to trust. Now she strained to keep her head in the air, gurgling and spitting the water that washed over her face. Helplessness overwhelmed her. Unless a miracle happened, she would drown, and her spirit would join the real, legendary Dragon King in his palace at the bottom of the sea.

"Somebody just jumped from that tower." As Sano crossed the lake in the boat he shared with Detectives Inoue and Arai, he leaned over the prow for a better look at the tower, where the plummeting figure and shrill cry had caught his attention. He squinted at the water near the tower's submerged base, where he'd heard the splash.

A thunderous premonition struck him. His heart began thudding; wild excitement surged in him.

"Row over there," he ordered, pointing at the splashes that still rippled the lake.

Inoue and Arai obeyed. The boat pulled ahead of the flotilla approaching the island. When they reached the spot where the figure had dropped, it had sunk below the surface. Sano reached into the water. His groping fingers found and grasped long hair. He pulled. Up came the head of a woman. She blinked water from terrified eyes; she wheezed through her gaping mouth. Her arms waved within the billowy folds of the patterned kimono she wore.

"Reiko-*san*!" exclaimed Sano.

As her gaze focused and she recognized him, Reiko moaned and clutched at Sano. He and Detective Inoue hauled her, drenched and dripping, into the boat. Filled with joy, he caught her in a tight embrace.

"Thank the gods you're alive," he said in a voice thick with emotion.

Reiko sobbed with relief, shivered from the cold. "This is a miracle!"

"You took a dangerous risk by jumping from that tower," Sano said. "You could have been killed."

"I didn't jump," Reiko said between chattering teeth. "She pushed me."

Sano removed his cloak and wrapped it around her. "Who did?"

"Lady Yanagisawa." Hysterical laughter bubbled from Reiko. "She did me a favor, and she doesn't know it."

"What are you talking about?" Sano said, fearful that the near-drowning had addled his wife.

"Never mind. We have to save Lady Keisho-in and Midori."

Another boat neared theirs. From it Chamberlain Yanagisawa called, "*Sōsakan* Sano! What's going on?" His face registered surprise as he beheld Reiko. "I see you've found your wife." He said to her, "Where is Lady Keisho-in?"

"We got separated," Reiko said. "The last time I saw her, she was in the castle grounds."

Yanagisawa ordered his men to row him around the island to the castle. Their boat sped away. Others were reaching shore, the troops disembarking. The siege had begun. Reiko turned to Sano. "I left Midori in the grounds, too. We must find her."

While Detectives Inoue and Arai rowed their boat after

the chamberlain, Reiko wrung out her wet hair. Sano said, "Where is Dannoshin?" Reiko looked puzzled. "The man who kidnapped you," Sano clarified.

"Oh. I didn't know his name," Reiko said, averting her gaze. "How did you discover who he is? How did you find this place?"

Sano summarized the events that had led up to his arrival. Reiko listened without comment, distracted by her own thoughts. "Did Dannoshin hurt you?" Sano said anxiously.

Though Reiko shook her head, Sano knew something was wrong, but he didn't press for an explanation. Right now, it was enough to have her back alive and apparently uninjured. And they had work to do.

Their boat rounded the island and drew near the castle buildings. "Have you seen Dannoshin?" Sano said.

After a moment's hesitation, Reiko nodded. "He was in the palace. I'll show you where."

Chamberlain Yanagisawa, accompanied by six bodyguards, hastened in the castle gate. Their lanterns illuminated the path through the overgrown garden, then the dingy, vine-choked palace and its gaping doorway. Although the sounds of shooting, scuffles, and clanging blades multiplied as the invaders stormed the island, an unnatural stillness cloaked the palace.

"Let's reconnoiter the area," Yanagisawa told his men.

As they stole around the castle, watching for signs of life, Yanagisawa's pulse accelerated and urgency fevered him. His purpose had evolved beyond rescuing Lady Keisho-in and scoring a point with the shogun. He needed more than to save his lover from execution. General Isogai's refusal to obey his orders had revealed the disturbing fact that he'd lost control of the army. Tens of thousands of Tokugawa soldiers would ally with Lord Matsudaira, Lord Kii, Priest Ryuko, and his other foes. Rescuing Keisho-in had therefore become a matter of survival. Success would allow him to maintain his hold on the shogun and country long enough to rebuild his power base. Failure would slide him farther down the slippery slope toward ruin.

He steered his retinue across the exposed foundation of a demolished building, toward the palace's interior. Suddenly he heard a raucous voice shout, "Get away from me, you filthy brutes!" Such glad relief buoyed his spirits that he laughed.

"That's her," he said.

The voice shouted more imprecations. Yanagisawa and his men followed it down a walled passage, into a courtyard enclosed by two-story buildings. In the center of the courtyard, three peasant hoodlums surrounded Lady Keisho-in. Their hands reached out to grab as they circled her. The old woman held a long sword that she'd somehow acquired. Clumsily gripping the hilt in both hands, she swung it at the hoodlums.

"Yah!" she cried.

The hoodlums leapt back. As the force of her swing sent Keisho-in reeling, one hoodlum charged at her. She whipped the blade around, slashed his chest, and laid him flat.

"That will teach you to kidnap me!" She chortled in triumph.

Her other attackers spied Yanagisawa and his men, and took off running. "Go after them," Yanagisawa told several troops. Then he said to Keisho-in, "It's all right, Your Highness. You're safe now."

"Hah!" she cried, flailing the sword at him. "Take that!"

Yanagisawa ducked just in time to avoid a cut to his head. Keisho-in obviously hadn't listened to what he said and mistook him for one of the kidnappers. Her watery eyes were crazed, her rotten teeth bared in a ferocious grin. Again she swung at him.

"It's Chamberlain Yanagisawa," he said as he dodged again. "I've come to rescue you."

Or he would if she didn't kill him first. Keisho-in spun

and tripped. Yanagisawa caught her from behind, locking his arms around her waist. They reeled and tottered together in a ludicrous dance.

"Let me go, you beast!" Keisho-in shouted.

"Help me!" Yanagisawa commanded his men.

Reiko, Sano, and the two detectives landed on-shore and climbed out of the boat. Sano called to troops arriving in another boat and told them to look for Midori. Then Reiko showed him and Inoue and Arai the way to the Dragon King. Around them in the forest, battles broke out between the invaders and defenders. War cries and the clash of steel blades shattered the night. A coil of apprehension twisted inside Reiko, because she dreaded returning to that chamber.

In through the palace's main entrance they hurried. The castle seemed a desolate ruin, abandoned by the kidnappers who'd scattered to fight for their lives. While Reiko led Sano and the detectives up the stairs, she silently prayed that they would find the Dragon King lying dead where she'd left him. If he was dead, he couldn't hurt her. Nor could he tell Sano what had happened between them.

She and her companions reached the second floor. Incense smoke wafted from the Dragon King's chamber. Reiko pointed at its door. "In there."

Sano and his men drew their swords. Detective Inoue cautiously entered first. Reiko and Sano went next. Detective Arai followed. The antechamber was vacant; battle noise drifted in from the balcony. They filed through the opening in the partition. Inside the bedchamber, the Dragon King was kneeling, fully dressed, before the funeral altar with its burning incense and candles. Dismay sickened Reiko. His head turned. His face was bruised and raw from their fight. Blood had run out of his nostrils, down his mouth. He regarded Sano and the detectives with wary unease, but as he spied Reiko, the smoldering light rekindled in his gaze.

"Anemone," he said.

Sano gave Reiko a questioning look. She said, "He thinks I'm his dead mother." She hoped she needn't explain any more.

The Dragon King's dagger lay unsheathed on the altar. He picked up the weapon. Sano leapt forward, pointing the blade of his sword at the Dragon King.

"Put it down, Dannoshin-*san*," he said. "You're under arrest."

The Dragon King ignored Sano; he appeared not to see the detectives surround him. He shifted himself to face Reiko. His open robes revealed his naked torso and his loincloth. "When you told me that our time together would soon end, you were right, my dearest," he said. "The evil influences around us have besieged me. Now I must commit *seppuku* and avoid the disgrace of capture."

Reiko saw two small, shallow knife wounds on his abdomen: He'd inflicted preliminary cuts, working up the courage to kill himself. The red-tipped dagger shook in his hand. Sano and the detectives held their positions, eyeing him warily.

"Before I die, there is something I must confess, Anemone." The Dragon King's voice quavered with emotion. "For twelve years I've kept a secret that has weighed heavily upon me. I must unburden myself to you." His eyes begged for Reiko's attention and sympathy.

"You don't have to listen," Sano told Reiko.

Much as Reiko would rather leave the Dragon King and never see him again, she felt obliged to let him speak. Sano needed to know what he had to say because it might bear upon his crimes. And although she feared he would mention what had transpired tonight, a samurai on the verge of ritual suicide deserved a hearing even if he was a criminal.

"It's all right," Reiko said. "Let him talk."

Hirata, Marume, and Fukida watched in consternation while burning torches lit up the night and an army of samurai charged through the forest around them.

"Where did they come from?" said Fukida, at the exact instant Marume said, "The island is under attack!"

"There's three more over there," shouted someone among the horde. "Catch them!"

Hirata recognized the voice. Gladness filled him, even while the attackers homed in on him. "It's our detective corps," he said, then called, "Wait, Kato-*san*! Don't attack! It's me—Hirata."

War cries gave way to happy greetings as the corps joined Hirata. "So you got here first," Kato said. "We wondered what had become of you three."

"Is Sano-*san* here?" Hirata asked nervously.

"Him and Chamberlain Yanagisawa, too. Where are Lady Keisho-in and the other women?"

"I don't know. We just got into the wing of the palace where we saw them imprisoned the day before yesterday. But they aren't there anymore."

Distant shouts echoed amid the thud of boat hulls against land. Kato said, "It sounds like the Tokugawa army has arrived. This siege is going to be chaos. We'll be lucky if we don't slaughter each other instead of the enemy."

Moments ago, Hirata had feared that the kidnappers had killed the women; he'd hoped they'd somehow escaped. Now he was alarmed to think of Midori wandering the island while a battle raged and troops running amok felled anyone in sight.

"Help me find the women before they're killed by accident," Hirata told the detective corps. Then he turned to Fukida and Marume. "Let's look around the palace."

They were foraging amid ruined structures and dense vegetation, when a plaintive wail halted them. "What was that?" Fukida said.

"It sounded like a cat," Marume said.

But the noise evoked wild hopes in Hirata that his mind hardly dared articulate. "Midori!" he yelled.

Pivoting in a circle, he scanned trees and rubble heaps. He heard an answering cry, and spotted her. She sat wedged between a broken wall and a shrub. Her arms cradled a small bundle. She leapt up from her hiding place and into Hirata's arms.

"You came to save me!" she cried. A torrent of weeping shook her. "I knew you would!"

Tears stung Hirata's own eyes. He embraced his wife, too overcome by joy to speak. Midori showed him the bundle. "This is our new daughter," she said, then cooed to the baby, "Look, it's your father."

"She knows," Hirata said. "She called to me."

He beheld the solemn eyes in the baby's wrinkled little face. Paternal love and pride warmed his heart. Then he heard a man shout, "There she is!" He saw Lord Niu, followed by a squadron of retainers, bustling toward him and Midori.

Hirata gaped in surprise. "What are *you* doing here?" he asked Lord Niu.

"Rescuing my daughter." Lord Niu barely glanced at the baby. "You're coming with me," he told Midori. He seized her arm and yanked her away from Hirata.

"No, Father!" Midori cried.

Incensed by the *daimyo*'s proprietary attitude, Hirata held Midori's other arm. Fukida and Marume grabbed Lord Niu and tried to break his grip on Midori. His men wrestled Hirata. As the opposing sides tugged at her, Midori screamed and the baby cried. Hirata marveled that even though his father-in-law wasn't the kidnapper, he'd ended up battling Lord Niu anyway.

"Let go of her, you piece of horse dung!" Lord Niu's crooked face blazed with anger.

"She's my wife," Hirata shouted. "You let go!"

"When you fell in love with that villain Hoshina, I thought that if my father knew about your affair, he would put an end to it," the Dragon King said to Reiko. "I thought he would use his influence to have Hoshina banished from the city."

The candles flickered; sweet, pungent smoke curled up from the incense sticks. Outside the chamber, the battle raged on while Sano, Reiko, and the detectives listened.

"It was a hot summer day," the Dragon King continued. "You were absent from home. My father was in his study. When I told him about your affair, he just thanked me, then sent me away. All that day I waited for him to act. When you came home at dusk, I watched him ask you to go boating with him. I thought he was going to confront you about Hoshina. I wanted to watch what happened. As you and my father rode to Lake Biwa in your palanquin, I followed on foot.

"It was getting dark, and the road to the lake was crowded with traffic. Neither of you noticed me." A bitter smile twisted the Dragon King's mouth. "But my father never did pay me much attention. He favored his older sons. He thought I was a stupid weakling. And your thoughts were too full of Hoshina.

"When we reached the lake, my father rowed you out on the water in his boat. I rented a boat at the pier and rowed after you. The night sky was lit up with fireworks. You and my father stopped far out on the lake where it was dark. I stopped some distance away. I could see the lantern glowing on your boat, and the two of you sitting under the canopy. There was no lantern on my boat. You didn't know I was there."

"No one knew," Sano said softly, and Reiko saw his startled frown. "The official records don't mention a witness."

"Then my father told you that he'd discovered your affair," continued the Dragon King. "You denied it. My father said he knew about your trysts. You tried to convince him that Hoshina meant nothing to you. But I knew better. So did my father." The Dragon King's tone scorned the lies. "Though you told him you loved him and you begged his forgiveness, he wasn't appeased. He shouted, 'You'll pay for betraying me!' And he threw you in the lake."

Horror glazed the Dragon King's eyes. "I swear I never

suspected that my father would hurt you, Anemone." He extended a pleading hand toward Reiko. "Had I known, I never would have told him about your affair. You must believe me!"

Reiko was astounded. By telling tales on his mother, the Dragon King had delivered her to her death. He was at least as responsible for Anemone's murder as Hoshina was.

"I watched you struggle in the water," the Dragon King said. "I listened as you called for help. I saw my father row the boat away. I was so stunned that I couldn't move." He sat rigid and stared blankly, as he must have that night. "I just sat while you fought for your life. I watched my father stop his boat and begin to weep."

Reiko saw the scene shimmering between her and the Dragon King. Sano and the detectives beheld him as though entranced.

"He drew his short sword," the Dragon King said. "I realized he was going to commit *seppuku*. And I was the only person able to prevent him from killing himself, or you from drowning. I drew a breath to call to him. I started rowing toward you."

The Dragon King pantomimed his actions. "But then, I remembered how my father never spoke to me except to criticize. I remembered that you had spurned me. My love for you, and my filial piety toward my father, turned to hatred. Suddenly, death seemed like a just punishment for the way you'd treated me." Vindictive anger blazed from the Dragon King. "So I watched my father slash his throat. I watched you disappear beneath the water."

His gloating satisfaction repelled Reiko. "I sat there, intoxicated by my revenge," he said. "But the intoxication soon faded. I was filled with horror that you'd drowned while I sat idle." The Dragon King's expression reflected his words. "I quickly rowed toward where you'd sunk.

"But the lantern on my father's boat burned out. The fireworks had stopped. It was so dark that I could see nothing. I plunged my oar into the water, feeling for you. I called your name." Tears poured from the Dragon King's eyes, mingling with the blood on his face. "I searched until dawn. But the lake was as smooth as a mirror. You had vanished without a trace. So I rowed back to shore and went home.

"Ever since that terrible night I've grieved for you, Anemone," the Dragon King said to Reiko as he wept. "For twelve years I've worshiped at your funeral altar. For twelve years I schemed to avenge your death."

Now Reiko understood why he'd pursued Hoshina's destruction with such excessive zeal. His father, who had killed Anemone, was beyond harm. The Dragon King had transferred his own share of the blame for Anemone's murder to Hoshina because he couldn't bear the burden. He'd hoped that by punishing Hoshina, he could assuage his own guilt.

"For twelve years my secret has divided my spirit from yours." He raised his hand, palm outward, fingers spread, as if against an invisible barrier between himself and Reiko. "It divides us still. I can't see nor touch you without remembering what I did."

Reiko also finally understood the reason for his impotence with her and other women. His guilt, not his love for Anemone, had emasculated him.

Sobs convulsed the Dragon King. "The only way for us to reunite is for me to join you in death."

He lifted the dagger, both hands grasping the hilt, pointing the blade at his middle. Reiko averted her face so that she wouldn't see the blade zigzag through flesh and vital organs. Sano took her arm and backed her toward the door. The Dragon King breathed in quick, sharp gasps. A groan of frustration and rage issued from him.

"I can't!" he cried.

Reiko turned and saw him grappling with the dagger. His hands shook violently. The blade's tip impinged on his stomach. Spasms wrenched his face as he tried to muster the courage to take his own life. Yet he could no more thrust the dagger into himself than he could enter a woman.

The Dragon King ceased struggling. He dropped his

hands and the dagger onto his lap. He looked up, his features a blur of tears, defeat, and shame. His gaze lit on Sano.

"Execute Hoshina. Grant me my vengeance," he said quietly, then gave Reiko a tender, wistful smile. "May our spirits reunite in the real Dragon King's underwater palace someday."

He bounded to his feet with a sudden, startling roar and charged across the room toward Reiko. The detectives grabbed for him, but too late. Reiko saw the Dragon King raise the dagger at her. His swift, unexpected motion froze her in terror. She saw the desperate intent in his eyes, and her death impending. But Sano moved even faster. He lashed his sword between Reiko and the Dragon King.

The blade gashed the Dragon King deep across the abdomen. His roar became a squeal of agony. He dropped, spilling blood and viscera from the wound. The dagger fell from his hand. Reiko saw consciousness flee his eyes, and death wipe the expression off his face, even before he crumpled to the floor and lay still. Sano turned her away and enfolded her in his arms. She swooned with horror, delayed shock, and gratitude toward Sano. When her racing heartbeat slowed and her mind cleared, she comprehended what the Dragon King had done.

"He was a coward to the end," she said. "He had his men kidnap Lady Keisho-in and the rest of us. He wanted the shogun to kill Hoshina for him. Then he attacked me so you would kill him, because he wasn't brave enough to commit *seppuku*. He wanted to die here rather than face a trial, scandal, and public execution."

"He's proved that a coward can do more harm than many a braver man," Sano said. His voice was hard; his sword dripped blood as he surveyed the scene. "There's no need to commiserate over his death. Let's go. He can stay here for now."

Before leaving the palace, Reiko leaned over the altar and blew out the candles.

• • •

Sano, Reiko, and Detectives Inoue and Arai exited the palace gate to find the square outside as brightly lit, crowded, and noisy as a temple precinct during a festival. Lanterns ringed the perimeter. Troops milled about or bandaged minor wounds; they swilled sake from flasks while bantering about their exploits during the raid on the island. Others guarded a few of the Dragon King's men who'd been taken prisoner and now squirmed on the pavement with their wrists and ankles bound. In the middle of the square, Midori and Hirata sat happily fussing over their baby. Near them, Detectives Marume and Fukida lay fast asleep, while Lady Keisho-in regaled General Isogai and the army with tales of her adventures. Reiko hurried to Midori. They exclaimed in delight to find each other safe. Chamberlain Yanagisawa approached Sano.

"Some of our men are continuing to search the island," Yanagisawa said, "but most of the kidnappers seem to have been killed or captured. Did you find Dannoshin?"

Sano nodded, still amazed by the Dragon King's confession. He had thought he'd learned everything about the man's crimes before he got here, but the murder that had inspired them had proved to have dimensions he'd never suspected. "I killed him."

"Then our mission was a success, and all is well," Yanagisawa said.

But Sano thought otherwise. He was troubled by questions about what had happened to Reiko during her imprisonment. He looked at Hirata, and their gazes met. The smile vanished from Hirata's face. His expression turned defensive. Sano knew he must eventually take Hirata to task for disobeying orders. A sense of unfinished business permeated tonight's victory.

Lady Keisho-in clapped her hands. "Listen, everyone," she ordered. When the crowd quieted and all eyes turned to her, she said, "Thank you for rescuing me. But don't waste any more time sitting on your behinds and congratulating yourselves. I'm sick of this terrible place. Let's go home!"

Amid the general stir of agreement, Reiko spoke: "Lady Yanagisawa is still missing."

Sano had forgotten about her; and so, apparently, had everyone else, including the chamberlain. A commotion ensued as the assembly realized that the rescue wasn't complete. Sano was about to organize a search for Lady Yanagisawa, when Keisho-in said, "There she is!"

Sano looked in the direction that Keisho-in pointed. He saw Lady Yanagisawa standing alone at the edge of the forest. Her hair and clothes were disarrayed, her posture and clasped hands rigid. With her furtive, wary expression, she seemed a harbinger of trouble yet to come.

32

Four days after the siege upon the Dragon King's palace, news sellers hawked broadsheets in the hot, teeming districts of Edo. "The shogun's mother has been rescued from her evil kidnapper and brought home!" they cried.

As the news spread through town, gongs rang at neighborhood shrines, where citizens offered prayers of thanks that fortune had spared Keisho-in. Priests garbed in saffron robes marched in processions through the streets, beating drums, to celebrate their patroness's deliverance. In the Hibiya official district, guards hauled fourteen captive, shackled henchmen of the Dragon King out from Magistrate Ueda's mansion and bore them off to the execution ground. The officials attending the trial departed the Court of Justice. Magistrate Ueda stepped off the dais and joined Sano, who had testified during the proceedings.

"Many thanks for saving my daughter," Magistrate Ueda said. "I hear that Chamberlain Yanagisawa claims the credit for finding and rescuing the hostages, but my sources contradict his story. I'm aware of your role, as are many other people."

"The honorable chamberlain is welcome to the credit," Sano said truthfully.

"I also hear you're back in the shogun's good graces," Magistrate Ueda said.

"For however long that may last," Sano said.

"And Hoshina has been released from prison?"

"The shogun issued the order two days ago—as soon as we returned to Edo and delivered Lady Keisho-in to him, along with the Dragon King's head as proof that her kidnapper had been brought to justice."

"It will be interesting to see what becomes of the liaison between Hoshina and Chamberlain Yanagisawa," said Magistrate Ueda. "But they must be thankful the crisis is past. And we can be thankful that Hirata-*san*'s new child survived. Her name-day celebration is this afternoon, is it not?"

"It is," Sano said. "Will you attend?"

The magistrate nodded; after a pause, he said, "When I visited my daughter yesterday, she seemed unusually pensive and subdued. How is she this morning?"

"The same." All his worries about Reiko assailed Sano. "She won't tell me what happened while she was captive, other than general details of how all the women were treated. I don't even know how she got them out of the palace. And there are bruises all over her. Did she tell you anything?"

Magistrate Ueda shook his head.

"But I have my suspicions," said Sano.

His mind pictured the scene in the Dragon King's chamber, with the rumpled bed and a woman's white under-kimono beside it. He thought of how Reiko had known where to find the Dragon King. He wondered what coercion or desperation had made her do. He didn't want to think about what could happen between a man and a beautiful woman he'd abducted. Rage, jealousy, and helplessness alloyed like hot, molten metals within Sano.

Magistrate Ueda's concerned expression indicated that he guessed the direction of Sano's thoughts. "Would you like some advice?"

Releasing his breath, Sano said, "I would."

"Give her time to open her heart to you, but understand that some secrets are better left untold," Magistrate Ueda said. "Remember that her spirit is as faithful to you as ever.

Don't judge her on what a madman did to her. Don't let him drive you apart when you need each other most."

Sano appreciated the wisdom of this advice that tempered his inclination to force the issue. "Thank you, Honorable Father-in-law."

He took his leave, rather glad that he needn't confront Reiko, for ahead loomed another confrontation that threatened a relationship almost as important to him as his marriage.

Inside Chamberlain Yanagisawa's estate, sunlight dappled a garden that displayed the lush greenery of high summer. But the smoke from funeral pyres hazed the air. Fallen leaves on the gravel paths, and withered blossoms on the lilies, portended the season's eventual demise. Cicadas shrilled in incessant warning.

Lady Yanagisawa and her daughter, Kikuko, stood hand in hand outside the private quarters. They peered up through the leafy branches of a plum tree at the chamberlain, who posed on the veranda, gazing moodily into the distance. This was the first time Lady Yanagisawa had seen her husband since they'd arrived home. After his troops had invaded the Dragon King's island, and during the journey to Edo, he'd not even spoken to her. His indifference pained her terribly. Reiko had said that the kidnapping would make him realize he loved her, but it hadn't. How Lady Yanagisawa hated Reiko for giving her false hope! She was glad Reiko hadn't drowned, but wished she had.

Police Commissioner Hoshina came walking around the corner of the veranda toward the chamberlain. Lady Yanagisawa's blood seethed with hatred for this man who'd usurped her husband's affections. She saw the chamberlain tense as he turned to face Hoshina. They bowed to each other, and his profile lit up with a joy that his dignified poise couldn't hide.

"Welcome back," the chamberlain said gravely to Hoshina.

Hoshina's features were set in a stiff, cheerless mask. "I'm here to fetch my belongings," he said.

The chamberlain frowned. "You're moving out?"

"Yes," Hoshina said.

Though she could hardly believe that anyone privileged to enjoy her husband's company would give it up, delight blossomed in Lady Yanagisawa. The kidnapping had brought her some benefit after all.

"But why?" the chamberlain said, his dismay evident. "What happened shouldn't drive you from our home. You must know I didn't want to abandon you. I did everything in my power to save you."

Hoshina folded his arms. "You let me suffer the worst humiliation of my life. You would have let me die."

"Surely you can understand that I only did what I had to do," the chamberlain defended himself.

"I understand that you were driven by political expediency." Hoshina softened his manner.

"Then stay," the chamberlain said.

All his persuasive power warmed his voice, but Hoshina backed away from his extended hand. "I'm not a fool to think you wouldn't cut me loose again if necessary," Hoshina said. "I'd rather separate than live in dread of the next time."

The chamberlain stared in shock. "Do you mean you're leaving me?"

Hoshina nodded, though reluctantly.

"For good?"

Unhappy silence was Hoshina's answer. Lady Yanagisawa felt Kikuko tug her hand. She motioned her daughter to keep quiet so that she could continue spying.

"I'll make up to you for all you've suffered," the chamberlain said. Panic laced his eagerness to appease Hoshina. "Do you want a higher position? Or a larger stipend?" He upturned his palms in a magnanimous gesture. "Anything you ask, I'll give."

Lady Yanagisawa watched Hoshina vacillate. She felt the current of passion that still flowed between the lovers.

She gripped Kikuko's hand while her lips moved in silent, incoherent prayer.

At last Hoshina said sadly, "Nothing you can do will make me forget that you would have sacrificed my life for your own self-interest."

The chamberlain dropped his hands. He turned away from Hoshina, and Lady Yanagisawa glimpsed naked desperation in his eyes. He took a few blind steps down the veranda, then rallied and faced Hoshina.

"All right, I should have defended you instead of deserting you," he said. "I made a mistake. I was selfish, and stupid." Lady Yanagisawa was astounded because she'd never heard her husband admit any fault. "I'm sorry I let you down. Please forgive me!"

Nor had she thought him capable of apologizing or begging. But now he clutched Hoshina's shoulders in urgent entreaty. Hoshina reached up, grasped the chamberlain's hands, and broke their hold on him.

"You're only making this harder than it already is," he said in a breathless voice that quavered.

The chamberlain looked stunned by the rejection. "Have our three years together meant so little to you that you would deny me a chance to make amends?" he demanded.

A wry, tortured smile quirked Hoshina's mouth. "If they'd meant more to you, would we be having this discussion?"

They gazed helplessly at each other. Lady Yanagisawa saw tears glitter in their eyes, and the restraint that kept them from succumbing to desire. Then the chamberlain cleared his throat and said, "Maybe a separation is a good idea. Take some time to recover from your ordeal. Come back when you're ready."

Hoshina shook his head. "I'd rather say good-bye today, while we still have more good memories than bad. I won't hang about waiting for some bitter end."

As he turned to go, the chamberlain said, "I forbid you to go!" The hurt and despair on his face turned to fury. "I order you to stay!"

Hoshina pivoted. "I'm not your man anymore," he said, his expression affronted. "You don't tell me what to do."

"You're mine to command as long as I control Japan," the chamberlain said scornfully. "Don't forget that everything you have depends on me. If you walk out of here, you'll lose it all."

Lady Yanagisawa marveled at how suddenly all the tensions in their relationship had exploded and their love had turned to enmity. Hoshina replied with equal scorn: "I haven't as much to lose as you think, because you haven't as much control as you once did. A lot has changed, in case you haven't discovered.

"While you were off rescuing Lady Keisho-in, the shogun got tired of your son. The position of heir to the regime is wide open. Rumor says Lord Matsudaira's nephew has the advantage. And I've been visiting the *daimyo* and army officers I befriended while I was helping you build your empire. They're my allies now. And now that you threaten me, I'll convince them that we should cast our lot with Lord Matsudaira's faction."

The chamberlain blanched with horror at the realization that he'd lost not only his lover, but his partner in political intrigue, many of his supporters, and his chance to rule the next regime. "So you'll punish desertion with desertion?" he said. "Well, you won't get away with it. You'll live to regret that you betrayed me!"

Hoshina's cocksure grin didn't hide his sorrow. "We'll see," he said, and walked away.

The chamberlain gazed after him a moment. Then he leaned on the veranda railing and buried his face in his hands. Lady Yanagisawa pitied him; but glee sang within her because his troubles afforded her an opportunity. Bereft of his lover, deserted by his friends, he needed someone. And who else could give him more loyal devotion than she?

Lady Yanagisawa stepped out from behind the tree, pulling Kikuko with her. The chamberlain looked up, and their gazes met. His reflected annoyance that she'd witnessed his defeat, but for once he noticed her; for once he didn't act as if she didn't exist. This miraculous event marked a new beginning. Lady Yanagisawa didn't know how she could replace Hoshina in his affections, or help him achieve his ambitions, but she swore that she would.

Someday he would love her and value her. Someday he would rule Japan, with her by his side. And when someday came, she need never be jealous of Reiko again.

Sano, seated behind his desk in his office, looked up at Hirata, who hovered in the doorway. "Come in," Sano said with quiet formality.

Hirata entered, knelt opposite Sano, and bowed. His face was taut with the same apprehension that Sano felt. Discord negated their five years of friendship. That this confrontation had been delayed by the aftermath of the rescue mission increased the strain between them. Although Sano hated to punish a retainer who'd served him so well as Hirata had, he must uphold his authority and enforce the discipline required by the Way of the Warrior.

"Your willful insubordination has dishonored us both," he said. "Disobeying your master is the worst possible violation of *Bushido*." Yet even as he spoke, Sano recalled the many times he himself had bent the rules.

"A million apologies." Wringing his hands, Hirata looked sick, terrified, and as ashamed of himself as devastated by the reprimand. But he met Sano's gaze and said bravely, "Will you please allow me to explain what I did?"

Sano frowned, offended that Hirata had the temerity to justify his behavior; but he owed Hirata for services rendered. "Go ahead," Sano said.

"When we found the kidnappers, I thought that if we came back to Edo to tell you, they might move the women off the island—or hurt them—before you could get there," Hirata said. "We had to choose between leaving them at the kidnappers' mercy or trying to save them ourselves. I made the decision that seemed right."

The merit of his rationale occurred to Sano, but so did

the risk Hirata had taken. Sano said, "The Dragon King had fifty-two men, by our final count. You pitted yourself and Marume and Fukida against them all. You knew the odds were that you would fail. You also knew the kidnappers had threatened to kill their hostages if they were attacked. You put the women in more danger than if you'd left."

Hirata breathed through his mouth; even though chastened by Sano's argument, he said, "We killed twenty-two of the Dragon King's men. By reducing their number, we allowed the women to escape from the palace, where he might have trapped and murdered them once you and the army came. We made your invasion much easier than it would have been if not for us."

"I realize that. But the outcome doesn't justify the action." Knowing he'd often followed the opposite belief and used it to rationalize things he'd done, Sano cursed himself as a hypocrite. "You couldn't have predicted what would happen when you disregarded my orders. That everything ended well was more a stroke of luck than a credit to you."

Hirata bowed his head. Defeat settled upon him like a visible, crushing mantle. "You're right," he said. "I did wrong. I don't expect you to forgive me."

"I already have." As Hirata looked up in surprise, Sano said, "If I'd been in your position, I probably would have done the same thing." He gentled his tone as he added, "I can't condemn you for wanting to save your wife and child."

"Then you're not going to punish me?" Hope vied with amazement in Hirata's eyes.

"If I were to follow protocol, I would dismiss you from my employ," Sano said. "But I don't want to lose you because you made one mistake."

Furthermore, Sano had always chafed at protocol. "Consider my reprimand and your shame as your punishment," he said. "Resume your duties. Use better judgment next time."

"Yes, *Sōsakan-sama*. Thank you!" Hirata exuded relief as he bowed to Sano. The color came back into his face.

Sano believed he'd made the right decision, and the bad feeling between him and Hirata had dispelled; yet the tension lingered. A line had been crossed during this episode. The kidnapping investigation had irreparably altered their relationship. What the future consequences would be, Sano couldn't predict.

The name-day celebration took place at Sano's mansion.

Midori reclined on cushions, holding her baby girl, whom she and Hirata had named Taeko on this sixth, auspicious day after her birth. While Taeko cooed and gurgled, female relatives and friends chattered around her. Little Masahiro offered her his toy dog. She waved her tiny hand at it, while he laughed and Midori smiled fondly. Maids served the women food and wine. A table was piled with red paper envelopes containing gifts of lucky money brought by guests attending the celebration.

Reiko drifted apart from the company and walked to the lattice screen that shielded the women from the male guests who'd wandered out of the banquet room to stroll and talk in the garden. Although she felt glad to be back in her own home, with her family and friends, a lingering unease haunted her. Lady Yanagisawa was somewhere in the house, determined to keep up their friendship despite the fact that she'd tried to kill Reiko. Furthermore, the kidnapping had taught Reiko that safety was an illusion. Not her husband's love and strength, nor the shogun's power, could protect her. Not even this festive occasion could brighten her mood.

Ever since leaving the island, Reiko had suffered nightmares in which hoodlums chased her through a forest and the Dragon King mauled her. She woke up with her heart pounding, convinced that she was still imprisoned in the tower instead of in her own bed with Sano beside her. During her waking hours, bloodstained visions of the massacre flashed into her mind. She saw the Dragon King's face; she felt his brooding stare and his hot, damp touch and breath on her. Beneath the samisen music from the banquet room she imagined she heard waves lapping, a sound that would forever signify menace.

Sano strode along the veranda past the room, glanced through the lattice, and stopped on his way to join the guests. "Are you all right?" he said to Reiko.

He spoke with the gentle concern he'd shown her since that night on the island. But the memory of what had happened there divided them just as did the lattice between them.

"Yes, I'm fine," Reiko fibbed, not wanting to worry Sano or spoil the party. Not even during their time alone had she wanted to tell the shameful story of her and the Dragon King.

Sano's expression said that her evasion didn't fool him. She saw the question in his eyes, and sensed his wish to know what she was withholding from him. Avoiding his scrutiny, she changed the subject: "How nice that so many important people have come to celebrate Taeko-*chan*'s name day."

"Unfortunately, that's not the reason they came." Sano's manner turned grim. "For them, this is more an excuse for a political confabulation than an event honoring the birth of a child."

As she and Sano surveyed the crowd, Reiko noticed the shogun sitting in the covered pavilion. Flushed and laughing, he downed cups of sake that fawning officials poured for him. Beside him, Keisho-in flirted with handsome attendants. Chamberlain Yanagisawa and several retainers hovered below the pavilion near the shogun. Priest Ryuko and a group of monks hovered on the other side, by Keisho-in. The two factions exchanged covert, hostile looks. Reiko watched Yanagisawa glance uneasily across the garden at Lord Matsudaira, Lord Kii, General Isogai, and Police Commissioner Hoshina, gathered together with their cronies. The Council of Elders circulated the crowd in a phalanx, paying respects everywhere, taking sides nowhere yet. Minor *bakufu* officials flitted nervously from group to group, like birds looking for a safe place to nest. Superficial gaiety masked the strife in the atmosphere.

"This might seem like a congenial gathering, but I can see the different factions as distinctly as if lines were drawn on the ground," Sano said.

Reiko nodded, sensing the storm brewing within the *bakufu*'s top echelon. Sano paused, as though searching for words, then said, "Should difficult times come, we must stand together."

An image of the Dragon King pierced Reiko's mind. Her fingers clutched the lattice. "Can we?" she murmured.

"Yes." Sano spoke with sudden emphasis as he turned to her. He lowered his voice beneath the noise of the party: "Now isn't a good time to bring up the kidnapping, but there may never be a better time. I want you to know that we don't have to discuss it unless you wish. And nothing that happened on that island will change my love for you."

Reiko bowed her head, thankful for Sano's forbearance and constancy. Tears filled her eyes.

"Whatever did happen," Sano continued, "the Dragon King bears the entire blame. Forget him. Don't give him more power than he had while he was alive, or more thought than he deserves."

Although Reiko recognized the merit in these words, she couldn't forget the Dragon King. She couldn't forgive herself for encouraging his attentions, especially when she still wondered whether she could have managed things differently and come home with a clear conscience.

"If the Dragon King ruins our lives, then he's defeated us." Sano said urgently, "Don't let him win!"

But neither could Reiko bear the thought of her marriage destroyed by a mad, evil coward. She raised her head and drew a deep breath of determination.

"I won't let him win," she said.

She slid open the lattice screen and reached through it.

Sano took her hand and held it tight and warm under the cover of his sleeve. They stood together, looking out at the discordant assembly in the garden, like two sailors on a ship heading into the winds of change.

Read on for an excerpt
from Laura Joh Rowland's next book

THE PERFUMED SLEEVE

Available in hardcover
from St. Martin's Press

*Japan, Genroku Period, Year 7, Month 10
(November 1694)*

News of trouble sent Sano Ichirō abroad in the city of Edo at midnight. Clad in armor and metal helmet, his two swords at his waist, he galloped his horse down the main avenue. Beside him rode his young chief retainer, Hirata; behind them followed the hundred men of Sano's detective corps.

Constellations wheeled around the moon in the black, smoke-hazed sky. Cold wind swept debris past closed shops. Ahead, Sano saw torches flaring against the darkness. He and his troops passed townsmen armed with clubs, standing guard at doorways, ready to protect their businesses and families from harm. Frightened women peered out windows; boys craned their necks from rooftops, balconies, and fire-watch towers. Sano halted his army at the edge of a crowd that blocked the avenue.

The crowd was composed of ruffians whose faces shone with savage glee in the light of the torches they carried. They avidly watched two armies of mounted samurai, each some hundred men strong, charge along the street from opposite directions. The armies met in a violent clash of swords and lances. Horses skittered and neighed. The riders bellowed as they swung their blades at their opponents. Men screamed in agony as they fell wounded. Groups of samurai on foot whirled in fierce sword combat. Spectators cheered; some joined in the carnage.

"I've been expecting this," Hirata told Sano.

"It was only a matter of time," Sano agreed.

As the shogun's *sōsakan-sama*—most honorable investigator of events, situations, and people—Sano usually occupied himself with investigating important crimes and advising his lord, Tokugawa Tsunayoshi, dictator of Japan. But during recent months he'd spent much time keeping order amid the political upheaval in Edo. The *bakufu*—the military government that ruled Japan—was divided by a struggle for control of the Tokugawa regime. One faction, led by the shogun's second-in-command, Chamberlain Yanagisawa, opposed a second led by Lord Matsudaira, a cousin of the shogun. Other powerful men, including the *daimyo*—feudal lords—had begun taking sides. Both factions had started building up their military forces, preparing for civil war.

Soldiers had poured into Edo from the provinces, crowding the barracks at *daimyo* estates and Edo Castle, overflowing the district where Tokugawa vassals lived and camping outside town. Although Chamberlain Yanagisawa and Lord Matsudaira hadn't yet declared war, the lower ranks had grown restless. Idle waiting bred battle fever. Sano and his detective corps had already quelled many skirmishes. Now, the city elders who governed the townspeople had sent Sano an urgent message begging him to come and quell this major disturbance that threatened to shatter the peace which the Tokugawa regime had maintained for almost a century.

"Let's break up this brawl before it causes a riot and wrecks the town," Sano said.

"I'm ready," Hirata said.

As they forged through the crowd, leading their troops, Sano recalled other times they'd ridden together into battle, when he'd taken Hirata's competent, loyal service for granted. But last summer, while they were attempting to rescue the shogun's mother and their wives from kidnappers, Hirata had disobeyed Sano's orders. Now Sano could no longer place his complete trust in Hirata.

"In the name of His Excellency the Shogun, I order you to cease!" Sano called to the armies.

He and his men forced apart the combatants, who howled in rage and attacked them. Blades whistled and slashed around Sano. As he circled, ducked, and tried to control his rearing horse, the night spun around him. Torchlight and faces in the crowd blurred across his vision. The armies drove him to the edge of the road.

"Behold the great *sōsakan-sama*," called a male voice. "Have you been demoted to street duty?"

Sano turned to the man who'd addressed him. It was Police Commissioner Hoshina, sitting astride his horse at the gate to a side street, flanked by two mounted police commanders. Fashionable silk robes clothed his muscular physique. His handsome, angular face wore a mocking smile.

"You shouldn't lower yourself to breaking up brawls," Hoshina said.

Anger flashed through Sano. He and Hoshina were longtime enemies, and the fact that Sano had recently saved Hoshina's life didn't ease their antagonism.

"Someone has to uphold the law," Sano retorted, "because your police force won't."

Hoshina laughed off Sano's accusation that he was neglecting his duty. "I've got more important things on my mind."

Things like revenge and ambition, Sano thought. Hoshina had been the paramour of Chamberlain Yanagisawa until recently, when Yanagisawa had betrayed Hoshina, and the police commissioner had joined Lord Matsudaira's faction. Hoshina was so bitter toward Yanagisawa that he welcomed a war that could elevate him and depose his lover. He didn't care that war could also destroy the city he'd been appointed to protect. A lawless atmosphere pervaded

Edo because Hoshina and his men wouldn't stop the fighting between partisans.

Sano turned away from Hoshina in disgust. Along the boulevard, more soldiers and ruffians streamed in as news of the brawl spread. Running footsteps, pounding hoofbeats, and loud war cries enlivened the night.

"Close off the area!" Sano yelled at his troops.

They hurried to bar the gates at intersections. The boulevard was a tumult of Sano's forces and the crazed soldiers colliding, blades flashing and bodies flailing, murderous yowls and spattering blood. As Sano rode into the melee, he feared this was only a taste of things to come.

It was dawn by the time Sano, Hirata, and the detectives separated the combatants, arrested them for disturbing the peace, and dispersed the crowd. Now a sun like a malevolent red beacon floated up from a sea of gray clouds over Edo Castle, looming on its hilltop above the city. At his mansion inside the official quarter of the castle, Sano sat in his private chambers. His wife Reiko cleaned a cut on his arm, where a sword had penetrated a joint in his sleeve guard. He wore his white under-kimono; his armor lay strewn on the *tatami* floor around him.

"You can't keep trying to maintain order in the city by yourself," Reiko said as she swabbed Sano's bloody gash. Her delicate, beautiful features were somber. "One man can't stand between two armies and survive for long."

Sano winced at the pain. "I know."

Servants' voices drifted from the kitchen and grounds as morning stirred the estate to life. In the nursery, Sano and Reiko's little son Masahiro chattered with the maids. Reiko sprinkled powdered geranium root on Sano's wound to stop the bleeding, then applied honeysuckle ointment to prevent festering.

"While you were out last night, the finance minister came to see you," Reiko said. "So did the captain of the palace guard." These were two of Sano's friends in the *bakufu.* "I don't know why."

"I can guess," Sano said. "The minister, who has recently joined Chamberlain Yanagisawa's faction, came to ask me to do the same. The captain, who has sworn allegiance to Lord Matsudaira, would like me to follow his example."

Both factions were eager to recruit Sano because he was close to the shogun and could use his influence to further their cause; they also wanted Sano and his detectives, all expert fighters, on their side in the event of war. The victor would rule Japan unopposed, via domination of the shogun. Sano could hardly believe that he, a former martial arts teacher and son of a *rōnin*—masterless samurai—had risen to a position where such important men courted his allegiance. But that position brought danger; both men would hasten to ruin any powerful official who opposed them.

"What are you going to tell your friends?" Reiko said.

"The same thing I've told everyone else who wants to lure me into one faction or the other," Sano said. "That I won't support either. My loyalty is to the shogun." Despite Tokugawa Tsunayoshi's shortcomings as a dictator, Sano felt bound by the samurai code of honor to stand by his lord. "I'll not join anyone who would usurp his authority."

Reiko bound a white cloth pad and bandage around Sano's wound. "Be careful," she said, patting his arm.

Sano perceived that her warning concerned more than his immediate injury; she feared for their future. He hated to worry her, especially since she was still suffering from the effects of being kidnapped along with the shogun's mother.

He didn't know exactly what had happened to Reiko while imprisoned by the man who'd called himself the Dragon King. But the normally adventurous Reiko had changed. During four years of marriage, she'd helped Sano with his investigations and developed quite a talent for detective work, but now she'd turned into a quiet recluse who hadn't left the estate since he'd brought her home. Sano wished for a little peace so she could recover, yet there was no prospect of peace anytime soon.

"This city is like a barrel of gunpowder," Sano said grimly. "The least incident could spark an explosion."

Footsteps creaked along the passage, and Hirata appeared at the door. "Excuse me, *Sōsakan-sama*." Although still free to enter Sano's private quarters, Hirata displayed the cautious deference with which he'd behaved since their breach. "You have a visitor."

"At this hour?" Sano glanced at the window. Gray daylight barely penetrated the paper panes. "Who is it?"

"His name is Juro. He's the valet of Senior Elder Makino. He says Makino sent him here with a message for you."

Sano raised his eyebrows in surprise. Makino Narisada was the longest-standing, dominant member of the Council of Elders, the shogun's primary advisers and Japan's highest governing body. He was also a crony of Chamberlain Yanagisawa and enemy of Sano. He had an ugly face like a skull, and a disposition to match.

"What is the message?" Sano said.

"I asked, but Juro wouldn't tell me," Hirata said. "He says his master ordered him to speak personally to you."

Sano couldn't refuse a communication from someone as important, quick to take offense, and dangerous as Makino. Besides, he was curious. "Very well."

He and Hirata walked to the reception room. Reiko followed. She watched from outside the door while they entered the cold, drafty room, where a man knelt. Thin and stooped, with a fringe of gray hair around his bald head, and clad in modest gray robes, Juro the valet appeared to be past sixty years of age. His bony features wore a sad expression. Two of Sano's detectives stood guard behind him. Although he looked harmless, they exercised caution toward strangers in the house, especially during these dangerous days.

"Here I am," Sano said. "Speak your message."

The valet bowed. "I'm sorry to impose on you, *Sōsakan-*

sama, but I must tell you that the honorable Senior Elder Makino is dead."

"Dead?" Sano experienced three reactions in quick succession. The first was shock. "As of when?"

"Today," said Juro.

"How did it happen?" Sano asked.

"My master passed away in his sleep."

Sano's second reaction was puzzlement. "You told my chief retainer that Makino-*san* sent you. How could he, if he's dead?"

"Some time ago, he told me that if he should die, I must inform you at once. I'm honoring his order."

Sano looked at Hirata, who shrugged, equally perplexed. "My condolences to you on the loss of your master," Sano said to the valet. "I'll go pay my respects to his family today."

As he spoke, a deep consternation beset him. Makino must have been almost eighty years old—he'd lived longer than he deserved—but his death, at this particular time, had the potential to aggravate the tensions within the Tokugawa regime.

"Why did Makino-*san* care that I should immediately know of his death?" Sano asked Juro.

"He wanted you to read this letter." The valet offered a folded paper to Sano.

Still mystified, Sano accepted the letter. Juro bowed with the air of a man who has discharged an important duty, and the detectives escorted him out of the house. Reiko entered the room. She and Hirata waited expectantly while Sano unfolded the letter and scanned the words written in gnarled black calligraphy. He read aloud, in surprise:

"To Sano Ichirō, sōsakan-sama to the shogun:

If you are reading this, I am dead. I am leaving you this letter to beg an important favor of you.
As you know, I have many enemies who want me gone. Assassination is a constant threat for a man

in my position. Please investigate my death and determine whether it was murder. If it was, I ask that you identify the culprit, deliver him to justice, and avenge my death.

I regret to impose on you, but there is no one else I trust enough to ask this favor. I apologize for any inconvenience that my request causes you.

Senior Elder Makino Narisada."

Reiko burst out, "The gall of that man, asking you for anything! After he accused you of treason last year and tried to get you executed!"

"Even in death he plagues me," Sano said, disturbed by the request that posed a serious dilemma for himself.

"But the valet said Makino died in his sleep," Hirata pointed out.

"Could his death have really been murder?" Reiko wondered. "The letter would have come to you even if Makino died of old age, as he seems to have done."

"Perhaps his death isn't what it seems." Sano narrowed his eyes in recollection. "There have been attempts on his life. His fear that he would die by foul play was justified. And he was extremely vindictive. If he was assassinated, he would want the culprit punished even though he wouldn't be around to see it."

"And lately, with the *bakufu* in turmoil, there's been all the more reason for his enemies to want him gone," Reiko said.

"But you don't have to grant his request to investigate his death," Hirata told Sano.

"You owe him nothing," Reiko agreed.

Yet Sano couldn't ignore the letter. "Since there's a chance that Makino was murdered, his death should be investigated. How I felt about him doesn't matter. A victim of a crime deserves justice."

"An inquiry into his death could create serious trouble for you that I think you should avoid." Hirata spoke with the authority of a chief retainer duty bound to divert his master from a risky path, yet a slight hesitation in his voice bespoke his awareness that Sano might doubt the value of his counsel.

"Hirata-*san* is right," Reiko told Sano. "If Makino was murdered, there's a killer at large who won't welcome you prying into his death."

"Makino's enemies include powerful, unscrupulous men," Hirata said. "Any one of them would rather kill you than be exposed and executed as a murderer."

"Investigating crimes against high-ranking citizens is my job," Sano said. "Danger comes with the responsibility. And in this case, the possible victim—who was my superior— asked me to look into his death."

"I can guess why Makino asked you," Reiko said in disgust at the senior elder. "Makino knew that your sense of honor wouldn't let you overlook a possible crime."

"He understood that justice matters more to you than your own safety," Hirata interjected.

"So he saddled you with a job that he knew no one else would bother to do for him. He tried to destroy you while he was alive. Now he's trying to manipulate you from the grave." Outrage sparked in Reiko's eyes. "Please don't let him!"

Even though Sano shared many of the concerns of his wife and chief retainer, he felt a duty toward Makino that superseded reason. "A posthumous request from a fellow samurai is a serious obligation," he said. "Refusing to honor it would be a breach of protocol."

"No one would fault you for refusing a favor to a man who treated you the way Makino did," Hirata said.

"You ignore protocol often enough," Reiko said, wryly alluding to Sano's independent streak.

But Sano had more reason to grant the request, no matter the consequences. "If Makino was murdered, the fact may come to light regardless of what I do. Even if he wasn't, rumors could arise that say he was." Rumors, true and false, abounded in Edo Castle during this political crisis. "Suspicion will fall on all his enemies—including me. By that time, evidence of how Makino died, and who killed him, will be lost, along with my chance to prove my innocence if I'm accused."

Understanding dawned on Reiko's and Hirata's faces. "Your enemies have tried to frame you for crimes in the past," Hirata recalled. "They would welcome this opportunity to destroy you."

"Most of your friends now belong to Chamberlain Yanagisawa or Lord Matsudaira," Reiko said. "Since you won't join either faction, you have the protection of neither. And if you're accused of murder, you can't count on the shogun to defend you."

Because the shogun's favor was as inconstant as the weather, Sano thought. He'd known that by resisting pressure to choose sides, he stood alone and vulnerable, but now the high price of neutrality had come due. "So I either investigate Makino's death, or jeopardize all of us," Sano said, for his family and retainers would share any punishment that came his way.

Reiko and Hirata nodded in resigned agreement. "I'll do everything in my power to help you," Hirata said.

"Where shall we begin?" Reiko said.

Their support gladdened Sano, yet misgivings disturbed him. Was Reiko ready to brave the hazards of this investigation so soon after her kidnapping? Sano also wondered how far he could trust Hirata, after Hirata had placed personal concerns above duty to his master during the kidnapping investigation. But Sano was in no position to turn away help.

"As soon as I've washed and dressed, we'll go to Makino's estate and inspect the scene of his death," Sano told Hirata.

Hirata bowed. He said, "I'll fetch some detectives to accompany us," then left the room.

"You must eat first and restore your strength," Reiko said to Sano. "I'll bring your breakfast." She paused in the doorway. "Is there anything else you need me to do?"

Sano read anxiety in her manner, instead of the eager excitement with which she usually greeted a new investigation. He said, "I won't know until I've determined whether Makino was indeed murdered. Maybe Hirata and I will discover that he died of natural causes. Maybe I can dispel suspicion of foul play, and everything will be all right."

Senior Elder Makino's estate was located on the main street of the Edo Castle official quarter. In accordance with his high rank, the estate was the largest of the compounds, surrounded by stone walls and retainers' barracks, that lined the road. The gate boasted a double-tiered roof; sentries occupied guard booths outside its double portals.

As Sano walked up to the gate with Hirata and four detectives, they passed officials hurrying about on business. A shrill pitch of anxiety rang from conversations Sano overheard between these men swirling at the periphery of the political maelstrom. The whole *bakufu* feared the consequences of the struggle between Chamberlain Yanagisawa and Lord Matsudaira. But Sano detected no sign of commotion around Makino's estate. He surmised that the news of Makino's death hadn't yet been made public.

After introducing himself to the guards in the booth, Sano told them, "I'm here to see the honorable Senior Elder Makino."

The guards exchanged uneasy glances. One man said, "I beg you to wait a moment," and went inside the compound. Evidently, the guards knew their master was dead but had orders not to tell anyone. Sano and his comrades waited in the chill gray morning until the guard reemerged, accompanied by a man whom Sano recognized as Makino's secretary.

The secretary, a pale, sleek man with a deferential air, bowed to Sano. "Will you please come with me?"

He led Sano, Hirata, and the detectives through the gate, between the barracks, through another gate to the inner compound, and up the stone steps to the mansion. Inside the entryway Sano and his comrades exchanged their shoes for guest slippers, then hung their swords on racks, according to custom when entering a private home. The secretary seated Sano, Hirata, and the detectives in a reception chamber and knelt opposite them.

"I regret to tell you that the honorable Senior Elder Makino just died," he said in the hushed tone reserved for such an announcement. "If you had business with him, perhaps I may assist you on his behalf?"

Sano said, "I already know about Makino-*san*. I would like to speak with whoever is now in charge here."

The secretary's face reflected startled confusion. He said, "I'll fetch Senior Elder Makino's chief retainer," then rose and edged out the door.

Soon, a man dressed in austere gray robes strode into the room. He knelt and bowed to Sano. "Greetings, *Sōsakan-sama*."

"Good morning, Tamura-*san*," replied Sano.

They were casual acquaintances, with a mutual wariness that stemmed from Sano and Makino's antagonism. Sano knew Tamura to be an old-fashioned samurai who considered himself as much a warrior as a bureaucrat; unlike many *bakufu* officials, he kept up his martial arts training. Although past fifty years of age, he had a hardy, muscular physique. His hands bore calluses and scars from combat. His features always reminded Sano of the carved wooden masks worn by villains in No plays: hard, shiny, prominent cheeks; a long nose with its sharp tip flattened downward; slanted eyebrows that gave him a severe expression.

"I am responsible for Senior Elder Makino's household and affairs," Tamura's voice—deep, raspy, and loud—befitted his appearance. "There are no male clan members in town, and until they can be summoned, it's my duty to handle any business concerning my master."

Sano recalled hearing that Makino had feuded with his four sons and numerous relatives, whom he'd suspected of plotting to oust him from power, and had banished them to remote provinces.

"I was just about to notify the shogun of Senior Elder Makino's death," Tamura said. "May I ask how you learned about it?"

"His valet came and told me," Sano said.

Disapproval drew together Tamura's slanted brows. "Everyone in the household was forbidden to spread the news until after the official announcement."

"Juro had permission, from his master," Sano said, then explained. Tamura stared, obviously disconcerted; Hirata and the detectives watched him and Sano in alert silence. Sano handed Makino's letter to Tamura. "The senior elder has requested that I investigate his death."

As Tamura read the letter, he shook his head in amazement. "I had no knowledge of this."

Was Tamura shocked, Sano wondered, because he'd prided himself on enjoying his superior's confidence, only to learn of secrets kept from him? Or were there other reasons for discomfiture?

Quickly regaining his poise, Tamura said, "I did know that the senior elder feared assassination. However, he died peacefully in his sleep." Tamura gave the letter back to Sano. "Many thanks for honoring my master's wish. You have no further obligation to him." He bowed and rose, concluding Sano's visit.

Sano thought Tamura seemed a bit too hasty to get rid of him. Perhaps Makino had had good cause not to tell his chief retainer about the letter. Sano, Hirata, and the detectives stood, but held their ground.

"I'd like to see for myself that Senior Elder Makino wasn't a victim of murder," Sano told Tamura. "Please take me to him."

Resistance swelled Tamura to his full height. "With all due respect, *Sōsakan-sama,* but I must decline. An official examination of my master would be a disgrace to him."

"The senior elder knew what my inquiries would entail. He cared less about disgrace than that I should discover the truth about what happened." Sano observed the angry crimson flush spreading across Tamura's shiny cheeks. He conjectured that Tamura might prove to be his first suspect in a murder investigation. "Now, if you'll show me to Senior Elder Makino?" Sano paused. "Or do you want me to think you have something to hide?"

Calculation flickered in Tamura's eyes as he measured the threat posed by Sano against whatever was his actual motive for barring examination of the death scene.

"Come this way," he said at last. His courteous bow and gesture toward the door smacked of disdain.

As they all trooped down the corridor, Sano experienced a growing sense that Makino's death wasn't as natural as it seemed. He anticipated that Tamura's unwillingness to cooperate was only the first obstacle his inquiries would meet.

Senior Elder Makino's mansion had the same layout as other samurai estates, with family living quarters at the center. A separate building, with half-timbered plaster walls, heavy wooden shutters over the windows, a broad veranda, and surrounding gardens, housed his private chambers. Tamura, Sano, Hirata, and the detectives crossed a covered walkway built above raked white sand studded with low shrubs and mossy rocks. Two guards stood outside the building. Inside, a corridor encircled the chambers. Tamura slid open a panel in the lattice-and-paper wall, admitting Sano and his men into a spacious room heated by sunken charcoal braziers. Across an expanse of *tatami* floor, a platform extended below a mural that depicted treetops and clouds. On a bed on the platform lay Senior Elder Makino, covered by quilt. But Sano's immediate attention focused on the people in the room.

Two women knelt, one on either side of Makino's head. A man crouched at his feet. All turned toward Sano, Hirata, and the detectives. Sano had a sudden impression of vultures feeding on a corpse, interrupted by a predator.

"This is Makino-*san*'s widow," Tamura said, introducing the older of the women.

Although Sano estimated her age at forty-five years, her face's elegant bone structure testified to the beauty she must have once possessed. A rich burgundy silk dressing gown embossed with medallions clothed her slim figure. Her hair fell in a long plait over her shoulder. She bowed to Sano, her features set in rigid lines of grief.

"That's his concubine." Tamura indicated the other woman.

She was small and very young—no more than fifteen, Sano guessed—yet voluptuous of body. Her scarlet kimono, gaily patterned with winter landscapes, looked out of place at a deathbed. But her round, pretty face was tear-streaked, her eyes red and swollen. As she bobbed a clumsy bow at Sano, she pressed a white kerchief to her nose.

"And that's the senior elder's houseguest." Tamura nodded at the man by the foot of the bed.

The houseguest rearranged his tall, agile figure in a kneeling position and bowed. He was in his twenties, clad in a plain brown robe, and stunningly handsome. His bold, lustrous eyes appraised Sano. Lively spirits flashed behind the somber expression on his strong, clean features. He wore his oiled black hair in a topknot above his shaved crown. Recognition jarred Sano, but he couldn't think where he'd seen the man before. He had a notion that the man wasn't a samurai, despite his hairstyle.

"Leave this building," Tamura ordered the three.

The concubine glanced at the houseguest. He jerked his chin at her, then rose and stepped off the platform. The concubine scrambled up, and together they hastened from the room. The widow glided after them. While Tamura stood by the door and the detectives waited at the end of the room, Sano and Hirata mounted the platform and gazed down at Makino.

He lay on his back with his legs straight and hands atop his chest under the quilt. A jade neck rest supported his head, which wore a white nightcap. His withered, sallow skin spread across his ugly face, delineating the skull beneath. Wrinkles wattled his scrawny neck above the collar of a beige silk robe; purplish shadows tinged his closed eyelids. He looked much the same as when alive, Sano thought. Except that Makino had never shut his eyes in the presence of other people because he was always on the lookout for threats, or for advantages to seize. And he'd had too much pride to let his mouth drop open like that. Sano experienced a mixture of sadness at the spectacle of human mortality and relief that his enemy was really dead.

"Who found him?" Sano asked Tamura.

"I did. I came to wake him, as usual, and there he was." Arms folded, Tamura spoke in tone of resigned forbearance.

Sano noted the quilt draped smoothly over Makino, his head balanced on the neck rest, his body in serene repose. "Was he in this exact position? Or did anyone move his body?"

"He was just as you see him," Tamura said.

Sano and Hirata exchanged glances, sharing the thought that Makino looked too neat and composed even if he'd died naturally, and that the person who discovers the body is often the killer. Now that he had more reason to doubt Tamura's word, Sano felt his heart beat faster with the excitement that a new investigation always brought him along with qualms about his next step.

In order to determine how Makino had died, an examination of the body was imperative. But Sano couldn't just strip Makino naked and look for wounds, as that would transgress Tokugawa law forbidding practices associated with foreign science, including the examination of corpses. Sano had broken the law often enough, but he couldn't do it here, in the presence of Tamura, a hostile witness. He needed to get Makino away from the estate. Besides, even if Sano examined the body, he might not be able to tell what had caused the death. He needed expert advice. His mind raced, formulating a ploy.

"Are you done?" Tamura asked impatiently.

"I'm not yet satisfied as to how Senior Elder Makino died," Sano said. "I must order you to delay reporting his death. No one will leave here." Sano sent one detective to begin securing the estate and another to fetch more troops to help. He didn't want the news to spread and visitors overrunning the premises before he could examine them. As Tamura gaped in outrage, Sano added, "And I must confiscate Makino-*san*'s body."

"What?" Tamura's outrage turned to incredulity. He stalked across the room to the platform and stared at Sano. "Why?"

"The funeral rites must be postponed until my investigation is done and the pronouncement of the cause of Makino-*san*'s death is official," Sano improvised. "Therefore, I shall take him into safekeeping."

Tamura's expression said he thought Sano had gone mad. "I've never heard of such a thing. What law allows you to do this?"

"Bring me a trunk large enough to carry the body," Sano said, eager to end the argument before it revealed his explanation as completely spurious.

Fists balled on his hips, Tamura said, "If you take my master, you'll displease many people."

Sano wondered whether Tamura was afraid of what he might see on the body. "If you stand in my way, you'll suffer," Sano said. "Get the trunk."

They were at an impasse. Sano knew that Makino's family and powerful friends—including Chamberlain Yanagisawa—could punish him for confiscating the body, especially if they guessed why he wanted it. But Tamura knew that Sano could have him stripped of his samurai status for disobeying orders. Hirata and the detectives moved closer to Sano, aligning themselves against Tamura. Evidently recognizing that the threat to him was more immediate than the one to Sano, the man visibly deflated. Surliness replaced his ire.

"As you wish," he said to Sano, then slunk out of the room.

Sano expelled his breath. The investigation had barely begun, and already the difficulties were mounting. He beckoned his two remaining detectives, Marume and Fukida, and whispered to them, "Take Senior Elder Makino to Edo Morgue."

The young, slight, serious detective and the jovial, brawny one nodded. They understood from past cases what Sano intended. They also knew the dangers involved and the caution necessary.

Tamura returned with two servants hauling a long wooden trunk. Marume and Fukida peeled the quilt off Makino, lifted his stiff body, placed it inside the trunk, and carried it away. Sano offered a silent prayer for its safe, secret arrival at Edo Morgue. Then he ordered Tamura, "Wait outside while I examine the senior elder's chambers."